Cover by Paragraphic Design

Staccato Publishing
Maple Grove, MN

First US Edition: December 2014

ISBN: 978-1-940202-13-6

Printed in the USA

To Jaime -
My friend and sister
Thank you for all that you do, without you this wouldn't have happened. xoxo

WHISPERS

BY HK SAVAGE

Chapter 1

"Your daughter is special."

For a long time nothing could be heard in the generic beige office but the loud tick tock of the industrial clock so typical of schools. Her parents stared across the faux wood topped desk, blinking at the balding man in a suit that cost more than her father made in a week. Paralyzed, they sat frozen by the confirmation that what they had been suspecting for months, since last summer to be precise. Something had happened to their little girl, happy and smiling no more.

It had started with long silences and glazed eyes when they'd thought she was daydreaming. Steadily it had grown worse, eventually leading to bouts of agoraphobia and panic attacks her pediatrician couldn't explain. They encouraged, cajoled, they'd even punished, but all to no avail. Natalie *was* different and no one knew why.

For a while they blamed it on the newly surging hormones. She'd only just gone through puberty and teens could be moody. Yet it had failed to ebb. Where hormones should have come and gone, Natalie's withdrawal was total.

Fearful, her parents had given money they didn't have to conduct every test the doctors recommended. All of them pointed to something permanent and having to do with a mental imbalance. Out of stubbornness and false hope that things would change in time, they hadn't said anything to the school. Once a label was in a child's file it was there forever and they were determined to fight the pitying looks and alternative classes sure to damage what was left of their once precocious child for as long as possible. Still no amount of avoidance could change the facts. Then came the "accidents."

Bob and Valerie Swenson, high school sweethearts who had settled in the same small Minnesota town where they'd grown up, were ill prepared financially to accommodate a child with special needs. Bob worked in a cabinet shop, Valerie was a receptionist at one of the two insurance agencies in town. They made a living just below modest but it was enough for their small family to get by and they had even traveled to the

Wisconsin Dells two summers ago for a family vacation. A rare treat they'd sworn they would do again. Until today.

Now, both of them sat across a cheap metal desk from the School Psychologist to meet with them. He stared benignly at them, seemingly oblivious to the fact he had just rewritten the course of their child's life in less than ten seconds with those four words. The Swensons watched with heavy hearts as the mantle of their daughter's new life settled heavy on her thin shoulders.

Natalie perched between her parents on a hard blue plastic chair letting her long dark hair hang forward in an attempt to hide her face, while she willed herself to become smaller. Self-consciously she tugged at her long sleeve to cover the edge of white bandage peeking out.

Swallowing to wet her tongue, Valerie spoke first. "What do you mean by 'special'?" Her voice broke on the word. Like any good mother, her first instinct was to protect her child. She had seen firsthand how cruel children and adults alike could be when someone was labeled as different. Try as the school might to keep that private the kids would find out and they would not be kind.

Dr. Spence clicked his pen rolling it around in his long, dexterous fingers, studying the name of the local company printed on its side. His slow deliberation before speaking fueled their already mounting anxiety.

"As we discussed at our initial meeting last month," he began in that slow doctoral manner meant to be comforting but just came off as condescending, "Natalie has exhibited certain *high risk* behaviors. We are required by the state to conduct an assessment when these things are reported. We have had the results analyzed by a Psychiatrist." He tapped the manila file folder laying in front of him with the end of his pen and showed a glimmer of interest, raising his brow encouragingly. "He's very good, he comes highly recommended in cases like these."

The dumbfounded parents nodded in unison, deferring to the expert's opinion. They had no experience in these waters. Natalie pulled again at the sleeve of her flannel shirt. It had become a nervous habit for her of late.

Her Art teacher had noticed these latest marks a few weeks ago when Natalie reached for a jar of paintbrushes from an upper cabinet and her sleeve rode up. He had reported the suspicious pattern of red, raised scabs right away to the counselors who had immediately contacted her parents. Natalie had told them all it had been an accident. "A cat scratched me," she'd said but cats' nails didn't leave marks in straight lines and the doctors recognized the cuts for what they were. Her parents could keep her secret no longer.

The bland Dr. Spence tapped the file folder with Natalie's name printed in bold black letters on the white stick-on label. Deliberately, he opened the folder and noisily thumbed through the first few pages while her parents unwittingly sat up straighter, craning their necks to see when the doctor slapped the folder shut and folded his hands over it. "Natalie's issues are relatively minor and there is no reason why with counseling and medication we can't keep her as a student at this school. I can refer you to a fantastic specialist who handles these sorts of cases for her ongoing care and monitoring. His office *is* in Edina. That isn't a problem is it?"

"Edina?" Valerie sounded worried.

Natalie shrunk further into herself. She knew a doctor an hour away would mean more time away from work for her mother. Valerie was already working part time to spend extra time with her daughter.

"What's wrong with her?" Bob was clenching his fists. Valerie slid a hand surreptitiously under cover of the desk to touch his arm. His jaw loosened at her gentling though his hands remained tight out of the doctor's sight.

Their daughter felt her chest tighten painfully at seeing her parents so upset. The whispering grew louder in her head and Natalie counted backward from twenty. Her fingers itched for something sharp. Something to help dull the whispers.

"She's always been so smart. Are you sure it isn't just some temporary thing? Something we can work through here, locally?" Valerie voiced her desperate hope. She rubbed the slumped shoulder of her daughter who had not looked up once since sitting down. Natalie tried to hide the way she cringed at her mother's touch but Valerie noticed and removed her hand

9

from where she'd attempted to lay it on her back. "This episode doesn't mean anything I'm sure."

Natalie had made it abundantly clear she no longer cared to be touched. On occasion her mother forgot, never her father. He was usually nearby, more than protective once she'd changed, though it was as if a barrier had been stretched between them he could not cross. Never did he come close enough to touch her.

Dr. Spence smiled, failing in his efforts to be reassuring. "This is a mental condition that has manifested itself in abnormal, self-destructive behavior. These sorts of things are often not diagnosed until the teen years. We are lucky to have caught it now before any permanent damage was done." Seeing the denials forming on their tongues, his expression grew dark and Dr. Spence leaned forward.

Reactively, so did Bill and Valerie.

"Have you looked closely at those marks? There are more scars underneath." He looked severely at them both lending gravity to his statement. "This is not an isolated incident and you are fooling yourselves if you believe that this behavior will just disappear." Dr. Spence gave them a few seconds to consider that before he cleared his throat and sat up straight. "We can put her on a few medications that will help her to better manage these urges. The specialist I'm recommending can help her to learn better ways to deal with pressures and stress." He tapped his pen and smiled at them again. "She can have a relatively normal life if you follow the treatment plan."

Scratching out a referral to the specialist, Dr. Spence stood, shook her parents' hands, and that was it. Natalie Swenson's world was altered forever. How people saw her was never going to be the same.

Of course people were polite about the whole thing. Everyone referred to her appointments as "checkups," and no one in her family commented about her clearly altered state thereafter. Frequently zoning out, a slight droop to her eye, and a shortened attention span were politely ignored or explained away as signs of exhaustion. Yet her parents knew, as did Natalie that her "issues" had nothing to do with sleep deprivation, nor were they as easy to cure.

***

The whispers had come on slowly at first, quietly. They had been only tiny rustlings at the edge of her hearing. Then, they'd amplified themselves to where she could make out words until they filled her conscious thoughts. They'd become a constant chatter filling her head. It was the worst when she was at school with all those people, forming her own thoughts became impossible. That was when she had started cutting. She wasn't really trying to hurt herself. It was hard to explain but it helped her stay connected with her body and the present. It helped to push away the noise.

When she feared she was going to lose herself in the whispers, she would take a small paring knife she had stolen from the kitchen and make a small inch to two inch shallow cut in the underside of her forearm.

The pain and blood reminded her that this was real. The world she was in, the body she was in, all real, all human. She bled red just like all the other children. It wasn't purple or green like the aliens she'd seen on tv. No, she was real, just not normal.

She had steadily withdrawn from everyone around her until she could count Auggie, their family doxie, her only friend.

Now, here she was with her parents walking her out of the school, guards escorting a prisoner to death row from whence there is no escape. Not a word was spoken between them. The pale, sick looks on their shellshocked faces got her started imagining she could hear what they were thinking again. She cursed her imagination, her sick, "special" imagination that wouldn't let her mind rest.

Edina? How am I going to explain this to my boss? Will the medication hurt her? How am I going to tell our friends? Would she really kill herself?

Chapter 2

The next few years went by in a medicated haze, the constantly evolving chemical cocktail they had her on made her barely more than the walking dead most of the time. Often, it only made things worse and the sessions with her specialist were a laugh.

Initially, Natalie had mentioned the whispering she heard and he'd gotten excited. Self-conscious, she had clammed up not to speak about it again. But oddly enough, she still enjoyed going to see him. The hour she spent in his office was the most relaxing time she had all week. By some strange circumstance, there was no noise in his office.

When the door closed, it was silent. He was content to ask occasionally if she wanted to talk. She would shake her head and they would sit quietly while he took notes or read for the remainder of their time. For Natalie it was the closest she felt to normal and a welcome haven for her tortured mind.

Natalie's grades dropped from A's to low C's and D's, even with her best attempts at studying. Her teachers gave up on her and her few remaining friends fell by the wayside. Word spread fast in her small town. Natalie became known as troubled. She tried to keep herself together. She felt her world steadily pulling away from her but the medications and the constant drain of hearing the babble and noise was exhausting. Struggling to cling to what was "her" through it all was too great a burden to maintain. She slept a lot and took the dog out to sit in the yard when it got to be too much. Even cutting, her once reliable tool, was not easily managed once they started watching her so closely.

One single bright spot remained for her outside the doctor's weekly visit. A teacher in her high school, Ms. Miller from her doctor assigned study classes took an interest in her and found different ways to keep Natalie precariously tethered to the world. She stayed after school to study with her, keeping her going when she wanted to give up and offering her a reason to want to come to school when high school had otherwise become a living hell. The combination of the noise of so many people packed together in a small space and her medications that had her experiencing more side effects than she could list. She couldn't remember the last time she hadn't had cotton mouth.

Natalie had another reason to enjoy being with Ms. Miller. It was the silence. Ms. Miller and her specialist were the only people she had found who she could be with and not hear all that noise. It was as though they had a protective bubble around them and when Natalie was with either of them it encompassed her too.

Ms. Miller was always trying to get her to try new age meditation or breathing techniques. For some odd reason she believed it would help Natalie to deal with the daily struggles she faced with her disorder. But, try as she might, Natalie could gain control of herself only long enough to breathe a few good breaths and then distraction would take her chances of success away.

"Ms. Miller," she huffed one day, tired of sitting in one of the quiet rooms the special kids had at their disposal in their resource center. "This isn't helping." Natalie was exhausted and frustrated with the exercise. All she could do was fidget when she was in the quiet, dark space the size of a closet.

Ms. Miller was ever patient. She smiled and jiggled her wrist to roll her gold bracelets back up her arm. "Nat, you need to learn to still your mind. Until you do, none of this will help you find peace."

Unable to stop the laugh that erupted, Natalie covered her mouth. "I'm sorry. This is just so Kung Fu Theatre. I'm waiting for you to call me Grasshopper or something."

Her more than forgiving teacher twitched her lips, only partially hiding an indulgent smirk, and ran a hand through her curly blonde hair. "You're right. It is a lot like that. Really though, it's going to make a huge difference in your life."

But try as she might, Natalie could not make it work. Whenever they would have their quiet sessions, about twice a week, Natalie would be rerunning things through her head she had "thought" earlier about herself or someone else. Sometimes there were strange ideas she could not find any personal reference to and other times there were just beyond crazy things like what it was like to have sex with the hot guy or even girl.

She thought about egging the house of someone she barely knew and trigonometry even though she wasn't in trig, all kinds of things she could not sort out enough to push aside. Instead they occupied her thoughts when she was supposed to be focusing on clearing them. It was like her mailbox was filling up with letters before she could read them all to sift through the junk.

Though Ms. Miller never gave up, Natalie never became reliable with the exercise the entire time she worked with her. It might work one day and not the next. Again she felt the sting of another's disappointment.

Then, in Natalie's senior year, the impossible happened. She received a letter from a tiny school in Northern California, Prestige College. Ms. Miller had been the first person she thought to share it with. She carefully picked her way through the halls, being careful to avoid touching anyone. After the initial crush of people at the front doors, she found herself in the significantly reduced traffic of their hallway on the first floor, just left of the stairs and outside the offices where students like Natalie took the majority of their classes. They were kept out of the mainstream but for the occasional elective. Their removal bothered some, but not Natalie. The fewer people around her, the better.

Finally reaching her favorite teacher's main room, Natalie knocked gently on the door with one hand, holding out the letter with the other.

Ms. Miller knew right away what Natalie was holding and her warm smile lit up her face.

She'd been so afraid to ask and didn't believe her parents would be honest with her. "Do you think college would be a good idea? For me?"

Ms. Miller's eyes welled up. "Nat, I think it's perfect for you. They're small, the campus is compact so you don't need a car and I can help you to set up a support network so you won't be alone."

"I'll miss you though." It was true. Natalie would miss her and her peacefulness most of all. Leaving would mean no more visits to the specialist as well. Natalie would lose her quiet places. That was no small loss.

"I'll miss you too, Sweetie." A tear leaked out from under her long black eyelashes. Ms. Miller's sadness at losing Natalie was heartfelt as well.

Nevertheless, they spent the year getting her application for financial aid together, Nat's parents having little experience on the subject. By some miracle, second only to the one that had brought her a letter from the college she had neither heard of nor applied to, Nat had not only gotten in but had been given a full scholarship.

With a lump in her throat and not a little amount of trepidation, Natalie drove with her parents out to the campus just outside the small California campus near the Oregon border and settled her into her room.

It was a twelve by twelve box with a large window on the back wall overlooking the sides of two other tan brick dorms flanking hers. It felt far too institutional for comfort, but through the gap between the buildings she could see the profile of tall blue mountains in the near distance. Though she hadn't seen it yet, Natalie knew the ocean was not far away nor were old forests frequented by tourists wanting to see and touch living history.

When her parents had gone on the heels of quite a few tears, blissful silence pervaded the room. Placing a small pink pill on the tip of her tongue and replacing the pill bottle back in her top dresser drawer, Nat fell back onto her tiny bed to let it dissolve and stared up at the white popcorn ceiling. Two small brown spots near the wall told her that the upstairs neighbor's window leaked when it rained. She stared at it without blinking. There were no other tiny details that gave the room any individuality. Only cinderblock walls painted cream with matching vertical blinds Nat intended to leave open as much as possible to let in the character of the location. It was the only thing the unit had going for it.

The evening dose made her drowsy. Natalie put her hands over her face and sighed. The noise she heard in her head was minimized by the solid oak door and her room's location at the far end of the hall. It was like the housing committee knew exactly what she needed, sort of.

Chapter 3

Her roommate was going to be a problem. She'd been sent a letter at the beginning of August informing her of her intended housemate. A quick Google search and Natalie had enough information to build a solid case for panic.

Avery Bluth was wealthy. Crazy wealthy. Her father had made his fortune creating a fantastic drug the majority of the world was using to make their overweight, overdrugged and overtired male members stand up and be useful once more. Natalie feared the worst in sharing quarters with someone who came from such a different place. Not only was Avery from money, she was also from Upstate New York.

Their relationship began much as Natalie feared. The very next morning after she had finally gotten a few hours of sleep after an anxious night, the door burst open to permit entry to a loud strawberry blonde tornado in a stomping snit. Natalie guessed the cyclone was her roommate and was soon to learn this was her typical modus operendi. Avery rarely failed to get her way and when she didn't, it was wise to leave before the storm broke.

"Who the hell are *you* and why are you in *my* room?" She demanded in a high, shrill voice, her big blue eyes wide and furious.

Natalie sat bolt upright, her three precious hours of sleep not nearly enough to deal with this banshee. Rubbing sleep from her eyes and blinking at the five foot nothing little terror, her hair frizzled possibly from the energy rolling off of her so strong the air hummed with it. Avery stiffly stood in the doorway full of her pink clad, slightly pudgy and pig nosed self.

Natalie sighed heavily. "I'm Natalie Swenson. Your roommate."

The small whirlwind threw a bag large enough to hold a picnic for five down on the nubby, dark brown carpet and spun on her heeled boot to storm from the premises. It was not until just before dinner that the poorly mannered girl made an equally dramatic *re*appearance.

Natalie's mind began buzzing just before the door whipped open, handle banging on the dresser behind it. Natalie startled backward, nearly jumping from the chair at the desk where she had been reading chapters from her Biology text.

"Look," the blonde started, setting herself in an aggressive stance with her hands on her hips, facing Natalie from a few feet away. "I'm supposed to have this room to myself. My father's secretary arranged it months ago." She rolled her eyes when she said "months" and Natalie got a good read on her right there. Never mind the whispering Natalie heard filling her head. She couldn't help herself as the rude thoughts ran through her mind of their own accord as they appraised each other.

Just wait until they find out, I'm sure Daddy will fire that stupid secretary for this. She's always trying to piss me off. Jealous much? From the looks of things she's not going to help me out in the social department. Biology, really? We don't even start classes until tomorrow. How am I supposed to have a fresh start when I have her here?

Natalie tried to shrug off the negative commentary running through her head. It was always the worst when she first met someone, but as she got used to it, she could usually could manage to tune it out to nothing more than constant murmuring. Sometimes she was so judgmental without even meaning to be, she wished she were a better person.

Blowing out hard and tucking a strand of her black hair behind her ear, it was just getting long enough now, Natalie stood up and faced the girl.

"I'm sure you're right and there's been some sort of mistake." She took the path of least resistance, confrontation was not her strength. "Didn't you get your roommate assignment in the mail?" The "duh" look on Avery's red face was answer enough. Natalie hurriedly continued, trying to smooth things over. "But no one's here to help us on a Sunday. How about we wait until tomorrow when the campus is up and running. I'm sure they'll figure it out." Though in truth Natalie was pretty sure nothing would change and she was going to be stuck with this obnoxious beast for the entire term if not the year. "So let's just make the best of it for tonight, okay?"

Avery considered her suggestion, tipping her head first one way then the other before finally giving a quick nod of assent, though not defeat. "All right. We'll give it until tomorrow." She kicked the door shut behind her with a small and expensive looking boot. "I've called to put a hold on my things. My bag has enough to get me through the night."

Natalie glanced over that the giant bag that had remained where it was chucked. It probably had enough for most people to stay a week. "Sure, whatever works for you." She wanted to be accommodating. Tension made her thoughts murkier, harder to control. It went from one voice to many, like when she was in a huge crowd and she couldn't keep her head straight. This particular time there was no crowd, just the one spoiled rotten girl who put out more hostility than Natalie had had aimed at her in a long time, but that was enough.

"I have a headache." She informed the unpleasant blonde hoping she would get the hint to dial it back. "I was just going to take something and go to bed." Natalie was going to take something her specialist had prescribed for occasions such as these when she felt like she was completely out of control and her head was swimming with noise. It would knock her for a loop but it was worth it to dull the buzzing.

Avery eyed her up and down, her demeanor softening slightly. "I get migraines." She offered. "Since I was a kid."

Natalie had the briefest thought that Avery might believe they had something in common. She lifted her weary expression. "Me too."

Looking around at the room, Avery put her hands on her hips and sighed expressively. "I suppose I could unpack a little. *I'm* staying no matter what." She leaned over to grab the handles of her giant bag.

Natalie waited until Avery was busy unpacking before she got up to find her stash of medications neatly hidden away in her dresser drawer. She was determined to keep her questionable mental stability a secret here.

"What's that?" Avery had come up for air and was looking over her shoulder at Natalie.

Startled, Natalie threw the pill into her mouth and hurriedly fumbled the cap back on the small bottle. "Nothing." She replied around the small pill already disintegrating on her tongue. She swallowed before the bitter pill could leave its lingering flavor on her taste buds. "It's a prescription my doctor gave me for my headaches."

"Really?" Now she was definitely interested. "What is it? My doctor has given me everything under the sun but nothing works. Does yours?" She peered around Natalie's shoulder.

I wonder if I could borrow some. For fear Avery might go through her things to do just that, Natalie lied. "I wouldn't recommend them. They help a little but they make me really sick. Sometimes I puke."

Avery's pig nose wrinkled in distaste. "Oh, never mind then."

Natalie was a seamless liar. It had grown out of necessity and she hadn't felt guilty about it for a very long time. Years ago when she had gone through a self-exploration phase, Natalie had researched mental illnesses trying to learn more about her mental disorder. Her findings didn't entirely fit with the doctor's dual diagnosis of ADD and OCD. Instead, they brought her to borderline personality disorder and her fingers had trembled where they traced the words on the page. "...depth and variability of moods... unusual levels of instability in mood; black and white thinking... chaotic and unstable interpersonal relationships, self-image, identity, and behavior; as well as a disturbance in the individual's sense of self... periods of dissociation..."

It wasn't perfect but it matched much better than what the doctor had surmised based upon what little she'd told them back in the beginning. Natalie could easily dissociate herself from others, the endless babble in her head, that couldn't be normal. And what about her continued lying? It clearly bothered other people to do it. Not so for Natalie.

She had gotten over that little hiccup shortly after the whispering started for her and people began to notice her unusual and often inappropriate behavior: avoiding crowds, ignoring friends, staring vacantly with a dazed expression when people spoke to her, like she was always listening to something else. That sort of thing tended to paint a picture of strange and unusual. Natalie had reacted accordingly; she had withdrawn further and become more antisocial, even causing several teachers to ask her parents if she was suicidal. Of course the Art teacher had let it slip about her little "accident" and word was out amongst the staff at her school.

Lying to *this* stranger presented no problem for Natalie. If it made things easier for her, she had no issue with it.

Chapter 4

The next morning was Monday. Natalie had her first class at ten, British Literature. As much as she enjoyed reading, classic literature was not a favorite. And she hated the English authors, so subtle she missed half their nuances and felt relatively certain it was intentional. Granted most of their audience probably wasn't medicated out of their gourds.

Natalie took her seat and, lo and behold, Avery crossed the threshold. She stopped in the doorway and caught Natalie's eye. Surprisingly, she slid into the seat right beside Natalie and spoke while she unpacked her books.

"I talked to the housing people and they said they were full this term so unless someone drops out, you *have* to stay in my room." Her tone was less acidic than it had been the night before yet did not fail to again assert her dominance.

"Sorry." Natalie mumbled, thinking that would be what the stronger personality would want to hear. Privately she prayed for a massive case of homesickness on campus.

Avery shrugged and glanced up. "We can try to make the best of it." She made a show of drawing herself up and putting on a brave face.

She doesn't seem that bad and she never argues. I can work with that. Natalie heard clearly through the rest of the noise in her head, imagining she was seeing herself through Avery's eyes, her refusal to fight back was pathetic. She wondered sometimes if she had more than one personality floating around in her skull, it would explain some of the things she came up sometimes.

Natalie smiled tightly at her new roommate, sure she was about as happy with the setup as she.

***

Class passed quickly as did the entire first day. British Literature, Biology, Calculus and Philosophy filled her first term requirements and as she was learning, college level classes were much more difficult than high school. Four was enough. When at the end of the day she made her way to her last obligatory stop in her schedule, she was exhausted but looking forward to it. She was going to meet the "special support network" Ms. Miller had helped her set up which consisted of a mandatory ten hours per week in the tutoring center. It seemed excessive to Natalie, but Ms. Miller was insistent.

The second she walked into the tutoring center and the door hissed shut behind her, Natalie felt her eyes well up. A blanket of silence enveloped her and peace washed over her.

A hand came up and rested lightly on her shoulder. Natalie was taken completely by surprise and spun on its bearer.

"Hello. You must be Natalie Swenson." The hand belonged to an older Hispanic woman with the beginnings of grey dotting her otherwise raven black hair and perfectly coordinated outfit down to the beaded chain on her glasses hanging around her neck. "I'm Ivy Santiago. I head the Tutoring Center." She lowered the hand left hanging in the air above where Natalie's shoulder had been.

Hesitant, Natalie took Ivy's hand noticing the woman's warm, dry skin felt oddly welcoming. With that one simple touch the constant tension in her body began to ease. It was a relief she hadn't felt since spring when she'd last seen Ms. Miller.

The smile she felt bending her lips into an unfamiliar shape came without effort, albeit a little stiff from disuse. "Ms. Santiago, it's a pleasure to finally meet you." Her hand lingered in the older woman's grasp.

"Please, call me Ivy." Her dark mauve lipstick captivated Natalie's gaze, drawing her eyes to the small gap between her otherwise even white teeth. "So, how are you finding things here at Prestige so far?" She motioned for Natalie to sit at one of the three small round white tables occupying the open space, each with four plastic orange chairs pulled up underneath them.

Somewhat regretfully, Natalie let Ivy disengage. "Nat." She clarified. "My friends call me Nat." No longer did that little falsehood cause her the pang it used to. In truth Natalie didn't have any friends, but when she had, they'd called her that.

Natalie let herself be guided to the nearest table. Glancing around, she saw that at present they had the center to themselves. In all, it was the size of a small classroom. In the center was a large, open, well-lit area with the three tables. One rectangular desk sat just inside the door behind her for the teacher or supervisor and on each of the two sidewalls were two closet sized rooms on either side. The rooms were mostly private except for the typical rectangular window schools put in doors so teachers can look in and confirm nobody is doing anything they shouldn't be. In between the doors outside each room were low bookshelves stocked with papers, workbooks, reference manuals and other various and assorted office supplies students might need.

The mostly white space, instead of being blinding, proved to be restful, devoid as it was of posters, books or any other stimuli. The only decorations were the furnishings and those were sparse and clean.

Natalie took the indicated seat and felt the cold plastic against the back of her jeans, its inherent static already making its presence known where her jeans gapped from her skin. Momentarily Nat was grateful she hadn't worn a skirt. Wiggling back, she sat straight upright against the hard curves of the chair, her long legs pushed out in front of her and crossed at the ankles habitually to present a false sense of relaxation Natalie so rarely felt.

Ivy took a seat across from her. She picked up her glasses and set them in place, reaching over to a manila file folder sitting on the table to her right. Natalie thought she recognized it even if she hadn't seen it since that fateful meeting in middle school. When she flipped it open, Natalie saw her high school picture staring up at her upside down. Her insides constricted, the sense of well being she had begun to enjoy evaporated leaving behind only the tense apprehensive feeling she usually operated under. Self-conscious, she tugged her shirtsleeves down.

Ivy caught the gesture, held up a hand and met Natalie's anticipatory gaze calmly. "Now don't worry about this. We are going to take a look at where you left off with Ms. Miller and then you won't see this again during your career here."

Her encouraging smile didn't completely erase Natalie's anxiety though she did feel her shoulders ease down to halfway normal. She nodded, uncertain what to say.

"Now, I see that you were having trouble concentrating until they added Depakote to your regimen and you're still on it." Her brows shot up. "How do you find that affects you?"

Shrugging, Natalie mumbled her response. They'd all made it hard to concentrate, after a while she'd given up complaining. "I don't know. It makes me feel fuzzy I guess. Better than the Thorazine or Haldol. It's been so long, I guess I don't remember what it was like before they put me on anything."

"Hmm." Ivy studied the pages in the incredibly thick file. "It looks like you've been underserved Nat." She snapped the file shut. "I would like to change that if you would be willing to try. We have a doctor here on staff that can work with us to step you down and eventually see about weaning you off of the drugs." She watched Natalie for a reaction. "But you would have to be willing to learn some skills that would help you to self-monitor in the future." Her eyes roamed Natalie's face in growing frustration.

Natalie wasn't sure what to say. Again she shrugged, non-commital.

Ivy raised an eyebrow archly. "Is that all you have to say about all of this?" She pointed to the file and the room around them. "Do you not have an opinion about anything regarding your future or your treatment these past five years?" She challenged expressionless, waiting for Natalie's input. To keep her mind on the question, Ivy's fingers drummed the folder expectantly.

Feeling pressured to explore parts of herself she preferred to leave closed off, Natalie squirmed. She uncrossed and crossed her ankles, sitting up even straighter and pushing the cuticles of her right thumb up with her left. "I don't know. It sucks I guess."

"That is a cop out." Ivy pushed back.

Natalie took a harder look at the matronly figure she had assumed was better at reading bedtime stories than teaching crazy students how to handle themselves without drugs.

Ivy met her eyes evenly and waited.

Under the bony, weak appearance lay a hard edged woman who had probably seen scores of students before Natalie pass through those blank white doors. Each of them somewhat jaded and unwilling to accept teaching or counsel at first. Natalie's case was nothing new to her.

With a sigh, Natalie delved a little deeper. "Okay, it has *really* sucked. I was doing well in my classes and with my friends and then everything got weird in middle school. They said I had this," she waved a hand by her head, "thing, and have been trying every mix of drugs since to make me less," she paused, searching, "less, I don't know what." Certainly not less dangerous to herself. "It's like it isn't even me in here anymore." Natalie couldn't be sure if it was a little homesickness or something about Ivy that perpetuated her moment of honesty, maybe she just needed to let someone know what it was like. Regardless, Natalie actually gave voice to one of her greatest fears. "I don't even know if I could tell you what's really me." Her voice cracked, giving away how real the anxiety was for her. It wasn't even the drugs, it was the disorder that had truly taken her identity. The thought of losing the drugs was exciting but frightening because if they were gone, she was terrified there was nothing left of her after all these years of deprivation.

Ivy's face warmed and she reached across the table to rest a comforting hand on Natalie's. "We're going to figure that out. That's what I'm here for after all." She gave her hand a squeeze.

Natalie sniffled back the emotion that had begun to wrestle free of her tight bonds just as the door opened. Her head jerked up at the sound of the latch giving way.

The boy, no man, that walked in was arresting. It was not that he was supermodel handsome, but there was something captivating about him. He had a presence that commanded attention. She felt her hazy mind work to focus on him. Shiny black hair fell thickly over his forehead in dark waves just long enough to brush his ears and eyebrows. His skin was olive and his eyes bright green, accented by thick black lashes. The man's build was nothing to sneeze at either. He was just over six feet tall with a well built chest, trim waist, and what she could see of his arms outside his black t-shirt were equally well developed. A hint of a tattoo peeked out from under one of his shirtsleeves and Natalie had an urge to push the fabric out of the way to see the rest.

Natalie stared, unable to stop herself from thinking of how beautiful he was and how she wanted to touch his skin.

As if he could tell what she was thinking, he cut his eyes over at her curtly, unimpressed no doubt with the sight of an average looking freshman like her.

Great, another cow eyed freshman streaked through her mind in a masculine "voice" that made her throat tighten. Chastising herself for getting caught ogling, Natalie assured herself she was not cow eyed.

His eyes grew wide then hard as he glowered back. His head jerked backward and she thought she detected a brief glimmer of something else in his glare.

Great, Natalie thought to herself. I'm staring at him and now he thinks I'm a spaz who forgot how to blink. She shifted nervously in her seat.

Ivy chuckled to herself. "Luka, please come in." She waved the handsome man over. Shifting his focus back to Ivy, his expression softened and he made his way to their table. "Luka Bailey is one of our tutors. Luka, meet a new student we'll be working with, Natalie Swenson."

Natalie felt herself blushing, not knowing what to do under his direct scrutiny. She tried to smile but all that came off was a quick flash of teeth closer to a grimace. Giving up, she stared awkwardly down at her hands.

Luka was quiet for a moment before speaking. "Pleased to meet you Natalie." When he spoke, his voice was multilayered, the richness of it confused her. She swore it was coming from inside and outside her head. Natalie once again found herself staring as his presence filled her up.

Ivy cleared her throat and Natalie jerked, remembering where she was. She felt the heat creeping up and flushing her face. Risking another glance at him, Natalie again swore she saw the same quick flash of shock before he hid it.

"Luka dear, your timing is impeccable." She tapped a fingernail painted to match her mauve lipstick against her teeth before speaking to Natalie. "Nat we have a tutoring program where we pair freshmen with upper classmen and I think that you would be an ideal candidate." She nodded to herself. "Yes, you two will work together splendidly." She waved her hand at him. "Luka, could you take over with Natalie here, say for an hour or two on Tuesdays and Thursdays?"

It would have been impossible for Natalie to miss Luka's lip curling under his slightly roman nose in distaste at her suggestion. But Ivy ran right over it before he could object. "Great. Then we'll see you," she pointed at Natalie, "back here every day. You choose when, except for the days you work with Luka. Those days you two will have to work out amongst yourselves."

Grudgingly Luka nodded and his multilayered voice became singular and hard. "Fine, I'll be in tomorrow at lunch." He stared at Natalie, challenging her. "Does that work for you?"

Mentally, Natalie ran through her schedule. She had about a three hour block of time between her classes on Tuesdays in the middle of the day and Thursdays she only had a morning class. "Sure. I'm open."

He nodded brusquely and spun on his heel to leave when Ivy called him back.

"Dear, I am sorry. Did you have something else you came in for?" She managed to look innocent as if she hadn't just ruined his semester.

"As a matter of fact, I did." He shot a dismissive look at Natalie. "I wanted to thank you for the recommendation. I was accepted for that internship."

"That's wonderful Luka. They'll be happy to have you. Have you told your father yet?"

"I haven't been able to reach him. They're traveling." He was uncertain and Natalie couldn't stop her eyes from searching his face, curious at his feeling.

Luka was troubled. *They're always traveling.* Natalie's whispers eeked their way into this quiet place.

"Well, I'm sure they are very proud of you dear." Ivy stood and put her arms around him, he hugged her back and Natalie saw the tension leave his big frame.

Their eyes met over Ivy's shoulder and Natalie looked away unable to hold his gaze. She wasn't used to making eye contact with people.

After Luka left Natalie had a hard time comprehending Ivy's remaining questions or answering competently. Exhaustion and overstimulation had her nearly dead on her feet. Several times she caught herself staring at the door. Looking for a distraction, she told herself. That's all.

Finally, Ivy harrumphed in frustration and stood. Natalie was caught unawares and blinked, bringing her mind to bear for a moment. "Since you're clearly not with me, let's call it a day." She gave a stern look over her glasses. "Come back tomorrow. Be rested and bring your books."

Natalie nodded and somberly and made a hasty exit. Finished with her classes, she hurried across campus to get back to her room. "And a cold shower," she muttered to herself only half joking.

Chapter 5

Except when she got back to the room, Natalie was not alone. Avery was already there and in a conciliatory gesture, she had a pizza box sitting on her desk. It smelled wonderful and, Natalie realized when her stomach growled audibly, it was the only food she had seen other than a granola bar since breakfast.

"Since we're going to be bunking together for the foreseeable future, I thought we could at least make an effort to be friendly." She flipped open the box, waving the top to fan the appetizing fumes in Natalie's direction. "Do you like pepperoni?"

Glad to have something less trying to think about than Ivy's notions or a stubborn pair of green eyes, Natalie laughed, "Yes." She sighed in relief and thought she felt one from Avery as well.

Already the whispers were starting. The barrage of thoughts Natalie's subconscious threw at her about a distant father and years of boarding school with no friends and lonely holidays in a big, empty house struck her as some sad movie script she must be associating with this girl based on some preconceived notion of what life was like for the rich. It was a common tendency of hers she assumed was a side effect of her disorder or lack of friends, this outrageous imagination she had. Nat could probably write a book if she could hold a train of thought long enough to make sense.

Come to think of it, the only people she hadn't made up stories for since Ms. Miller and her specialist were Ivy and Luka. Odd, especially Luka considering he'd affected her so strongly.

As the girls ate pizza and talked and joked, the subject eventually turned to family and Natalie was shocked to learn that her guesses had been accurate. Avery had a distant father, her mother was dead and she spent most of the past seven years at various boarding schools on the East coast. Her prickly exterior made a little more sense as her life was put into context.

"What about you?" Avery asked, peeling a piece of pepperoni off of her third slice of pizza and tossing it into her mouth. "What's your family like? Are they nice?"

Natalie appreciated the phrasing of the question. It let her answer without lying. The realization that she didn't want to lie to Avery if she could help it caught her unawares. And in a weird way it was liberating. If she was beginning to feel some sort of guilt or remorse then maybe there was hope for her. Maybe Natalie wasn't such a lost cause after all.

"My dad works at a cabinet shop and mom is a secretary at an insurance company." She glossed over her parents' careers. It embarrassed her to think of telling this rich girl about her working class family. They were good people and worked hard but not everyone knew that about blue collar jobs like her dad's. She didn't want Avery to think less of her or her parents and didn't see her answer as a direct lie. "They're really cool. I'm lucky to have them."

"Any brothers or sisters?"

Natalie had a mouthful of pizza and shook her head.

"So what did you think of your first day?"

Natalie's mind didn't go to her classes or professors or even the fact that she'd stumbled up the stairs into another student nearly bringing them both down. No, she saw a pair of eyes that made her heart skip a beat. There must have been something in her reaction that gave her away because Avery lowered the remaining half of her pepperoni denuded slice and leaned forward. "Spill."

Natalie was uncertain how to go on without hinting at her hopefully temporary infatuation but did want to talk about the strange exchange with Luka earlier. Never having had any sort of boy meets girl situation before, she didn't know if hers was normal or if, like a wolf senses defect in another and kills it, maybe he sensed hers and hated her on sight.

"Well, I don't know if you know this but to qualify for my scholarship I need to spend a certain amount of time in the tutoring center."

Avery shook her head that she did not. Natalie had to keep her grades up to keep the scholarship and the only way to do that was to be tutored. Avery didn't need to know *everything* about Natalie.

"I went in today and met the guy who's supposed to tutor me or mentor me or whatever."

"Maybe I should stop in. My aversion to Calculus is clinical. It won't be long before I'm in there under orders." Avery rolled her eyes.

"Really?" Natalie had been out of the mainstream for so long she had forgotten that other people didn't always understand the lessons either.

"Yep." She was still staring pretty intensely. "So? What happened? Did you meet someone hot?"

Natalie felt her face flush and Avery's jaw dropped.

"What? It's the first day and you already have a crush?" She grinned. "You work fast woman."

Natalie felt her lips lifting again into a smile at the memory of Luka's dark features and she could hear his voice in her head.

"Wow, that good huh? I *definitely* need tutoring. I want details." Avery took a bite and stared at Natalie, clearly waiting for more.

Nervous, she picked at her pizza. "His name's Luka Bailey and he's older than us." She shot a look at Avery and, although very interested, she was making no move to interrupt. Natalie continued. "He's pretty good looking and we've been paired up for some mentoring program between freshmen and upper classmen."

"Is he cool or does he know he's a hottie and make you suffer?"

She furrowed her brow, remembering his confusing coldness. "I think he's okay but I don't think he's big on the whole big brother, little sister thing." She confessed.

"Don't think of him as your brother or it makes it weird that you totally want to jump him." Avery said straightfaced.

Natalie flushed flaming red and defended herself. "I do not."

Avery dropped her chin to properly look down her nose. "If you don't want to admit it that's fine, but nobody gets that flustered about someone they just want to study with I'll tell you that." She continued to stare pointedly at Natalie. Her upturned nose, round face and eyes slightly too close together gave her more than a passing resemblance to a pig.

Still, Natalie was beginning to like Avery. Underneath her spoiled, prickly façade, she had the potential to be a reasonably friendly person and rather astute as well. She was gleaning things from Natalie she hadn't intended to let slip. Though she did have to admit Avery was probably light years ahead of her when it came to social nuances. As it was, she was well on her way to making her first friend in a very long time and it felt good.

Chapter 6

The next day's morning class couldn't wrap up fast enough. Never mind it was Calculus, a point of constant confusion for most of the class. For Natalie, anything that required much concentration was nearly impossible under the influence of the chemicals flooding her system.

Finally, it was ten to eleven and she packed up her books in a rush and slung her nondescript brown canvas backpack over her shoulder to head to her tutoring session. Natalie was nearly all the way across the campus when she heard her name being called by a familiar voice. She stopped and glanced around. The source was easy enough to find.

Avery was jogging up, holding her bag's strap so it didn't slip off her shoulder. A good idea considering she never packed light for anything, her book bag probably weighed a good twenty pounds. Her red-blonde ponytail bounced with every stride. By the time she reached Natalie her cheeks were pink and she was puffing from the exertion.

Natalie found herself mildly annoyed to be slowed in her progress yet still smiled in welcome, pleased to be sought out. "I *know* you only have two classes in the morning. What the hell do you have in that thing, a small car?" She pointed at the bulging bag currently tipping Avery's shoulders with its bulk.

"You never know what you're going to need. Someday my overpacking will come in handy." Avery shot back, not offended in the least. Her eyebrows wiggled, "Are you off to meet tall dark and dreamy?"

Natalie felt her face flush hot. "I have my tutoring session if that's what you mean."

"I'm going that direction, mind if I walk with you?"

There was no reason Natalie could think of for Avery to be going that direction. The building that housed the tutoring center was at the far edge of campus with nothing else around it. Still, it didn't matter if she saw him or not. Natalie had no claim on him. "Sure."

The walk to the building was quick. Avery followed Natalie through the double glass doors and down the short hall past two classrooms and into the wooden door on her right. Ivy glanced up and smiled in welcome from her desk. The Zen-like tranquility of the place wrapped itself around her and Natalie felt her defenses relaxing.

"Hello Nat, who is your friend?" She eyed Avery curiously.

Natalie could see Avery swiveling her head to and fro, though whether she was taking in the contents and setup of the room or searching for a handsome stranger Natalie couldn't be sure.

"Ivy, this is my roommate Avery." It was too soon to call her "friend" and it had been a long time since she had used the term. Honestly, she was a touch nervous to say the wrong thing and be corrected.

Ivy stood, extending her hand over the desk. Avery shook it firmly, giving a brief businesslike smile. Ivy was not who she wanted to meet and Natalie could see the disappointment written plainly on her face.

"Natalie, Luka called to tell me he's unable to make it today so it will be just the two of us. I hope that is all right with you?"

It was difficult, but Natalie managed to keep her own disappointment from showing. Instead she shrugged, "That's fine. I've had one day of Calc and I'm already feeling lost."

Eyeing her curiously, Ivy nodded and glanced back at Avery. "Would you like to study with us Avery?"

Avery shook her head. "No, not yet. I'm sure I'll be back though, give me a few weeks and I'll be needing everything you've got." She laughed at herself.

"Don't let yourself get too lost. You're welcome to come along with Natalie any time."

"I will." Avery turned. "Nat, I'm heading back. Will you be around later?"

"Yeah, this won't be but a few hours."

Avery left with a wave. After the door closed and they were alone, Ivy rose and came around her desk.

"Are you ready to work today?"

Nat puffed her cheeks and blew. "Guess so."

Together they attacked the complexities of algorithms and logarithms for nearly an hour until Ivy felt certain Nat had a tenuous grasp on it. Next they explored Alice's adventure down the rabbit hole, Ivy translating and pointing out the nuances Mr.

Carroll had layered into his work that Natalie had completely missed.

Finally, they had gone through everything and Ivy leaned back in her chair, taking her glasses off to let them hang by their chain. Today's was a red beaded chain to match her red cardigan wrapped around her lean shoulders clad in a plain white tee tucked into jeans.

Ivy's long tan fingers rubbed her eyes. "Now that we are done with that, I would like to start working on something else with our last twenty minutes." Her fingers remained on her face, blocking her features from Natalie's eyes.

"Okay." She felt her heart skip a beat.

"Don't worry." Ivy smiled warmly. "This will be the first step for you in learning to control yourself and getting off of your medications."

That said, Natalie agreed despite being doubtful Ivy's plan would really work. She sat back, hands folded on the table and crossed her ankles in her familiar pose of attentiveness.

Ivy's brows drew together and she frowned. "Don't patronize me. Who has done this more often, you or me?" She did not wait for an answer. "Right. So when I say I can help you, believe me. If you work hard, there is no reason this can't work for you too."

Natalie nodded once, lips pulled tight against her gritted teeth.

"Now, I want you to open your mind. This is going to seem strange at first but it has proven effective in cases like yours."

Staring in disbelief, Natalie asked. "You've worked with people who have what I have?"

"I have indeed. It is a specialty of sorts." She smiled strangely but before Natalie could ask her what she meant, she got down to business. "Now uncross your legs and put your feet flat on the floor. Hands palms down on your thighs."

Confused but curious, Natalie did as she was told.

"Now I want you to pick a spot on the wall and stare at it. Let your eyes lose their focus and your mind go blank."

It was almost exactly the same exercise Ms. Miller had given her to try in high school. "I've done this before. It doesn't work on me." She explained, starting to bring her hands back up to the table. "I can't make my mind go blank."

Ivy was prepared for her arguments. "No, you *haven't* done this before. I spoke with Ms. Miller and you actually were *supposed* to do this but you didn't. You hemmed and hawed, making excuses every step of the way about why you couldn't or why it wouldn't work for you. In the end, you quit. Here, you will not quit." Ivy made her expectations very clear. Something no one had been bold enough to do for fear of setting her off.

Without another word Natalie slid her hands into her lap to rest lightly on her thighs, her feet uncrossed themselves and   her feet were planted firmly on the floor.

That done, Ivy went on to instruct her on the proper methods of breathing. Knowing she wasn't going to be allowed to talk or stubborn herself out of it, Natalie gave it an honest try.

Once she gave it a chance and began breathing properly, as easy as that sounded it was actually very difficult, Natalie found herself relaxing. Her mind quieted.

Ivy caught it. "It isn't enough to count on someone else to calm your nerves. You need to be able to do it yourself Nat."

Natalie gasped in surprise. Ivy knew the effect she had on her. On the surface that fact was alarming, but only a minor amount of thought on the subject and Natalie realized it didn't really surprise her that Ivy would know that. In much the same way a mother knows when a child is lying, Ivy knew she could quell students' nerves. It wasn't so strange when she looked at it that way.

Ivy's only response was to smile serenely.

For the next twenty minutes, Natalie worked to clear her mind. She was nearly there several times but then sounds from outside or a random thought and her concentration was lost.

Just as she was about to give up, Ivy called their session over for the day.

"That was good progress Nat. This is hard work and your mind is undisciplined. Some of that is from your medication and some is you too." She patted her hand where it lay on top of the table. "Don't worry, you're doing fine. You'll get this. I want you to cut your dose in half starting tomorrow. It will take some time for it to clear your system."

Natalie started to object and Ivy intervened holding up a finger.

"Trust the teacher. I think you've fallen back on excuses out of laziness and we are going to break that as well as some of your other habits. Agreed?"

"Agreed." Natalie bit back any arguments seeing they would buy her no slack.

The walk back to her dorm to meet Avery was a surreal one. Natalie was still working to practice her breathing as she walked. It was challenging over the uneven terrain but that only made Natalie grit her teeth and try harder. By the time her hand grasped the handle she was impressed with herself for maintaining as much focus as she had. A small flicker of confidence lit itself within her breast.

Chapter 7

"There you are!" Avery nearly bowled Natalie over when she opened the door.

She almost saw the bubble around herself burst and Natalie felt the familiar rising of the cacophony of sound that so typically followed her. "I told you I would be two hours." Avery's maternal welcome elicited Natalie's automatic snappy response.

Avery put her hands out, palms up defensively. "Easy Nat. It's just been hard to sit still. I've got some cool news." She was bouncing on the balls of her feet less than a foot from Natalie's nose. Natalie stuck out her hands to pretend push Avery back as the whispers took over.

Oh my God. A party with guys and beer is just perfect. It's been so *long since I've been to a party and I've never been to a* college *party before. Those guys probably really know what they're doing. I should tell Dad, boy would he be pissed if he knew I was out partying again.*

"Nat, I heard about a back to school party off campus. On my way back here I stopped off in the store to get some gum and this girl I was talking to said when *these* guys throw a party you *have* to go. They're amazing!" She was so excited she practically vibrated. As much as Natalie did not want to go to a party with a bunch of college kids, she didn't want to offend Avery either and it was pretty clear she felt strongly about going.

"Okay." She caved before Avery could build up a head of steam and argue with her. The thought of a long emotional debate with her did not appeal. "When is it?"

Almost defeated by her unexpected victory, Avery snapped her mouth shut and stared at Natalie. "O-okay." She said slowly. "I had no idea you were so easy to convince. I figured you wouldn't want to go."

Natalie shrugged. "It can't hurt and it might be fun to get out for a while." She lied adding quickly, "I don't want to go for long though."

Avery gave her a queer look as she agreed without argument. "Not a problem. We'll just go for one or two." She winked.

"Unless one of us meets someone." Avery's preoccupation with the gruffer sex was becoming apparent.

In order to sound like she was less of a social mutant, Natalie agreed to both of Avery's stipulations. Better to go along than argue, however, if she got there and it was as bad as she assumed it would be she was not above pleading a headache.

Together they headed down to dinner, an interesting and unfulfilling kitchen creation called a "Bread Bar." It was completely unappetizing so Natalie went for the cereal always available on the back counter. Avery tried her luck with a slice of banana bread, also grabbing a bowl of Cocoa Puffs just in case. With their stomachs only barely sated, the girls went back to their dorm to get ready.

Natalie hadn't been to a party before so deferred to Avery's guidance as to what she should wear. On their way out she began to have second thoughts. Tugging at the hem of her fitted red tee to bring it closer to the top of her jeans and silver studded black belt.

"Relax Nat, you look great." Avery walked beside Natalie, it was only a few blocks to the party. "If I had your body I would run around naked. I don't know why you don't show more skin than you do."

Natalie offered a quick, tight smile before concentrating on the quake damaged sidewalk. They were in a residential area populated by 1920's bungalows so popular in California. While these were probably very lovely homes years ago, now that they had been turned over to student housing they were tired, unpainted and most had some of the ugliest furniture she'd ever seen since they'd cancelled "All in the Family" residing on their front porches.

The house they approached, joining in with several other small clusters of people converging on its dry front lawn was in good company with its neighbors, complete with a set of mismatched and weatherworn chaise lounges minus their cushions.

Like its streetmates the tan stucco exterior had several cracks in it, effects from suffering repeat earthquakes. Its few surrounding bushes were unkempt, arguably on the verge of death and to the side of the front step in the place of a lawn jockey was a female mannequin dressed in a sexy maid costume with a small silver lunch bucket dangling from her wrist.

When she forced her reluctant feet up the two concrete steps and looked into the bucket, Natalie saw that it held car keys though there were only a few. Most of the attendees appeared to be walking with the intention of stumbling home.

She hung back letting Avery enter first. Without knocking or ringing a bell, Avery walked through the door propped wide open. Natalie could almost hear Avery's excitement.

Oh, this is cool. There's the keg and who is that standing there with the cups? He's hot.

Natalie's reaction was the polar opposite. The loud music hurt her ears and the noise was tremendous. Her mind was swirling with thoughts about sex, tests, a cheating girlfriend and something darker.

The dark thoughts revolved around sex as well but not with a willing partner. She shook her head trying to get rid of the image of a girl drugged and bleary eyed lying naked with her head lolled to the side while male hands worked at the button of her pants. How could she ever hope to live with herself off of her medication when she suffered such depraved thoughts that would only get stronger without the fog? The weird thing about it was that even *she* was disgusted by the thoughts yet there they were in her head, being thought by her. Natalie wondered if Ivy would want to help her get off her meds if she knew how her mind *really* worked. She would probably *up* her dosage instead.

Natalie stumbled away from the crowd gathering at the keg including Avery and wandered through the house, instinctively heading away from the people. Her need to get away and clear her head drove her straight through the house and out the sliding glass doors standing open to the fenced back yard.

A pool was the centerpiece of the tiny yard ringed by citrus trees and tropical bushes. Off the corner of the house to her left was a small shed with a life preserver hanging on its side. Natalie guessed it was a changing room or cabana or whatever they called those things. To her it promised the oasis she needed from the maelstrom inside the house and her head.

She went straight for it. The thump of the music was fading and then the whispers began to swirl upsetting her equilibrium.

Feeling faint, her feet sped up, eyes fixed on the door standing slightly ajar.

He can't leave me. I'm sure he's just trying to prove a point. We'll see if he can say no to this.

She is delusional. I can't do this anymore for them.

Natalie clutched at her head, wishing she could be home in her room with the world shut away from her. Her eyes welled up at the thought. Home hadn't been much better but at least when she had been in her room with the music on and no one at home she didn't feel like she was going to burst. It hadn't seemed like enough but now, by comparison, it was paradise. For the first time in months, her hand itched for a blade, fingers traced the inside of her forearm. The urge seductively rolled through her mind, offering her the release and moment of control she craved. It's addiction pulled at her. Nat hoped to find something sharp inside the shed.

Her hands reached for the door and she shoved it open, slipping inside and leaning back against it to close it behind herself. Most of the noise was gone but for the new one she had just heard. She instantly felt around for something with an edge to it, not waiting for her eyes to adjust.

What the hell?

Natalie screamed, striking her head with her fists. "Leave me alone!"

"You're the one who barged in on *us*." An angry female voice hissed from the shadows.

Natalie froze. The voice had come from outside her head. Desperate eyes searched the darkness.

It proved unnecessary. The speaker moved, her shoe scraped the wooden floor of the building. Natalie squinted to see the woman.

A light from the house shone through a small side window casting a shaft of light inside the poolside shed. From the other side of the light, the woman's form stalked into sight.

She was a gorgeous woman with raven black hair falling down her back. Her shoulders were shrouded in a dark sweater thrown over the top of a similarly colored dress. It was too dark to see any more detail than that.

41

Her olive skin and dark hair reminded Natalie of someone. The woman's dark eyes narrowed, her lips pulled up into a snarl. Even angry this woman was beautiful. Natalie pushed herself harder against the door, willing it to open backward so that she could escape. Casting her glance to the side, by chance a glint of light struck on a metal object lying on a shelf beside her.

"What are you doing in here? Can't you see we wanted to be alone?"

"I'm sorry." Natalie reached over to snatch the short sharp object from its perch. Prize in hand, she reached behind her back trying to turn the handle. It was stuck. "I didn't know anyone was in here."

The woman's sneer turned cruel. *It's almost too easy to make this one squirm.*

Natalie imagined she was enjoying her cruelty.

A male voice, one she would know anywhere, spoke from the darkness and Natalie felt her breath catch in her throat.

"Leave her alone Ericka." He stepped forward. Natalie didn't need the light to know what face she would see.

Ericka turned her head and her harsh look did not alter with his approach. She was not to be put off the hunt, she smelled blood. He stepped up next to her and she slid an arm possessively around his waist. He let her.

Chapter 8

Natalie's heart sank. The last person she wanted to catch her here crying and being homesick was Luka yet here he was and she had just interrupted him with his girlfriend. Her stomach twisted, the tool in her hand made its presence known with its weight. She prayed it was sharp, her need for it was terrible. Natalie's eyes roamed what she could see of them both but they appeared to be fully clothed. She would rather die than walk in on him having sex with another woman.

Mentally she kicked herself for presuming to know anything about him after a five minute meeting. He was her tutor. Nothing more. Ericka was his girlfriend. Luka did fall a few rungs down in her eyes for having such a bitch for a girlfriend though. It was a let down to see that he was not so perfect after all. A nice guy would never have a girlfriend like that.

He was staring at her, she was grateful for the shadow darkening his eyes. Ericka had pulled herself in close to his side and had her other hand up on his chest clearly staking her claim.

Natalie slid over another step changing her angle and tried the stubborn handle again, this time opening the door. "I'll leave you two alone."

Luka said nothing, continuing to stare at her. The way he looked, so troubled and haunted, hurt more than it should have and Natalie couldn't wait to get away from here too. She wanted to find Avery and go back to their room.

She whipped the door open and took a sidestep back out turning as soon as she was clear. Natalie shoved her weapon up her sleeve and ran back inside the glass doors and was again hit by the wave of noise. Her eyes scanned the impossibly crowded house that felt volumes smaller now that it was shoulder to shoulder. In her head she heard someone crying for help. It was desperate. She feared she was going mad. Her other hand lay protectively over her salvation to prevent it from slipping free as she scanned for somewhere she could be alone if only for a few minutes.

"Nat! Over here!"

43

Avery's voice sounded far away despite the fact that she was only a few heads away. Natalie followed the voice until she stood in front of her. People bumped into her back and pushed her into Avery. Natalie jumped sideways, trying for a small space bubble around herself with no luck.

"Let's go." She shouted over the noise inside and outside of her head.

Avery shook her head, her eyes slightly out of focus. The cup in her hand told Natalie why. "No Nat. I want you to meet somebody." She held out her other hand and Natalie saw that it was attached to the hand of the shaggy blonde surfer dude standing next to her. He had an equally unfocused pair of blue eyes.

"This is Jason. Jason," she nodded her head toward each one with their introductions, "this is my roommate Nat."

"Hey Nat. Can I get you a beer?" *Man she looks freaked out. I wonder if she's tripping. She'd better not need Avery to take her home.*

Natalie shook her head at the offer but also at the whispers in her head. Still, the thought did have merit. She was being selfish for trying to pull Avery away from a good time and a new... what? What do you call this thing, a hookup? Casually, she let the lump slide down her sleeve into her hand and tested the side of the metal tool on her finger and found it to be sharp. She slid it into her pocket wondering if she could sneak away to the bathroom. If she didn't get herself grounded, she was afraid she was really going to lose it.

Taking her choice away, Avery spoke first. "Sure Jason. Why don't you grab a beer for Nat?" She gushed a big smile at him and he grinned back, kissing her cheek before he released it to disappear into the crowd fighting his way valiantly to the keg.

Avery's tongue was lazy with beer. "Nat please. Give me another hour. Jason is sooo sweet and super cute." She pleaded, batting her mascara darkened lashes.

Against everything screaming inside her to run from here, Natalie felt herself nodding her head and returning Avery's smile. "Sure. We'll stay a little while."

Squealing, Avery wrapped her newly freed arm around Natalie for a fast hug.

Jason returned shortly with a red plastic cup for her. Natalie took it and held it to her chest so she didn't spill on anyone. Several people in the crowd were dancing nearby to the fast techno and increasing the jostling.

This is hell, Natalie thought to herself closing her eyes for a moment to try to use some of those breathing exercises Ivy taught her today. It was no use in this environment.

"Come on, drink up. You'll feel better." Jason was watching her eagerly when she opened her eyes.

"I don't drink." She told him honestly. Glancing around, she tried to keep her curiosity mild as she inquired, "Where's the bathroom?"

"See that line?" Avery pointed to a row of people going all the way up the stairs.

Natalie's heart tightened.

Jason flashed her a smile. Natalie saw what Avery found charming about him. He had dimples and a certain charm to go with his wavy hair and outdoorsy good looks. "Well what else are we here for if not for drinking?" He waggled his eyebrows.

If it weren't for their combined contagious enthusiasm, Nat might have found it creepy. Instead, she found herself being swayed.

Maybe if she had a few she'd loosen up.

She took the thought as the impetus to push her toward a decision. Natalie raised her cup to her lips and parted them. A mouthful of the bitter golden alcohol flowed in and she swallowed hastily before her throat could object.

The initial bitterness was tolerable, even tasty. Natalie couldn't help feeling a little guilty, like she was breaking the rules. However, her parents had never had that talk with her and had not actually ever prevented her from drinking alcohol or doing drugs or even having sex. They had been more concerned with whether she would slit her wrists or end up in an institution. Apparently the other stuff was not as great a concern.

Natalie took another gulp. She had heard about being drunk and knew some people used it as an escape. If she had to be here with all this noise and no chance at getting her preferred method for another hour, an escape like this might be exactly what she

45

needed. Things couldn't be worse than they were at this very moment, millions of people couldn't be wrong.

As the beer began to make her head fuzzy, Natalie, Avery and Jason moved toward a quieter corner with less likelihood of one of them getting slammed into by a wiggling body. Jason went back for refills all around and Avery spun on Natalie when he'd taken their cups.

"What do you think?" Her eyes were huge and glassy. "I'm going to see about going back with him to his place."

The idea was no longer shocking to Natalie in her dulled state. "Didn't he say he has a roommate?" She couldn't remember his exact words but thought he had mentioned one.

Avery's brow was furrowed in thought. "I don't remember. What if he came to our place? Would you mind?"

As a matter of fact, she did. Then, looking at Avery's huge hopeful eyes, Natalie couldn't say no. "Sure."

Avery threw her arms around her again and Natalie got a picture in her head of what Avery was thinking in far more detail than she would have cared to. *There is something wrong with me.* She accepted the glass Jason brought back and took another long, grateful gulp.

"Me thinks she likes it." Jason said with a laugh.

Avery laughed heartily and Natalie took another gulp. The beer dialed the noise back to a buzz, each thought running into the other, too confused to make sense. It wasn't the silence she needed still it beat back the distinct voices she usually heard.

"Look, it's the little spy."

Natalie spun but stumbled up against Jason as she lost her footing.

She feels good too.

Natalie blinked, trying to focus and clear her head. It was failing.

Little girl can't even hold her liquor.
Where is it?

Natalie's stomach lurched. She tried to revisit the calm breathing. Except once her vision settled on the source of the jibe, she nearly lost more than her focus. Ericka stood planted firmly in front of her, her glare a direct challenge although for *what* was beyond Natalie.

"I told you I was sorry." She mumbled, watching the light and shadows play on her hair. Natalie wished she had beautiful hair like that, hers was just flat.

"Ericka, I think it's time for you to go." Luka grabbed her arm to pull her away.

She shook him off. Natalie would guess she wasn't the only one of them who had drunk too much to be reasonable. "No, I want to show her what I think about people who spy on other people." *I'm dousing the bitch.*

She raised her glass while Natalie watched it happen in slow motion, not believing her bleary eyes as she turned it upside down, and spilling the contents down the front of Natalie's shirt. She had only been saved from it going over her head by the dizzy backward stagger she'd mustered when she'd seemingly guessed the woman's intentions.

"That's enough!" Luka's angry tone was easy to hear over the sudden musical lull as someone changed tracks.

Ericka was not the only one who stopped. There were a number of people around them that turned to stare curiously.

"What the hell lady?" Avery stepped forward putting herself directly in Ericka's face. "Where do you get off being such a cow?"

"What are *you* her guard dog?" Ericka jutted her chin out, preparing for a fight.

Jason licked his lips in anticipation.

Natalie had a fleeting thought about a cat fight. She lunged forward to shove Avery out of the way as she had another thought. Sure enough, Natalie got her out of the way just as Ericka's hand came up and connected with Natalie's face.

Natalie's vision went dark with spots of white light dancing in front of it as she stumbled backward, hand coming up to rub her stinging cheekbone. Avery started forward again to defend Natalie when Luka moved between them.

"Please." He turned his gaze to Avery and she faltered. *Wow.*

"Natalie are you alright?" He asked without turning his head.

She nodded. Then, realizing he couldn't see her, she answered thickly, "Yes." Her face wasn't the only thing that stung. She blinked rapidly. She wouldn't cry in front of him or his nasty girlfriend.

She isn't my girlfriend.

"Then what is she?" She forgot that the words were coming from her own head. There was no way anyone but her would know what she was asking. The alcohol had caused her to make the mistake she feared. Feeling foolish, Natalie turned and pushed her way out of the house. Her pocket felt heavy.

Don't hurt yourself.

Avery called something from behind her and she thought she heard Ericka's mean spirited voice growing shrill. Luka growled something low and angry in response. Still she pushed until she reached the door and broke into a run.

Chapter 9

Natalie woke up alone in her dorm room. She sat up to get a drink of water and regretted it as soon as she was upright. The pounding in her head was incredible. Fortunately Friday mornings were quiet with most people not in class having gone home or, like her, were slow to get up after a late night.

Taking a quiet and much slower assessment of herself and the room, Natalie pieced together what she could remember from the night before. The scent of stale beer on her clothes brought to mind Ericka, Luka's beautiful yet psycho girlfriend and the gigantic ass she'd made of both of them.

"He sure can pick them." She muttered bitterly under her breath.

Wiggling over to the edge of her bed, Natalie was able to reach a bottle of water from under her bed. She kept them there in case she wanted one in the night and didn't want to go all the way down the hall to the bathroom or kitchen for a drink.

Slowly she sat up and sipped delicately at the bottle testing her stomach. This was a first for her and she didn't know what to expect but thought going slowly was a good plan. Something hard poked her hip. Turning, she saw the wooden handled tool she'd picked up last night. A quick inventory revealed she had not used it. Nat's hangover was providing all the grounding she needed to her physical being at the moment. She was in no danger of doing anything to herself just yet.

Natalie's cell phone buzzed in her other front pocket. She'd slept with it on her. Her mother would say she was going to get cancer.

"Hello." She knew the number but it didn't register until she heard the voice that went with it.

Avery did not sound any less herself than usual. She was better at morning afters than Natalie. "Nat! Oh my God. Where did you go last night?"

Holding her phone about a foot from her ear, Natalie answered quietly hoping to send a message. "Nowhere, I'm in our room." She wasn't too hungover to roll her eyes. Obviously her roommate didn't look too hard for her if she was at home.

Sadly, Avery did not copy Natalie's subdued tone. Instead she shrieked. "What? We went and knocked for at least ten minutes last night after you ran out of the party. You never answered and I lost my keys somewhere so I couldn't get in."

"Oh."

"Are you there now? I need to get in to change and grab my books. I have a class in like an hour."

"Yeah." She kept it simple.

Avery hung up and Nat clicked the cover closed on her phone. She had passed out and locked her roommate out. That was great. At least Avery didn't seem too upset by it. She had said, "we" so maybe the evening had gone well for her after all.

Twenty minutes later Natalie woke up in the exact same position with her phone on her pillow and Avery knocking softly on the door.

She swung her legs over the edge of the bed and got up to let Avery in. No sooner had she flipped the latch on the door that she felt her stomach do the same thing. Spinning, Natalie ran back and stuck her head in the garbage can while she heaved up the contents of her stomach, which thankfully wasn't much.

"Whoa Nat. You really can't hold your liquor." Avery commented from the doorway.

She cut her eyes at her before going back to throwing up again only this time was a painful dry heave. "I told you I'm not a drinker."

Avery chuckled from across the room. Her hangers rattled tinnily as she selected her clothes. "You could have fooled me last night. You sure held your own for a while there."

Natalie sat down on her haunches, laying her face on the edge of the garbage and liking the coolness of the plastic can liner against her sweaty skin. She rolled her face toward Avery, wanting the cool against her painful eye.

"Who was that girl? And that guy knew you. Are you holding out on me?" Avery was staring at Natalie and trying not to be caught so kept averting her eyes.

It seemed to Natalie she was going to get a cramp. "That was Luka and his girlfriend, I guess."

"That was your dream guy? What was up between his lady friend and you?" She no longer was trying to hide the fact that she was staring at Natalie. "Does she have reason to be jealous?"

Natalie snorted. "Weren't you there? Did you see the same thing I did? She was just pissed because I walked in on them in the changing room out by the pool."

"Huh." Avery wore an unreadable expression.

"*She* was the one who came after me inside and all *he* did was to tell her to go. It had nothing to do with me and him." Her voice was muffled as she put it back in the garbage. "It isn't my fault he's dating a nut ball." Pot calling the kettle black, she thought acidly as her stomach tightened again and came up empty.

"Well, you missed the fireworks after you left."

Natalie sat back, peeling her eyes open to see if Avery was serious.

She nodded at her. "That's right. After you stormed out, she got really mad at him. She called him a few choice words having to do with his misplaced loyalties. Then she hit him and stormed out."

"What did he do?"

Avery smiled slyly. "He asked Jason and me to go make sure you were okay and that was the last I saw of him. He didn't look like he was going to go after her, I think he was going upstairs." She looked off, thinking. "Other than the bathroom which had a humongo line, the only thing up there were bedrooms. Don't know why he'd go up alone." She shrugged and glanced back at Natalie.

Natalie wanted to be away from Avery's scrutiny and the smell from the garbage was horrendous. She tied up the bag and pointed at the door. Avery chuckled.

"Two aspirin and a warm shower will make you feel like a whole new woman. Trust me." She grabbed her robe and shower caddy as Natalie walked out to take the garbage to the chute in the center of the floor by the kitchen.

When she returned, Avery was gone. She followed her advice and got into a robe, grabbed her towel and caddy and headed to the showers.

By the time she got out, she heard a phone ringing from her room. Jogging the last few feet to her door she pushed the door open and heard the land line on her dresser ringing.

"Hello?" She panted, praying her nausea would stay gone so the aspirin had a chance to work. Her head was killing her.

"Were you coming in today dear?"

"Ivy?"

"I have your schedule and although you do not have any classes on Fridays, you do still owe me two hours for the day."

Natalie groaned. "Ivy, I'm not feeling well."

Her tone went icy, "Natalie I will tell you this once. My expectations from you will not ever change. If you owe me ten hours per week, you will give me ten hours per week whether you are *ill* or not." The way she said it, Natalie had the distinct feeling Ivy knew better than to be taken in by a story about having the flu.

"Okay Ivy. I'll be in in half an hour."

Pleasant once more, Ivy chimed back. "We'll see you then dear."

Chapter 10

Natalie slid on a pair of jeans and a loose blue sweater her mother had given her for her birthday last year. Try as she might, it was very hard not to be homesick. Everything had gotten so complicated all of a sudden. Dutifully remembering Ivy's orders, she cut her usual dose in half and swallowed it dry, a skill one develops after years of constant medicating.

On her walk to Ivy's, Natalie's thoughts rolled around the jumble of events that had taken place in the past few days. Avery was definitely a friend but was she a good one? She had gotten her drunk for the first time as well as into her first fight if you could call being slapped and doused with a beer a fight, one sided as it was. However, if she was honest, she had to admit she would not want to be here if it weren't for Avery.

Her spirited and unpredictable manner was infectious. Natalie had enjoyed herself more in the last few days than she had in the last five years.

She had made peace at least with her decision to stay in the dorms with Avery when she opened the door and was greeted by the sight of Ivy calmly going over papers with her glasses resting on her nose.

Natalie was liberated from her oppressive whispers as the door shut behind her and the center enveloped her with its solace.

Looking up, Ivy's mauve bow shaped lips curved into a smile and she removed her glasses. "So pleased you could come in." She frowned. "You do look a bit pale. Are you well?"

"I woke up sick." That was true. Natalie came to a stop at Ivy's desk.

Ivy's mouth tightened, her nose twitched. "Could it have anything to do with the alcohol I can smell coming out of your pores?"

Natalie felt her mouth fall open. "Uh."

"You shouldn't drink while you are on the types of medications you are. They can make you violently ill if they don't put you in a coma or worse."

"Sorry." Legitimately busted, Natalie didn't want to fight.

Ivy held up a hand and shook her head. Their conversation was over. "Shall we pick up where we left off yesterday?" She motioned toward the table closest to them. Again, no one else was in the center.

Natalie felt only a relief at not seeing Luka when she entered. Knowing he had such bad taste to be with a cruel person just because she was beautiful was a huge bucket of cold water for her.

She and Ivy worked together on her homework for a while until Ivy asked her if she was well enough to work on her "alternative medicine."

Natalie liked the sound of that. "I think so."

They did. They worked together well over an hour. So distracted was she with her focus inward on calm, Natalie didn't hear anything in the vacuum of silence until the door latch clicked into place.

Startled, she craned her neck to see behind her.

"Hello Natalie." Luka stood with his back against the door.

She held her breath. "Luka." Natalie wasn't sure if she was angry at him or ashamed of herself as she saw his face from the night before in her mind's eye.

He turned to face Ivy. "Ivy are you two almost done?"

"As a matter of fact dear, we were just finishing up."

Surprised, Natalie looked at the digital clock on Ivy's desk.

"Wow, I've never been able to focus for so long." She said in disbelief.

Ivy nodded in her usual unaffected way. "You are doing very well. I would like for you to practice both days this weekend and then I think we can talk to the doctor about starting to cut out your medication altogether over time."

Ignoring the embarrassment at Ivy's mentioning of her meds in front of Luka, she was both excited and scared at the prospect but held back. Ivy seemed trustworthy yet even trustworthy only went so far in the face of safety. Ivy most likely had a duty to report any serious mental illness and Natalie knew hers was serious. It could mean Ivy's job if she didn't report the severity and she harmed herself. Given her history, it was a definite possibility. Her thoughts returned to the tool she'd stored in her room. She had to hide it to keep Avery from finding it.

Ivy pushed herself away from the table and rose, removing her glasses to let them hang from today's purple beaded chain that matched her long sleeved knit dress. "Are you here for me dear?"

"No."

Natalie's heart rate picked up. Best case scenario, he wanted to apologize for his girlfriend's bad behavior. More than likely, he was going to yell at her about eavesdropping regardless of the fact that listening to him with her was the last thing she would have wanted.

Exhaling loudly for show, Natalie stood as well. "I really have to run. I have plans this afternoon."

Stepping into the room, Luka shoved his hands in his pockets. "Natalie, I would like to talk to you."

Shooting a sideways glance at Ivy, Natalie found that she was entirely preoccupied with gathering her papers and pen into a pile. Clearly she was trying to convey her disinterest. Natalie wasn't buying it.

"I don't think there's anything we need to discuss."

Really? Nothing?

Natalie had years of practice hiding her reaction when she heard things. But this time was different. This felt like it was aimed at her. Not just that she was overhearing or describing something, but actually hearing something meant for her. The other thing, the thing that made her heart skip a beat was the fact that this voice had *his* timbre. It was like he was speaking only it was in her head. She could hear him so clearly she shook her head to clear it.

"Is something wrong, Nat?" Ivy asked gently.

"I...I have to go." She grabbed her things in a sloppy pile and jammed them into her backpack, not caring the rumpling of the papers she heard or crushing of the book corners. "I'll see you Monday." She waved over her shoulder to Ivy not giving Luka a second glance.

Rushing out of the building, trying to get her backpack up on her shoulder she fumbled it in a rushed bout of clumsiness and cried out in frustration as she watched it fall to the ground.

Natalie didn't have to look up when she heard the outer door of the building swing open. Sure enough, Luka had followed her outside.

"Natalie I want to talk to you about last night." He hunched down next to her and picked up one of her books.

She grabbed at her papers, jamming her fingers on the sidewalk in her anger. "I don't know what *you* think happened last night, but there is nothing about any of it I want to rehash. Let's just agree that it was nothing, because that is *exactly* what it was. Nothing." Natalie stuffed her papers in a book and shoved it in her bag.

"It wasn't *nothing*. You heard something, I know it."

"Like I told your crazy pants girlfriend, I didn't hear anything. I didn't know anybody was in there. I went in to get *away* from people, not find them." Natalie's lips tightened in frustration. She was so flustered she'd told him more than she had intended.

Luka's voice rose in irritation. "I told you she wasn't my girlfriend."

"No, you didn't." She retorted, equally annoyed. "Avery and I were just talking about it this morning and she never heard you denying it." Damn, she did it again. Why did she let him get so far under her skin? "It doesn't matter. Just leave it alone. I'll see you Monday and we can study. Okay?"

He reached out and Natalie skittered sideways, losing her balance in the process. She landed on her butt with a thump and skinned her palm catching herself. "Damn it." Natalie balled her fist against the sting, glowering at Luka. "Why can't you leave me alone?"

"Because Ivy asked me to help you." He still held his hand partially extended. "Because I was just like you once."

Irritation turned instantly to self-pity. "No one is like me."

I disagree. Popped into her head.

Natalie felt her back stiffen though this time kept her face blank. "I have to go." She snatched her book from him and jammed it into her bag, zipping it as she stood.

No, you don't.

The beer messed with the meds more than I thought. These are getting worse. Natalie thought to herself. Her thoughts went to the metal edge promising to keep her tethered. It had been a while since she'd given in but the pull was getting too strong, the line between reality and fantasy was shifting.

"The medication is working just fine, you don't need to do it."

She started to argue that he had no idea what he was talking about when she stopped. "What did you say?" She dared not face him.

"You heard me." Luka's voice softened.

"N-no. You're messing with me. I don't know how but you are." Her hand went to her temple and rubbed at the throb beginning there.

Luka came up beside her and lay a gentle hand on her shoulder.

Natalie cried out at his touch. The jolt that ran through her was electric. He didn't remove his hand. Quite the opposite, he let his hand settle more firmly on her.

You aren't the only one who hears voices Natalie.

Choking back her denial, Natalie listened. Either she had finally gone completely nuts or this guy was telling her an improbable truth.

You aren't nuts. He chuckled out loud. *At least not because of this.*

How do I know this is real? Natalie ventured to ask of his voice in her head. It was far less incriminating to ask inside her head should this all be a delusion.

Think of something you haven't told anyone and I'll hear it.

No. It won't work like that. Not if this is all in my head. I'll just think you answered me but it'll be me.

Fine. Think of something and I'll write it down.

Holding her breath, she tried it. Natalie let herself think of something personal. Something there was no way Luka would know or Ivy would have seen in her file. That meant it had to be *really* personal.

When I cut, it's the only time I don't feel like I'm just going to float away.

Luka blanched as he watched her, fishing in his pocket and coming up with a receipt from his wallet. "Can I borrow a pen please?"

Natalie bit her lip, anxious, and reached into the side pocket of her backpack and handed over a pen.

Luka scribbled on his receipt using his leg as a table and handed it to Natalie.

It took a minute for the words to register but there they were staring her right in the face. Word for word he had copied down exactly what she had consciously thought adding, "Please don't hurt yourself anymore. Throw away the tool."

Chapter 11

"How is this possible?" Natalie stood transfixed, staring at the paper in her hands. Her mind was busily running through all possible options for how Luka could have rigged it or tricked her yet there was nothing.

Everyone thought she had stopped cutting under threat of confinement after several particular deep ones she made when she was a sophomore. They had bled through her bandages at the dinner table and her parents had flipped out. It was a bad memory from an even worse time.

Natalie had never breathed a word otherwise. That was the deal they had made as a family. Bob and Valerie would not tell the psychiatrist about the deep cuts if Natalie would promise never to put blade to flesh again. She had kept it for the most part. Only a handful of times had she done it since and she'd had to promise again before they'd let her go off to school, away from their watchful eyes.

"I know how you feel right now."

She twisted her head to peer up at Luka's face. He was not looking at her, but was staring off at the forested hills beyond them. Feeling her gaze, he nodded toward the tree line. "Want to take a walk with me?"

A few days ago those words would have held a promise for Natalie now worlds away. Yet her answer was the same as it would have been then although for very different reasons. "Sure."

They set off across the street and quickly reached the edge of the trees marking the base of the hills.

"How do you feel about a little hike?" Luka asked, hands on his hips, staring out at the trail into the forest.

Natalie shrugged her backpack more securely into place and stepped onto the trail without answering. She heard a chuckle behind her accompanied by the crunching of his shoes.

They walked in silence, the severity if the incline making it impractical to speak. Natalie appreciated the quiet, noticing she could only hear the crunching of their feet on the leaf litter and the sounds of skittering woodland creatures mixed in with the singing of birds she didn't recognize from home.

She was with another person and heard nothing. She stopped, breathing heavily. Luka only took one of his long strides to come abreast of her.

"What's wrong?" he panted. A light sheen of perspiration trapped some of his hair against his forehead. He used the back of a hand to push it back.

Swallowing to wet her throat to speak, Natalie gaped. "I can't hear you."

Luka flashed an enthusiastic grin at her. "I know. Give her a chance and Ivy will teach you how to do the same thing." He started walking, calling over his shoulder. "Come on, I want to show you something."

They continued up the trail another quarter mile or so before Luka stepped off the path taking a sharp right turn. Their footsteps were muffled by pine needles and underbrush as they stepped over fallen trees and down branches.

After a solid fifteen minutes of steady trudging, Luka stopped. Natalie had been walking behind him with her head down and ran right into his back.

"Oops. Sorry." She muttered.

Luka didn't comment, he only stood staring ahead. Natalie eased over to stand next to him and followed his gaze.

They had come to a clearing, the pines opened up to reveal a still somewhat green patch of waving grass at the top of the hill which ended abruptly at a cliff.

"It's a place I found my first summer here." He spoke softly.

"You didn't go home?" Natalie realized she didn't know the first thing about him.

Luka shook his head, black waves shining in the sun's rays. "No. I don't have much reason to go home. Not since Andjela died." Stepping out, he made his way to the cliff edge.

Natalie followed a few steps behind and paused. "Who's Andjela?"

The breeze picked up when they got close, bringing the salty scent of the sea with it. Luka stopped a few feet from the edge and lowered himself onto one of several boulders set in a half circle overlooking the small downtown and the Pacific beyond.

Motioning her to sit as well, Luka rested his forearms on his thighs. He had picked up a small stick and now scraped at it methodically removing its bark. Natalie chose a rock two away from his and sat. They both watched the waves as they whitecapped, overlapping each other as they advanced tirelessly. They pressed forward as though if they continued on their course they would push their way up the beach and into the streets of the town itself.

"My sister. Andjela was my sister. She died when I was a kid."

Birds' occasional tweeting was the only sound that punctuated the silence, the roar of the surf being too far to reach them on their hilltop island. As her breathing returned to normal, Natalie felt her tension ebbing as well. It was a unique experience to be sitting so easily with a stranger and be able to relax. The whispers she now knew had been the thoughts of others, were blissfully gone. All she had to listen to were her own thoughts, some of which strayed to the handsome man beside her.

Luka laughed softly.

Natalie flushed. "It is not okay for you to listen in." She chastised. "It's not fair either. I don't know how to keep you out."

You're not so bad yourself.

"Don't give me that." She sounded more annoyed than she really was. Natalie held no illusions about being more attractive than she was, certainly not enough so to draw a man so much older and already involved. His compliment after hers meant nothing.

"I'm pretty well off too." He added out loud, teasing. "Well, my parents are anyway."

The change in Luka's attitude toward her was more curious. Until today, he had treated her as a burden. Not someone he would come all this way to have a heart to heart with.

"What's with the new attitude? Did Ivy tell you to play nice?" She half teased.

When he didn't answer right away, Natalie twisted to see his expression. Gone was his levity, in its place was shadow and grief.

Feeling a twinge for causing him pain, Natalie spoke sincerely. "I'm sorry."

"You should stop apologizing for things that aren't your fault. You do that a lot." Luka bristled, picking at a spot on his jeans. "Yes, Ivy told me to take you under my wing. She's worried about you. She sees that you have a strong talent and she wants to be sure you learn how to handle it. She thought I would be especially interested in you." He glanced over, seeing Natalie's confused expression he smiled kindly. "My sister had this ability too. She was the first of us to develop it. She didn't know what to do with it." He nodded at her arm. "She did the same thing for a long time. We thought she was okay when she stopped in her junior year of high school. She really seemed to get it together." He itched the side of his thumb. "She killed herself when she went away to college. Nobody saw it coming."

Natalie looked down at her arm. The cuff had slipped up and she could see the edge of one of the many white lines that crisscrossed her forearms. She saw them in her mind's eye for a flash before she pushed it away. That was private.

Too late, Luka had seen them too. His expression slipped before he righted himself, his thoughts were better guarded. "I should have seen it coming but I believed her when she told me she would be okay. Then she went away to school. The calls and visits were less and less as the months went on. After the first year she stopped coming home altogether. She was dead within two years." His voice was barely audible. "I never told my parents what I knew even when I got older and got more confident in my own ability."

A new need, the need to ease his suffering tugged at her. "You were young, it isn't your fault for believing her. It was her choice." Natalie said softly.

His fingers rolled a strip of green wood from the stick he was rapidly mangling. Stopping, his eyes bored into hers. The pain in them was heartrending. "You stopped for a while, why?" He'd learned more than she'd intended the night before.

"I told my parents I would stop and I did for the most part when I was sixteen. They were worried and I didn't want them blaming themselves." She rubbed her thumb over a particularly thick scar she could feel through the thin fabric of her shirt. "I didn't want to leave them feeling like failures. I was the only child they had." She was mostly honest with him.

"Andj might as well have been their only child. After she died, they gave up. My father's business takes him away a lot and my mother started to go with him. Eventually, between business and vacations, they were gone all the time. I finished school mostly because of my father's influence. Dad was just starting to think he needed to buy my way into college when I got my letter from Prestige, *and* this is where Andj went so there was never a question. When I got my letter, I went."

"Are there a lot of people like us here? Does this school specialize in these sorts of things?"

Luka shook his head, moppy waves moving with him. "It's not *just* us, there are regular kids here too. I've only met a few others, no one exactly advertises, but no one else like me or you."

That explained his surprise when she had picked the cow eyed Freshie comment out of his head, Natalie thought. Luka snorted.

"Yeah, I'd never met anyone else who could do it. The couple of people I 'heard' thinking about any sort of weird differences like ours were during my freshman year before I'd learned to block them out. One guy could tell if someone was lying but he never took it beyond party tricks and the other one, hers was cool. She could heat or cool things by touch. Some sort of 'current impulse' was how Ivy described it."

"Whoa. Did they *like* having them? Either of them?" Or were they like her, misunderstanding it and seeing it as a flaw.

"Neither one liked it, but I don't think it was as difficult as this one. The girl did have a few unfortunate scenarios before she got here and Ivy helped her but nothing a pair of gloves and made up germ issue couldn't fix in the interim."

"Where did they go from here? What does someone like that do with their future?"

"Most people go to a research company, Optimax not far from here that's really big. My understanding is they do just about everything and the owners are Prestige grads so tons of people end up there, although I don't think it has anything to do with us being like this. There just aren't too many big companies in this area so it makes sense. It's just over the border into Oregon and

I have an internship starting there this summer." He was staring at his hands, "Maybe you could look into going there too. I could put in a good word for you. It might be nice to have someone looking out for you."

Natalie bit her tongue. He had already started on her about the cutting. Natalie let her head roll back, feeling the tethers of obligation once again. Still, thought of him worrying enough to look out for her filled her mind with fodder for daydreams.

Luka continued to stare at his hands, politely ignoring what she knew he was picking up. There was a heck of a visual that went with what she was thinking. Struggling to bring her thoughts back under control only made it worse.

Standing suddenly, feeling incredibly uncomfortable, Natalie walked the few feet to the edge of the cliff and looked over. The quaint town of Eureka lay below them, the streets laid out in a grid with low buildings fading to soft shades of their original colors from a lifetime near the harsh ocean climate. She wondered what it would be like to live a normal life in a sleepy town like this one. The natural backdrop drew her and she knew she would not be going home to Minnesota. Oregon was probably a lot like this.

"Ivy wanted me to help you." Luka stood too, his eyes were half closed, a crease formed between them. "If you're willing, I'd like to do just that."

She picked up what he was thinking. Whether he was letting her or he had dropped his guard she couldn't be sure but she got a definite thought about saving her somehow redeeming him for having let his sister slip away.

Emboldened and feeling close to him in a way completely foreign to her, Natalie closed the distance between them and laid her hand gently on his forearm. She dipped a shoulder and craned her neck to look under his bowed head and make eye contact. "It wasn't your fault. You had no idea what she was going through after you'd lost touch. There was nothing you could have done to stop her." That much she knew was true.

His green eyes met hers, troubled but hopeful. Luka's raw need to be absolved of his guilt was painful to see. "Thank you, Natalie. That's kind of you to say."

Natalie decided to take advantage of their new honesty. "So are you going to tell me who Ericka is? Because you may not think she's your girlfriend, but she has different ideas if I 'heard' right last night."

Luka sighed, shoving his hands in his pockets and staring out at the sea. "Our parents are friends. Ericka is a little emotional," he ignored Natalie's choked laugh. "Our fathers have always hoped we would end up together. I would assume because I have taken care of her, more so after my sister died. So when I got accepted here, they sent her here as well and asked me to keep an eye on her." He shrugged. "Nothing has ever happened despite her repeated efforts and last night she decided to make one last push to argue her case. I had just turned her down when you found us poolside."

"So what was with the aggression *inside* later? As I recall, she gave me a beer shower when I was minding my own business." Her recollection was a touch fuzzy although she did remember that one clearly.

"Oh that. Well," Luka rubbed the back of his neck and scanned the horizon. "That was just Ericka being Ericka. After you left the cabana she tried to follow you and I told her to leave you alone. When we went in, she was mad at me and saw you. She figured she could get away with it since you didn't fight back before *and* she was trying to get a rise out of me."

His discomfort struck her as odd. She assumed it was embarrassment at being associated with that woman in front of her, when she was supposed to see him as a mentor. "Thanks for keeping her from fighting with Avery. I don't think Avery has much in the way of self-control."

Luka laughed. It was a full, generous laugh and Natalie felt her cheeks warm. He stopped. "Speaking of self-control. Natalie, you have to practice those techniques Ivy is teaching you. They keep out the voices, and they block yours from me too."

Natalie flushed again. "Sorry."

"I'm flattered, but that's the last thing you need right now. Let's concentrate on getting you in control of yourself and then you can figure out dating from there. We don't have much time, I have to leave in May and September is nearly half over."

"That's a long time," Natalie sniffed.

"It's not as long as you think. You're going to be very busy."

Chapter 12

Luka was right. For the next three months Natalie's every second was spoken for between her studies, tutoring sessions and practice sessions with Ivy and Luka. Ivy taught her occasionally at first, but Luka was actually able to work with her unique talents specifically and test how well she was able to control her thoughts. As great as Ivy was at teaching Natalie how to wall herself off, she had no way of detecting how effective she was.

Luka, however, was great at finding the holes in her defenses.

"We'll eat dinner after you hold me off for five minutes." He tossed a pen at her. "Come on, *anyone* can do five minutes."

She deflected it easily, irritated with Luka for picking her mind while physically distracting her and making her job infinitely more difficult. In a fit of malice, she brought up a mental image to give him something else to pick out.

"Ha ha, I don't *need* to do that to myself. There are usually takers should I find the need." He narrowed his eyes.

Natalie flushed as he fed her a flash of exactly what he meant. Out of decency he kept it to a quick glimpse and hid the woman's face. Luka's constant exposure to her mind had given him far more details about her than she would have preferred. Typically he was respectful of her privacy, but there was no way of keeping him from everything. As a result, he knew exactly how best to embarrass her.

She threw a pencil back at him. "Damn it Luka, I'm tired and I'm hungry and we've been at this for hours. Can't we get a pizza or something? I'll concentrate better when I've eaten."

Sitting back, he regarded her steadily before nodding. "I guess you've earned that."

"Gee thanks." Natalie sneered sarcastically. She was frustrated more with herself than him. Intellectually she knew he was helping her, but at times his constant barrage was exhausting and she wasn't above occasionally snapping.

For his part, Luka maintained his temper very well. He had only once lost his cool with her and that had been entirely her doing. It had been in the first few weeks and Luka had come over in the morning, bringing her coffee and looking incredible in a pair of designer jeans and charcoal tee under a sleek leather jacket. Her thoughts continued to run in only one direction until, after half an hour, Luka had slammed down his book.

"If you want to think about sex all day that's fine but leave me out of it." He had been honestly upset and Natalie had fought back her desire for him from that point on. If she ever had even a glimmer of a thought about him, she would make herself think about being surrounded by a crowd. That was unpleasant and confusing enough to shut her down and scramble her thoughts.

Now, as much as Natalie's feelings for Luka had evolved from a crush into something far more significant, she had developed enough of a defense system to keep that part mostly locked away until he was out of her general vicinity. Only on a rare occasion did Luka give any sort of hint that he "heard" her on that front. Then only giving her a look to let her know she had to work harder to tuck that away.

Natalie knew he didn't reciprocate her feelings. Not because of anything he'd said or shared with her. He was far too kind to her for that, obviously thinking of her as the little sister in this relationship. She couldn't blame him. He had had enough access to her head to know she was his junior in more than just years. There were a number of life experiences she was lacking. It was only natural for him to treat her as his pupil.

Without fulfilling his "five minute" stipulation, she unfolded her legs and stood, stretching before she picked up the phone from her desk where he had been sitting and returned to her perch on the edge of her bed. While she ordered their favorite, pepperoni and banana peppers, Luka stretched. He failed to comment on her breach of contract.

The edge of his shirt lifted enough for her to see his flat, tan skin above his belt. He shot her a look and mouthed cautionary words, "Control yourself."

As usual, Natalie blushed and locked down her thoughts. It was always worse when she was tired, her hunger only exacerbated the problem.

Avery's key noisily rattled the lock as she announced her presence before entering. For as often as Natalie had assured her friend that Luka remained her tutor only, Avery still held out hope that she would walk in someday to find them lip locked or better if her thoughts were any indicator.

Upon entering Avery was disappointed, as usual, to see Luka standing with his arms crossed looking out the window and Natalie seated alone on her bed. The one downside to Natalie's constant "tutoring" was that Avery had to think she was a complete idiot by now.

Attempting to preserve some amount of respect from her roommate, Natalie had told her she screwed around a lot in high school and had to maintain at least a 3.0 GPA to maintain her scholarship. That was somewhat true. In actuality she had to maintain a 2.5 but Natalie's pride told her studying with tutors five days a week should get her more than that.

"Hello my studious little friends. How goes the battle of the books?" Avery dropped her trademark giant pink bag on the floor next to her dresser.

The room was set up in a mirror image with dressers and closets on the wall flanking the door. Both of them had agreed to put their dressers inside their closets in favor of more floor space for their microwave and mini fridge. Their desks sat on the wall at the far side of the room on either side of the window. Only their beds were not symmetrical.

A few weeks after classes started Avery found a flyer selling a wooden loft and she had dragged it home, excitedly exclaiming she had found the answer to their prayers. It wasn't an answer to a prayer though it certainly did help their space issues quite a bit. Avery slept on top, Natalie below. Avery had insisted that she get choice considering this was supposed to be her room anyway. As usual, Natalie didn't disagree.

"We just ordered a pizza. Care to join us?" Luka asked her benevolently.

Natalie appreciated his continued inclusion of Avery in the social aspect of their relationship despite the fact that as a result he had to put up with some rather racy fantasies from Avery. Only occasionally now did Natalie forget herself and hear them. She caught Luka a few times "listening in" and chastised him for it as well. He argued that if they were about him he should be allowed to hear.

69

"No thanks. I only have like ten minutes before I'm supposed to meet Jason at the basketball game." She answered distractedly over her shoulder, digging busily in her closet.

"Since when do you like basketball?"

She caught Luka's eye and saw he was wondering the same thing. Avery had been bending over backwards to please Jason, the blonde she'd met at the party where Natalie had been baptized as her friends now referred to the beer dousing. The night they'd met Ericka.

That had been another ongoing saga. Unfortunately for Luka, and even more so for Natalie, Ericka had been doing poorly in Biology and was coming in for tutoring sessions almost daily. She seemed to have an uncanny ability to predict when Natalie was trying to study with Luka, thus their relocation to Natalie's room for study sessions.

When they had at first tried to use Luka's apartment since he had no roommate, they had gotten as far as sitting down when Ericka had appeared. Two more such "oopses" and they moved. Ericka didn't dare come to Natalie's so they had been safe.

Avery wheeled around and stuck her tongue out at Natalie, her hand on her hip. "I happen to be a woman of many interests." She glared at both of them separately. Satisfied she had sufficiently made her point, Avery stuck her head back in her closet and continued to rummage.

When she emerged, a very soft looking off the shoulder sweater in hand, Avery stared at Luka. "I suppose I have to go change in the bathroom instead of my own room?"

Luka gave her a grin and hid his reaction to what Natalie guessed he heard unless he had his mental "earmuffs" on. "No, I have to use the restroom anyway so I'll leave you a few minutes of privacy." He winked at her on his way out and this time Natalie caught the twitch at the corner of his mouth as he walked past. Avery was staring down at her sweater, hiding the flush creeping up her neck.

You jerk. Why do you insist on doing that to her?

Come on, she's already thinking it.

Yeah, but you're just encouraging her. Natalie "heard" Avery thinking how lucky Natalie was that she was the one Luka wanted, and promptly threw up her defenses fast before he caught wind of her disappointment that she would again have to explain to her friend how they were just "study buddies."

Luka's shoulders tightened as he reached for the doorknob and she knew he'd caught at least part of that. He didn't stop the door from shutting hard enough to rattle on his way out. Natalie sighed heavily. Having a talent in common was not making this friendship easier, quite the opposite.

Avery didn't waste a minute. She jerked her sweatshirt over her head and stood facing Natalie in her bra and undershirt. The cool fall breezes off the ocean usually gave the student body cause to dress in layers nearly year round from what Natalie had heard. They were no exceptions.

"You can *not* tell me you haven't closed the deal with him yet." She accused, reaching for her deodorant.

Natalie shook her head, speaking slowly for effect. "For the millionth time Avery, Luka and I are assigned to each other for studying. That's it. Case closed."

Avery threw her hands up in the air looking skyward. "See what I have to work with?" She asked of the heavens. "Look, I know guys and I'm telling you *that* one has it bad for you." She wiggled into her sweater very carefully so as not to mark the sides with her deodorant, stretching the sides out as she pulled them down one at a time. The sweater hung loosely on Avery, accentuating her generous bust and recent few pounds of weight loss, giving her an enviable figure.

Frustrated, Natalie didn't answer, but chose instead to straighten the rumpled blanket where she'd been sitting. When that was done, she grabbed the canister on top of the microwave that held napkins and flatware. She plucked out what they needed for them both knowing Luka preferred to eat his first piece of pizza with a knife and fork. She, on the other hand, liked to eat her last piece by picking it apart with her cutlery.

Natalie had reached under her bed for the plastic tote they kept their dishes in to extract two plates and cups. Luka had to walk right past the kitchen and soda machine in order to use the men's restroom on the opposite end of the floor and would grab a Dr. Pepper for himself and Wild Cherry Pepsi for her.

Pointing at Natalie's place settings on the desk waiting for each of them to grab when the pizza arrived, Avery rolled her eyes.

"Christ Nat, you two are practically married as it is. You know each other's habits down to how you blow your nose. He isn't into that chick and I've been doing some digging." She waved her hand. "Don't get all wide eyed at me. I've checked and he hasn't been on a date or anything yet this year. Not since he met you." She was giving Natalie a meaningful look and Natalie was almost choking as she bit her tongue.

"I appreciate what you're trying to do Avery but please leave Luka alone. The man deserves his privacy." Natalie sank down into the chair at her desk. "His not dating this year is none of your business, mine either." She smoothed her jeans on her thighs. "But I assure you it has nothing to do with me. And who says I want to date? I barely have enough energy to keep up on all my schoolwork."

Avery sighed heavily and picked up her hairbrush to fix her wind tangled locks. "I just don't want to see you let a good thing pass you by because you're too shy to say anything."

"He knows how I feel about him." Natalie mumbled.

The hairbrush hit the dresser with a bang. Natalie looked up and saw Avery's eyes bulging at her. "You told him?" She smiled broadly. "Nicely done Nat. I didn't know you had it in you."

Not in as many words, but he'd gotten the gist of it. Natalie shrugged. "So will you leave it alone now? He knows I'm interested and he's not. Let's let it go, okay?"

"Wait, 'he knows I'm interested' is not the same as telling him you loooove him." She lectured, pointing the brush at Natalie and advancing on her.

Suddenly paranoid at the use of *that* word, worried Luka might be coming back, Natalie hurried to change their conversation. "It's not an issue Avery. Why don't you tell me how things are with Jason? Are you coming home tonight?"

Often times when they had a date, Avery spent the night at Jason's. He lived off campus and had his own room in a house he shared with Natalie lost track of exactly how many guys.

Wiggling her eyebrows, Avery turned and sashayed back to the dresser to take a look at herself in the mirror hanging over where the dresser had originally sat against the wall. "One never knows." She reached into one of her drawers extracting a clean pair of underwear to put in her giant bag. "But one can hope."

Natalie laughed. Avery had that effect on her. Avery lived larger than life and was unburdened by many governing social mores. Not that she was truly rude, more like she lived on her own plane. She got away with just about anything. It was hard to say no to her and it was exhilarating just being with her. Natalie thoroughly adored her.

Just as Avery put her hair up into a messy clip with some hanging loose for a soft look she knew accentuated her huge blue eyes, Natalie heard the doorknob jiggle.

"Come on in, you're too late to see anything good." Avery teased.

Luka entered and twisted his neck to shoot her a disappointed look. "Ah, to the victor go the spoils. Tell Jason he has a good woman."

Avery's smile was genuine and Natalie was surprised to see she even appeared to be a trifle embarrassed at Luka's sincerity.

"Thanks." She grabbed her bag and hefted it onto her shoulder. "You two partiers don't get too wild now. We can't have the neighbors complaining again."

"Don't worry Mom. We'll be good." Natalie joked back, moving toward her closet to grab her wallet.

Luka had paid last time and it was her turn. She had insisted on being equals. He knew she was poor, still she had her pride.

Just as Avery settled her hand on the doorknob and Natalie got close, she turned and mouthed in Natalie's ear, "Be honest with him. Tell him you love him."

She kissed Natalie's cheek and waltzed out, closing the door gently behind her. Natalie was left standing frozen with one hand on the door, unwilling to turn around.

It didn't matter that she could effectively block off that part of her thoughts from Luka most of the time, she couldn't block off the fact that Avery had run those words through *her* head. Whispering didn't help when one was in the presence of a mind reader.

Damn you Avery. Natalie cursed silently. She entertained the thought of sneaking out the door and waiting until Luka left before she came back but they were stuck together the rest of the school year. Ivy wouldn't let them split before then. She'd have to face him eventually anyway, running now would do nothing.

Natalie's chin quivered, her eyes filled up. "I'm going to run to the bathroom, will you pay if the pizza comes while I'm gone? I'll be back in a minute." She slammed her drawer shut, a twenty laying on top of her wallet and dashed out the door without waiting for an answer.

Chapter 13

By the time Natalie had composed herself enough to return, Luka was standing with his back to her looking out the window at the sun setting behind the mountains. His shirt was pulled tight against his back, arms crossed in front. The sight of him was almost physically painful. Natalie locked away her private thoughts.

Without turning around, Luka spoke low and clear. "Natalie, we need to talk."

She hated that tone. It was the same one her father got when he was going to lecture her and she didn't want it from him. Not now, not ever. "No, we don't." She replied petulantly.

"I know you are attracted to me, but that isn't practical. You know that." His tone remained even.

"Never mind what Avery says. You know she says whatever goes through her mind." Literally.

He turned his head halfway, offering her a glimpse of his profile. Luka's brow was knotted. "You don't... feel that way?"

Natalie answered truthfully. "I've never told her that."

Luka turned all the way to face her. She had splashed water on her face but worried her eyes were still pink from the few tears that had snuck past her. Years of hiding her feelings could almost completely manage her slip, though not entirely. Natalie ducked her head.

"Did the pizza come yet?"

"No." His voice was soft.

Snatching her wallet from the dresser, Natalie announced, "I'll go wait at the door. Why don't you grab the sodas?" Oddly he hadn't picked them up on his way back from the restroom. That was a first. She didn't bother to ask why.

Without waiting for a response she tucked her wallet against her chest and, leaving the door open behind her, went down to wait at the locked doors for the delivery guy.

She came up less than five minutes later. Luka had already cracked the tops on their drinks and sat paging through her Biology book. He glanced up when she walked in with the pizza box.

"Do you remember how hard this was for you before?" He held up the book for her perusal.

She nodded, smiling as she remembered back to those first few weeks. Already her studies were making her parents proud, she called them every week for an update. But the real reason she was doing so well was not just Ivy's academic tutoring. It was the medication free lifestyle that enabled her to concentrate. She'd been off entirely for nearly six weeks and counting.

That one small change had returned her love of learning. Natalie once again was happy to go to class, gloried in teachers' praises and high marks in all of her classes. Having the ability to shut out people's thoughts while she was in class had given back the confidence in herself she used to have.

Of course it was good she only had two classes on her heaviest days because holding her concentration for an hour long class period was mentally exhausting. She had to rest afterward before going to the tutor center or trying her homework or her protections would be Swiss cheese.

Yet the progress was invigorating and she anticipated what it would be like to be as good at it as Luka. He said he could hold his focus for most of the day with only a few breaks here and there.

"Yeah, I didn't think I was going to make it here a week." She set the box down on the microwave and held out a hand for a plate.

When her hand remained empty for longer than it should have, Natalie glanced over at Luka. He was giving her a curious look. His eyes were troubled. She let her arm fall back to her side.

"She was right you know. My lack of dates this year does involve you, though not how you might think."

Natalie's heart pounded in her ears while she kept her breathing steady so he couldn't see. "I would imagine it's hard to date when you have to work with me all the time." Her feigned laughter fell flat.

"Before we met Ivy said there was a new student this year that I could help. She said you had an ability but she left out the part about you being like *her*."

Natalie knew he meant his sister. She rubbed a thumb over her arm, encased as always in long sleeves.

"May I?" He held out a hand.

She held her breath, dark eyes wide in fear. No one but her parents and doctors had seen her scars. They were a visual reminder of her private pain and now that she was gaining control over that, she had grown even more self-conscious of them.

The pain on his face stayed her objection. Gently, he stepped closer and reached for her arm hanging limp at her side. His lightly calloused hand cradled her wrist, bringing her arm to his chest height. Very slowly, as if he was afraid of what he would see, Luka used his other hand to pull her knit sleeve up to her elbow.

She watched the fabric roll back, exposing what she could have described by heart. One large scar ran nearly from her mid forearm to her wrist. That was crisscrossed by a number of lighter scars that could only be seen as her skin hit the light. Several others were deeper and all together they made a patchwork of silver lines reminiscent of a spider's web or fisherman's net. A few were still purple. They were the last from the summer before she'd come here. Their proximity to the veins in her wrist showed how close she'd come in her dance with death.

Luka held her forearm facing up with one hand letting the other slide down, tracing the largest of the lines lightly with his fingers, coming to rest on the purple line less than half an inch from her dark blue vein. A little deeper and she would have never come here, never discovered this new life.

When he spoke, his voice was a choked whisper. "When you 'heard' me and I realized you were like us, I was scared. I didn't want to think about her but every time I looked at you how could I not?" He gave one short, sharp laugh. "I told Ivy I didn't want to work with anyone this year, I wanted to concentrate on finishing up my classes. That was when she told me about these." He brushed his thumb against her wrist. "I couldn't say no."

Natalie had pictured him touching her a thousand times, not like this. Not this worst part of her. Yet his flesh on hers made her heart race. She willed herself to calm down. "I know I remind you of her. I'm sorry." He started to say something but

Natalie hurried to add, "I'm glad you said yes. Without you I wouldn't have made it. You saved me Luka."

Natalie wasn't sure if she would have killed herself or not. It was also a strong possibility she would have slowly gone insane. Regardless one thing was for certain, Luka had saved her life. If not literally, he had saved her from living a tormented shell of one. For that she could not thank him enough. Again she felt her eyes welling and opened them wide to try to keep the tears from spilling over.

Just as gently as he had pulled it back, Luka reached up and pulled her sleeve back down while one hand remained, cradling her hand in his. "I made a promise to myself that I would make you strong enough to protect yourself like Ivy did for me. Any sort of distractions from that would be a great disservice to you. I couldn't live with myself if I cheated you." He looked up, meeting her gaze with clouded eyes.

"I know you think of me as her but you have to know I'm already so much stronger than I was. I'm not going to do what she did. I meant it when I said you saved my life."

Flicking his eyes down to where he still held her hand, Luka stepped forward and drew her against him. His warm arms wrapped around her, his chin rested lightly against her head.

Natalie's emotions were on a roller coaster. Here she was, exposing her feelings to him like Avery suggested except in a very different way. Instead of telling him she loved him, she was exposing her vulnerability. At the same time, he had confirmed for her how he felt.

She was a second chance at saving his sister. Nothing more. How could she be? He was obviously still haunted by Andjela's suffering and loss. Still, standing there with his arms holding her to his chest, smelling the fresh scent of the outdoors he loved and the mixture of his cologne with his pleasant scent, Natalie was happy. Even if they felt different ways about his embrace, she was in it. She inhaled once deeply before pushing away. "Now that we've both bared our souls, let's have some pizza before it gets cold," she joked flicking her eyes up at him.

Luka hesitated only a moment before releasing her to ruff up his hair and reaching behind him to hand her a plate. "Sorry.

The holidays are hard for me. Maybe *I* should be the one practicing a little control." He snorted.

Natalie startled. Christmas was coming in just another week. She had been so busy getting ready for finals at the beginning of next week she had forgotten entirely about their month off. She hadn't intended to go home, hopefully that wouldn't offend her parents.

"Are you going home?" She asked Luka, sliding two pieces onto his plate.

He switched plates and she slid two smaller pieces on it for herself.

"No. They always take a vacation over Christmas to keep their minds off of it." He sat down heavily. "Andjela died the week before Christmas. None of us has celebrated it since."

"Oh," she sat back on her bed. "I had no idea. I'm so sorry."

He shrugged, picking up his utensils. "How could you know? I've never told anyone that."

Natalie let that detail settle in as she chewed her first bite. He obviously considered her a close friend if he was comfortable sharing such intimate details of his life with her. Even if it was mostly because he thought of her like another sister, she enjoyed the closeness they shared. Luka was a good person and, like Avery, he made her life infinitely more full by being a part of it.

Chapter 14

No sooner had Natalie blinked than the calendar had changed from December to April. Natalie's heart was heavy as she counted down the three remaining weeks before Luka left for his summer internship at Optimax.

Avery would have noticed Natalie's glum mood if not for the fact that she was in love. She and Jason had become inseparable since they had both stayed home over winter break. Whatever had happened between them Natalie didn't know because Avery was never at home to ask.

Once in a while she would stop in to do laundry, pack new clothes and collect her mail but she was for all intents and purposes living with Jason. Natalie was happy for them still missed Avery. The weekends were the worst. During the week she was so busy with school and Luka and Ivy she didn't have time to think.

On this particular Saturday the sun had come up especially bright and Natalie had wanted to feel less alone. Not having any good reason to call Luka away from his own intense studying, he was carrying a heavy load this semester hoping to finish his last year early, she made up her mind where she could go and packed a lunch and book intending to stay most of the day.

Natalie stepped outside and took a deep breath. She watched a couple approaching and tested. Nothing. Good. Feeling satisfied with her progress, Natalie made a wide sweep around campus before heading for the edge. She waved at Luka's apartment, letting her guard down for a minute to send him a hello for her own private amusement just before she reached the tutor center. She wondered what he would think of that little trick if he happened to be home and had his down as well. Her path took her around his building toward the trailhead they had taken that day last fall.

Natalie had just gone past the front door and was nearly to the curb at the back of the building, trailhead across the street in sight and thinking about lying in the grass. Most likely greener than it had been in the fall, it must be beautiful. When her skin on the back of her neck prickled in warning, she turned.

Just as Natalie was turning something very hard hit her in the side. Fortunately her backpack absorbed some of the impact, however, the searing pain in her side took her breath away.

Natalie spun the rest of the way to face her attacker, stumbling with the impetus of the blow and went down on one knee, catching herself with one hand. She felt her palm scrape the concrete and pushed herself up.

Ericka's eyes were wild. She held a racket gripped tightly in both hands. Raising it high, she swung it down and hit Natalie's outstretched hand held protectively to shield her head. Pain surged through her limb at the impact but Natalie let her defenses down and "heard" Ericka's enraged mind.

She'd been finishing tennis practice across the street from the center and staring as she was, she saw Natalie waving at Luka's window. She had jogged over and when she saw her go around, she followed, sure Natalie was going to a secret rendezvous having signaled him to follow. Her twisted thoughts had Natalie and Luka hiding in some love nest from Ericka, laughing at her attempts to win Luka for herself. She blamed Natalie for stealing Luka from her. She wanted vengeance.

More important, Natalie heard Ericka's next move and countered it as best she could not having a lick of self-defense training beyond watching action movies with her dad.

When Ericka lifted the racket again she hauled it back to her shoulder like she was setting up for a backhand. The racket went up and Natalie jumped to her feet, the pain in her side nearly unbearable and tore her backpack down one arm and into her hand. She had just lifted it to block her shoulder when Ericka's racket came down hard on the canvas shield. It slid up and glanced off her head. Furious at being thwarted, Ericka switched her grip in the air and brought her weapon back toward Natalie's head.

Before it could reach her this time Natalie swung her bag, not as a block, this time as her weapon. The weight of her book and lunch was not great but swung at full speed with the additional twisting of Natalie's body, when it hit Ericka in the stomach she dropped, gasping for air.

Natalie's side was instantly ablaze with sharp, fiery pains. She dropped her bag clutching at it. When her hand touched her body, her fingers that had stopped the racket were tender. Glancing down, Natalie saw that her ring finger on her left hand was crooked. Broken.

The attack had shaken her, the blow to her head left her foggy and confused. Natalie couldn't think clearly to decide the most reasonable course of action. Instead, she sought only refuge. Taking one last look at Ericka, still curled up on the sidewalk face down on the ground, Natalie made her choice.

She slung her bag over one shoulder and jogged unevenly across the street holding her muscles tight in an effort to reduce the pain throbbing there. Once across, she slowed to a brisk but stiff walk, holding her upper body very still.

The steep but easy hike she remembered was far more difficult and rapidly becoming more so with each step. Natalie stopped several times to rest, thinking she had made a mistake. She was considering turning back when she heard footsteps on the path below her.

She bit off her cry as she jumped up and headed off the trail following the path Luka had shown her only once. In her picture of how the day would go, she'd had a lot more time to consider her course and make sure she was remembering right. In actuality, Natalie was now plunging through the deadfall hoping like crazy she was on the right track.

After what seemed an eternity, she reached the edge of the trees and crossed into the green clearing she had envisioned so often in her dreams after experiencing it with Luka. The dream visit was far more intimate than the real one.

The blue of the ocean beyond the cliff edge reflected the sun now high in the sky above. Natalie staggered up to the stone arc and let her bag slide down her arm. Her knees buckled and she let herself fold to lay on her side with her sore hand protected against her stomach, right hand cradling it protectively.

Being alone, she was free to let her body and mind hurt. Here she was, sore, stupid, and alone. Avery was never around to talk to and Luka was soon to be gone as well. She couldn't imagine her days without his company. She loved him more deeply than she dared admit even to herself. Groaning, she raised a hand to wipe at a tear and stifled a cry when the movement made her ribcage shift.

Now she was going to have to try to make her way back down and she knew that was going to hurt as she stiffened up. As soon as she could move, she would have to tape up her finger as best she could. For now, she was torn between whether she should try to make it back down tonight or give it until morning when she was sure her attacker was gone. She was in no shape to face Ericka again. For now she was too tired to try.

Giving herself sufficient time to catch her breath and to realize just how stupid it had been for her to come up here as her head cleared, and even more stupid to have left her phone behind for today's little adventure, Natalie knew she had to try to tape her finger. She'd seen basketball players tape two together when they jammed one. She knew she had enough bandaids in her bag for that. The ribs were another story, she was determined to deal with what she could manage for now.

Slowly, she tried to sit up and gasped when pain ripped through her side. Gritting her teeth stubbornly, Natalie rolled herself up to her hands and knees. She pushed herself with her knees as much as possible the few feet to her bag. She fought the urge to collapse when she reached it, knowing that would hurt just as much as getting there had.

Instead, she carefully unzipped the bag's inner compartment where she kept her backup "woman supplies" as well as several bandaids, tweezers and ointment. It wasn't a real first aid kit but it had always been enough for the few tiny maladies Natalie had been faced with.

Two bandaids was all it took to strap her ring finger to her middle. When she pulled the fingers together and bit down in pain she tasted blood. Angry, she spat on the ground and lay down again trying to find a comfortable position.

Ignorant to her small worries, the sunset was incredible. Natalie lay facing the cliff, her body growing cold when the breeze picked up. She hadn't intended to be up here this long or she would have packed a jacket or something heavier than the usual long sleeved tee she found herself in now. The sweatshirt in her bag would only provide her a small amount of protection. Whimpering at the knowledge of how it would feel to shrug into, Natalie pulled it from her bag. Unable to bring herself to wiggle this way and that into the sleeves, she merely lay it across herself and lay back on the soft grass.

She lay staring at the horizon, turned sideways by her awkward position. Natalie watched the golden rays steadily, seamlessly, shift from yellow to orange to pink in brilliant shining layers, finally splitting into a lavender bottom half, peach top. The colors scrolled slowly up, credits rolling on the day. No birds nor airplanes complicated the sight. Natalie felt like the last person on earth.

She stopped herself from crying again. In her world, she *was* the last person. Only Ivy remained and theirs was a relationship without more than superficial warmth. Natalie hadn't minded before, having Luka and Avery had been enough. Now she was going to face the summer here alone and she was beginning to doubt Avery's previous promise that they would room together and get jobs in town so they could stay through fall.

Weariness made her limbs sluggish and her thoughts slow. The final few moments of her sunset faded away, the stars had not yet made their appearance in force leaving her world dark. Natalie closed her eyes letting the peace of sleep take her.

Chapter 15

"Natalie."

She dreamed she heard Luka calling for her. They were hiking and she had fallen behind. Branches obscured her vision. She couldn't see him and started to panic, fearing she had lost the path entirely.

"Natalie."

He called for her again. He was looking for her. Luka wouldn't leave her alone. She wasn't scared, knowing he was trying to find her. Smiling, she muttered his name.

"Natalie."

His voice was closer, she turned her head expecting to see him, yelping when the muscles stretched and moved over her bruised side. Instinctively her hands moved to protect her ribs and she felt her fingers throb in protest.

Without opening her eyes, Natalie knew she was awake now. She was not hiking, and no one was looking for her. The breeze picked up from behind her and she smelled a familiar smell just before she heard his voice again.

"Natalie, what are you doing up here?" His hand hovered over her shoulder so close she could feel its heat.

"I'm an idiot." She stared straight ahead, unable to see in the darkness. He had set his flashlight down beside himself when he crouched down. "I figured it was safer up here than down there."

"What happened to you?"

Natalie was still groggy. "I wanted to come up here, it was such a beautiful day and I was alone so I thought I'd spend it here." She cracked a smile without opening her eyes. "I even brought a little picnic for one."

"Did you fall on the trail?" His fingers touched her makeshift bandages tentatively. Her eyelids shone red as he shifted his light to set it on the ground in front of her. "God Nat, your hand's purple."

"I didn't fall, Ericka hit me."

"Ericka *hit* you? She came over a little while ago going on about how she's missed our friendship. Her mind was all confused but I heard your name a lot. It felt wrong, I thought it was a good idea to look for you." His hand lay gently on her shoulder. "Ericka saw you go up the trail. I hoped I might find you here."

"She's crazy. I 'heard' her when she was hitting me. She *really* hates me." Natalie stifled a giggle but not before her ribs made her gasp and grimace.

"How badly are you hurt?"

"You sound worried." She teased. "It's just a bruise."

"Can I take a look?" He grabbed the bottom of her shirt.

Natalie couldn't stop her lazy smirk. "You wait until now to sneak a peek?" She shot back giddily.

She's like ice and that hand looks broken.

Distantly Natalie knew she heard him and that he was also hearing her. Her sketchy faculties were as bad as when she had first met him. Who knew what he was hearing. It didn't escape her notice he must have thought she was pretty far gone to let his own guard down. Maybe he thought she was going to pass out or maybe this really was a dream. How hard had she hit her head?

She reached out and touched the flashlight. It didn't feel like much, "Definitely dreaming," she mumbled.

"You should stay awake Natalie. It's best if you don't fall asleep."

His fingers were warm against her skin as he pulled up her shirt to expose her ribs. He made a distracted sound and Natalie shivered at the cold. The thin shirt and sweatshirt went back to cover her, Luka got up and she heard a rustling of fabric then a zipper.

"I didn't know what I'd find up here and it was getting cold so I grabbed a blanket." He laid it over her, Natalie shivered anyway. Her body was having a hard time dividing its dwindling resources. It hadn't done her any good laying immobile, letting her blood pool, while she exposed herself to the cold night wind coming off the still winter chilled water below. Coming up here had been poorly planned.

Luka cursed. "This wind is going to make a fire almost impossible."

She mumbled something unintelligible, her tongue too lazy to respond. Luka cursed again and moved his bag to use as a pillow, pulling her bag under her head. The world around Natalie grew dark again as he picked up his flashlight and trotted off.

When Natalie came back to consciousness, it was to a much brighter and warmer world. Not only was a fire burning in front of her, but she was leaning up against something much warmer than a rock or log. Luka had made their camp by the stones. From their positioning, she could tell he was leaning against the stone and had pulled her up to lay back against him, his legs stretched around her, the blanket covered them both.

Natalie didn't move when she woke, consciousness was too stubborn to come back all at once. Her hair moved when his hand touched it, stroking it aside as he rested his face against the back of her neck. The warmth of his breath sent goosebumps racing down her arm.

It didn't take long before he felt her body stop shivering. She relaxed against him and he heard her sigh, her breath finally coming in deep regular intervals while she stared into the fire, uncertain exactly when she came and went from sleep. Luka "listened" to her and heard her dreams slide from rambling and confused to more normal patterns. He let himself listen longer than he should have, hearing some things he wanted to be true yet finding it painful to hear the longing behind them. Natalie knew he was listening because when his defenses were down to hear her, she could hear his.

Luka was relatively certain Natalie was going to be okay, he had gotten to her in time. Knowing that, he remained where he was, feeling her body against his gave him pleasure. The fact that he was enjoying it bothered him. He'd thought himself beyond that.

Her fear of losing him touched him as did her fear of being alone. She had enjoyed the intimacy they shared by the uniqueness of their talents. Like him, she could be herself with someone else who could block thoughts. It did give him a guilty pang to know she trusted him, despite knowing he had picked through her mind when they had worked together.

He hadn't meant to, it was difficult to avoid much like having someone sitting next to you on the bus talking on his phone. Even when they were quiet it was hard not to listen. But he hadn't dug as deep as she'd imagined. He had stopped himself every time.

Now though, now was different. He was having a terrible time keeping himself from her mind having overheard her feelings for him, complicated by his own for her. He'd heard Avery that night when he'd gone to the restroom. Natalie's repeated deflections when love was mentioned had flustered him enough he had forgotten their sodas.

It was a long night for Luka. He kept vigil the last few hours before dawn, only partially grateful when at last the sun broke on the horizon.

Chapter 16

Morning finally came. Luka remained motionless for fear of jostling Natalie. When finally she stirred, he put a hand on her leg to tell her not to move. It had the opposite effect.

When Natalie jumped at his touch, she shrieked and clutched her side setting off the pain in her hand. In less than a minute she had gone from blissfully asleep to lying curled up and gasping in agony.

"I didn't mean to startle you. I was trying to get you to stay still." Luka's voice was pained.

Natalie's mumbles were impossible to decipher against the blanket tucked up against her face.

"What?"

She lifted her chin only slightly. "I said, how often do you think I wake up with someone?"

Luka was embarrassed. "I guess not often."

"Try never," Natalie snapped. She was in more pain than she could ever remember having and knowing she was going to have to get down the slope today was giving her incentive to jump and pray for sharks.

"Don't even think it," Luka cautioned darkly.

Can't you give me some amount of privacy? This is already bad enough.

You aren't blocking very well. It's hard not to hear you.

That is because all of my energy is going to not crying like a baby knowing I'm going to have to crawl down this damn hill as soon as I can get up.

She took a series of shallow breaths and leaned over to catch herself on her good hand, rolling forward onto her hands and knees. Luka watched her, impressed with her fortitude. She had even brought her blocks up tight. He couldn't hear a peep coming from her.

Luka folded the blanket, hoping to keep his hands busy to avoid moving to helping her. If she wanted help from him, she wouldn't be so intent upon blocking him out. Unzipping Natalie's pack he saw the lunch she had packed had survived for the most part. Thank you Tupperware.

"Are you hungry?" He shook the container rattling the crackers against the plastic.

Natalie glared at him but they both heard her stomach growl. It had been nearly twenty-four hours since she'd eaten. Luka grinned at her.

"Don't be stubborn. You need it if you're going to get down there under your own steam."

Rolling her eyes at him, she halfway kidded. "You could carry me."

"I would if I thought it wouldn't hurt more," he replied honestly.

Natalie felt her anger dissipate. "Thanks for coming to find me Luka."

He ducked his head, pairing a piece of cheese with a cracker. "They're a little warm but they'll do."

"I'd eat anything right now." She shot him a tight smile letting him place the food on her upturned palm.

They ate in silence but for the sounds of their crunching. Luka offered a bottle of water for them to share. He chuckled to himself. "I guess you got your picnic."

Natalie snorted.

When they had eaten and drank their fill, Natalie could put it off no longer. Luka had not said a word about moving, leaving it to her. Finally, she groaned and he saw her gathering to stand.

"Wait." He bolted to his feet. She did and watched as he collapsed her bag into his, shouldering the load to leave his hands free. Luka held out a hand for her, not missing the tightness around her eyes indicating how much pain she was in and how frightened she was. "Come on, let me help."

"Thanks." Natalie closed her eyes briefly, gathered herself and reached out to take his hand as she gained her feet. She clutched at his hand, squeezing in pain before it hit her she was hurting him.

She glanced up at him and caught him squinting before he straightened his face. She eased up, flushing, "Sorry."

Luka's grin temporarily knocked back her pain though its effects were woefully short lived. He eased her right arm around his waist, being too tall to support her easily with his shoulders. His right hand held her right arm to his side, the other rested against her back, ready to catch her if she stumbled yet unable to touch her left side without causing more discomfort.

They traveled down the hill making slow but steady progress. Natalie kept her lips pressed tightly together, only crying out a few times when she misjudged a step and came down hard jarring herself. Luka couldn't believe this was the same fragile girl he had met seven months ago.

Impressed, huh? Natalie commented, pulling it out of his head.

"So the student has become the master," Luka joked uncomfortably. He could see her strength fading, her body shook from fatigue and sweat had drenched her shirt.

Eventually they made it down. As soon as they did Luka took control, directing their path toward his apartment. He had a unit in a four square available only to those lucky few who could afford them. It had a private bathroom, no roommate and most importantly, it was closer than her dorm.

She saw where they were going and didn't object. It didn't matter where they ended up as long as she could stop moving. Her legs failed crossing the street and Luka swept an arm under her legs to hold her loosely against his body, keeping the jostling to a minimum now that they were on flat ground.

Natalie hurt all over by the time Luka locked his door behind them. He gently lay her down on his queen size bed. She had never been in his room before and looked curiously around herself with minimal head movement, grateful for the distraction.

"This bed barely fits in here. Kind of overkill don't you think?" Even backed up against the far wall the edge of the bed left less than two feet around it on three sides.

Luka shrugged. "I like to stretch out when I sleep. I have a King at home but that won't fit in here."

"I sleep curled up, I could sleep in a chair if I had to."

"Well, for now you can use this one." He stepped around the corner and came back with a blanket he used to cover her.

"I'm getting your blankets all sweaty and gross..."

He gave her a severe look, "Don't you apologize." He wagged a finger at her. "I told you, you have to stop doing that."

"S... well, it's a habit." She blushed.

Grinning at her, relieved she was well enough to joke around still, Luka moved to smooth her hair from her face and stopped himself short. "Get some sleep. We'll worry about everything else when you wake up." He shut off the light and closed the door partway behind himself leaving her alone.

Natalie was asleep before his footsteps faded.

Some time later she awoke to loud voices and a fading sun glowing behind the drawn curtains. It took her a minute to remember where she was. She was in Luka's bed, remembering only barely in time not to move or stretch. Nothing else to do, Natalie listened to the voices. One was Luka and he was really mad. She'd never heard him like that before.

The other was female. Natalie's heart skipped a beat. It was Ericka. Here. Natalie could not defend herself like this. She started to panic, her skin prickled with sweat between her shoulder blades. It took all of her self-control not to try to run out of there or hyperventilate, though she wasn't sure which would hurt more.

"You have to listen to me, Luka." She was pleading. "I was worried about you. She's been distracting you, taking you away from all of us who love you. Your mother hasn't heard from you in weeks. Someone like her can't understand you like I can. Who knows you better than I do?" Ericka's shrill voice was on edge.

Luka growled back at her. "Ericka I have been nothing except patient with you, but I have had enough. She could have died out there if I hadn't found her. Do you realize what that would have meant? Do you want to go to jail? Do you want someone's blood on your hands?"

"I don't care if she dies. She doesn't mean anything to us. You have to know I only did what I did for you. You just don't see her like I do. She's after you for your money. You can't trust a *poor* girl like that. She only has one way to change her standing in the world and that is to sleep her way up." Ericka whined.

"The only one trying to sleep her way up is you."

Natalie heard a loud crack.

"You may have money but you can't buy class Ericka." Luka's cold voice was low and harder to hear. "Go home and pack. I'm calling your father to let him know you're out of control and I don't want anything to do with you ever again. I refuse to be your keeper any more."

Ericka howled angrily, her thoughts swirling in anger and hurt so quickly they were hard to untangle. The door slammed a few seconds later.

Natalie waited a few minutes for him to calm down before calling his name softly. It hurt to take a big breath or shout so it was more about practicality than tone.

He ducked his head inside, visibly concerned. "I'm sorry, did we wake you?" He didn't mention names.

"Yes. Thank you, Luka."

He stepped inside the door to come sit on the bed. "For what?"

"For standing up for me. I'm sure it was hard what with the connection between your families and your history and all."

Luka rubbed her foot through the blanket. "The only connection between our families beyond our fathers golfing together anymore is me managing her chaos and I'm done. I meant what I said. You could have died up there." His hand stayed on her foot.

As much as she didn't want to do it, Natalie held her breath and started to slide out from under the blanket.

Luka's demeanor changed immediately. "What are you doing? You should rest."

"I would like to go home and shower, and eat, and feel human again."

Pointing to her head, he argued. "Fingers aside, you have a nasty bruise on your head and your ribs are at least bruised. The only place you should be going is to the hospital." He stared her down, daring her to disagree. "You could have a concussion."

Natalie was determined. She rolled onto her stomach, leaning on the right side and slipping her feet to the floor to reduce any need to use the muscles across her ribs. "Us poor kids can't afford to go to the hospital for every bump and bruise and it's nothing a little tape can't cure. I'm going home and I can either send Avery to the store or I'll go."

Luka shook his head in bewilderment. "You are so stubborn. Who knew under all of that insecurity was such a hard head."

"I am not hard headed. And who are you to chastise me for being able to take care of myself? Aren't you the one who said that was exactly what I needed to learn how to do?"

93

Taken aback, he blinked at her. "I did say that and you're right, you are doing a great job. Up to the part where you hiked up to the top of a mountain, injured, and then you nearly froze on it."

Natalie was frustrated with him for being right and for her body for screaming at her to listen to him. It fueled her uncharacteristically tense response. "You are a big, fat hypocrite. You want me to be strong and independent but as soon as I don't need you, you try to undermine me." She was on her feet and shuffling stiffly toward him. Her body hurt but it wasn't impossible to move around if she was careful. "Which one is it Professor Bailey? Meek and needy or strong and independent? To be fair, you should go with the latter considering you'll be leaving soon and you won't be around to help the former." Natalie stopped, glaring at Luka.

She wasn't usually one to go off like that, not since she was a kid. Yet here she had unloaded on Luka when he wasn't entirely at fault. He had just spent the night keeping her from freezing or going into shock. Sure, he was going off for the summer, but that was not a surprise nor did he owe her anything. He was a friend and a tutor who had taught her a lot. She could hope that he would return to finish his last three classes next fall but if not, oh well. Maybe they could have dinner once in a while or exchange emails. He owed her nothing nor could she demand more.

Luka's eyes burned, he was still furious from his argument with Ericka and now Natalie had baited him. She was embarrassed and the need to get home became more urgent. More to put distance between herself and Luka than any screaming desire to be back in her dorm.

Natalie shuffled to her right trying to go around him but Luka blocked the doorway.

"Where are you going?" he asked roughly.

She slowly tried to ease past him, pressing her point. "Away from here."

"Please stay." He held out his hand, blocking her path.

"Move," Natalie insisted halfheartedly. She *was* being stubborn but she didn't want to see her cry and she knew she was going to. Now that she was thinking of losing her two friends at the same time, she was feeling weepy again and wanted to be alone before she humiliated herself further. When had she grown so weepy? Sometimes she missed her lonely life. It hurt but she'd learned to control that hurt. This kind was harder.

Luka stepped over, putting his body between her and the door, his hand sliding up her cheek. Natalie froze. He was trying to make her look at him only she wouldn't. She continued to hide her eyes. Luka's other hand came up to cup her face.

Natalie jerked her head up in surprise. His hands weren't forceful, yet they were insistent as they guided her. She watched his face come closer to hers, not figuring out his intention until his lips touched hers.

She stared up at him when he withdrew, his hands sliding down her neck to her shoulders. "Why?" she whispered in shock. "I thought you thought… I mean, you said you didn't want to…I mean why me? Why now?" Natalie didn't know what to say.

Luka leaned in again, this time sliding his hand up under her hair at the base of her head and holding her firmly against him. Kissing her again, this time more demanding. When he let go of her, Natalie's head was spinning.

"I didn't want to be with anyone." He brushed his lips against hers lightly. "But that was before." His hand slid down her back, holding her, supporting her carefully. "I can't explain why or when it started for me, but when I heard Ericka and imagined you out there, hurt…" His voice trailed off. "And now here we are." Luka stepped a half step closer, his chest touching hers while he gently massaged her back. When he ducked his head down again, Natalie leaned her head back and returned his kiss. "Oregon isn't far." Kiss. "And it's only for twelve weeks." Kiss. "And we have three weeks before I leave." Kiss. "Are you game?"

As an answer, Natalie rested one hand against his chest, spreading her fingers to feel the body she had longed to caress for so long. She closed her eyes, unable to stretch up or pull him down and felt him come to her. When he did, she parted her lips to him, tasting his warmth and a hint of peanut butter. He'd had a snack while she slept.

The gentle kiss wasn't enough and, forgetting herself, Natalie slid her left hand up to touch his neck but the sharpness of the pain in her ribs made her gasp.

Luka broke off immediately. "We should tape those. I have some from last summer when I sprained my ankle playing Rugby. Let me get it." He rubbed his thumb over her shoulder.

Natalie bit her lip, fighting with her body to let her have just ten minutes but it was no use. As soon as Luka came back and escorted her to his couch, she sat and inhaled sharply. She would not be experiencing any other fun today.

"Take your shirt off." Luka ordered her, sitting on the coffee table in front of her.

Chapter 17

"Excuse me?" Natalie blinked at him. He was a fool if he thought she could do that with bruised ribs.

Luka rolled his eyes. "I meant so that I can tape your ribs. They go pretty high so I figured it would be easiest without your shirt. I promise to be a gentleman."

Self-conscious but seeing the logic and not wanting to go to the doctor and have to explain the bill to her parents, Natalie nodded. "I'll need your help getting it off," she mumbled shyly.

True to his word, Luka helped her to get her arms and head out while minimizing her need for movement. Before long Natalie was sitting in jeans and an all too practical white bra covering her small and uneventful chest.

Natalie kept her breathing shallow, though some of it was from nerves. She thought it best to let him think it was all a pain response. Luka's hands were steady and firm, pressing the tape against her skin. When he was done, she took an experimental deeper breath. Although not back to normal, it was significantly better. Exhaling carefully, Natalie smiled at him. "Thanks, that's a lot better."

"Can I see your hand?" He pointed at the swollen one and she handed it to him. Luka grasped her wrist and twisted her hand back and forth to see both sides. He glanced up at her. "Can you bend it at all?"

Snorting, Natalie answered incredulously, "Not if I can help it. It hurts."

"I know it does," he jibed. "But I am wondering if its broken or sprained."

He reached for the scissors he'd used to cut the tape and sliced off her makeshift wrapping job. "This is pretty bruised. It'll be hard to move it even if it isn't broken." Tenderly, he probed the joint. "I think it was just dislocated and it feels like it's back in now. Nice job. I bet that hurt."

Natalie tried not to be sarcastic. "You bet right." Tipping her head, she watched him rewrap her fingers loosely with two strips of tape. "How do you know all of this stuff?"

He flashed his teeth at her. "I was accident prone when I was a teen. Sometimes I'd be so busy listening to the voices in my head, I'd walk right into a wall. I paid attention to what he was thinking when I went to the doctor. Curious mind, you know."

"Well I'm glad you were a klutz. At least I am right now." The looser wrapping already felt loads better.

Bumps and bruises properly tended to, Natalie was suddenly feeling foolish for being half naked in his living room. She rose and Luka backed up to give her space.

"I still want to wash my hair." She reached up her hand to touch it afraid she'd find pine needles in it or something. It wasn't that bad, but it didn't change how she felt after spending the night on the ground and sweating like a pig. "It's been a rough night."

"Why don't you shower here? I have a spare shirt you can wear and we can wash your clothes." He offered. *I don't want you to go.* He added in her head, picking an imaginary piece of lint off of it.

"Okay," Natalie agreed softly. She didn't want to go either.

She stepped past him to go across the hall into the bathroom. She turned on the water and waited for it to warm up. Peeling off the rest of her clothing was difficult though once it was off she climbed in and breathed a huge sigh of relief.

The water was incredible. At first it was too hot still she let herself burn for a few seconds as her skin adjusted to the sudden change in temperature. After the world's longest shower, Natalie finally felt clean again. Thank goodness for waterproof tape, she hadn't compromised Luka's ministrations.

She stepped out and saw that her dirty clothes had been removed, a shirt and sport shorts left on the edge of the counter. A hairbrush sat on the edge of the counter, as did a glass and a large blue gel tab.

She stepped out into the main living space feeling refreshed. "You thought of everything. Thank you." She wandered through the open area to the far right wall where the small kitchen was located. Luka stood at the stove. Natalie sniffed, "That smells good. What is it?"

Luka turned around and let his eyes run up and down, appraising. Natalie's body remembered the feel of his hands, warming at the recollection. "It's a sauce my mother's mother taught her back in Serbia. She had to pass it to me or let it die." He shrugged, "It's usually served with little minced meat sausages but with our time constraints, I thought pasta would be good."

"Sure. Pasta sound fine." Natalie broke off from watching him, not trusting herself to be so close. "Do you need me to do anything?"

He motioned with his elbow toward the counter by the fridge. "If you want a glass of wine, I have an open bottle over there."

It was a Petite Syrah. Natalie didn't know much about wines but was willing to try it if Luka said it was decent. He'd set two glasses by the bottle.

She poured, he stirred and they talked about family while the sauce simmered and water boiled. It wasn't long before any awkwardness evaporated and they were again at ease in each other's company.

Natalie tried to reach up and grab plates except they were unwieldy and she sucked in her breath sharply. Luka was behind her in a flash, catching the plates as she bobbled them.

"Thank goodness for small kitchens," she joked.

He lowered the dishes to the counter top and wrapped his arm around her. She felt his lips brush her neck as he mumbled against her.

"You have to take it easy with any sort of lifting, especially over your head."

"O-okay." Natalie closed her eyes and let her body melt against his. Her back felt cold when he pulled away to serve dinner.

The first bite of home cooked food she'd had since Christmas tasted better than anything her mother had ever made. *Sorry Mom.* She thought penitently at the disloyal thought.

Luka set down his glass, guessing at her reaction. "Do you not like it?"

She shook her head, chewing quickly to answer. "No, I love it. It just made me realize what we're missing with all of this cafeteria food." She pointed at the food with her fork. "When you told me you like to cook, I had no idea it was like this or I would have fished for an invitation way earlier."

"How about tomorrow then? I would like to make you something with more heart. Something appropriate for our first real date." His eyes rested on her, waiting. "If that would work for you."

Natalie could see that he was actually waiting for her to agree to a date with him. Would wonders never cease? She counted to three before answering so as not to appear overly eager. "I'd like that."

***

After dinner Natalie insisted upon helping him clean up the kitchen, enjoying the luxury of time and idle chatter the lack of a dishwasher gave them. Their friendship had allowed them enough knowledge of each other to be extraordinarily comfortable around each other. The only difference now was that the sexual tension was now two sided instead of just one.

It had been there all through dinner, reminders each time their hands touched accidentally handing off dishes and when Natalie stifled yet another yawn and announced she wanted to go to bed.

"In *my* room." She blushed hotly. "I should go."

Luka wiped down the sink to avoid her direct gaze. "You could stay here."

As much as she wanted to stay, it was almost a physical pull, she knew the right thing was not to jump into bed with him. They had been friends the entire school year without him saying he was interested, on the contrary, he had been assuring her he was never going to be interested in anything more. Now, in less than a day she was not going to hop like a grateful little freshman into his bed glad to have his attention.

She did not question his sincerity of emotion, but his commitment to it might be less so than hers and she wanted more than just a fling. Especially considering this could potentially be her first boyfriend as well as her first sexual experience *and* he was due to leave in less than three weeks. For her part, she intended to take things seriously and slowly. It was far simpler to make that decision when he wasn't kissing her.

"No, I think it would be better for me to go." She made a move toward the door and Luka laughed.

"Like that?" He pointed at her outfit.

Looking down, Natalie groaned inwardly. She had forgotten all about the fact that she was wearing his clothes. Luka walked past her, disappearing into his bedroom for a minute. She heard a drawer shut and he emerged carrying a gray sweatshirt.

Holding it up, he walked toward her and placed it in her hands. "If you wear this, no one will even notice. You'll look like half the student body."

"Thanks." She took it and carefully pulled it over her head, the tape helped. The scent of his fabric softener reminded her of how he smelled. Close though not quite him. Natalie inhaled deeply wishing it had *that* smell, the one that was all him.

He grabbed her bag from inside his. They were still sitting by the front door with the shoes. While Natalie put her shoes on, Luka surprised her by stepping into his as well. When she looked askance, he stared at her before clarifying his intentions.

"I can't let you walk across campus alone at night. Even if you weren't hurt I wouldn't be comfortable."

He shouldered her bag, opened the door and waited. Smiling tentatively, Natalie accepted and secretly approved of his gentlemanly gesture. Patiently she waited for him to lock up before allowing him to escort her across campus and to her dorm.

They strolled slowly, Luka taking her hand after they were through the narrow elevator doors. Natalie rubbed her thumb against the backside of his, enjoying every minute she was touching him. All too soon they arrived at her doorstep.

She squeezed his hand and released it long enough to fish her keys from her bag and unlock the door. He opened it and held it for her, letting her take the lead.

"Would you like to come in for a few minutes?" Natalie offered once they reached her door. She wanted to hold on to him as long as she could, fearing his feelings were fleeting and whatever magical spell they were under would dissipate when they parted.

"I'd better not." He squeezed her hand. "I still need to stop by the center before it closes and let Ivy know you won't be in for a while." Seeing Natalie's anxiety he added. "Don't worry, I'll explain everything. I'll keep her off your back by telling her we'll keep studying here."

Natalie's heart skipped a beat and she questioned her resolve. Right then it didn't matter whether her first time with a man was with someone she was involved with or a friend who had a temporary break from reality and just liked her for now as long as it was him. She kept a grip on his hand and stepped closer, tipping her face up.

Luka was momentarily startled by her boldness but recovered promptly. His hand went around the back of her neck and held her face against his while he kissed her goodnight.

"So that's where you've been!" Avery exclaimed from the far end of the hall where she stood, laundry basket in hand.

Reluctantly they let themselves be parted by her intrusion. One glimpse at his face before he focused over her head at Avery told Natalie he was just as displeased for the interruption as she was. She kept her mind closed to Avery's thoughts, not wanting to get too complicated at the moment.

"Rest well, have Avery keep an eye on you and don't forget to take something for the pain in a few hours when the other one wears off." He kissed her nose and let their hands drift apart as he walked past her to the stairwell and disappeared. "Avery." He nodded as he walked past.

Avery on the other hand stalked down the hall to her, throwing the door open around Natalie. "Next time you decide to go on an all nighter you could at least call and tell me not to worry." She stepped over the pile of dirty staged laundry sitting outside her dresser and closet area. "Or you could have the decency to take your cell phone so I can call you." Avery pointed to Natalie's phone still sitting on the edge of her desk where she'd left it, thinking she wanted to be unreachable for her afternoon picnic. That had almost been a fatal mistake.

"It wasn't like that." Natalie stopped herself, not sure what to say. She guessed it was okay to tell Avery about Ericka except she wanted to leave out the part where she decided to hike to her potential death. That had been dumb and she didn't care to share it, even if she could blame it on having her bell rung by a tennis racket. "Do you remember Ericka?"

"How could I forget? She knows how to make an impression." Avery rolled her eyes sarcastically.

"Well, I went for a walk yesterday and she caught me off guard and hit me with a tennis racket." Natalie held up her hand, still impressively purple and swollen. She lifted her hair and showed Avery her forehead, which also sported a multicolored lump.

"Holy crap!" Avery jumped her pile of colors to investigate further.

Natalie felt the weight lifting from her shoulders already as she recounted the events for her. "That's not all." She took her good hand and raised her shirt enough to show off her white strips of bandage. "She bruised a couple of ribs too."

Reaching out, her fingers touched the bandage on Natalie's side only for a second before Avery clenched her fists at her sides. "I don't know why that idiot keeps her around if they're not screwing."

"Not anymore. He told her he never wants to see her again and it sounds like he's got some pull with her dad so he's going to see about having her shipped home."

"Good." Avery snorted. "That woman is unsafe at any speed." Rapidly, typical Avery, she changed gears. "So what happened between your walk yesterday and showing up here in his clothes today? That has to be close to a full day left to the imaginations of degenerates everywhere. Mostly me. What do you have to say for yourself young lady?" She put her hands on her hips in a mock accusatory pose.

The whole truth of how she'd been found was too hard to believe unless she shared something about Luka and herself she chose to keep private. Partial truth would cover what she needed it to. "She saw me outside the center on my walk and assumed I was going to meet Luka who was inside. Then, when I came by, she jumped me. She still had her tennis racket from practice."

"Let's be happy the nutter isn't in archery," Avery quipped dryly.

"Luka was inside and saw it. He came out and brought me back to his place so he could check me out. Make sure I was okay."

"You spent the night?" Avery watched her closely.

Natalie rolled her eyes heavenward. "Yes, with bruised ribs that hurt when I breathe too deep." She backed up and when she felt the edge of her bed against her legs, eased herself down into a prone position and sighed, closing her eyes.

The thin mattress depressed beside her. "Is it safe to say you guys are a thing now?"

"Yeah, I think so. For now anyway," Natalie replied, knowing even with her doubts that it was true. She just wasn't sure how long it would last. "We have our first official date tomorrow."

"Oooh," Avery teased.

Natalie didn't answer. Her mind was on someone taller and far more handsome than her roommate.

Chapter 18

Saturday was a great day. No classes. Unfortunately for Natalie that meant no distractions to busy her before the grand event of the evening and, after what had happened with Ericka, she was unwilling to go on walkabout alone.

She went with Avery to breakfast and lunch. Since Natalie was "convalescing" she heard her friend tell Jason she was going to stay with her until that night when she could hand her over. Natalie wasn't convinced Avery's intentions were that innocent still she appreciated the company as well as the pedicure and manicure Avery gave her.

By the time dinner rolled around and Natalie had been on a constant diet of anti-inflammatories and pain reducers, she was feeling pretty good. Avery had even helped her to style her hair, giving it some soft curls around her face and pinning her bangs out of her eyes.

"It gives you that innocent girl just waiting to be tarnished look men find so appealing." Avery said as she sat back to survey her handiwork.

"Thanks Avery. You've done wonders." Natalie appraised herself, picking up her makeup bag. A little brown eye shadow, some black liner and a hint of soft pink gloss and she was ready.

"You can't wear that though." Avery looked down her nose disapprovingly at Natalie's jeans and standard issue long sleeved tee. She pointed at the sleeves. "Show some skin, come on. Do you want to look like you're a little girl going on a play date or a woman looking to be taken thorough advantage of?"

Natalie's hand instinctively went to her cuff, clutching it close to her skin. "I like this. Luka knows me, there's nothing I can do with clothes that is going to change how he feels about me."

Avery threw back her head and laughed. "I knew you hadn't really dated, but you haven't dated *at all*, have you?"

There was no point lying. "No."

"There's nothing to be embarrassed of. I think that's pretty cool that you haven't been throwing yourself out there at guys who aren't good enough." She smiled gently.

Natalie detected some introspection but said nothing. She was interested in the soft underbelly Avery had started to show lately. Jason seemed to be bringing out a part of her she liked to keep hidden behind her brash façade. Commenting on it might stop her from opening up.

"So, can we mess with this a little bit?" Avery pointed at the ensemble, the hopeful look on her face saying it all.

"I can put on something more feminine if it will make you happy," Natalie offered.

Avery jumped up and clapped excitedly. "Yeah!" She glanced at her watch. "We don't have much time. When did he say he was coming? Six?"

"Yep." Luka wanted to pick her up. He said he was old fashioned, she believed it was more of a protective measure.

"Well that only gives us a few minutes." She tugged at the edge of Natalie's shirt. "Take this off."

Her nerves jumped instantly to the foreground. "No," she said too fast. Avery eyed her questioningly. "It's too late for the shirt, I don't want to mess up my hair or anything."

Slowly Avery nodded. "Good point." She pointed to her jeans. "Then at least take those off."

Natalie obeyed and allowed Avery to rummage through her closet, pulling out a denim skirt and black footless tights to match the black graphic tee she wore.

Sitting back, Avery nodded approvingly. "It's perfect. Now you need shoes."

Natalie made a move toward the black Converse she had taken off to replace her pants.

"Not a chance." Avery stopped her short. "You have to wear a uniquely girl's shoe to be considered feminine." She pointed disgusted at Natalie's choice. "And a basketball sneaker is not a girl shoe."

Shrugging, Natalie replied, "I don't have anything else."

"You're my size. Let me see what I have." Avery's digging turned up a plain pair of black heels.

Natalie shook her head. "I'm too tall for heels."

Avery argued that with Luka being taller than her it was okay, Natalie countered that she never wore them and didn't trust her balance. Neither gave until finally they agreed on a pair of black ballet slippers that caught Natalie's eye in the back of the closet.

A knock on the door announced his arrival and Avery stepped up to answer.

Of course Luka wasn't surprised. "Evening, Avery. Are you heading off to see Jason tonight or are you going to manage a whole day without each other?" He teased her.

Natalie took a moment to drink him in. Luka had put on black dress pants and a green Cuban style shirt with a cream geometric pattern running vertically up the lapels and he had topped it off with a pair of black shoes she was willing to guess cost more than her father brought home in a month. Normally, as a friend, his money didn't bother her, but as a girlfriend she wasn't sure she could handle being with someone from a significantly higher tax bracket.

Avery put her hand on her hip. "I find that absence makes the heart grow fonder." Then added with a smile, "Actually we thought for a change of scenery we would hang out here tonight since Nat will be out. His roommates are kind of slobs so we can only hang in his room or risk being overcome by the scent of unwashed man sock and Frito farts." She stopped, seeing Luka staring past her. He wasn't listening. "You two kids behave now. Don't do anything I wouldn't."

Natalie resisted the urge to shoot back the obvious fact that that was not all that limiting. Her view of Avery was under construction. Impulsively, she reached out and gave her a limp one armed hug on her way out.

Avery smiled warmly back and gave Luka a severe look. "Don't turn out to be a dick."

Luka inclined his head at her, offering Natalie his arm. "No ma'am."

The door closed behind them and Luka smiled down at Natalie. "I had no idea I would be meeting your mother so soon."

A strange new shyness stifled Natalie's usual wit and she merely smiled back at him.

He rubbed her hand where it rested on his arm and she became painfully aware of their public display. No one was in the hall, still she felt herself blushing. They walked down the two flights of stairs. Luka kept her hand, helping to balance her as that was obviously still painful for her.

"How are you feeling today?" He asked her halfway down when she still hadn't said anything.

Without taking her eyes from the steps, Natalie answered. "A little tender but the tape helps a lot. From what I read that must mean they're bruised and not cracked, so that's good."

"Yeah, no offense but you would have to be pretty damn tough to have a broken rib and still have been able to make it up that hill. I'm glad you're feeling better."

She wasn't offended at all that he would have more knowledge of injuries than she. Having never been to a doctor for anything beyond a checkup nor had she known anyone who really had hurt themselves like that, Natalie had no resources but the internet and her own perceptions. From what she had read, it was a painful injury and one a doctor would only tape so Luka had saved her a trip but the recovery was the real silver lining. Bruised ribs resolved within a week or so, the worst of it only lasting a few days. That beat the pants off having to nurse broken bones. She might have let Avery take a few retaliatory swipes at Ericka like she had offered to after watching Natalie wince on the steps this morning on the way to breakfast.

They walked nearly the entire campus without saying anything beyond Luka's few failed attempts to make conversation. He had stopped trying to touch her after she became increasingly uncomfortable with each passing witness to their "togetherness."

Finally they reached his apartment and took the elevator to his floor. Just before Luka was going to turn the key, he paused and let go, leaving his sparse keychain dangling in the lock.

"Do you want to be here with me?" His face was an unreadable mask. Physically he was as locked away as his thoughts.

Natalie was tongue tied from the unexpected question. "Well, yeah. Of course I do."

"Would you like to tell me if this makes you uncomfortable?" He waved his hands between them to denote a relationship. "Because if you don't want this to go any further, now would be a good time to tell me. We can just shake hands and say good night, still friends with no harm done. But I thought after last night we both wanted to try this out. Was I wrong?"

Glancing around at the other doors in the hallway, Natalie dropped her voice and asked him pleadingly, "Can we talk about this inside please?"

Luka cocked his head to the side and studied her for several long heartbeats. "Are you embarrassed to be with me?"

She was flabbergasted. *Her* embarrassed to be with *him*? Was he conscious? Natalie stammered awkwardly. "N-no. I-I, um... I just don't... I mean... I've never..." She exhaled loudly in frustration before she let the truth gush out. "I've never been on a date and I'm not sure what I'm supposed to do. I don't want all of these people looking at me." Finished, she pursed her lips and exhaled slowly trying to calm herself down. She could feel her defenses slipping and didn't want him in her head tonight. It was important to her that her first date be normal.

Eyes still focused on her, Luka reached out and turned the knob, pushing the door inward and motioning her inside. Grateful, Natalie ducked through and scooted stiffly inside, not sure whether to sit or stand. Or leave for that matter. So far her first date was a near bust and everything she was doing was just sending it down the tubes faster.

Shutting the door, Luka jingled the keys in his hand absentmindedly. "Please, make yourself at home. I'll be right back." He disappeared into the hall. Natalie thought he had gone into his bedroom and her anxiety tripled. This was not going at all like she had hoped.

Luka's apartment was small by Midwestern standards. The front door opened into a short hall. In front of them lay a great room that was bordered by another short hall that led to its one bathroom and one bedroom. To the right was the modest kitchen separated from the living room by a half wall, the small table on the other side of it. At the far end of the living room, opposite the front door were sliding glass doors. They were hidden behind the chocolate drapes currently standing closed. The common flooring was older hardwood, yellowed with sun and time. The smooth plaster walls rose to coved ceilings typical in California if Natalie's limited knowledge was accurate.

His furnishings were sparse though of a higher quality than those of a typical college student. A few multicolored earth tone knobby rugs Natalie guessed his mother had contributed were scattered through the hall and kitchen. The couch was leather, worn and comfortable, not beat up like a hand me down, this wear was designer.

Natalie had been here a few times before but not for long enough to explore and she had been far too distracted last time to check out his view. The bathroom she knew was decorated in white subway tiles and chocolate linens; his room a dark blue. That newest discovery brought on a slight twirl in her stomach. She breathed deeply to steady herself.

At first glance, Luka didn't seem wealthy. He didn't wear labels yet his clothing was well made and of a high quality, apparent to someone who knew to look at the details. It was the same with his apartment. He could have lived off campus in a nicer place but he had rejected his parents' repeated efforts to buy him one of the condos nearby. He never talked down to people who came from less but sometimes he mentioned things most kids aren't exposed to if their parents are working all the time just to put food on the table.

Luka had been to the south of France on spring break, the Swiss Alps to ski over Christmas and on two trips with his mother's favorite charity to the Philippines. That was all before Andjela had died. After that there had been no more family trips and his mother had stopped working with all of her organizations.

Now Luka held his parents' money at arms length, only accepting help when it pleased his mother. She so rarely stepped in to his life that when she did engage, he mostly let her do whatever she wanted and if that meant brightly colored rugs, then so be it.

Natalie padded to the floor length drapes across the room, eager to see how the view would be from up here. They were facing the trail by her figuring. Her hand had just touched the brushed twill fabric when Luka spoke from where he had just come back into the room.

He held two glasses in his hand. "Go ahead, I'll be right there."

He was so at ease, Natalie envied him that. She had yet to see Luka lose his cool with the exception of Ericka. The only thing helping her not see him as far above her equal was that Natalie knew he was jittery about "them" as well even if he hid it better.

She swept back the curtain and saw that the glass door opened out onto a small balcony, at present set with two rattan patio chairs with bright floral patterns. A small table between them held a champagne bucket with a bottle already chilling. Soft light illuminated the space from several candles surrounding the chairs.

Natalie took in the view over the backside of campus, the tutor center lay just to their left and straight ahead was the hillside where already so much had happened. The sun was beginning its descent in preparation for its setting in an hour. It would disappear behind the hill giving them a perfect view from there.

"What do you think?"

Startled, she spun and saw him standing in the doorway. "It's beautiful. You're so lucky to have all of this."

The corner of his mouth twisted. "Yes, I am."

Natalie started to feel uncomfortable again.

Luka held out the glasses in one hand. "Could you take these? I have something else I wanted to grab."

"Sure." She set them on the little table and removed the bottle from the ice bucket and felt a nervous twinge. She was not much of a drinker. Hopefully, she hadn't given him the wrong impression on the only social outing she had ever seen him at which would have been the party when she was drunk and got assaulted by Ericka. Plus there was last night's glass of wine, she realized.

But when she examined the label, she saw that it was a bottle of sparkling lemonade he had placed in the bucket. She found herself smiling that he knew her better than she gave him credit for and relaxed as she poured two glasses. Taking hers, she leaned on the railing to watch the sun drawing even with the top of the tall hill, not quite a mountain by California standards but bigger than most of what they had back home. Wherever Natalie ended up after she was done with school, she wanted mountains to look at or at least foothills like these. They were so beautiful and peaceful, she had grown to love them for their stillness.

The glass was nearly to her lips when she heard music and lowered it. Turning, she saw that Luka had set an MP3 dock on the balcony behind their chairs.

"You've certainly thought of everything again." She teased, feeling her tensions evaporate now that she was here and with him, no one else watching to see if she did things right or answered questions no one else could hear.

He gave her a boyish grin, she saw his dimple he disliked so much and smiled back. Luka raised his glass.

"You weren't going to take a drink without a toast I hope."

"*You* had better have one in mind." There was no way she was setting the tone for this evening.

Luka took a step around their seating area and stopped next to her holding up his glass. "To taking chances." He took a drink and lowered his glass.

Natalie liked the freshness of the lemonade and the carbonation kept it light, not too tart. It was a perfect summer drink, suited their spring evening just as well. "I like this."

"Good." He motioned for her to sit, putting a hand under her arm to let her lean if she needed to. "I noticed you aren't much of a drinker."

"How? I was thinking you must consider me a drinker for sure since the only time you saw me outside of our sessions I was loaded to the gills."

Luka broke into a huge grin. "You *were* a mess that night but remember I knew how many you had." He tapped his temple. "Once I knew you were there I kept tabs on you. I wasn't sure about that Jason guy though. I'm still not. There are some strange ideas that float around the heads of some of these guys at parties sometimes."

Natalie recalled hearing someone thinking about using drugs to take advantage of someone and she shivered. At the time she had thought it was a disgusting side of her personality. What an amazing relief to know that she was not the person she feared, but was in actuality a somewhat sane human being. She realized she'd left that girl to that man's foul intentions and felt sick. "I heard a guy there. He'd slipped something in this girl's drink and took her upstairs. I didn't do anything to help her." Her hand went to her mouth. "If I'd have known that's what I was hearing..."

Face growing serious, Luka took a drink. "He didn't do anything. That was why I asked Avery and Jason to follow you back instead of going myself. I had to wait to find out who the guy was so I could put some other ideas in his head."

"Can you project your thoughts into people's minds?" Natalie whispered, leaning in to him.

"No," he shook his head. "But once you know how to listen, it's pretty easy to convince someone they've been caught and there's someone's cop boyfriend looking to kick his ass. It seems to have done the trick. He had never done it before and he sees it as too risky to try again."

Natalie was studying him, glass resting on her leg pulled up on her chair. "You're very protective of women, aren't you?" She asked appraisingly.

His eyes widened in surprise yet he didn't answer right away. Putting his glass down on the table, he watched her. She was just starting to squirm when he finally replied. "When we first met I didn't know if you could handle the strength of your talent. For months I told myself it was a lot to ask of someone so emotionally sensitive."

She started to object but he held out a hand to stay her.

"I don't mean that as a bad thing. Quite the opposite really. In my opinion, your talent is strong, but your real strength comes from the way you combine what you 'hear' with what you sense from watching people like you do. It's very good, really. I wish I was that good. You could make a fortune as a therapist or magician." He teased lightly.

"Wow, thanks. I don't know if I deserve all of that but thanks anyway." Natalie felt her face grow hot from such high praise. It was arguably the biggest compliment she'd ever gotten. To have it involve her ability made it harder to take.

"Is it still weird to talk about it?" He prodded gently, sensing the source of her discomfort.

"Yes, I've spent so long thinking it was all in my head and now in such a short amount of time it turns out it wasn't me at all. There was kind of a 'getting to know you' stage I went through at the beginning when I learned what it was I'd been hearing all those years. Sorting through what was me and what was outside." She waved a hand.

"What did you think? Do you like what you came up with as 'you'?"

"You know, I do. It's still all shifting, what with being at this place in my life, but I think it's good." She rolled her eyes. "Now don't ask me what I want to be when I grow up because I have no clue. Although I hear there's a future for me in therapy." She winked.

***

They watched the sun set and went inside to have an inspired meal of diver scallops over a bed of greens with a tangy, sweet sauce drizzled over them Luka said was a balsamic glaze of sorts. They had one glass of pinot noir with dinner and then he served coffee with a sweet bread for dessert.

Natalie sat back, stuffed but happy. "Luka, color me impressed. You must have worked on this all day. You didn't have to do all this for me. The balcony was plenty. You could have made this two dates."

"Does that mean you would like to do this again?" He set down his coffee cup.

She couldn't help her wide smile. "Yes, it's been wonderful. How about for you? Is it weird or are you worried you didn't get enough of a return on your investment?" Natalie teased lightly.

Without a word, Luka pushed back from the table and rose. When he was standing next to her, he held out a hand.

Feeling her pulse quicken, Natalie took it and rose beside him. His hand slid around her back and the other came up to brush her hair from her cheek. She watched his eyes, hooded as they were with what she instinctively recognized. She couldn't look away. Transfixed, she watched him lower his face to hers and discovered her body was as reactive as it had been the night before.

She had assumed it had been because it was her first kiss but maybe this was all that "initial bliss" she had heard so many girls talk about in the beginning of a relationship with a new guy. No wonder they were always so eager to jump into a new one.

"What?" Luka withdrew, confused at her smile.

"I'm sorry. I was just thinking no wonder women and men are always chasing each other if it's like this."

He frowned and shook his head. "It isn't always like this."

Letting that sink in, Natalie went up on her tiptoes to touch his lips again and he responded by lowering his face to make it easier for her to reach. Their heights were perfectly complimentary as were all of their curves, she noted. Not that she would say it out loud, but it was like they were made for each other. They just fit.

Their kissing led them to the couch where they continued for some time without coming up for air. Luka's hand rested on her hip, hers on his shoulder and neck where it mostly stayed. But after a while, she felt Luka's hand moving and her body began to respond, a whimper escaping her lips in answer to his body's question.

He lifted his head. "We're at that place. Is this what you want?" His words were those of a gentleman, but she could see in his eyes the wolf that waited just outside the door.

Not trusting her voice, Natalie tightened her lips together and shook her head nearly imperceptibly.

"Then we should stop before we do something we're going to regret." He ran his hand through his hair and leaned up on his elbow allowing her some space to catch her breath.

Natalie finger combed her hair, imagining Avery's expression if she saw what they had collectively done to all of her hard work. "Avery's going to be pissed. She was on my hair for almost half an hour."

Smiling calmly though he hadn't completely banked the fire in his eyes, Luka ran his hand over it. "Your hair is so soft. I'm glad you let it grow, it suits you."

She was still breathing hard, trying to keep her panting shallow to avoid too much rib movement. Her hand throbbed some from the increased blood flowing through her body. Otherwise she felt amazing, more alive than she had felt in a long time. The sexual pull she felt to his body was incredible; she wanted to possess him physically, knowing somehow what that would feel like. That was weird considering she no idea what sex really felt like. Books and other people's thoughts couldn't begin to accurately describe something that differed with each person.

Layered underneath those strange feelings were more some more appropriate to her. Elation at having Luka care for her, physical excitement and a sense of security and comfort knowing that he cared for her.

"Luka you can't hear me can you?" Her eyes were wide in alarm. *Please don't let him be able to hear me right now.* She put her energy into that one specific thought as well as keeping her defenses shored up.

His face was non-reactive to her directed thought. "No." He shook his head, smiling, "You're keeping me out even with all this distraction."

She caught a little of what he was thinking about more distractions. "You're not doing as well as I would expect though."

Luka blushed. His tan skin pinked all the way up to his ears. "You heard that?"

Fascinated, she stared at him as she answered with only an affirmative head bob. His face tensed and she saw him concentrating, the extra thoughts "popped" right out of her head.

Chest heaving with the effort, Luka rubbed his neck. "That was very strange. It's not usually like that for me."

"We must have slipped a little while we were, you know."

"I don't know. This is foreign territory for me but I don't think that was normal."

"As opposed to how normal our situation is otherwise?"

He laughed. "I suppose normal is a relative term. I've never been with someone like you before."

Natalie remember what he'd said about her ability being stronger. "I wonder if I can pick up more when I'm physical with someone. That would be an interesting experiment." She thought about other people, like those he'd said were there at Prestige. People who could also keep telepaths like them out. Maybe it was no good once she had a physical connection to them.

His face snapped up to hers, amiable expression replaced by an angry one. "That would certainly not be an interesting experiment. You are not going to…" Luka stopped himself.

"Are you jealous?" She asked playfully, putting her hand on his arm.

"Does that bother you?" He didn't deny it.

Natalie smiled shyly. "No, I kind of like it."

The walk back to her dorm was so much shorter. It seemed like they had just left Luka's when he stopped at the door of her building, resting his hand on the door handle, prepared to open it after she unlocked it.

Only Natalie didn't take out her keys right away. Instead, she stepped into his space and put an arm around his back, wishing she could fast forward a few days and use both hands.

More than willing, Luka put his arms around her and brought her in close, resting his face against her head before sliding his mouth to hers. Releasing her, he was grinning broadly. "What happened to not wanting to have an audience?" They both heard the distant voices of students out and about.

Shrugging, Natalie stared at his chest. "I guess it doesn't seem like as big a deal anymore. I wanted to say good night out here where Avery can't see us."

"Do you really think she's looking through the peek hole waiting for us?"

"At this point, nothing surprises me with her." Natalie giggled at the picture in her head of her roommate waiting and watching for her.

Luka's hand stroked her back. "I had fun tonight. What are you doing tomorrow? Brunch?"

Leaning back, Natalie pulled her brows together in mock concern. "So soon? Isn't there a rule about when we can call each other, like how many days or something?"

"Did you want to wait?" he asked seriously.

"No."

"Then I'll call you in the morning."

Not wanting to part ways yet, Luka walked her upstairs and had just planted a chaste kiss on her lips at her door when Avery's voice reached their ears. "I'm just saying she'd better not stay out all night."

The deep hum of Jason's reply was lost through the thick door. Natalie shot Luka a playful smile which he returned as Natalie unlocked the door. Inside, she could hear the forced hush so obvious when the person being discussed enters the room.

"Hi Mom, I'm home." She found Avery sitting at her desk, Jason stood at the microwave making popcorn. The scent of artificial butter was already permeating the air of the small space.

"Did you kids have fun?" Avery's eyes scanned Natalie up and down. She smiled knowingly when she reached the hair and winked at Natalie.

"We did. How about you? Jason, are you staying here tonight?" Natalie took in his flannel pants and tee. After having come so close herself this evening, Natalie didn't want to have to listen to the sounds of her roommate doing what she wasn't.

"Yeah, you're just in time. We were going to watch a movie. Want some popcorn for the lower balcony seating?"

Exchanging a quick look, Natalie smiled and raised a brow at Luka who answered for them. "Sure. What are we watching?"

"Dial M for Murder." Jason sounded excited.

"Jason's a Hitchcock fan," Natalie volunteered. Personally she appreciated Jason's taste in movies, preferring a good thriller to a hack and slash horror movie any day.

Jason poured one bag of popcorn in a bowl and threw a second into the microwave.

"Anybody want a soda or something?" Luka jiggled some change in his pocket.

Avery and Jason gave their orders, Luka pointed at Natalie, "The usual?"

She nodded.

No sooner had the door closed behind him than Avery started.

"So? What did you do? Was he nice? What did he make? Did he like your hair? Did it work? Looks like it did."

"Easy there." Natalie laughed at Avery's enthusiasm, secretly happy to have someone to have "girl talk" with about her date. She gave Avery a quick synopsis of the evening's events, only pausing for Avery to give an "awww" here and there. She stopped when she heard Luka's quick double knock before he opened the door.

How much of that did you just hear?

He didn't answer, presumably to convince Natalie he hadn't been listening although she saw his lips twitching when he set the sodas on her desk.

Nosey.

Yeah, but think of the possibilities. My parents used to have card parties all the time, we could annihilate them.

Natalie did consider the possibilities and was wondering if she would ever meet his parents. She stopped, not wanting him to hear that yet wanting to "keep the line open" while everyone settled in. Then she had another fleeting moment of shyness considering the logistics. The tv was in front of their beds which meant that was the only place to watch from. It was hard for someone Natalie's height to sit and watch, much less Luka's. The only option was to lie down. She felt her neck heat up at the thought.

The lights went out, Avery and Jason snuggled up on their bunk leaving Natalie and Luka some amount of privacy.

He had heard her thoughts on the subject. *I promise I'll be good.*

Oh I know you will. But could she trust herself? He was kind enough to block any response to that. Natalie waited for Luka to get in first and scoot back to make room. When it was her turn, she tentatively lowered herself to the thin mattress.

Luka's arm was there to catch her, easing the burden on her muscles in lowering herelf. He lay back behind her and, true to his promise, he left space between their bodies. Hand propping his head and the other across his hip, Luka made absolutely no contact with her for almost half an hour. Grace Kelly was not the only one getting tense as the movie unfolded.

With a pointed thought that she was getting chilly, Natalie scooted her leg backward. Luka was hesitant, testing the waters with actions only, he slid his legs forward to line hers. Though they had the option of speech audible only to them, neither attempted it.

When Natalie tipped her shoulders back, she bit back a curse as her muscles pulled and Luka came forward to catch her. Their bodies molded to each other automatically. His hand draped over her hip where it stayed the remainder of the movie.

By the time the credits rolled and Grace Kelly had successfully outwitted her would be killer, soft snoring was drifting down from their fellow movie watchers.

"Could you reach up onto Avery's desk for the remote?" Natalie didn't relish the idea of twisting her body to grab it herself.

Obliging, Luka reached a long arm up and shut off the movie, putting on a late night talk show for noise so they wouldn't disturb the others if they spoke out loud. His torsion created friction and Natalie bit her lip to quell the sound she made in her throat.

Did that hurt?

No

The beauty of being in each other's heads was that it was nearly impossible to misinterpret what the other person meant because the feeling behind it was transmitted with the words. Luka heard Natalie's meaning loud and clear, lowering his head to kiss her neck. In that one kiss, her body was back at the level it had been at when they had called things off at his place.

Letting herself fall backward into him, Natalie's body knew from thousands of years of programming what it wanted and how to tell him. Luka understood and lowered his head to kiss her exposed neck.

Within minutes, Natalie was desperate to lay her hands on him and feel his skin under her hands. Turning her head, she offered him her mouth and his closed on hers, equally insistent. Natalie shifted and gasped in pain. Mentally cursing her conflicted systems, she closed her eyes and took shallow breaths waiting for the pain to pass.

I think it's best to take a raincheck until those heal. He was trying to hide his own frustration although she felt it both mentally and physically.

Oh, I'm sorry. She contemplated trying again, eager to know what it would be like to be intimate with him.

His blocked feelings slipped at her thought and she caught her breath at its intensity. An image of his hand on the skin of her leg, running slowly up her side and the mounting desire he felt imagining them going farther, flashed in her mind.

Natalie closed her eyes at the strength of the vision and the clarity of the emotion behind it. *Is that really what it's like?*

Luka was fighting for control over himself. She could feel his disturbance at giving her free access to his feelings for her. She felt his muscles held tense against her and opened her eyes to see him. His clenched teeth and tight lips spoke of his physical struggle. The combination of body and mind assaulted her senses.

Natalie had given up on getting an answer when she felt his muscles easing, his mind again clearing.

You really haven't ever done anything?

You know I haven't.

No, I don't. He was affronted by her assumption. *I tried to be selective about what I heard. Mostly I picked up only what you were shouting.*

Well, that's unfair.

How is that unfair? You're certainly getting enough from me right now. Again his irritation at himself flared.

That's physical. Of course it's going to have a strong response. It's not like it's as personal as hearing me obsess over you.

Obsess is a strong word. He touched her hair, brushing it off of her forehead while his eyes searched hers. *It isn't just the physical that's making this so difficult.* He was deliberating telling her something but now that he was calmer, he was effectively blocking most of it. *It's how I feel about you. You're special to me.*

Natalie stared at him, seeing a wavy piece of his forelock falling down on his forehead and catching in the tips of his matched black eyelash. Her insecurities kept her from believing his sentiment entirely. Surely she was making more of his feelings for her than he meant by his comment. They shared a talent that made their relationship easily definable as "special." It was far from common.

"I know perfectly well how I feel and it is not because of that." He sounded offended, pulling back to give her a disapproving glower.

She kicked herself for her misstep. Of course he had heard her discounting his feelings. "I didn't mean to insult you, I was just trying to figure out what you meant."

"You shouldn't have to figure anything out. It just is." He sat up abruptly, scraping his head on the board of the upper bunk. "I think I should go."

Natalie heard his curse and felt him shut her out. She tightened her lips, mad at herself for being so insecure and mad at him for being so sensitive. In a fit, she threw her legs over the edge of the bed and pushed herself up in a rush. Natalie gritted her teeth, stubbornly cutting off any external reaction to the jolts of pain she felt. "I think you should too."

Luka stood and turned to face her turning his back to the tv and casting his features in shadow. "You're wrong."

Not wanting to get in a bigger argument about what she saw as a matter of perspective, Natalie folded her arms.

He spun on his heel and roughly tore the door open, stopping short of slamming it shut.

See you Tuesday. She effectively took back her acceptance for breakfast in the morning.

Sounds great. He growled back.

"Did Luka leave?" Avery asked sleepily.

"Go back to sleep, Avery."

Chapter 19

By Tuesday Natalie had run through their argument a thousand times and was too embarrassed to bounce any of it off of the more experienced Avery, who was infuriatingly stuck on the subject of praising Luka for being such a great guy and a wonderful catch.

Ivy was waiting for her when she walked in, tired from getting three days of bad sleep yet repentant for her part and ready to talk things out with Luka.

"Is everything alright Nat?" She asked mildly. Trust Ivy to pretend to be out of the loop while she picked up on absolutely everything.

"I'm on the mend. Thanks for giving me Friday."

"It was nothing."

"Well, I appreciate it anyway." She knew Ivy's expectations. The break this time raised her humanity in Natalie's eyes.

Ivy slid a packet across her desk at Natalie. "Why don't you work on this today?"

Her heart sank. "Isn't Luka coming?"

"He's been called away on family business. He's hoping to be back in a few days."

"Oh." She tried in vain to hide her disappointment. "Okay."

***

Luka was not back by Thursday and Natalie refused to call him but she told herself it wasn't stubbornness, she was letting him have his time with his family, knowing how rare that was. Yet she worried that he was still angry with her. Certainly he would call if he needed any sort of support from her. Wouldn't he?

It turned out Luka was not back for two more weeks. Avery had decided Natalie was bad company and had gone back to staying with Jason all the time, apparently over her aversion to "sock smell and Frito fart."

When he finally did return, Natalie was in her room studying and jumped at a knock on her door.

"She's not here." She called out thinking it was one of their neighbors looking for Avery, now actively involved in "floor activities planning" though she never attended any of the activities for longer than ten minutes. Natalie had jokingly accused her of wanting something to orchestrate and Avery's correlating foot stomp confirmed it.

The door opened and Natalie repeated her diversion without looking up from her Biology. Mitochondria were occupying her entire brain at the moment. "Avery isn't here but you can leave a note on her desk." She indicated unnecessarily behind her with her pencil.

"I'm not looking for her," Luka's low voice replied from the doorway.

Natalie's head came up in surprise. "Luka. When did you get back?"

"Yesterday. Sorry I didn't call, it's been a little hectic." He sounded tired. He looked tired. Natalie took in the new bags under his eyes and lines in his face.

She closed her book and remained in her seat, not sure what to do. The pencil twisted round and round in her anxious fingers. "Is everything okay?"

"My dad died." He spoke simply, his rough voice unable to hide his feelings.

Natalie went to him, hugging him without the burden of relationship baggage. As a friend she had a need to comfort him that trumped the nuances of a lover's quarrel. "Luka I'm so sorry."

He hugged her back, tentatively at first then tighter, desperate. It wasn't sexual, he was swimming in grief. She could feel it bleeding through his shoddy defenses worn thin from exhaustion.

They held on to each other, Natalie giving him all the support and warmth she could push through their unique channels as well as her physical body. Finally, his arms loosened and he pulled away, wiping at red eyes.

"Come on in." She withdrew to close and lock the door behind him. Should he have a breakdown they didn't need any intrusions.

124

Obediently, Luka crossed behind her and flopped down on her bed. Natalie leaned against the loft's wooden upright support. She waited, wanting to apologize for being stubborn, choosing instead to keep her mouth and mind closed, letting him steer the conversation.

He was silent for a long time. Lying with his eyes closed, one arm behind his head and one hand thrown casually over his stomach. Natalie watched the steady rising and falling of his chest. She thought he had fallen asleep and quietly moved past him to return to her studies, as if she could concentrate, when his hand reached out and caught her wrist.

Glancing at it, Natalie peeked under the top bed and saw Luka's bright green eyes focused intently on her.

"Lay with me?"

Without saying anything, she eased in beside him, he moved over to let her in. Natalie lay next to him, her head on his chest while he softly stroked her arm lying across his body.

Natalie started to feel what had to be him and lowered her defenses wanting the intimacy of this type of exchange more than simple words.

Dad had a tumor on his liver. He'd known for a while but didn't tell anyone. Mom's a wreck. He was still trying to justify his father's actions, anger flavoring his grief.

Is she going to stay in the house in Santa Barbara? Santa Barbara was where he had grown up although they had a vacation house in Colorado his mother enjoyed quite a bit.

I don't know. She's there now but she might go to Colorado as soon as she gets the rest of the legal matters settled. I told her she could do it with a computer and a phone but she wants to do it her own way. I guess I understand. His mother liked working at her husband's desk in their study. Luka could smell the leather of the chair and some of the books, the warmth of the dark rich woods made him feel safe. It was a place rife with memories of his father. He was in there a lot.

Luka kissed the top of her head. *I meant to call you but I didn't want to talk over the phone where we could have another misunderstanding.* He laughed softly. *This is so much easier. You've ruined me for anyone else.*

Don't be silly. Natalie laughed him off. *I've seen you in action.* She sent him a reminder of his flash of another woman's mouth, the same image he had made for her jokingly. *You'll be just fine.*

That was stupid of me. He felt a pang of remorse.

Don't worry about it.

Natalie, I mean it. I've been thinking about you this whole time. We shouldn't have left things that way.

I wanted to tell you I was sorry for discounting you.

You believe me then? That you mean more to me than I can say?

She still couldn't get all of her doubt out of her mind. *Yes.*

"Natalie. Please believe me. You were on my mind the entire time I was gone. It drove me crazy thinking of you here, wondering if I'd left you because of our fight."

Saying nothing, Natalie listened as he echoed exactly what she had been thinking.

"I wanted to call you." He switched to speaking out loud. "I didn't think you would listen to me unless it was in person." Luka shifted his chest out from under her to better see her face.

Natalie saw his eyes were dark and troubled. "It's okay, you're here now and everything's back to normal." She avoided his perseverance on the subject, not wanting to argue again. A big part of her knew Luka was telling the truth, he did care deeply for her. Except there was a small nagging piece that didn't want to believe him. She was afraid.

It was Natalie who was in doubt. She knew she loved Luka and he cared for her, but was it love? To get into that conversation would open her up to him and set her up for a colossal rejection she never wanted to face.

In answer, she reached up and wrapped a hand behind his shoulder to bring him back to her. Their kisses started slowly and built. Completely healed, Natalie was able to throw a leg over and slide herself astride. His eyes opened in surprise and Natalie gained confidence from the reaction she felt underneath her.

"We can't keep doing this." Luka started to pull away.

Only Natalie wouldn't let him this time. She had been doing some thinking too while he was away. She had thought of no good reason not to have her first time be with a man she loved no matter how brief. Depth of emotion outweighed longevity in her mind.

"We're not. I don't want to stop this time." She perched herself on her knees and put her hands up above his shoulders on the bed. Looking him directly in the eyes, her hair falling around her face, Natalie was painfully honest with him. "Luka, I want to do this with you. Now. No more waiting for a perfect time because being with you is enough for me."

Luka's eyes scanned hers and she watched him register her words as well as what they meant. Neither one had the courage to take down their barricades though. This was already more vulnerable than either one was comfortable. He wrapped his hands around her shoulders and brought her to him, rolling to bring her down as he covered her neck and face with kisses.

Hands on the bottom edge of her shirt, Luka began to pull and felt her freeze. "It's okay."

Hands trembling, Natalie pulled her shirt off exposing her scars for the first time. Luka had seen one arm to the elbow but to see the whole picture was a greater test. For not the first time she felt shame at being weak, for being different.

She watched his face, waiting for an indication he was disgusted or thought her a fool for her self-destructive coping mechanism that had nearly cost her her life and her freedom.

Judgment didn't come. Luka took in the lines, big and small that crisscrossed her arms. Though her forearms were the worst, she had marked the rest up to her shoulders as well. There was no possible way to explain the need to cut to someone who has never done it. To explain how she had been so angry that she turned her rage upon herself, why a person would "self-mutilate" as her psychiatrist termed it. It was easier for most people to understand destroying oneself with drugs or alcohol, even sex or outward acts of violence. But to slowly hack away at that which offended herself the most, her own person, was the only way Natalie had been able to maintain a barely sane and reasonable facade to the outside world when she had thought herself mad and unworthy of anyone's compassion.

Luka leaned down, kissing her arms alternately. His soft hair tickled her stomach and chest but she did not laugh. Finished with her arms, he came back to her lips and kissed her again, both their eyes damp. She imagined for him it was painful to think of his sister's pain and even his own. All of them not understanding their ability had caused so much hurt.

One of Natalie's pale arms tightened his face to hers and her love for him grew with his acceptance. The other came up under his shirt, fingers pressing his flesh. It was no longer enough to lay with him. She wanted to feel his skin on hers. Her hands hinted at his shirt and he removed it, following that up with her bra. She traced the ink on his arm she'd been curious about when she'd first seen it. Giving it a moment's study, she saw that it was a band of Celtic knotwork with his sister's initials worked in so she missed it at first glance.

The new series of sensations their bare contact was sending into Natalie's brain and body were dizzying. Fearing she would lose control, Natalie tried to calm herself. Luka felt her withdrawal and broke off again.

"Is everything alright? Are you sure?" His concern did not entirely cover his reluctance to stop.

She shook her head against the pillow. "No, I'm fine." He understood her strategy, he was doing the same, pacing himself. She watched him working to cover his raw need, neither completely successful yet their strongest feelings were toned down by the time they touched again.

When they both lay naked and Luka's body covered hers, Natalie felt a fierce burning pain but it was gone in a moment with his gentle persistence. He distracted her mind, moving his hands over her body and taking care to find the things that brought her the most pleasure. After they both lay satisfied and panting, Natalie finally understanding what all the fuss was about and already thinking of doing it again, Avery's keys jiggled in the lock.

"Avery, no!" Natalie managed to shout just as Luka threw the blanket over them both and the door swung open.

Avery took one step in, her earphones firmly shoved in to block out all other noises and glanced up after removing her keys from the lock.

"Oh my Christ!" She jumped back, hand pressed against her chest.

Natalie imagined what she was seeing. Her hair was a mess, Luka's wet with sweat at the roots had been pushed back and now he lay with his back to Avery in an effort to shield Natalie's yet uncovered breasts with his shoulders. The blanket had gotten hung up on their feet and legs, only reaching Luka's hips and Natalie's waist.

Earbuds popped out of her head, hanging from one tightly clenched fist and Avery's eyes bulged. "Welome hooome Luka." She drew it out sportscaster style.

"Avery." Luka calmly greeted her. His grace under fire was something Natalie could take lessons in. "Do you think we could have a few minutes please?"

She bobbed her head, eyes running up and down the lovely shape his form made through the thin blanket. "You'd better take longer than that. I'll be back tomorrow. Just needed this." She reached into her closet and pulled out a hanger with some sort of bright pink sweater on it. "We're going out to dinner with his parents."

Avery backed out, clothes hanger pressed against her chest and tore her eyes away only when she couldn't find the doorknob behind her back after her first flailings.

The lock slid home and Natalie threw her arm over her eyes. "How humiliating. My first time and I get caught. What are the odds?"

His head dipped to trail his mouth over her neck, teeth nipping at her jaw. Natalie sucked in a breath.

"Want to better your odds?" His tongue flicked against her ear.

Chapter 20

The next week flew by. Natalie and Luka were beyond busy with finals. He was taking his early and she was studying for hers the next week. He had been able to test out of two of his last three classes leaving him only one course to graduate.

Every spare minute they had was spent together though now they mostly stayed at his place where there were no intruders. Luka was leaving for his internship in Oregon in less than four days and though neither one mentioned it, it was never far from their minds. Already she had heard him on the phone with his mother's friends he would be staying with, pushing back his arrival date twice.

They spent less and less of their time in one another's heads choosing instead to concentrate on less complex feelings and actions.

Finally, on Friday night, they could put it off no longer. Luka was scheduled to start at Optimax on Monday morning. They lay together before bed.

"It's only twelve weeks. It'll go by before we know it." He made the usual false promises.

She played the part of the one being left behind. "I wish you didn't have to go. It'll be weird sleeping alone. Funny how fast I got used to it."

He ran his fingers lightly up and down her bare back, "I was thinking the same thing. You'll be busy though. Ivy told me you signed up for two classes each summer session. You're not even going to notice I'm gone."

She snorted, playing with the few shorn hairs on his chest. "I think she's glad you're leaving. She was practically drooling when I told her I wanted to double up. She says it jumps me up a whole semester."

"Good, maybe we can get you graduated sooner." He stopped as soon as he said it.

Their relationship was wonderful and it was fulfilling and all of that, but it was also locked in a state of suspension. Talking about anything in the future was taboo. Luka was leaving for a great opportunity with a huge employer with their hands in many different pots thus allowing for an employee to change directions if he didn't know exactly how to use his newly earned degree. And now with only one class left, Natalie doubted he would come back here if it weren't for her. She knew they were in a good place and maybe even in love but was it enough to make a long distance romance work? Especially with it only in its beginning stages. It was hard not to be skeptical.

Saturday was to be their last full day together. They could have been weepy and sad, they could have finally spoken of what was to come. But no. Instead, Luka served omelets and Natalie was responsible for the coffee. They ate on the balcony, watching the sky light up with the sunrise behind them. Its vibrant morning rays shone golden and burnished copper on the leaves of the trees in their view. The hillside, their hillside, appeared luminescent and grand. Were Natalie a big believer, she would have called it a sign. Once the idea came to her, it grew.

"What would you think of a hike to our overlook today?" She suggested after breakfast as they sipped their coffees and watched the world change around them.

"Sure."

***

After a second cup he threw a load of laundry in and they set out on the trail for "their overlook." Natalie sat on the ground and leaned against his legs where he sat perched on a rock facing the ocean. Clouds had rolled in during their trip up and now cast the sea in an ominous shade of gray, the ever present wind busily whipping the waves into an impressive white frothy display.

Their afternoon was anticlimactic. Mostly they held hands a lot and spoke little. Luka, feeling the pressure of his impending departure, cut their stay short to return home and finish laundry so that he could pack.

The plan was for him to leave the majority of his things for fall but that was before he had nearly finished his course load. Now he might not need to return in the fall.

By dinner, Natalie was feeling the strain and Luka had gone mute, only making the occasional grunt or forcing a tight smile when she asked for a response. Neither felt up to the challenge of cooking, one of their usual pleasures was to cook together. Tonight, they ordered Thai and stayed in.

"Do you want to watch a movie?" Natalie suggested, eager for distraction.

"Sure." He took another bite of his Rama Thai, chewing slowly so as not to be asked to speak again.

Though he was bordering on sullen, Natalie had felt his eyes on her all day. She knew he was entirely focused upon her. That and the fact that it was their last day was the only reason she hadn't snapped at him or gone back to her room. They couldn't leave things badly again.

Natalie walked away from her Pad Thai and flicked on the tv on the wall opposite the couch. She ran through the channels though their choices were significantly limited. She didn't want a romantic comedy nor anything in the horror genre. Her nerves were frazzled enough without throwing in bad dreams.

She settled on an action movie, The Transporter. Luka sat against the arm of the couch, Natalie leaned against him. His arm was wrapped around her shoulders holding her near him. After the credits rolled, Luka shut off the set and kissed her head.

"Should we go to bed?"

Natalie didn't answer, following him into the bedroom where they made love in silence and lay together, not sleeping for a long time. Yet even with keeping her wet eyes open as much as possible, Natalie still thought morning came too quickly.

***

After a light breakfast Natalie helped Luka zip up the last of his luggage, choosing to stay in the apartment while he walked to the far student lot to pick up his car where it had sat parked since he'd come back from his father's funeral.

The door opened, Luka walked in, water spots on his tan polo shirt. The clouds had finally opened up and given them a long overdue spring shower. "They're expecting me."

"I know." Natalie dipped down to grab the handle, pulling it up to haul out his smaller bag. Luka followed behind with the larger one, stopping when his feet hit the threshold.

"I don't want to do this Natalie. I know it's stupid and it's impulsive and it's not part of my dad's plan and that sucks to say right now because it's the last thing I promised him I'd do is go work for this 'great company' even though I have no clue his infatuation with them." He rubbed at his forehead in agitation. "But this isn't what *I* want."

"What do you want Luka? You can't hang around here waiting for me." As she said it, she realized it was true. Luka had to move forward with his life. He had to do this last thing for his father or he would always regret it. "If you don't do this, you'll hate yourself and someday you'll hate me too." She blinked back her tears, hating them for blinding her, hating them for reminding her she was giving her lover permission to leave her, hating them for showing him how hard this was for her. Natalie's entire life had been spent hiding her emotions until she had met him. And in those first few heartbeats, she had felt something other than shame and self-loathing. Things that had filled her world since her body went from child to woman and her ability had forever changed her.

Luka's green eyes shone wet but he said nothing. His bag fell where he dropped it, his feet carrying him to Natalie who took two steps back inside and threw her arms around him. He picked her up, kissing her hard and demanding, a drowning man finally come to water, he reveled in her return kisses, sweeping her up and kicking the door shut behind him as he carried her back into what had been their bedroom for one perfect week.

***

Their diversion solved nothing. Luka still had to leave, hope as he might to stay they both knew it wasn't the right thing. Natalie was dressing and glanced up. The picture on the dresser caught her eye.

It was one Avery had taken on the sly while Natalie and Luka had been studying in the center one afternoon. Their heads were together, Luka's finger pointed to a spot in her book and Natalie had her eraser in her teeth, forehead wrinkled in thought. She hated the picture, even asked Avery to get rid of it but Luka had her make a copy for him.

She picked it up, tracing his profile with her fingertip. He stood next to her and put a hand on the frame too.

"I can't believe I almost forgot this." Applying pressure, he freed it from her grasp and held it.

"I don't know why you like that one," she said softly.

Grinning absently, Luka peered at the people framed in his hand. "That particular day we had been working for so long on that problem. Do you remember? Avery wanted to go out, you wanted to stay. It wasn't enough that you had the answer, you had to figure it out for yourself. That's how I see you. No matter how difficult something is, you stick with it until you figure it out, until *you're* happy with it. You aren't a quitter Natalie. No matter what you might think sometimes."

Luka slid the picture in the front of his bag and picked it up again. Holding hands, they took the elevator down to the front of the building where his blue Honda Coupe was still parked. Thankfully it hadn't been towed yet, despite being parked in a no parking zone while they were upstairs having a prolonged good bye.

Natalie handed him the bag she'd been holding. While he put them in the trunk, Natalie ran up to grab her bag she had left by his bed. She took his key to lock up for good. She stopped before she walked out of the bedroom and smoothed the blankets where her bag had made an indentation on the freshly made bed.

On an impulse, she grabbed his pillow and shoved it into her duffel. The fact that it was down made it easy to punch down to fit. Dashing out, the strap slung across her chest, Natalie locked up after one last look around. She hoped so much to be back here again with him, she closed her eyes and made a wish, something she hadn't done since she was a kid.

The rain had picked up to a steady downpour when she got to the car.

"Get in," Luka insisted.

He drove her back to her room and after a short and awkward exchange in which neither one trusted themselves not to say too much, they kissed and Natalie stepped out into the rain.

Chapter 21

At first they talked every night before bed. Luka liked the job but didn't quite understand the company. It was too big to wrap his head around just yet, he said. Still, he liked his boss well enough. A blue eyed second generation Scot named Bradley Whiting. There was something about him he couldn't quite put his finger on though. So far all he had allowed Luka to see in paperwork were his newspapers. Most of Luka's time was spent making travel and dinner arrangements for Mr. Whiting as well as several other executives, though he had only ever met Mr. Whiting. The others must work out of other offices, he said. Bradley was in his mid forties with close cropped salt and pepper hair and a penchant for young female assistants if the office rumors were to be believed. It was too early for him to tell for himself, he said. Mr. Whiting was very secretive.

"You are not going to work for this guy." He had laughed before he caught himself.

They were still maintaining their rule of not discussing the future or "them." He had nearly broken the rule by suggesting she might come there when she was done with school that summer before it started again in the fall. She let it go but he was careful not to mention it again.

"Whenever I see him, he asks me about myself. He seems genuinely interested too." His tone changed, he was troubled. "Do you want to hear something really strange? I can't 'hear' Mr. Whiting."

Natalie stopped pushing Avery's mattress out of the frame above her with her feet and sat up. His change in tone worried her. She wished she were there so she could feel what was behind it. "Is it that uncommon? I've had a few people I can't hear but I can't say I've ever paid attention to *everyone*."

"No, not everybody so I don't know what sets them apart. I only asked Ivy once and she made it clear she wasn't going to answer that one." She could hear his frown, picture him rubbing his neck as he tried to work it out in his head.

"I should go." Luka finally said. "I have to be in an early meeting tomorrow and help Mr. Whiting with a presentation.

Looks like I'm finally going to get to do something more than gopher."

"That'll be good. Maybe you'll learn some more about the guy and what it is he does." She had tons of homework and needed to go too. Three weeks into the first summer term was nearly halfway. "I was going to try to get to the beach tomorrow after classes. Do you realize I've been here almost a year and still haven't dipped a toe in?"

"Really? I should have taken you." Remorse colored his words.

Natalie shook her head out of habit. "It's okay. I don't mind." It was all she could think to say. She couldn't say, "when you get back" or "when I come up" or even "when we see each other again."

"Yeah. I hate to cut it short, but I really do have to go Nat."

"I know." She hated this part. The good byes they gave without saying anything. "Good luck with the presentation tomorrow. Let me know how it goes or what you learn." *I love you and I miss you so much I ache.* She told him in her head knowing the distance made her thoughts more private than her best defenses could.

The next day was incredibly busy with classes and she ended up spending an extra hour in the tutor center with Ivy. She swore the woman was working her overtime trying to burn out her brain.

"Come on Ivy, I'm just going into my second year. I'm not even halfway to done. If I keep going at this pace I'll be exhausted in four years." She exclaimed when she was given another set of parables to which she was to apply the rules of philosophy. Natalie had already done the professor's required five.

The orange glasses came off her nose and hung by their matching chain. Natalie could not recall the woman ever wearing the same pair. Ivy's eyes narrowed. "You have great potential Natalie. If you work hard and excel, I can fast track you and have you out in two more years. All it takes is a commitment from you and I can do the rest."

Natalie was taken aback. She had only ever seen Ivy get her back up once, Luka said he had only seen it a few times, so when she did it demanded attention. The fact that it was in response to *this* conversation was disproportionate. Natalie had been far more frustrating and lazy in past sessions and Ivy had barely batted an eye. Now she was upset about this?

Plus, what kind of connections did a tutor have that would allow her to move Natalie through the system in three years? Even with classes over summer and winter breaks she figured she would still fall short on credits. Natalie eased up on her mental barriers hoping to hear something from Ivy. She didn't.

"Why can't I hear you, Ivy?" Natalie asked her outright, hoping for a better reception than she had given Luka. Maybe she could learn something about Luka's boss for him. It obviously troubled him not knowing. It would be good to feel like she could do something to help ease his mind.

Nothing. Ivy didn't react to the question at all. She put her glasses back in place and continued to review her stack of papers while Natalie worked her problems. Determined to get an answer, Natalie got up from her table and approached Ivy's desk where she was resuming her seat.

"Ivy, why can't Luka or I hear you?" Keeping her voice from becoming too demanding was hard, but Natalie held back.

Ivy's pen paused and tapped her paper several times as if she was going to say something, then she aimed it back at her papers and continued.

Irritation growing quickly to anger, Natalie bit her lip and with a boldness she hadn't known existed within her, she reached out and snatched Ivy's pen from her hand. Ivy did not look up.

"Tell me. What is it about you we can't hear?" she demanded, voice quaking with emotion. "Why can't we hear people like you? Is that what *you* can do, block?"

Ivy slowly brought her eyes up to Natalie's. Her face was impassive, her eyes glowed in a fiery anger. "Don't." Her one word answer came out low and ominous.

A feeling of dread settled in Natalie's stomach. She saw Luka's face, his forehead lined in worry and rubbing his neck, unable to figure out the why's and how's of his new situation. She had so hoped to be able to allay his fears.

Natalie changed her tactics. "Ivy, please. It's for Luka. He's met someone, like you maybe. He isn't saying, but I can tell he's worried. If I could just tell him something, about how this works maybe he would feel better." She hoped Ivy would relent. After all, she had known and worked with Luka for three years.

"I think we are done here," Ivy told her crisply, settling her orange glasses back on her nose and taking another pen from the cup holding several of the exact same Bic ball points.

Natalie gathered her things and slid them into her backpack. Ivy didn't look her way again even when she opened the door and mumbled an uncertain good bye.

It probably wasn't a big deal, she told herself slowly, making her way across campus. Certainly they would both run into people they couldn't hear over the course of their lifetimes. Natalie was going to start paying attention to the people around her, listening for specific voices and see if it was really all that unusual not to hear some people. Having failed with Ivy, she ran through different options for helping Luka feel better about his situation. Maybe things would be clearer after his meeting.

Chapter 22

"He knows."

"What?" Natalie was pacing in her room. The sense of dread that had taken up residence in her gut yesterday reared its head, and she felt her stomach roll threateningly.

She hadn't made it to the beach that day. Instead, she had walked straight from her last class into town where she had crossed paths with as many people as she could, walking into stores, fast-food restaurants and gas stations. Everywhere she could think of an excuse to go. All told, she had purchased four sodas and used the restrooms in three different gas stations. It being such a small town, she guessed she must have seen every resident in it.

She had heard each and every one of them. Only the infants didn't have a voice in her mind. She had decided to tell Luka nothing of her experiment.

Panic readily apparent in his tight voice, Luka went on. "Whiting. He knows. That presentation was a test of some sort. He had a guy in there. He stared at me the whole time. I was getting weirded out and I 'listened' to him. He was *thinking* things. Things I was *supposed* to hear. And Whiting was watching me out of the corner of his eye. I saw him."

"Are you sure?" She hoped he was just being paranoid, that *she* was being paranoid. Please don't let him be in trouble she chanted silently, fingers clutched tightly on the phone. Its plastic casing cracked under the pressure.

Luka forced himself to take a breath, exhaling slowly before answering. "He was talking to me in his head. He was direct and told me 'look at me' to see what I'd do and 'I know you can hear me.' He just stared at me the whole time, completely calm about it like it was no big deal that I could read his mind."

"S-so what does that mean?" She could hear her own heart hammering in her ears.

Sighing, he replied exhausted. "I don't know. But I can't work there anymore. They know I can hear them and Whiting has me spooked. There's just something about this guy. Tomorrow I'm going in there and giving my notice."

Natalie's stomach knotted in fear. "You don't think they would do anything do you? They wouldn't hurt you or anything, would they?"

He hesitated without meaning to. "No, I don't think so. It's not like this is some communist country or something where they make dissenters disappear." He tried to make light. "I can quit a job without getting shot or thrown into some pit somewhere." His words were meant to be reassuring yet their effect was just the opposite.

His caution did not help her doubts. "Just be careful okay? Are you going home after that? I would feel better knowing you were far away from them, and not alone." She didn't want him to think she was pushing him to come back to her. Still she knew she wouldn't feel better until she could touch him herself. There was something amiss. She had started to feel it when Ivy refused her, now her apprehension worsened.

"Yes, I'm coming home." She heard his smile in his tone. "What are you doing tomorrow night? Are you up for a late dinner?"

It would have been impossible for her to keep the excitement out of her voice. "I'd love it! Call me when you get close?"

"I will. Sleep well Natalie."

"You too Luka."

They hung up but Natalie didn't lower the phone right away. Avery let herself in and gave Natalie quick glance.

"How's Luka?" She threw her keys on her dresser.

"Coming home," Natalie replied, distracted.

"What?" Avery whirled. "Aren't you thrilled? Or are you not allowed to be excited? What do the rules say?" She thought their topic limit on the subject of "them" was ridiculous. Avery and Jason talked about their relationship all the time.

Natalie lowered her phone and let it rest on her lap. "No, I'm very excited."

"Yeah, I can tell." She rolled her eyes.

"He's quitting tomorrow and I'm worried about him."

Avery caught on to Natalie's serious tone. "Is everything okay? Why is he quitting?"

Clearly Natalie couldn't tell Avery exactly why, so she paraphrased. "His boss is a jerk and really put him on the spot today in front of a bunch of people just to see what he would do."

Avery's allegiance to Luka immediately put her on his side. "What an ass!" she agreed. "When is he quitting?"

"Tomorrow. We're going to have a late dinner tomorrow night when he gets in."

Her pale, freckled arm wrapped itself around Natalie's angular shoulders. "You just need time to adjust yourself. Here you got used to the idea of being alone all summer and now he's coming home two months early." She rubbed her arm. "Watch, by tomorrow you'll be walking on air."

Natalie nodded and hoped her roommate was right. "Yeah."

"Come on, I was going into town to see a movie and you're coming with me."

Scowling in confusion, Natalie twisted to see Avery's face. "Where's Jason tonight?"

"What, can't I spend time with you?" She let go of Natalie's shoulders and leaned away in feigned offense.

Natalie met her look with a steady stare.

Avery didn't lie well. She laughed, "His parents are in town for a few days so tonight he's with them and tomorrow we have dinner."

"You're seeing his parents again?" Natalie was excited for her friend and at the same time jealous. Avery and Jason had so much figured out. She and Luka had this separation hanging over their heads for so long they had put off talking about their future. And now that it was upon them, Natalie was fearful they might not want the same things. Forcing a smile, she tried to sound enthusiastic. "What movie?"

"It's an old Hitchcock movie, Rear Window."

She thought back to the night of their first date and the movie they'd watched that night, also Hitchcock. "All right." She didn't want to go, but told herself to "suck it up" and smiled again. "Great."

Avery saw through it. "What about pizza and renting something?"

Natalie's relieved smile was answer enough. Avery grinned back.

Chapter 23

The next day could not pass quickly enough. Natalie checked her watch every half hour it seemed, wondering if Luka had told Mr. Whiting he was leaving. Wondering if he had told his host family what was going on or if he was packing. They were friends of his parents so she figured he would be mostly honest with them, maybe they would try to make him stay for the night. She checked her phone for texts and messages in case he had changed his plans. A missed call from her mother, she would call her tomorrow maybe. Right now she had no desire to talk to her parents. Soon though. Soon she would have great news to share with them. It would feel good to share a happy, normal, thing with them. So far she hadn't said a word about Luka although now, providing they could figure out their relationship, she could tell them all about how wonderful he was and how happy he made her.

At two she was done with classes and went for a hike up the hill. She sat a few feet back from the edge and lay on her back to watch the clouds. Natalie zoned out and enjoyed the silence around her. She had brought a book and unpacked it from her bag.

She read for an hour before she noticed the air had cooled. Shivering, she looked up at the sky and saw that the clouds had gathered and grown darker. Rain drops spattered her book and began to fall steadily on her thin summer clothes. Hurriedly, Natalie tore off a blade of grass for a bookmark and shoved her novel into her bag, zipping it as she jogged into the woods.

The rain was cool at first. As Natalie rushed down the hillside her blood warmed her and the crispness in the air felt good. She laughed as she ran, joyfully thinking that each stride brought her closer to Luka.

He was coming home and she would sleep beside him tonight. Panting but invigorated, Natalie broke out from the tree line and hit the street. She moved briskly, enjoying the feeling of the rain on her skin. Drenched and hanging in ropes, her hair clung to her face and she shook it free.

A flash of dark hair to her right as she passed the tennis courts and Natalie jumped three steps left. Ericka was standing outside the court spinning her racket in her grip, the murderous glare left no room for misinterpretation. She slapped the racket in her open palm and pointed it at Natalie, a sneer twisting her otherwise beautiful features into an ugly mask. Luka's dad had been unable to persuade hers to pull her out of school. Apparently she had told her father she liked it here and was doing well. He let her stay.

Natalie forced herself not to speed up, averting her eyes to stare straight ahead. She didn't think Ericka would come for her this time but dropped her defenses and allowed her mind to act as her early warning system should she be wrong.

It was almost six by the time Natalie ran up the steps to her room and stripped off her wet clothes. The hot shower felt spectacular on her cool skin and she reveled in it, allowing herself the luxury of imagining the pleasures tonight would bring as she took extra care in her cleaning and hair routines.

By the time seven o'clock rolled around Natalie was clean, dressed and hair piled up on top of her head in an elegant knot that framed her dark, sharp features so well. She had put on a light purple summer dress with a matched shrug that covered her arms and could be removed in Luka's presence where she didn't have to hide herself.

Seven came and went, Natalie had her phone next to her on her bed and tried to read to no avail. She put away her book after she reread the same page three times. Next she tried the tv, nothing was on. It didn't matter she would be leaving soon anyway and didn't need to watch anything for long.

She found a movie. French Kiss, a personal favorite was starting and figured it would keep her attention for long enough to pass the time more quickly. At ten to ten when the credits were rolling, Natalie called her voicemail and checked to see if she had somehow missed the call. The call log was empty.

"There's nothing wrong with me calling to see where he's at." She told herself. "The rain just slowed him down."

Natalie got his voicemail. "Hi Luka, it's me. It's getting late and I, um, I was wondering if you were still planning on coming home tonight or if you got hung up. I'll be up for a while so you can call late. Bye."

She had no idea what time she fell asleep. Natalie woke up at two and checked her phone again. Nothing. Telling herself it was the weather that had kept him, she hung her dress back up and put on her pajamas and lay down though it was a long time before she fell back asleep.

The next morning broke rainy and brought no word again from Luka. Natalie grabbed a coffee at breakfast to make up for the lack of sleep from the night before. At lunch she left him another message asking if he had decided to stay and by dinner she was praying he would call by bedtime.

He didn't. Nor did he call the next day or the next. By Saturday morning Natalie was beside herself with no one to talk to except Avery, and she was no help.

"I'm betting he went in to tell them he quit and they gave him more responsibilities or a raise or something so he would stay. I'm sure they saw what a smart guy he is and kept him. He's just super busy now." She suggested, shrugging off Natalie's concerns.

"And that would stop him from calling?" That was the part that didn't make sense. "I can see him staying there." She couldn't. "And I could see him being busy, but how could he not call all week." She pointed to their wall calendar they used to visibly schedule their obligations for better coordination between themselves. "Today is Saturday. He can't be working on a Saturday." Natalie heard her voice growing shrill as panic crept in and stopped herself.

Avery was sympathetic. "Look. You and I both know Luka adores you and he was coming back here to be with you. But he's also a man and men are proud. Maybe he told you the boss was a dick and he was going to storm out but then they made him an offer he couldn't refuse and he can't bring himself to call and admit that just yet."

Her suggestion made perfect sense for anyone else. But not someone like Luka, working for someone like Mr. Whiting. That one small detail changed everything. Natalie shrugged and dropped the subject. Without telling Avery everything, their conversation on the subject could go no farther.

On Sunday morning, at eight fifty-three in the morning, Natalie's phone rang. It woke her from a dead sleep and she tripped on the edge of her sheet where it had wrapped around her foot when she jumped up to grab it off of her desk.

Without checking the number, Natalie excitedly answered. "Luka!" She couldn't hide her relief. It was short lived.

"Miss Swenson?"

Natalie did not recognize the mature woman's voice and looked at the number, it was unfamiliar.

"Yes," she answered hesitantly.

"My name is Marta Bailey. I'm Luka's mother."

Natalie's stopped breathing and pulled out her chair to sit. Her knees felt weak. She couldn't speak. Moms don't call before nine a.m. or after ten p.m. for good news.

Marta's voice was tightly controlled making her speech halting. She was unhappy to make the call.

"He's told his mother about us and she's mad because I'm not right for him." She told herself. Natalie had worried about that but had at least hoped she would be able to meet her and make an impression before judgment was passed on her. "Or he told her he was leaving work and she's blaming it on me." She thought.

"Miss Swenson, I found your number in my son's phone." Her voice quavered. "The police gave it to me Wednesday night. After the," she paused and Natalie heard the catch in her voice, "accident. I haven't been able to look at it up to now."

Her head swam and her stomach churned. "Accident?" she whispered.

Marta Bailey sniffed. "Wednesday night he was driving down to see you, I would assume, and with the rain," her voice trailed off. "The police said he swerved for something in the road, maybe an animal, and he lost control of his car. He went off the road and rolled down an embankment. My son is dead."

Natalie couldn't find her voice to respond. The air was gone from her lungs.

"I am sorry Miss Swenson, I thought you should know. I am calling the contacts in his phone. He didn't put many in, he never did. Seeing your name in here I would assume you two were close?"

She had no idea Luka and she had been seeing each other. He had never mentioned her to his family. Natalie took a shaky breath.

"Yes, Mrs. Bailey, Luka and I were friends." If Luka hadn't wanted to share the nature of their relationship with his mother then Natalie would respect his wishes. "Mrs. Bailey?"

"Yes?"

"Did he suffer?" She imagined him alone and in pain, a knife twisted inside her.

"His neck was broken," she replied, calm and detached. "The police said he died instantly." His mother's voice was hollow.

Natalie felt a kinship with the woman she would never meet. They had both lost a man they loved more than anything. Both of them were alone now. However, Natalie's isolation was self-imposed. She chose not to have contact beyond a weekly call to her family. Luka's mother had not had a choice, her family had been taken from her.

"I'm so sorry for your loss." She didn't know what else to say. "Will there be a service?" She needed to say goodbye to him.

"We will be having a small family service. Take care of yourself." She replied politely before hanging up the phone.

That was it. She was cut off from him forever. Natalie replaced her phone on the desk and numbly climbed back into her bed, wrapping her blanket around herself in a cocoon intent on keeping the rest of the world out forever. Her face was buried in the pillow she'd stolen from him and she inhaled his scent, wanting to call his ghost to her.

Of course that was out of the question. Avery came home mid morning to grab a different pair of shoes for some sort of outing and had Jason in tow. One glance at Natalie's bunk and the blank eyes staring out of the swaddled mass of blankets and Avery asked Jason to wait for her in the hall.

"Natalie?" She knelt by the head of the bed. "Natalie, what's up? Did Luka call?"

She blinked. Her eyes were dry. Natalie couldn't cry. To cry would make it real. If she lay here and didn't go out into the world or talk to anyone it wouldn't be real.

But Avery wasn't the sort to be put off. Her voice rose and she touched Natalie's shoulder. Still no response and she shook her. "Did that prick break up with you?" Avery ventured a guess.

Rage instantly flowed hot through Natalie's mind, fueled by the righteous anger Avery was feeling for her supposedly jilted friend. Natalie could not have her friend, or anyone, thinking ill of Luka. Certainly not now when that would be their last thought of him.

Sitting up in her blankets, Natalie fixed her wild eyes on Avery and shouted. "He's dead!" Saying the words aloud made it real and, just as she had feared, Natalie felt her world crack open and swallow her whole. "His mother called this morning. He was in an accident coming home to see me and he died." The guilt and pain sapped her rage and Natalie's fire was extinguished. The spark in her eyes went out, again they were flat and dead as she stared emotionlessly at Avery. "He's dead." She repeated, expressionless.

Avery stared at Natalie, mouth open in shock. She blinked and stood, mumbling through the door to Jason before closing it and locking it. Avery came back to sit next to Natalie and put her arm around her.

Natalie gave a shaking moan, her defenses unable to hold back Avery's thoughts.

Poor thing. She loved him. I was so sure they were going to end up together. Bet she feels bad he was coming to see her. I can't imagine how I'd feel if it was Jason. What a loss.

The sentiments Avery would never have shared willingly with Natalie while doing so unwittingly were absolutely correct. She was feeling guilty. She was feeling like it was her doing. If he hadn't tried to drive all that way just to see her he would still be alive. His mother would still have a child left in this world.

Avery put her other arm around Natalie and she couldn't help the wracking sobs that shook her as she cried on her only friend's shoulder. Natalie cried until her eyes were dry and sore. Entirely spent, she let Avery lay her back down and tuck her into her covers without objections.

Chapter 24

For three days Natalie lay in bed, getting up only for the once daily trips Avery forced her to take to the shower and down to the cafeteria where she stared at her food before throwing it away and going home and to bed.

By Tuesday evening Ivy called. Avery answered.

"It's your tutor lady." She held the phone out.

Natalie held a hand out from her nest of blankets to take the phone. She hadn't even thought of Ivy and wondered if she knew.

"Hello?" Her voice was thick and strange in her ears.

"Natalie." Ivy's by contrast, was soothing. No trace of the irritation she had displayed at their last meeting. The meeting where Natalie had been trying to help Luka to no avail. Again, guilt washed over her. "Natalie, I know that you are upset right now but we can get through this together. A return to normalcy will help, believe me."

When she didn't answer, Ivy sighed and tried another approach.

"You are doing so well, I would hate to have you throw that away just because you miss Luka." Her tone hardened. "You need to finish your classes. I don't have to explain to you how important it is that you finish, especially these condensed summer sessions. If you fail a class, you'll be kicked out of Prestige."

"I don't care." Her reply was honest. "There's nothing left for me here."

"You don't have the luxury of being dramatic," Ivy chastised her. "You cannot throw away your future on a boy no matter how close you were. You may be sad now but you *will* get over it."

There was no fight in her to argue. She merely hung up her phone and dropped it on the floor.

Avery took matters in her own hands. "Are you going to class today? You have finals next week."

"No." She mumbled from under the safety of her blankets.

"Do you want me to call your parents?"

The blankets came down from her face and she stared at Avery. "What?" She knew her parents would yank her out of here and drag her off to some psychiatrist and maybe even lock her up if they saw her like this. They would remember her scars all too well and assume she was capable of the worst. They might have a point. Natalie had felt her fingers starting to itch for her tether again. One cut would help her feel connected to her body. The only thing stopping her was her unwillingness to *be* connected to her body. It would only make things hurt even worse.

"Please Avery. I'm not ready to face the world yet," she pleaded.

Avery was practical on top of her many other defining characteristics. "Who else knows? Really, you'll be the only one who is thinking of it and no one else is going to be talking about it. Finish out these classes and take next summer term off if you need to but don't throw this one away." She knelt down beside Natalie and stroked her hair gently. "What would he want you to do?"

The arguments all made sense in her head yet Natalie's heart had a great big empty hole in it and it was sucking all of her energy and taking all the color in her world with it. Still, she nodded her head against her pillow. "I'll go tomorrow."

Avery smiled gently. "Promise?"

"Yeah."

Thursday she did go to class, explaining to her professors she'd had a death in the family. They were somewhat understanding and told her they would not let the absences affect her grade if she made up the work, which actually turned out to be a blessing in disguise.

Natalie was so busy in the run up to finals she barely had time to grieve. Her studies kept her busy until after. Her mother had left two more messages, both of which went unreturned. Then after finals, she came back to her room, flopped down on her bed and felt the hollowness in her chest, curling protectively around it wanting to keep it because it was where he lived inside her. To lose it was to move on from him and admit he was really gone and she had nothing left of him. There was no evidence of him in her life. Not a gift he'd given her, not a special song they'd had. Not even a picture.

Natalie sat bolt upright. The picture. He'd taken their picture with him. She was guessing his mother or host family would have it. She slid out of her bunk and grabbed her phone, scrolling back through her received calls. There hadn't been many with him gone and Avery knowing she was not in the mood to talk on the phone.

There it was. The area code was California and who else did she know here but his family? "You don't know her." She reminded herself, dialing with her heart in her throat. Natalie didn't know why she was so nervous to call her, surely she would give her the picture. It couldn't mean anything to his mother, she had to have many others.

"Hello?"

"Um, hi Mrs. Bailey, this is Natalie Swenson. Luka's friend." She had to force herself to say his name. When she did, she was glad. She hadn't said it in so long and it made her smile to feel it on her lips now. "I was wondering if the Van Slykes, the family he was staying with, if they sent you his things?"

Marta's reply was deliberate. "No. He only had clothes and I've asked them to give them away."

Natalie was surprised. She hadn't considered that his mother wouldn't want his things back even if it was just clothes. "Oh, well, he had something else with him. A picture. I was kind of hoping that I could have it."

"I don't know anything about that." Oddly, she didn't sound interested. "If that's all, I really must be going. I have company."

"Well, actually I was wondering if you could maybe give me the number for the Van Slykes? I would like to find out if they can send it to me if they still have it."

"I would rather not. After all, he was like a son to them and it would only upset them right now. Good bye Miss Swenson." Click.

Her phone went silent and Natalie stared it in disbelief. Mrs. Bailey was strange. She had lost both her son and her husband within three months yet she was dismissive of his friends and uninterested in a girl she had to have guessed by now he'd been dating. If Natalie had a child and he had died, she would have wanted to find out more about his life and who his friends were. Especially after being so detached for so long.

Natalie supposed that was it. She had so detached from Luka after she lost her daughter that she was hiding her grief away. Suddenly feeling the need to stretch her legs and think, Natalie jumped up and slipped on an old pair of sneakers and strode out the door.

She walked into town and traversed the streets for over an hour. Again, she found herself cutting across the most populated areas in town, listening for "blank spots" but heard none. It really was rare not to hear someone.

The fact that the only people she'd ever come across, Luka either to her knowledge, they couldn't' hear had been people heavily involved in their lives. That couldn't be coincidence, could it? Natalie felt that heavy feeling in her stomach again. That nagging feeling that she was missing something.

Ms. Miller had been just like Ivy. She had been her only friend in high school. The specialist had been content to let her merely sit and not be bothered to explore her problems or treat her. Ivy was an ordinary woman with a unique ability and had shown nothing except kindness to Natalie and Luka here at Prestige. Yet when they asked her why they couldn't hear her she had grown aggressive. Luka had gone to work for a company his father had recommended and his boss had the same ability. Then, when Luka tried to quit, he was involved in a car accident. Was there something bigger going on, some way these people were related? The flesh on her neck prickled.

No way, she shrugged off the idea as paranoid and absurd. There was no connection between these people other than the fact that Natalie had paid attention and noticed their commonality. It was all perfectly normal, her brain was just trying to put things together that didn't belong. There was no greater coincidence than if they had all been interested in horse racing.

With a shake of her head, Natalie pushed all of that behind her as nonsense. There *was* something that wasn't nonsense. There was something that she was latching onto as a lifeline, the only thing left linking her to the all too brief happiness she'd had with him.

She rushed back to their room and burst through the door in a flurry. Avery looked up surprised from her desk. Jason lay on the top bunk paging through a sports magazine. They had been spending a lot more time around here since Luka had left.

He spoke up first, it was the first time he had seen Natalie since hearing about Luka. "Hey Natalie. I'm sorry to hear about Luka." From the way he watched her, Natalie knew Avery had shared her concerns about her mental well being with him.

"Thanks Jason." She nodded somberly and went straight for her laptop sitting on her desk.

"What's up?" asked Avery, spinning in her chair to watch Natalie.

Without answering, Natalie flipped open her computer and typed in "Van Slyke" in Klamath Falls, Oregon. "Yes!" She hissed victoriously, oblivious to the look Avery and Jason exchanged behind her. She copied down the address and spun back to Avery, deciding how crazy her idea was going to sound.

"Avery, could I borrow your car?" she opened benignly.

"For what?" Avery was eyeing her suspiciously.

"Well," Natalie tried to tone it down to sound as non crazy as possible. "I was going to drive up to Klamath Falls for the day." She saw Avery register the name of the town, she started to open her mouth. "Wait, before you object, let me just say this. I don't have anything to remember him and he has, I mean had, that picture of us. I want it, that's all."

Avery wisely didn't point out that Natalie hated that picture. *I don't see anything wrong with that but she's nuts if she thinks she's going alone.*

"You can come with me." Natalie threw in. She thought maybe having Avery with her would give her a second opinion in case she was being paranoid about this whole thing.

"Do you think I could come along? I've never been to Oregon." Jason was watching their exchange with interest.

Natalie regarded them both. Seeing that this was the only way for her to accomplish her goal, she acquiesced. "Okay. Can we go soon?" Her mind made up, Natalie was itching to get on with her mission.

Avery glanced at the clock. "Natalie even if we left now we wouldn't get there until late."

Natalie glanced up at the clock and saw her opening. "It takes less than five hours to get there. We'd get there in time for a late dinner." Avery was wavering. "Please Avery? I'll buy." She didn't have any money aside from the *very* limited credit card her parents had given her for emergencies. She had never touched it but considered this as close to an emergency as she had ever experienced.

Jason answered. "Yeah, let's go now. I'll run back to my place and throw some stuff together. Can you guys pick me up in half an hour?"

Seeing she had been defeated, Avery bobbed her head. "All right. Half an hour Jay, no more."

Jason slipped off the bed and gave her a mock salute before he leaned in to kiss Avery on the cheek. "Of course." He grinned and rushed out of the room, closing the door behind him.

Their exchange, although brief, nearly took the wind out of Natalie. She felt the hollowness in her and saw his green eyes as clear as if she had him right there with her. She could almost feel his lips on her skin. She hugged herself trying to feel less empty although it didn't help. Her eyes felt full.

"Sorry Nat, I didn't think about that." Avery was ashamed to have been so thoughtless. *I'll have to talk to Jason about the whole affection thing in front of her.*

She offered a weak smile and shook her head. "It's okay. I'm happy for you guys. It isn't your fault about Luka."

Avery hugged her. "Come on, let's get some stuff together. Oregon or bust." She held a fist high.

Natalie gave a brief laugh. "Thanks Avery."

Chapter 25

They were on the road within forty minutes, due to arrive in Klamath Falls by seven if Google proved reliable, which sometimes it was not. Avery drove and Jason sat in the back. Her father had given her the car on her sweet sixteen and Avery had taken care of it, loving the freedom but she had also made some modifications to the gray Camry.

For example, the seats and steering wheel were now covered in hot pink fur. A glass skull hung from her rearview mirror.

"It pisses my father off. He thinks I'm going goth." She had explained to Natalie when she'd asked about the totally *not* Avery decoration.

Attached to the dash were a laser radar detector, compass and notepad. Avery might be absentminded but she planned ahead for it. She had installed an after market satellite radio while refusing GPS, telling everyone she preferred the adventure and challenge of finding her way back herself.

Natalie hadn't wanted any delays so she had not only copied the directions, she had printed a quick map as well.

They drove straight through, only stopping once to "empty and refill" as Jason put it, sipping his Starbucks macchiato.

They made incredible time mostly due to Avery's heavy foot. Natalie couldn't help but wonder as she watched the road go by, where Luka's car had gone off the road. She wondered if she would feel something or have some sort of premonition when she passed the spot where he had died.

The car passed the city limit sign at six thirty and Natalie fished out the directions to the house. They were pretty straightforward and accurate. The Van Slykes lived in a white colonial house with black shutters and a red door. Very East coast, it looked out of place here on the opposite side of the country. Natalie thought they might be transplants just like their house. Never quite letting go of their roots. Like her; a Midwestern girl muddling through here on the West coast in a totally different culture.

Avery put the car in park on the street in front of the house. There were several lights on in the house. People were home. Now that she sat here in front of the house, Natalie was scared.

How did she approach total strangers, the unknown girlfriend looking for a picture their friend's dead son had left in their home?

"Do you want me to go with you?" Avery put her hand on Natalie's arm.

Natalie shook her head. She wanted to do this alone. She shored up her defenses tight, not wanting to feel anyone else's grief, took a deep breath and opened her door.

A petite woman, probably three inches shy of Natalie's 5'7" answered the door drying her hands on a perfectly white dishtowel. She wore a pink shell and cardigan combination, gray trousers and a small gold cross around her neck. "Can I help you?" She looked up expectantly at Natalie, hazel eyes wide and unassuming.

"Hi, Mrs. Van Slyke. I'm sorry to bother you but I'm Natalie Swenson."

By the stricken look on her face, Natalie knew Luka had at least mentioned her. It made her feel strangely better. She had a connection to his world.

Uncomfortable, she persevered. "I spoke with Luka's mother and she said that you hadn't sent back his things. I was wondering if you still had any of his personal items."

Mrs. Van Slyke recovered herself. She touched her neatly coifed sandy brown hair, smoothing back any strays that might have come loose from her chignon. Natalie doubted that happened very often.

"Like what dear?" She tried to smile, Natalie thought she saw the woman's hands clenching the towel and felt a twinge of guilt to remind her of her loss. She was clearly distressed.

"He had a picture. It was the only one of us together. I was hoping if you didn't want it, that maybe I could have it?"

"Certainly." She stepped back and opened the door to allow Natalie passage. "Please come in."

Natalie stepped in and looked straight up at the biggest crystal chandelier she had ever seen in person. The foyer floor was grey marble laced with black veins leading to a dining room on the left, furnished in dark cherry. To the right, she caught a glimpse of a formal sitting room, cream and floral Laura Ashley looking furniture. With the gently curving staircase in front of her and oak banister, Natalie thought she was in an edition of Better Homes and Gardens. Nothing was out of place.

"You have a lovely home." She remembered her manners. Her mother had taught her growing up that if you were clean and well mannered no one knew how much money you came from.

"Thank you." Mrs. Van Slyke smiled a little more easily. "His room is up here." She put a hand on the banister and led the way.

Natalie caught her use of the present tense when she referred to his room. Feeling guilty, Natalie followed. Inside, she was glad at least this woman was feeling something in the wake of Luka's death. Unlike his mother who was completely cold. She has her own way of dealing with pain, Natalie reminded herself.

At the top of the stairs, there were a number of doors. Mrs. Van Slyke led her to the second door on the right and stepped back to stand at the doorway. Natalie stared, frozen. This was where he had called her from every night while he had been away. She touched his bed, running her hand over the pillow.

"I'll give you a minute." Her host announced and backed away from the doorway.

Natalie nodded and turned back to his room. She wanted to feel close to him and lowered herself to the bed, laying down on it. Rolling over, she smelled his pillow. Even after two weeks, she could smell his cologne mixed with shampoo and *his* smell stronger than on the pillow she'd taken from his apartment. Natalie closed her eyes and felt tears leak out. She stroked it and patted it before she pushed herself back up.

She had come for the picture. Glancing around, she saw evidence of him everywhere. It was as if he was going to come walking through the door any minute. Change lay on top of the dresser, his cologne beside it. A desk under the window had a laptop and printer set up. The printer's green light was glowing "on."

Freshly washed clothes sat folded in a basket in the corner. She could smell the fabric softener as she stepped closer.

Wouldn't the smell dissipate after two weeks? Had it been that long since she'd lost him? It had been closer to three.

Giving the room a closer evaluation, Natalie noticed there was no dust on the dresser or desk, footprints and vacuum tracks marked the carpet.

She heard footsteps in the hall announcing Mrs. Van Slyke's return. "Did you find what you wanted?" She asked quietly.

Natalie looked around again, realizing she hadn't seen the picture. Frowning, she asked, "Did he bring it to work?"

"Oh, isn't it in here?" She stepped in to help look.

"No." Natalie watched the woman's back, her shoulders pulled together tensely. "Have they sent his things back here yet? His office?"

Mrs. Van Slyke shook her head slowly. "We haven't seen anything."

Natalie's warning bells were going off in her head. Carefully, she lowered her defenses.

I have to get her out of here. She can't be here when he gets home.

Natalie gasped. Mrs. Van Slyke spun and narrowed her eyes.

Out. Out. Out. She repeated in her head, effectively controlling what Natalie heard.

Her mouth dropped open. "What's going on?" she demanded. This woman not only knew who she was, but what she could do as well. Luka had to have trusted her implicitly to share that. "What has Luka told you about us?"

Mrs. Van Slyke was not to be distracted. She moved toward Natalie, hands outstretched. "My husband will be home soon. You can't be here." She ushered her back. Natalie had no choice but to be herded or physically run into the woman.

She turned and let herself be rushed down the stairs and out the door. After it slammed behind her and Natalie stood on the stoop, mind swirling in confusion, she heard her name being called.

Avery stood on the sidewalk staring at her, eyes wide in alarm. "Natalie, are you okay?"

Completely lost in her own thoughts, Natalie shuffled across their lawn toward the car and walked past Avery. She sat down, shut her door and stared straight ahead. Jason didn't say a word and Avery got in, shutting the door. The engine remained silent.

"Nat, what happened in there?" Her voice was full of panic. *Oh my God, she's cracking up. I knew we shouldn't have come.*

Natalie brought her guard up to concentrate. What did it all mean? "Avery," she continued to stare out the windshield. "Can I see your cell?"

"Um, yeah, I guess. What's wrong with yours?" She handed Natalie her pink swaddled phone capable of everything but landing a commercial jet.

"How do you find an address on this thing?" She asked quietly.

"What do you need to find?"

"Optimax."

Avery was silent. Natalie turned her head only, seeing a green faced Avery staring at her.

"Natalie what are you doing?"

"The picture isn't here, it has to be at his office." She needed to go there. This was more than a picture now. There was something else going on she was sure of it, the hair on the back of her neck was standing straight up. Had Luka been murdered? Had someone else been in his room recently looking for something? Maybe he had found something out about Mr. Whiting. Natalie pictured Mrs. Van Slyke wiping down the room like they did on those forensic cop shows to hide the evidence and fingerprints.

Concerned for her friend's stability, Avery tried to soothe her. "Natalie, I know this is hard for you. I know how much you loved him, but this isn't healthy. We're taking you home and I'm calling your parents."

"No!" Natalie shook her head emphatically. "No, you're not. All I want to do is go to his office and see if they have it." She pointed at the house. "That woman is hiding something and maybe I'm paranoid but there is something wrong. Really wrong here. I think Luka tried to leave and they killed him."

Once it was out, she realized what it sounded like to them. They didn't know about the ability to read minds or to block one's thoughts. They didn't know about his sister's suicide while she was at Prestige. Had she figured something out? What about the cultivation of their talents with Ivy? Luka was being groomed for whatever this company did and maybe so was she. And when he had tried to get out, they had killed him. Had that been what had happened to Andjela as well? Natalie's mind was in hyperdrive, making connections she'd refused to see before.

Avery and Jason stared at her like she was mad. Natalie found the handle and she let herself out shutting the door behind her.

"Natalie get back in the car." Avery got out and tried to talk to her over the roof.

"No. Go ahead and go back, I'll call a cab." She backed away from the car until her shoes scraped on the cement of the sidewalk. "I'm not leaving this town until I find out what she's hiding." She crossed her arms, feeling a chill that was out of place in the warm summer air with her long sleeves holding her body's heat in. Instead of sweating, she was shivering.

Jason stepped out on her side of the car and walked toward her, palms out. "Natalie, get in the car." He spoke softly, soothingly. "If it will help you put this away, we can go to the office and I'll go in with you to find his stuff." He exchanged a look with Avery and shook his head slightly at her silent objection.

Natalie heard him thinking exactly in line with what he was saying and believed him. He was not trying to trick her, he saw no harm in checking things out. "Okay." She said slowly and reentered the car. Avery got in last and sighed. Natalie saw her hands shaking while she punched in the name of the company on her phone. She jotted down the address and some notes that must have been directions on her dashboard notepad.

The car started and pulled away from the curb, all of its occupants lost in their thoughts while they all had a common thread. Natalie was very possibly going off the deep end and someone was going to have to be there to reel her in if it wasn't already too late.

Chapter 26

"Wow. What did you say these guys did again?" Avery asked as they sat parked outside the enormous glass fronted white behemoth of a building, two times wider than it was high. Perfectly manicured lawns nearly a half mile long flanked the long drive. No cars sat in front of the building; all parking was directed to the rear. A fact made abundantly clear by a large white sign partway up the approach directing them to do the same.

"Research and clinical trials are what Luka was going for. Although he said they were huge and into just about everything." Natalie stared at the enormity of the place and was discouraged. She wasn't sure how she was supposed to find out anything in a place so daunting.

The car crept forward and Natalie turned her body to see Avery. Her jaw was set and she was strangely focused.

"What's up babe?" Jason was watching her too.

She answered without averting her eyes. "My father works for a company like this one. The kind that says they're one thing but another entirely. Things fell apart as soon as I started connecting the dots and figured out his tech company was funneling money into some experimental stuff. I told him it was wrong. That's when he sent me away."

All three of them stared at the building growing larger as they approached.

Avery let them out at the main doors. "I'll park around the corner in the visitor's lot. Call me when you're done." She stared at the building. "Careful. It might be nothing, but this place gives me a funny feeling."

Natalie nodded, Jason said, "sure thing." She was glad she wasn't the only one intimidated by the heavy presence of security cameras and lack of external activity. It was strange how having no cars in front made it feel abandoned and unreachable.

Jason opened the heavy glass door for Natalie. They walked in and looked up. It was impossible not to. The foyer was large, crisp and white. Sterile was the word that came to mind. The open entry was rounded, open sided stairways and walkways circled up above the enormous receptionists' desk. There were three staffing phones and all appeared busy. Security guards were positioned on either side of the front doors as well on both ends of the front desk. What *did* they do here that required that much security?

Natalie's gaze went up, noticing the spiraling white walls that served as a barrier to the stairs. They were open from the waist up reminding her of indoor parking ramps at home. It was probably supposed to make the giant building feel open, it made her squirm. Feeling that everyone could see her made her feel nothing but exposed and extremely small.

Jason led her by the elbow toward the long white desk, approaching the lanky young Indian man on the end of the desk curved toward them.

He glanced up expectantly. His name tag said Jonathan. "May I help you?" Very vanilla.

Jason nudged her when she didn't respond right away.

Swallowing, she kept her nerves out of her voice. "I'm here to speak to Bradley Whiting."

Jonathan smiled blandly, taking in her casual tee and jeans. "Do you have an appointment?"

Natalie shook her head. "No, but I only need a minute. It's about an employee of his, Luka Bailey."

His face didn't change as he picked up his phone. "Your name?"

"Natalie Swenson." Her eyes met Jason's, his brow was furrowed and he shrugged. He also seemed to have noticed the lack of an effect her request had on the man. She glanced over at the nearest guard out of the corner of her eye and swore he was staring at her. She would have liked to listen in to what they were thinking, but if they had people like her or Ivy here it probably wasn't wise to announce her ability. For now she would have to keep any additional means of getting information locked down.

Jonathan murmured into his earpiece so low Natalie couldn't hear him over the sounds in the open swirling area. Natalie was reminded of a beehive with all the busyness and humming of activity.

Instead of looking at her, Jonathan glanced over at the guard nearest him. Young and well muscled, he smacked of former military down to the neatly buzzed blonde hair. His glasses were black and unattractive.

"Derrick, could you bring Miss Swenson up to Mr. Whiting's office on eight please?" Derrick nodded and motioned for Natalie to follow. Jason moved to follow and Derrick held up a hand. "Just Miss Swenson sir."

Natalie felt her stomach warning her not to go alone. "Please, this is difficult for me. He's here to help."

Staring at them both, he finally nodded and exchanged a glance with Jonathan. Natalie hadn't seen him dial again but definitely saw his mouth moving as he spoke into the boom mic he wore as part of his uniform. Derrick led them down a white walled hallway that had been hidden behind the tall, blank wall behind the receptionists' desk. Against the opposite wall was a bank of elevators.

Derrick pushed the button and waited silently, staring straight ahead. Natalie looked over at Jason again and saw that he was apprehensive as well. She was paranoid maybe, but there was a growing possibility that at least some of her suspicions were grounded in reality. That did not make her feel any better at the moment.

The light went on for the shiny metal box in front of them. Derrick stepped inside as the doors opened on a graphite paneled interior. Natalie and Jason followed, turning to face the front. Derrick stood beside the door and pressed the button for eight.

Eight was not as sterile as the entry by far. It was painted in a soft green color, plush cream carpet muffled their steps and frosted glass doors marked both ends of the hall running left to right. Neither door was marked with a name. Derrick led them left and flashed the card attached to his belt on the black box beside the door and the lock clicked softly.

He opened one of the doors and held it for them both, following them in. The décor within matched the freshness and color of the area outside the doors. A short hallway of six frosted glass doors sat on either side, one solid metal door marked the end. Derrick motioned for them to sit in the cream upholstered chairs in the small sitting area. The usual variety of magazines littered the glass coffee table making it feel like a higher end doctor's office.

Not like Natalie's doctor back home. Their sheetrock had some random crayon marks, the chairs were worn and aged yet it felt comfortable. This most definitely did not. Natalie didn't want to sit nor did Jason. They both stood exactly where Derrick left them and watched him disappear into the third door on his right.

Muffled voices could be heard and Derrick reappeared.

"Miss Swenson, Mr. Whiting will see you now." He turned to Jason. "Just Miss Swenson please."

Jason looked at Natalie and she nodded her head. He was close by; that was all she needed. He was already witness to the surreal way this was all unfolding, he no longer doubted her questions about Luka's death.

"I'll be okay. Stay here?" She said it more for Derrick than Jason. He wasn't going anywhere without her but she wanted the guard to know she expected him to be there when she got back.

"I'm not going anywhere." He sat down in silent protest to any plans Derrick had for escorting him out.

Shrugging, Derrick took up a position next to the frosted doors leading to the elevators.

Suddenly uncertain the wisdom of her pursuit, Natalie walked into the office of the man who had so frightened and possibly killed her Luka. Her control had gotten stronger with practice, but so had her ability without medications. She could feel them both straining to cancel each other out as did her curiosity and caution. It took tremendous effort to keep her guard up, denying her ability free rein to search the man's mind.

"Miss Swenson, so good to meet you. I understand you are a friend of Luka's?" He walked around his desk to take her hand in both of his, smiling warmly.

He was exactly as Luka had described him. Attractive enough, she would argue he was closer to his late forties and a little heavier than she would have wanted but otherwise she could see Luka's point that he could turn the heads of the young

163

impressionable women working here. Most young women were drawn to confident men and Whiting was absolutely commanding. It was hard to look away from him. He exuded power. She wasn't normally affected by that, but *she* even found herself drawn to him.

She had to break off from his gaze, redirecting it to his desk searching for anything that might tell her something about Luka's death. It was neatly composed with a computer on one side its cover closed, a lone file sat in front of where he had just been sitting, the rest of his desk was spotless. She could see nothing.

There were no other indicators of his personal life. No pictures of loved ones, no knick knacks that denoted hobbies or personal interests. Even the wall over the back of his desk was blank but for a map of the United States.

His greeting struck her as odd for the situation. He expressed no condolences. Maybe he had so many people working under him he had forgotten which one she was here for.

"Mr. Whiting sir, I know this is going to sound strange, but I wanted to get something Luka had on his desk."

His brow furrowed as he stared at her for a long, tense moment before he deliberately motioned toward his door. "If you'll follow me." He walked out and down to the last door on his same side.

Natalie walked in and covered her mouth. He had been there nearly two months and had obviously made the space his. Behind his slightly smaller desk was a set of encyclopedias that had formerly resided on his living room bookshelf at home. His father had given them to him. Luka had always preferred them to internet research. He must have sent for them after he'd arrived, they'd been on his shelf when last she'd been there.

She walked straight over to touch them, knowing he had been the last to do so. Her eyes were filling up again, threatening to spill over. She didn't care if Bradley Whiting saw it or not, she realized as she felt her cheeks growing damp. Sitting down in his chair, she turned and there, next to his computer was the picture.

She reached out to take it. It didn't bother her how she looked in it. That wasn't what she had come for. She had eyes only for him. His profile just as handsome as it was in her memory. Now that she had this, the memory of him and what they had would never fade. There would always be evidence that they had been happy once. She held the frame against her breast and glanced up.

"Mr. Whiting, I wonder what you're going to do with the rest of this?" She glanced around her thinking they must have a lot of offices not to need this one back. A man as important as Mr. Whiting must need an assistant and she couldn't imagine they would hold the desk out of respect for an intern after all.

His smile faded from his eyes. "Nothing." He pointed at the picture. "Is that what you came all this way for?"

Nodding, she stood. She didn't like this guy and knew if she tried to hear him, she couldn't so she kept herself blocked off. Sidling around the desk, she clutched the picture. "Yes, sir." It came out choked. "It's the only one of us."

"How long have you known Mr. Bailey?" He stared at her, his focus so intense and predatory she squirmed, daring to go no closer.

"We met at the beginning of the school year."

"And what was the nature of your relationship?"

"I'm not sure how that's pertinent, sir." It felt blasphemous to tell him about what they'd had.

Whiting nodded toward the picture in her hands. "You interrupt my day, walk in here, into my employee's office, and take personal property from his desk. I am merely trying to determine what right you have to that." He crossed his arms and leaned against the doorframe.

Not willing to give up her prize, Natalie fought to keep a civil tongue. Her mother would have been proud. "Luka and I were together sir."

His eyebrows went up. "Was his mother aware of that fact?"

The question confused her coming from him. She wondered if he knew Marta Bailey. "No sir, she was not."

"Intriguing." He watched her with a decided interest. "When was the last time you spoke with Luka?"

"The night before the accident." She could feel the rage beginning to get the better of her. Here she stood being grilled on personal matters by the very man she believed responsible for his murder and that belief was growing stronger by the second. Her lips curled in an involuntary snarl. "I talked to him the night before he was going to quit and come home."

Unaffected by her emotional display, Whiting smiled again. "So he told you he was going to quit did he. Did he tell you why?"

She said nothing. Instead forcing herself to shake her head. She couldn't give him that. She wouldn't. "I don't know."

Pushing off from the doorway, Whiting approached her. His steps were silent on the carpet, her attention was entirely focused on his eyes. They had gone cold and flat. His mouth set firmly. Natalie was afraid to move.

When he was within reach he extended his hand again, this time he touched her forehead with one finger. "I *know* what Luka can do, and I think you do too."

Chapter 27

As soon as he touched her, she felt her defenses shake and she reeled backward to get away. Just as Luka had said, there was only a blank spot where Whiting's "voice" should have been. "Don't touch me!" She shouted as she patched up her blocks as quickly as possible.

The sounds of an argument reached her from the sitting area and she guessed Jason had heard her. Whiting had heard it too. "He won't come to any harm. Derrick can restrain without injury and no offense to your friend, he's outmatched." He refocused on her, eyes searching her face. "What accident are you talking about?"

Natalie closed her eyes, wishing herself away from here. "His mother called me and told me he drove off the embankment in the rain. He died at the scene." How did he not know that about his own intern?

"Did she seem upset to you?"

Squeezing her eyes shut tighter, Natalie saw white lights against her lids. "I don't know her well enough to tell."

"So, no." He read into her deflection. "Was there a funeral?"

"Family only." She could barely hear her own voice it was so quiet. He was making her relive the worst day of her life and she hated him for it. Not only was he a murderer, he was cruel.

"Did you ever wonder at the timing of this *accident?*" Whiting sounded amused.

She opened her eyes again to glare at him and lied. "No."

Whiting shrugged, non-committal. "I would suspect one of two things if I were in your position and knew what only you know." He gave her a meaningful look. "I would assume either the fates had conspired to keep the two of you apart, or, I would imagine his boss didn't want him quitting and arranged for something to happen to him."

Natalie's teeth pulled up showing her teeth. "How dare you!" She hissed. "You killed him and now you have the nerve to taunt me?" Blood roared in her ears as she fought to keep her hands clenched around her picture when she wanted to wrap them around his neck and choke the very life out of him.

He laughed out loud. "I think you should recheck your facts." He backed up and turned, giving her the door.

When she was nearly to the sitting area, Whiting called out quietly. "If I were you, I wouldn't have taken Marta Bailey's word for it."

Natalie froze. "What?"

"You gave up awfully easy. One call from a woman you've never met who doesn't let you see the body and you give up? From what Ivy has said, I figured you for more of a fighter."

Her body shook with fury but her mind was spinning. Was this guy messing with her or did he know something? Why would a mother ever make up her child dying? That was sick. Did he just say he'd spoken to Ivy? She felt her defenses slipping again.

Jason shouted from the front room. She didn't hear what he yelled, but his exclamation tore more of her concentration from where she needed it right now.

Natalie felt her defenses come tumbling down and in rushed a horrible wave of confused sadness that took her breath with it. She sagged and had to stick a hand out to catch herself on the wall.

A glance at Whiting showed him watching her with a renewed interest. Natalie couldn't help herself. She heard the others on the floor without exception.

I wish she'd hurry up. This muscle is starting to piss me off.

I wonder if I could still go to work in Jimmy's shop. Sure would beat this rent-a-thug gig.

She's better off thinking I'm gone. No one can ask someone to give up everything on a maybe. I miss her though. I still hear her in my head.

Natalie jerked back as if she'd been struck. She recognized all the voices and felt the blank spot where Whiting stood. Except the last one didn't belong. Her eyes were wide, she put her hands on her head trying to drown out the delusion she was hearing. She stared at Whiting, his head was cocked, watching her intently.

"He's dead," she whispered, telling herself inside and outside her head in an effort to clear the hallucinated voice from her mind. "Whiting's playing some sick joke."

She's here? No.

She shook her head, still clutching at her ears even though the sound came from *inside* her head.

You're not real. Leave me alone.

Hearing what she thought was his voice brought her heartbreak rushing back as raw as when she had heard Marta utter the words, "My son is dead."

Whiting brought a phone to his ear. "My office. Now."

No. This isn't happening.

Natalie sank down to her knees, too exhausted and confused to concentrate on blocking off the voices. Part of her didn't want them to go away. Maybe it was a delusion, but it sounded just like him and she hadn't known exactly how much she missed hearing his voice in her head. The sadness it brought with it was crushing. Her eyes welled up and tears ran down her cheeks as Natalie sat with her back against the wall holding her knees tight to her chest. Let Whiting have Derrick throw her out. It didn't matter. At the moment, she didn't have the strength to stand no matter who gave the order.

A heavy door opened down the hall. Natalie assumed it was more security here to throw her and Jason out on their ears.

Whiting's furious voice pierced the silence. "Why did you keep this from me? Do you know what this means? How rare this is? Ivy has some explaining to do."

The voice from inside her head sounded like it was outside too, answering Whiting quietly. "You don't want her. She's unstable. Look at her."

Natalie raised her head off her knees and looked down the hallway. There, next to Whiting stood a ghost. She blinked.

"*You* did this to her. I'll decide if she's too unstable to use, not you."

Luka shook his head, his displeasure obvious. "No. She doesn't have a strong enough ability to make it worth it. She's a head case. You're better off sending her away before she gets to be a problem."

"Luka?" Confused, Natalie put a hand on the wall and eased herself up without taking her eyes off of him. "How?"

He kept his eyes on Whiting. "Let her go. We talked about this, you don't need her."

"Luka, look at me," she called out softly, still not certain what she was seeing. Her mind tried to piece it together. Whiting was right. She *had* never seen a body. There had been no funeral, no service. No one else had ever spoken a word of his death. Ivy had been the only other person who had even mentioned it.

He kept his eyes on Whiting, she saw his jaw twitch. Whiting was staring at her.

"Luka, look at me."

Her blood was boiling. How dare he ignore her, how dare he put her through that. She wished he could know for just one second how that felt. To think that the person you love more than anything, your best friend in the world was suddenly gone, taken by a horrible accident. Or worse yet, murdered. She had come here and made a fool of herself all for him. And he had lied to her. Why? To get rid of her?

Luka, look at me! Natalie glared at him and felt her rage focusing on him. She let it gather, running through her body like an electrical current. Furious, she sent it all out at him in a ball of rage, screaming as she released it.

Luka's face registered surprise and then horror as he was suddenly knocked backward off his feet. "Nat, no!" He shouted before the impact forced the wind from his lungs.

Whiting's face lit up. He took one look at Luka and leaned over. "I think I can judge for myself who I want." One finger jammed over his shoulder toward Natalie, still fuming ten feet away. "I want her. Get rid of the other two and be back in my office for orders."

Redirecting his attention back to Natalie, Whiting strode forward and extended a hand, a huge grin on his face. "Welcome to The Company Natalie. I'll make the calls and arrange everything, you start today." He jerked his head over his shoulder to where Luka lay, his chest moving was the only indication he was even alive. "Luka will tell you what you need to know."

In a fog and making sense of none of it, Natalie shook his hand dumbly, barely registering it when he left. She was still staring at Luka. Had she done that? Had she actually physically attacked him? It wasn't possible. Narrowing her eyes, she glared at his prone body. If she had, she didn't feel bad. He deserved it.

By the time she recovered herself enough to go back to the seating area where she had left Jason, it was empty. She reached for her cell phone and dialed Avery.

"What's going on?" Avery's panicked voice answered on the first ring. "You guys have been up there forever and I'm getting ready to call the police and report bodies."

"Everything's fine. Jason's on his way out." She could guess that even if Derrick's thought hadn't registered at some lower level in her mind during her face off with Luka. "I was wrong about this place. I'm going to stay for a while and go through his things. His boss invited me to take my time." She didn't let Avery interject. "I'll rent a car and get back when I can." She hung up amidst Avery's loud objections.

Natalie approached Luka's unmoving body and stood next to his head. It was him. He was more pale than before and he had dark circles under his eyes but it was definitely him. Slowly, he opened his eyes and his dull gaze fell upon her. It wasn't friendly.

"Why did you have to come here?"

She felt her hurt turning to anger once more. "You know, decent human beings break up when they don't want to be with someone anymore. Do you have such a low opinion of my 'stability,'" she used air quotes to mock him, "that you have to have your mommy call me to fake your death?" She clenched her teeth. "A simple breakup would have sufficed. This was cruel." Natalie drew back a foot and kicked him in the ribs. "You're an asshole!"

There was nowhere for her to storm off to so Natalie went in to his office. The hard wooden frame still in her hand reminded her of why she had come. In a rage, she pitched it against the back wall, disappointed in the anticlimactic tinkling noise the glass made as it shattered. Sitting down in one of the chairs facing his desk, she kept her back to the door wishing she could go the rest of her life without having to look at him again.

Chapter 28

His knuckles rapped softly on the door.

"Go to hell." Natalie sat with her arms crossed, staring at the wall over his desk.

She felt him coming closer until he took a seat behind his desk. He kept his eyes from her and closed his computer, straightening the few things at his desk unnecessary as that was considering it was tidy in the first place.

"I didn't want you here," he began.

Natalie laughed. "Yeah, you've made that *very* clear."

Luka pressed his finger against the edge of his desk, choosing to watch the tip turn white to avoid making eye contact with her. "It's not what you think." He eased the pressure and watched the blood return before pressing it down again.

Natalie waited, keeping herself locked away. With her initial reaction passed, she was embarrassed now that she had shown him with her outburst exactly how much he had hurt her. That wouldn't happen again.

"Do you know what this place is or its relationship with Prestige College?"

"No."

Sighing, Luka finally looked up. She was shocked at his appearance. He looked terrible. The bags under his eyes accentuated how dull they were. Luka was running on empty. For a minute she felt bad for him then stubbornly she clung to her anger and pushed away her pity. "Optimax is a front for a government agency like the CIA or NSA. It's so underground it doesn't have a name. They just call it The Company."

Natalie rolled her eyes, keeping her arms crossed. To think, she had started to feel bad. Here he was making up more stories. She couldn't believe a word that came out of his lying mouth.

"Prestige is a culling ground where they have people like us shipped to from all over the country. Ivy works with everyone and mainstreams the ones who either don't have a strong ability or can't handle the strain of working for the Company. Only the few who are a good fit are offered these internships with

Optimax where they test us further. After we pass, we're brought on board."

At his description, Natalie snapped back. "Would that be the strain you said I couldn't handle? My instability?" She remembered what it had taken to show him her scars from that time in her life when she really had been unstable. That he would so easily put that up for public display was a betrayal of the worst sort. Natalie subconsciously rubbed the inside of her arm. "How could you?"

Something flickered behind his eyes though he kept his face impassive. "You can't work here," he said firmly.

Sneering at him, Natalie channeled her hurt into a safer emotion, anger. "My ability is stronger than yours, you said so yourself. Or was that a lie too? I would bet you've never blasted anyone like that before."

His eyes blazed and he shot back. "Did you hear nothing I said to you? Why would you show him what you could do? *Especially* that. Christ, the guy was practically drooling over you. Now there's no way to get you out of here."

"I don't need your help getting me out of anywhere. I'll leave when I'm good and ready."

Frustrated, he growled and his hand came up to rub his neck.

Natalie took his agitation personally. She pulled out her phone, turning her back on him.

"What are you doing?"

"Calling Avery. I changed my mind. I want to get out of here."

He lowered his voice. "You can't."

Turning around, Natalie felt a sense of foreboding. "What do you mean?"

"Did you not hear anything I've been saying? Once you're here, you're here. They don't let you go. Why do you think I wanted you to think I was dead?"

Her legs were weak. She sank back down in the chair. "Say that again?"

Luka came around the front of the desk and sat on the chair beside her. Natalie didn't object when his knees touched hers. "I was telling you the truth that night. I went in the next day and told Whiting I quit. He told me that wasn't an option." He put

173

his head in his hands and Natalie had to concentrate to hear him. "He said my father found out about Prestige's association with Optimax through a business contact after Andjela died. Whiting convinced him my ability made me an asset to the country. He told dad that if I could train with them I would embrace my ability. That I would never do what Andjela did. Mom knew too and as much as she hates this place she was willing to help me lie to you. She never agreed with Dad that I belonged here." He turned his face back up to meet her eyes and reached out tentatively for her hand clenched at her side.

She let him, mind spinning too fast to argue.

"We have to live a double life. It's not one I wanted you to be pressed into. He'll force you to give up everything and everyone important in your life. Your ability is really strong and now that Whiting's seen this new psychic blast of yours, he's going to keep you for sure. I was trying to protect you, let you live a normal life and hoped when your offer came you would hate the place so much you'd refuse."

"What if I don't want to be protected?" she asked calmly. "What if I would like to have an opportunity to have my ability be of some benefit to someone?" Natalie put her other hand on top of Luka's. She pulled her defenses down and stared at him, waiting. He did the same and she could feel that he was telling her the truth this time. Relief washed over her hearing what he wasn't saying as well. "I appreciate you trying to protect me, but did you honestly think that was a good idea? You've said it yourself; I don't leave things alone until I figure them out on my own. You had to know I would check it out."

Luka let his hand fall back to her knee. "I had hoped you would be so upset you'd leave it alone. You were so busy with classes I thought you might forget and move on eventually."

Natalie tore her hand from his and shot up out of her chair. "Are you kidding me? You think I would forget about you because I was taking some *classes*? Are you blind as well as stupid?"

He watched her walk away and got up to stand behind his chair facing her. "I had to do *something* and I didn't have a lot of time. I couldn't think of any other options or anyone else I could trust with your safety *and* your secret."

174

She whirled. "You told your mother I could read minds?"

Luka nodded unhappily. "It was the only way. She didn't want to do it until I explained how you were like Andj. You've got no idea what kind of risk she took helping me to hide you. You saw Whiting. If it weren't for my mother's influence she would be in real trouble."

"What about Ivy? She knew."

He shook his head. "She knows that you have it, not how strong you are. They don't start testing you until your second year at least. The first year you just learn how to control it. I never told her exactly what she was dealing with. She seemed… weird about it. Like she didn't *want* to know." He remained perplexed at the memory, displeased with it.

"Why?" She asked quietly, shaking her head in disbelief. "Why did you do all of this?"

"Because I love you," he replied softly, resting his hands on the back of the chair and fixing his eyes on her.

Natalie felt her heart skip a beat. "You love me?"

Luka took a step around the chair and held out a hand uncertainly. She took it and let him pull her into him. His hands stroked her hair, hers his neck while she buried her face against his firm, thinner chest, reveling in his scent and warmth.

"I love you too," she said softly before adding more severely. "Do me a favor and don't die again."

Luka threw back his head and laughed. Natalie could sense his joy both in her head and through his touch. His hand rubbed against her back, one slid up to cup the back of her neck. She leaned back and turned her face up. Just as their lips touched, the intercom on Luka's desk phone buzzed.

"Mr. Bailey, Mr. Whiting would like to see you and your guest in the blue room." Where was a receptionist? Natalie hadn't seen one.

Groaning softly against her neck and giving her goose bumps in the process, Luka tried to hide his frustration. "Thank you Janelle." He smoothed her hair and pecked her forehead. "We can't make him wait."

Natalie followed Luka into the hall and they went out the metal door through which he had entered the floor. The concrete in the stairway led them down. Luka exited on the sixth floor and, sure enough, it was a carbon copy of the eighth floor only painted blue.

This hall, however, only had two doors on either side. Luka led her into the first one on their left. Already waiting inside the blue conference room were two strangers and Mr. Whiting was settled at the head of the large rectangular dark wooden table.

Luka stopped inside the door. Natalie followed his lead, halting beside him. Having been informed of the folly of her decision to pursue her instincts and come here, and knowing any control she had over her future was lost, Natalie did not regret any of it. Here she was standing with Luka who was alive, she knew her place was with him. Wary of the three people seated at the head of the table and watching her, vaguely interested, Natalie trusted Luka to guide her. She realized at that moment she always had.

Whiting rose halfway out of his chair and waved them to sit. "Luka you can shut the door, we're all here."

With a brief nod, Luka did as he was told then took his seat at the foot of the table. Natalie sat beside him.

Whiting resumed his seat while he did the talking. The other two, a man and a woman sat with blank faces, only their eyes moved as they shamelessly assessed Natalie. She shifted nervously in her chair and felt Luka's hand on her leg. Eagerly she took it.

"You have already met our newest recruit, Mr. Bailey." Whiting was speaking to the unknown pair.

They did not move.

"I thought you would be interested in meeting a friend of his, Natalie Swenson." The amusement in his tone at her expense was starting to grate on her. "She is quite the little detective." He explained how she had come to be there.

They still did not move.

"The interesting part of Ms. Swenson's story is that she has telepathy like Mr. Bailey as you will recall. Because of their like abilities, their potential value in the field is extraordinary. Although I admit I'm not sure the distance limitations."

"Luka," Whiting looked askance of him. "Where in the building were you when you became aware of Ms. Swenson' presence?"

The other two watched him, mildly interested.

"In the lower facilities when I first thought I heard her, Mr. Whiting."

Natalie didn't understand where that was, but the other two did. The woman, petite, oddly smooth faced and blonde with spiked hair raised her brown eyebrows. The man, tall angular reminded Natalie of a black Ichabod Crane from Sleepy Hollow. He leaned forward and rested his hands on the table, clearly intrigued.

Whiting turned to the others, his pleasure plain on his face. "The lower facilities, that is six floors of concrete and steel. Very impressive." He continued, positively beaming like he had something to do with it. "But what was most impressive, was the physical manifestation of her mental abilities. Ms. Swenson attacked Mr. Bailey, knocking him off his feet with a psychic blast."

The woman wrote something in her black notebook lying on the table in front of her. The man stared at Natalie and she swore she felt a breeze ruffle her hair, raising gooseflesh on her arms before he turned to Whiting. "I cannot get anything from her, she feels guarded." His voice was soft, nearly inaudible.

Squeezing Luka's hand, Natalie tried to keep her face from showing just how nervous she was growing with the passing of each dreamlike second. Luka rubbed the back of her hand with his thumb. Neither dared use their telepathy. Clearly the others all had abilities and would know they were using theirs.

Whiting answered. "I've spoken to Ivy Santiago, the head of the program at Prestige. She paired these two at the beginning of the school year. Mr. Bailey was Ms. Swenson's tutor." He let his tone grow heavy with meaning. "According to Ms. Santiago, they developed an attachment almost immediately."

"How well can you focus your attacks?" The woman asked Natalie, interested though unemotional.

"Um, I'm not really sure. That was the first time that's happened."

"What pre-empted the incident?" The man asked, again she felt the breeze over her skin. This time she shivered in its wake.

Answering the questions of the nameless authorities now wielding control over her life was intimidating to say the least.

Throw in the fact that she had no idea what would be good or bad in their eyes and she was uncertain the level of honesty she should take. Luka squeezed her hand.

"Please. Natalie has had some terrible shocks today, most of which are my doing. If we could be so bold Sirs and Madam, would it be possible to reconvene tomorrow? Natalie will be better able to answer your questions to your satisfaction."

She did her best to look submissive and beat, not hard to do at the moment. When they had been silent too long, she risked a glance up and saw that the men were watching the woman. She was in charge. Good to know.

Finally, she nodded. "Tomorrow at nine we will meet back here and Ms. Swenson, come prepared to give us an example of what you can do." She did not wait for an answer, returning immediately to outlining the details of Natalie's fate in her notebook, her presence already forgotten.

"Luka, why don't you take Ms. Swenson home for the day." Whiting instructed. As they started to rise, he coughed. "Oh and one more thing. Please do something about your friends currently being held in Security please. They refuse to leave until they see that I haven't murdered Ms. Swenson as well." He chuckled, thinking he was actually being funny. It was far too soon for Natalie to share his humor. He had a ways to go before she could consider him anything other than a bad guy.

"If you don't, I will."

Yep, still a bad guy.

Chapter 28

"Natalie!" Avery rushed off of the chair where she had been seated against the far wall of the large office. Jason remained seated beside her, watching the girls embrace. He stared at the ghost who stood silent behind Natalie.

Avery wasn't so silent. She drew back and made a move to strike him but it didn't take mind reading capabilities to see what she was prepared to do. His hand was waiting for her and deflected her easily.

Physically he could stop her, but not verbally. "I could kill you Luka Bailey!" She stuck an accusatory finger in his face. "Is it your idea of a joke to go around telling people you're dead? That's so wrong I can't even begin to explain it to you!" She moved protectively in front of Natalie. "Do you know what you put her through?"

"Let's just go." Natalie cut in sharply. Having Luka hear how she had mourned him when he wasn't dead was too much.

Avery wanted to continue, Natalie could see her catching her breath for another tirade when Jason got up and put his hands on her arms from behind. "Come on Avery. I think we can talk about this outside." He gave Natalie a look that said he fully expected her to follow.

Natalie was surprised. She had never seen Jason be anything more than easygoing Jay, following in Avery's wake. It appeared there was more steel to him than met the eye. Jason led the way while Avery let him guide her with a hand on her arm. Natalie and Luka followed them out the doors to the lot where the lights were coming on as dusk fell.

Once outside, Jason released Avery who instantly wheeled on Luka to finish what she had started. Natalie heard the crack before she registered that Avery had stopped. Luka did nothing to defend himself. Jason let her get one more in before he restrained her again.

"*She* may be too blind to see you for what you are, but *I'm* not. You are a manipulative ass and I won't stand by waiting to pick up the pieces when you do something awful again." Avery's blue eyes burned hot, her teeth exposed in a furious snarl.

Natalie had never seen her so angry. "Avery…" She let her voice trail off. She had no way of explaining what had really happened. There was nothing she could say to anyone. Both Avery and Jason, the two who had at her grieving request driven five hours straight through, would not be able to understand why Luka had done what he had nor why she was going to stay.

"You're right."

Natalie looked over curiously at him. Avery and Jason appeared equally interested in what he had to say.

He held out a hand, telling Natalie he wanted to explain. "You two have been good to Natalie and to me. You were there for her when she needed you the most and although I can't explain why I had to do what I did, please trust me. It was a necessary evil." He watched their reactions.

Jason nodded slowly, unconvinced and Avery continued to glare. It wasn't enough.

"I can't tell you everything about this place, but suffice it to say it isn't as it seems. Avery, please believe me when I say everything I did was to keep Natalie away from me for her own good. But now that she's here, the best way for me to protect her is to keep her close." He looked at Natalie standing next to him. "I can't give her up again, I know that now."

Can you tell them that? Her mind reeled at his confession both at the hint of Optimax's false front and his unwillingness to let her go.

It's probably too much but if I don't tell them anything, they might snoop around and it would end badly for them both no matter what kind of pull Avery's father has. He felt her surprise. *You know he ran their names as soon as they stepped into the building. There's no way he's going to bring on the wrath of a wealthy man like Bluth should anything happen to his little girl. If Whiting told me to talk to them and he knows they think I'm deceased, he knows I'll have to tell them something. He trusts me. He knows he's got me.*

What do you mean?

Luka took her hand, his eyes filled with grief. *He can get to the two people I love most in this world. I'm in this for life.*

Avery eased her aggressive posture only slightly and Jason relaxed his grip on her, beginning to trust that she wasn't going to strike Luka again. "I don't get why you couldn't just tell her that."

"I knew that if I told her that, she would probably come anyway and I didn't want her here. It's not a good place." Luka explained cryptically.

"Why, is this one of those, 'I could tell you but then I'd have to kill you' things?" Jason joked nervously.

Luka shrugged, giving them a look.

Avery and Jason's eyes bulged. "Are you kidding me?" Avery glanced over at the building, a renewed reason to dislike it. "Natalie you have to come back with us, you can't stay here." She reached out for Natalie's arm.

Natalie stepped back, holding Luka's hand tight. "No. I'm staying here." She said firmly.

"No! You heard him. It isn't a good idea for you to be here." Avery pleaded with her friend to see sense.

Stubbornly, Natalie shook her head. "I fully understand the risks but this is where I want to be." It was hard to refuse her friend but her love for Luka held her.

Avery opened her mouth to object again when Jason spoke up.

"Avery, Natalie is a big girl and she knows what she's doing even if we're fairly sure it's a dumb move." He stared daggers at Luka before turning his attention to Natalie. "Nat, if you change your mind you know where to find us. Call and we'll be here in a few hours. Okay?"

Natalie felt her eyes filling up yet again. She swore she had cried more in the past twenty-four hours than she had in the last year. "I will." She offered a smile to Avery. "Avery, I'm going to be okay. Please don't leave here mad, I can't handle that." Natalie held out a hand.

Hesitating, Avery stared hard at her proffered hand before finally taking it. "Be careful Nat. Don't let your heart get in the way of your head, huh?" Her voice cracked.

Natalie silently shook her head and reached out to give Avery a last hug. She knew better than her friend that this was probably the last they would share in a while. Jason cleared his throat.

The girls glanced up and saw a security guard had stepped outside the building and was watching them.

"Are you sure?" Avery confirmed tensely, ill at ease for good reason. She could sense that something was amiss about this place without Luka's scant admission. It went against everything in her to leave her friend here.

"I'm sure."

"That's it then." Jason offered Luka his hand. Luka shook it once firmly. "Take care of each other you two." He took a step back and grabbed Avery's hand to help her break away.

One more backward glance from Avery and they were gone. Luka and Natalie let them go before they themselves headed to Luka's car. Unlocking the door for her, he remained mute until he had the car moving down the road.

"This isn't the way to the Van Slyke's." Natalie commented as they turned the opposite way onto the main road.

Luka glanced over at her.

She shrugged. "I went there first to see if they had our picture."

"So now it's 'our' picture?" He couldn't resist the opening. "I thought you hated it."

Natalie flushed. "It's the only one in existence with us together and I wanted it."

"Is that what brought you up here? The picture?" He was incredulous.

She nodded. "That and I figured your boss had you killed. Then when I went to Van Slyke's, your room still looked lived in and she was in a panic about my being there. I knew I needed to meet Whiting to figure it out for myself."

Luka ran his hand over his face. "Nat, I think I was wrong about you. I think it's the other guys who have to worry, not you.

Chapter 29

They pulled in at a chain hotel, Luka called his host family on the way explaining he and Natalie had a lot to talk about and wanted to be alone. He would be by later but wasn't sure when. She told him she would leave a light on.

"So what does she know about all of this?" Natalie asked when they got into their generically pastel decorated room and the lock slid home behind her. The small room was clean and she sank down on the bed, her day weighing heavily on her shoulders. She tucked a leg under the other hanging over the edge.

Luka tossed the keys on the dresser and sank down facing her on the king sized bed in the middle of the room. Only a bathroom sat off to the side and the one window faced out onto the parking lot from their second floor elevation. "Elise and Bill Van Slyke have been friends with my parents since before I was born. With my parents traveling so much, they had a will drawn up that had my sister and me going to them should anything ever happen. When they did, they had to tell them about us."

"I could tell she knew something when she knew how to block me out. What did you tell her?"

He did something rare for him, Luka blushed. "It's something they've learned out of necessity. They couldn't be around us and not be able to have private thoughts. Elise and Bill are like a second family to me. After my mother lied to you, I thought I was never going to see you again." He rubbed his neck. "I was upset and she wouldn't leave me alone until I told her about you. I never thought she'd meet you so I didn't think any harm would come of it. But I explained how you and I had something special because we shared this ability." He met her eyes while he explained. "How I would never meet anyone else who could be with me like you could."

"What did she say?" She was mesmerized by the sound of his voice and what he was saying. She'd never thought she'd hear him speak again.

"She said I was a fool for not going home to you."

Natalie was shocked out of her trance. "She doesn't know the truth about Optimax?"

He shook his head. "No. All she knows is that I chose my career over you."

"No wonder she thought you were being dumb," Natalie teased. "Giving up love for a job?" The woman's lack of sadness made more sense too, she'd been distressed to have Natalie there, never supporting the false pretense that Luka was no longer among the living.

"It's not a mistake I intend to make again." The look in his eyes changed. "Any of it."

Natalie felt the room get warmer, she saw only Luka's green gaze boring into her. His black hair was shorter than when he had been at school, it no longer interfered with his eyes. Luka's golden skin filled her vision, the outward curve of his nose casting a small shadow on his cheek, nearly obscuring the small freckle that lay just to the left of his nose. It was almost invisible except Natalie had studied his face for months, first from across a desk, then a pillow. She could trace his features with her eyes closed.

Luka leaned in, only his mouth touched hers and he backed off.

Confused, Natalie opened her eyes and raised an eyebrow.

He seemed to gather himself, touching his tongue to his lips before sliding an arm behind her back and pulling her over and across his legs. The temperature in the room grew intensely fast. Natalie's chest rising and falling rapidly as she found it harder and harder to breath.

Sliding a hand down, smoothing her hair, Luka leaned in again and kissed her firmly. Kissing him back, she slid her arms around his neck and putting her hands in his hair to push his mouth hard against hers. She couldn't get close enough to him. The need to be with him was urgent. She shifted against him, making her want clear.

Natalie hesitated, her mouth hovering over his and pulling back. Luka watched her, eyes dark with passion. She slowly lowered her defenses and waited, unable to tell him she was completely exposed for him.

His desire was the first thing that hit her. Then guilt and love slammed into her.

You should *feel bad.*

You know I do. It was horrible leaving you, lying to you. You have to know I thought that I was saving you from this life.

By choosing for *me, you did the same thing you wanted to keep me from with Whiting.*

She felt the impact that statement had on him, felt it roll around in his head. She let it. *I want you to understand that I make my own decisions.* Natalie was no longer angry with Luka, she knew to go forward with no more doubts he had to know how vital this was for her. Whiting and The Company might not let her choose her career path, but she insisted that he let her have her say in their relationship.

I can live with that but there's a lot about this situation you don't understand. Things you'll have to do that you don't want to.

Natalie saw a flash of something she wasn't supposed to. A hint of fear that she wouldn't go along with The Company's orders, that she would refuse them when they asked her to use her developing ability again. Uncomfortable with her seeing his fears, she could feel him trying to pull back and throw up his defenses.

Don't. Natalie put her hands to his face, capturing his eyes with hers. *I won't do that to you again.*

You have to understand, those two have to see you as an asset or they see you as a liability. Once you get this far, you can't fail or that's it. He flashed again on her body, lifeless on the floor in the very same conference room where they'd met Whiting and the two mysterious partners today. Luka standing helplessly by.

It's not going to happen like that. We'll think of something else. I'm not hitting you like that again. I can hit Whiting. I don't like him.

Don't kid about that. You need a target that can evoke enough of an emotional response to bring that out again and your dislike of Whiting isn't going to be enough.

What if I can't get it to happen again? What if it was just that one time and I can't do it again?

Luka couldn't hide the trepidation he felt at that prospect as well. *We'll redo it. All you have to do is remember how you felt, all that hurt and rage and hit me with it once. That will buy us enough time to figure out how to control it for future use.*

Natalie shifted, Luka's body responded. Tomorrow's business was tomorrow's business. Pushing it aside left only tonight. Should tomorrow go badly, this would be their last time together. They might as well enjoy it.

Don't think that way.

The downside to being unguarded was the free rein they had inside each other's minds. Natalie took advantage. Her hips rolled over his slowly, her lips making their way down his neck, nipping playfully at his jaw and scraping against his shoulder.

He shivered. The groan she heard echoed inside and outside her head.

Then distract me.

He did. And then he did again.

***

When they came up for air, Natalie lay with her body curved against Luka's. His arms held her tightly to him, not wanting to let her go again. Natalie trailed her fingers back and forth across his forearm, feeling his coarse hair roll underneath her skin.

Luka tipped his face down to nuzzle her neck. "I've missed you."

"Me too." She brought his hand to her lips. "We should stay here all night."

With his nose in her hair Luka's response was muffled but she caught enough.

"Can't we go in the morning before work? I don't want to move."

He shifted against her. "At all?"

"Well, not *out* of this bed I don't." She wiggled back.

"I know Elise and Bill won't sleep until they've heard from me." Luka reluctantly released her and sat up, beginning to dress himself. "I'd like for you to meet them."

Natalie watched the muscles in his back as she followed suit. Had he always been so ripped? "Do you think meeting them like this is a good idea?" She pictured herself with sex hair and imagined what kind of state her clothes were in after riding in a car for over five hours. "Women talk, she's going to tell your mother I'm a hobo."

Luka's rich laughter filled the room. Hearing it made her heart flutter. She hadn't heard his laugh in so long; she hadn't realized how much she'd missed it. "Nat, she will adore you just like I do and so will my mother. We're not the sort of family that hangs out a lot, but we care about each other and she supports my decisions." He gave his belt a little too much attention. "We've been talking a lot since I came out here, I forgot how cool she is."

His affection for his mother made her think of her own parents. Since she'd left home, Natalie had spoken to her parents for the most part every week, calling either Wednesday or Thursday. After she had heard about the accident, she had stopped calling them altogether. Natalie felt guilty, worried for the first time they might be upset. Thinking for the first time about them at all really.

"I owe my parents a call tomorrow." She donned the last of her clothing. Glancing around the room, Natalie determined they had what they'd brought. The clothes on their backs. That was it.

Nervous and excited at the prospect of meeting some of Luka's people, no matter the less than opportune circumstances, Natalie walked out the door and heard him pull it shut behind them. The only way to go was forward.

Chapter 30

The house was dark except for the outdoor light and a faint glow from the interior. Natalie was caught unaware by how disappointed she was at the fact she was not going to see Mrs. Van Slyke again, this time with Luka hoping for some level of redemption in the woman's eyes.

"I figured you would be happy not to see anyone." Luka opened her door.

Stepping out, Natalie grinned self-consciously. "She probably doesn't see me in a very positive light. The last time I was here I was pushy and not quite myself. I was hoping to try again."

Holding out his hand for her, Luka escorted her inside and lowered his voice for the hush of the house. "There's plenty of time for that."

Natalie felt her heart flutter at his mention of a future. With their separation over, it was no longer taboo.

At the top of the stairs, a woman's voice called out. "Luka?"

"It's me Elise," Luka answered softly. "Natalie is with me."

Sounds of clothing rustled, they waited. Natalie ran her fingers through her hair and fidgeted with her clothes.

Luka lay a hand on her arm and kissed her temple. "You look wonderful." She felt his lips curve at her shiver.

"Luka is everything alright?" Elise's voice was concerned. Her gaze fell upon Natalie, appraising anew.

"Elise, I believe you met Natalie already." His fingers found hers. Natalie appreciated his show of affection lest the woman think she was a stalker and poor Luka was stuck having to put up with her until he could send her away.

Elise's broad mouth split into a huge smile as she looked at Natalie. "I'm pleased to see you've reordered your priorities Luka." She leaned in and gave Natalie a hug. "I don't want to have to lie for you again."

Natalie was too shocked to react.

"Are you staying here tonight?" She turned her attention to Luka. "It's getting late." She glanced at Natalie. "Or are you taking tomorrow off?"

He shifted his weight, Natalie felt him stop his hand from going up to his neck. He was aware of his nervous habit. "We're due in at nine. Natalie is meeting with our HR department. She has some experience that might get her in."

"Is that wise?" Elise asked. One eyebrow lifting as the only indication how she felt about this new development.

Luka's response was cryptic. "It has to be this way."

Elise stared at him, oddly deciding her better chance was with Natalie. She shifted her focus. "I am merely suggesting you two give it more time before you throw it all in together. Optimax is a good company, one of the hardest to get into. Bill has checked it out." She shot a sideways glance at Luka, his jaw was set firm. Elise saw it as stubbornness, Natalie knew it was frustration. "If things don't… work out, you don't want to have thrown away your opportunity with them."

Natalie nodded. To someone who didn't know about the secret identity of The Company, her advice made perfect sense. Elise most likely thought they were being stupid kids, turning this into a drama when it didn't need to be. "I agree Mrs. Van Slyke. But I've been tapped for an internship with Optimax as well already." She fought the urge to look at Luka. "The liaison at Prestige thought I had some things they might be looking for. All we're doing is asking to move up the timetable if they'll work with me."

Luka stood motionless, disturbed by how easily lies rolled off Natalie's tongue.

Staring at her a moment longer, Elise turned back to Luka. "Just promise me you'll think things through before you make any big decisions?" She crossed her arms and waited.

"I promise Elise," Luka agreed solemnly.

"Good night then." She flashed a more forced smile at Natalie. "Good night Natalie." Elise disappeared into the shadows back in her room.

Once inside his room with the door closed, Natalie sighed and leaned up against the wall. "That went well. She thinks I'm wrecking your life."

His lips were tight, Luka was not happy either. "I don't lie well. This is going to be harder than I thought. At first the lies were vague and harmless. 'Oh I don't know Dad, I thought I

189

heard that somewhere,' 'No, I never would have guessed you got me a bike.'" He ran his hands roughly through his short hair. "Now we have to keep track of all of it, make up this whole elaborate story. If people get suspicious and do any checking they could get hurt." He threw the contents of his pockets onto his dresser.

Watching him, Natalie wasn't certain what to do. Her lips twitched nervously. He saw it and turned to face her.

"Do you find this amusing? I have to lie to almost everyone I know. They trust me. They have no idea." He cocked his head. "*You* don't have a problem with it. You do it so easily." His eyes narrowed.

Natalie's lying had never bothered her. As a matter of fact, after the first few years, she hadn't given it a second thought. Coming to Prestige and meeting Avery and Luka had been the first time she'd tried to be honest.

Hearing the accusatory tone in Luka's voice she faltered in her surety that there was no harm in the one she'd told to Mrs. Van Slyke. She fought to keep the indecision from turning to anger. That was always a safer emotion for Natalie, far less painful to lash out than let it touch her.

With a conscious effort, Natalie kept her voice low. "Luka you just admitted having to lie to explain away how you knew something you shouldn't. It comes with the territory."

"Not necessarily. My sister chose to lie about everything, to keep people out, and look what happened to her. A little honesty and trust would have saved her. *I* could have saved her. I'm not going to live that way." Luka's chest heaved from the physical toll of his mental battle. He feared for them both and now that she was here, taking her first steps into this new life, he was second guessing the wisdom of having her stay.

Natalie already had her hackles up at his unfavorable comparison to Andjela. "Well, some of us didn't have someone else's mistakes to learn from, we had to figure it out on our own." She took personal offense at his condemnation. She felt her anger combining with hurt, a dangerous combination. "You had the luxury of knowing what you were dealing with. I didn't and neither did your sister. You have no right to sit in judgment of either one of us."

Luka's nostrils flared, he ground his teeth. "I'm not judging, I'm just sitting back and observing the carnage. Look what she did to herself by keeping secrets. Look what *you* did." His eyes went to her arms.

There was no more hurtful comment he could have made. Natalie's body stiffened as though he'd physically struck her. It was an effort to whisper, her breath was heavy in her chest. "You have no idea what it's like to feel that alone, to think you're crazy and have to hide everything you are from the people you want most to ask for help. To hear them beg you to let them in and knowing you can't. The few times I did try, all I got in return was more medication. I don't even remember two years of my life from all the drugs."

Natalie felt betrayed by his low blow. Luka bringing up her deepest hurt and shame and throwing it in her face was more painful than the cuts themselves. He had no idea what it took for her to open up to him about that part of her life. He wasn't allowed to judge her for it.

Luka jammed his hands in his pockets, his features dark with fury. Natalie swept past him, his voice caught her as she opened the door.

"Where are you going?"

She did not turn around, not wanting to look at him. "I can't sleep here with you." Her defenses were up tight. Let him try to sort this mess out the old fashioned way. No short cuts this time.

"It's late. You can't get a cab out here for at least an hour."

That he didn't ask her to stay or that he didn't apologize did not escape Natalie's notice. Sadly, what he said made sense. She was exhausted and it was late and if she was too tired to function tomorrow, Luka seemed to think it would not go well for her.

"Then I'll sleep on the couch." Padding down the stairs, Natalie picked the smaller of the two Laura Ashley sofas, camping out on the loveseat and pulling the decorative throw down to cover her.

Eventually the anger dissipated and gave way to fatigue. Natalie let herself be pulled down into a deep and dreamless sleep.

Chapter 31

Rain. It suited the day's outlook.

Natalie rose with the sun, or what little light shone through the clouds and draperies at a quarter to seven. More likely it had something to do with the smells coming from the kitchen. She crept to the lower floor bathroom and cringed at the image in the mirror. Second day hair having been thoroughly tousled the night before in ways Natalie failed to see in the same light this morning, did not improve with sleep. Nor did the bags under her eyes, the wrinkles in her shirt or jeans. Natalie looked terrible.

"Rough night?" Elise walked past her carrying a load of folded towels to the base of the stairs and up. She failed to stop for an answer, going on about her business and inciting a fresh surge of vexation in Natalie.

At her return, Natalie was still stewing impotently in the same spot until Elise put a stack of clothing in her hands. "Go get washed up. I'll save some eggs." Off she went bustling past, treating this morning like any other.

Natalie retreated into the bathroom, locked the door and did as she was told. When she emerged, dressed in a tasteful black sheath dress and sling back sandals that handled the slight difference in foot size commendably, she felt human and hoped she at least looked ready for anything they threw at her.

As soon as she came out of the hall and glanced right at the table, her spirits fell. Luka was sitting at the table eating the last of his toast, a full cup of coffee at his place. To her left, Elise was moving efficiently about the kitchen, a pale orange William Sonoma apron protecting today's powder blue sweater and jeans.

Smiling encouragingly, Elise pointed with an elbow as she put the finishing touches on Natalie's eggs. "Sit. I'll bring your plate in a minute. Coffee? Luka pour her coffee."

Grudgingly Luka complied, pouring into the cup at the setting beside him but shoving it down a place setting. He barely looked up as she thanked him just as coldly.

Natalie was debating excusing herself without eating when Elise placed her dish before her. "Oh wow Mrs. VanSlyke. That smells amazing." She meant it. Luka could deal with it. She was not leaving without breakfast.

"Elise." She said it without looking up from her tasks at the counter.

He drank his coffee, staring at the same page of newsprint until Natalie was finished and thanked Elise. Rising to clear her plate, Natalie heard Luka clear his throat.

"We should go," he muttered.

"Thank you for breakfast and for the clothes Mrs. VanSlyke. Elise." She corrected herself at the woman's sideways glance.

Luka waited for her at the door, wordlessly holding it open for her. She walked past him equally mute, waiting for him to get in the car.

It was a short and silent ride to Optimax. The only sound to be heard inside the car was the steady swish swish of the windshield wipers. When they arrived on the grounds, Luka stopped the car at the front doors and put the car in park.

Natalie's throat tightened convulsively. A long conversation was not something she needed right now. She began to panic when she saw him twist his body toward her, leaning over.

"Here." His arm had reached behind her to grab an umbrella from the back seat. Poker faced, he held it out for her.

She snatched it from his hand and replied with a crisp, "Thank you."

To add insult to injury, Natalie had to wait inside because she did not have clearance to go beyond the reception area without Luka. Waiting for him to park and walk through the rain gave her time to ponder.

In the last twenty-four hours she had regained her boyfriend, had him confess he did in fact love her *and* committed herself to a lifetime with a mysterious covert governmental agency known only as The Company. And of course the fact that they would kill her if she didn't perform to their satisfaction.

Though, oddly enough, the only thing occupying her mind at the moment was the sting of the barb he had slung at her the night before. The other things were almost too big to worry about whereas Luka's treachery was right there, easy to latch onto with all of her fears and anxiety.

Natalie watched the influx of people just beginning their workday wondering which few or maybe more had abilities. Did all of them work for The Company or were some plain old normal people who helped to keep up the front of a boring research facility?

She maintained that she dared not let down her guard here until requested. If anyone did have an ability, she would potentially be announcing herself to them and she would have to know more about this place and the people in it before she brought that kind of attention to herself.

"Come on." Luka's voice was suddenly next to her.

Mad at herself for letting him sneak up on her and more so at him for startling her, Natalie followed after him in a huff, dragging her feet to make him have to wait for her at the elevator.

They boarded with three others, making any meaningful discussion impossible. They were alone from floors five through eight and maintained their awkward silence. It was awkward to Natalie anyway. Luka had no outward appearance of discomfort. Drawing herself up, Natalie stepped off the elevator and allowed him to swipe his card and open the door for her. Once inside their office area, she took a seat in the waiting room and he continued to his office, closing the door behind him. She could neither see nor hear Whiting through his closed door and assumed he was already in the conference room waiting for her.

Natalie checked her watch. They had ten minutes before she had to be at her "interview." Luka may have had some work to do in his office but she didn't, nor did the idea of having him lead her around appeal to her. Now that she was inside the building, Natalie knew from yesterday's path through the stairwell a key card would not be necessary.

She stood and smoothed out the dress that fit her slender build well. The height difference between her and Elise made the skirt a hair shorter than she would have liked, but it was a good look for her and she was ready. Maybe.

Retracing her steps from the day before to the blue conference room, Natalie checked her watch again and saw she was still five minutes early, a perfectly acceptable amount of time. Nervously she smoothed the skirt again, running a hand over her hair just brushing her shoulders.

"This is as good as it gets." She muttered under her breath and knocked.

"Come in." Came the muffled reply.

Natalie entered and saw Whiting again sitting at the table flanked by the same two nameless individuals. She thought she saw him peer behind her, looking for Luka. The others showed no interest. Their notebooks sat open on the table the same as before.

"Welcome back Ms. Swenson. I hope you've come ready to show off your talents." He grinned broadly at her.

His efforts to be personable were disingenuous. She was suspicious of him, her father would have called him a snake oil peddler. Mr. Whiting was willing to say whatever he needed to in order to get people to sign on. Her guess was that after they belonged to The Company he got real. She had seen a small hint of it in the exchanges between he and Luka and presumed the same would go for her.

"Please, have a seat." He indicated the seats they had taken yesterday.

Natalie pulled out the chair and swept her skirt under her as she sat.

"We have some questions first."

Whiting pulled a file out of a bag at his feet, it was several chairs away across the long table but she would have recognized it anywhere. Ivy had sent her file from school and it had grown significantly larger over the past year.

Whiting again made no introductions, leaving Natalie to wonder at the identities of the two observers though they obviously outranked Whiting, apparent in his frequent sideways glances seeking approval.

He opened the file, flipping through pages until he reached a point he wanted to discuss. His familiarity with it brought back Natalie's ball of dread, landing it firmly in her stomach.

"Ms. Swenson, do you mind if I call you Natalie?" He folded his hands on the desk, leaning over the pages as he blinked innocuously at her.

Swallowing, she nodded once.

"Great." He leaned back, flipping again through the sheets, trying to appear lost in the file. However, she was watching closely and saw him flipping around then coming back to the same page he had opened to initially. Whiting cleared his throat and began. "So your talent showed itself when you were twelve?"

"Yes." She offered nothing more. She needed no prompting to know the less she shared, the better.

He caught her strategy and gave her a curious look. Wondering, she was sure, what Luka had done by way of coaching.

She forced her lips up into a serene expression she had seen Ivy give countless times. It worked to hide her real expression while still appearing pleasant. Natalie thought it a good defense for now.

"Has anyone else in your family ever shown signs of a talent similar to yours or otherwise?"

"No." Not that she had ever seen and she *had been* looking. However, she had been watching for mental illness, not psychic abilities, she assumed she would have noticed either one.

"Did you ever discuss what you could do with anyone? Parents, doctors, friends?"

Natalie was not going to open herself up. She'd done that once and the hurt still stung from it backfiring. "I discussed it only a few times with my psychiatrist and the school specialist."

Whiting turned his head to speak to the woman. "Dr. Spence was sent in when she started to show signs." He shifted back to Natalie now growing more uncomfortable, guessing at what he was going to say next. Nodding, Whiting informed her. "Spence is one of ours. We keep tabs on the school psychologists' reports nationwide. When we hear something interesting, we dispatch one of ours for further analysis." He glanced back down, tracing the page with a finger. "I see you've been on a number of medications, they switched you often and played with your doses almost constantly but you continued to have symptoms." He nodded his head approvingly at the man beside him.

Black Ichabod nodded his head as well mumbling, "She is very strong."

Natalie felt the breeze and knew he was "sensing" her. It was unwelcome. Natalie was glad to be sitting. The air was thin, she felt increasingly dizzy. Even sitting she wasn't sure she was safe from falling over. They had been involved in her life from the very start. They had been responsible for her "treatment," medicating the hell out of her her whole life. It was ridiculous not to feel like her entire world had been contrived from the start. She asked her own question, terrified the answer that would destroy her.

"Did my parents know?"

"No. We find it more convenient to keep our distance until we're more certain of the value of your abilities." He looked back down and frowned. "It appears Ivy paired you with Mr. Bailey almost immediately." Again the approving nod. "You were fortunate to have someone with a similar skill to work with Ms. Swenson. Yours is very rare and Mr. Bailey has astounding control for someone so young."

She fixed her serene expression back in place. "Yes, his control is admirable." What didn't they know about her? She hated that file. She felt her face growing hot as her blood heated.

Whiting smiled. "How fortunate indeed." He thought she was blushing at his mention of Luka but the cause was incorrect.

As if on cue, a hurried knock echoed on the door. Whiting didn't break his gaze from Natalie.

"Come in."

Chapter 32

Natalie knew without turning who was had entered. She felt him approach, her skin tingled at his nearness. Roughly she pushed off the relief she felt at his presence telling herself it was only because he had been her sole ally here.

"Not anymore" she told herself although it didn't ring true.

"I apologize for being late." His voice was tight in anger. "I thought I lost something."

Natalie imagined him searching the offices, upset to have lost track of her. She had proven to be uncontrollable, certainly that bothered him more than anything.

"That's fine Luka. Have a seat."

He took the seat beside her, keeping his hands to himself. She didn't want to admit it, but Natalie felt stronger with him here.

Whiting glanced between them, seeing she was sure, the distance new since yesterday. Natalie felt the breeze again and glanced over at the thin dark man. He flashed slightly yellowed teeth at her. The gesture surprised her.

Natalie was already off balance, Whiting's next question took her legs out from under her.

"Do you still inflict harm upon yourself or has that stopped with your teachings at Prestige?" His expression remained curious, the others were back to blank.

Natalie could feel her pulse pick up, sweat prickled her back and underarms. Some day she would get hold of that file and burn it. "No." She replied thickly. Her tongue felt heavy. She wished for a glass of water. Her hand rubbed at her sleeve.

"Sir, I have worked with Natalie intensively for nearly a year and I can personally vouch for the fact that she is stable. My reasons for saying otherwise were purely selfish."

Glancing sideways, Natalie saw he was staring straight ahead, his face blank. The tension she saw in his jaw the only sign he was upset.

She bristled at his defensiveness. "Mr. Whiting, if you have not seen it in the file already, I would like to point out the specialist noted when the 'habit' stopped. It stopped nearly three years ago."

The woman wrote something in her notepad and set down her pen. He fixed her eyes on Natalie and said calmly, "You're lying."

"Excuse me?" Natalie froze.

"You're lying," she repeated. "Please answer the question honestly." She stared unblinking at Natalie, her unnaturally smooth skin and dark eyes gave her a reptilian air.

Natalie stared at her for a long minute deciding how she knew Natalie was lying. She was correct. Although Natalie had made the agreement with her parents she had honored for the most part, she had found there to be times up to her senior year in high school when she fell off the wagon and dealt with her emotional pain the only way she knew how. The lizard woman was not to be messed with. "The last time was spring break my senior year." The admission was hard. It was one she had withheld from her doctors, her parents and even Luka. His hands twitched beneath the table. She could tell from the way Luka shifted in his seat he was hoping they wouldn't ask him about the subject, he might not be able to lie about knowing she had tried to the night she'd met Ericka at the party. Again, the twinge of guilt nagged at her conscience. She reminded herself that Luka had lied to her too.

Lizard woman made another note in her pad, disengaging herself from the interview for the time being.

Concern lining his forehead, Whiting took over. "I must tell you Natalie, there is some talk of you being mentally unsound. It happens often with your particular ability, which is why it is so rare to have an adult who can competently do the job we ask of them. That is also why we try to medicate enough to beat it back until we can work with you." He folded his hands over her file. "However, yours is a special case which is why we are willing to look at you now, see if you're ready. I get the impression that with your special treatment, your training has progressed more rapidly than most." He sought confirmation from Luka.

Luka nodded once, saying nothing.

"I think we're ready to see what you can do." He looked left and right receiving an affirmative nod from both parties. "We already know that you can read a mind through ten floors of concrete and steel but what I am more interested in is the attack

199

that I saw yesterday. Would you care to demonstrate that for our guests?" He motioned to the side of the table where there was a wide path between the chairs and the blue outside wall.

Without waiting to speak to her, Luka rose and walked around behind her, down the length of the table to stand nearly at the head of the table just out of the path of their audience.

Natalie's earlier doubts about hitting Luka returned. She sighted down the table and saw him standing alone, evenly on his feet with his hands by his sides and staring straight ahead. It reminded her of pictures of men facing a firing squad.

She started shaking her head. "I can't do it. I'm sorry."

"This isn't a request Ms. Swenson." Whiting's voice grew teeth. "You must give us a display of what makes you special and worth considering. Without that, I am sorry but you will be rejected for employment. I would assume Luka has informed you what that means?"

She continued shaking her head. Luka was glaring at her. When she had hit him before it had been an accident. This was different. It was on purpose and now she knew she would have to "show" him something when she opened up, she would reveal her motivation to him and that felt too revealing under the circumstances.

The dark skinned man spoke in his quiet way. "You are blocking him out. You must not do this if you are to succeed." He could sense when she was using her ability and not. She would have to ask Luka if this was the man who'd been in *his* meeting.

Luka stalked toward her. Natalie watched his body move, his temper evident in his taut muscles. She stood and drew herself up, throwing her shoulders back and daring him to make her submit. He did not stop walking until he was a mere matter of inches from her. She could feel the heat coming off of his body. His hands remained at his sides.

He lowered his head and spoke softly in her ear. The air moving past his lips tickled her ear, the hair on her arms rose not just from trepidation. "Natalie, you have to do this. You don't have a choice in the matter."

"I don't want to talk about it with you." She stared stubbornly at his chest. The thrum of his heart was moving his white shirt.

It was going fast. Letting her eyes roll up to catch sight of his face, Natalie saw him staring down at her, his creased forehead and tight mouth sending her a very clear message. Sighing, she reluctantly gave in.

Why do I need to do this? Why don't you just get up there and jump backward? You can pretend I hit you.

Do you think this is the first time they have done this? Everyone has to prove themselves and you've got them pretty excited. The guy can sense your strength and *when you're using your ability. Whiting can block people's abilities.* He hesitated and she felt his radiating anger. *And as you've learned, she can tell if you're lying. You have to do this.*

I don't want to hit you again. She repeated stubbornly.

Luka saw through her simplistic excuse. *If you need to be mad but don't want me to see anything, think of something less personal that pisses you off. I can help.*

She glanced up and saw that his tension had eased as he sensed she was giving in. *Did you have something in mind?*

"Please, it is rude to whisper amongst yourselves and we *are* waiting." Whiting was annoyed.

"Yes, sir." Luka backed away from Natalie before he turned around and made his way back. When he took up his position, this time he let his shoulders relax and he made direct eye contact. With a wink, he hit her with his image.

He was right. It pissed her off. Luka was able to picture her the night of the party, Ericka had just dumped the beer on her and Luka, although angry with Ericka for picking on her, had found it funny. Ericka had been thinking what a silly fool the sad little freshie was. She felt drunk on more than just alcohol. It was a bully's high.

Her wrath was near the surface to begin with and this image filled her up. Natalie let the ire swim through her and gave it free rein in her body. Her heart slammed in her chest, her breath came in ragged gasps and she could only see Luka. Standing right in front of her, taunting her with a humiliating memory. With a snarl, she let it go.

Luka was ready this time, he had known what was coming and had braced himself but there was nothing he could do to stop a psychic burst. His body flew backward and for a few long seconds, he lay very still.

As soon as the burst had left her body, Natalie's vision cleared and she felt drained. She also saw Luka lying flat on the ground, unmoving. Her feet were moving before she made the conscious decision to go to him. The three remained seated. All she could hear was the steady hum of their voices. They could be comparing staplers for all the excitement they showed.

It barely registered with her. All she could see was Luka and she ran to him, kneeling down beside him. At first she looked him over, surveying him for outward signs of damage. Seeing none, Natalie tentatively reached out a hand to touch his and gasped.

His skin had gone cool and clammy. Growing frantic, Natalie lowered her head to put an ear to his chest. The heartbeat she heard was much slower and weaker than the one she had grown to know as well as her own.

The memory of laying her head on his chest at night pushed aside her bruised ego and she placed a hand on his cheek, feeling for warmth there.

Luka, are you still with me?

She could hear a jumble of thoughts coming from him but they were jumping around so much she couldn't make sense of them. It was like he was having a seizure.

Luka please wake up. We did it. She glanced over at their huddle. The three wouldn't have noticed if she picked him up and walked out, which she would have done if she could have managed it. *Come on, get up. Please Luka.*

Still seizing, his mind was running too fast for her to hear. What she could get from him were racing images. Paying close attention, she tried to make sense of what he was thinking from what she could see. She caught a flash of a young female version of Luka that must have been his sister, and Natalie that night on the hill when he had lay with her by the fire. A tall man, older with salt and pepper wavy hair, Luka's nose and eyes lay in a casket. Luka was thinking of loss.

It hit her. When she had blasted him, she had sent some of her feelings of anger from last night, how enraged she'd been when she'd been ready to walk out. Unintentionally, Natalie had sent him a message of her own. He thought she was leaving him. As soon as she was confronted with that thought as reality, she regretted even thinking it. He hadn't been intending to be cruel, he was terrified he wouldn't be able to protect her. That he would lose her too.

I'm not going anywhere. Wake up and we can talk about it. Luka please. Rising up on her knees, Natalie leaned in regardless of who might be watching. Gently, she pressed her lips to his. *Luka please come back to me. I love you.*

His mind flashed on her face just as she hit him and Natalie gasped in shock. Her unnaturally pale face and cold black eyes were straight out of a nightmare.

Nat. His hand turned to clasp hers where hers had now fallen loose. *It's okay. You did it. Good job. They're impressed.*

A shaky sigh of relief bubbled up, mixing with a laugh. Natalie turned to the three and spoke without caring if she was out of line. She had just bought herself some small amount of credit with them and she was going to use it.

"Can we go please? I'd like to take Luka to lie down in his office."

Whiting gave her an irritated glance before waving her away. She took that as a yes.

"Sit up Luka. Can you walk?"

Bright, beautiful green eyes opened and blinked slowly at her. Natalie's deep brown eyes were full as she smiled tearfully down at him. Together they got him up and onto his feet. Whiting called out as Natalie opened the door, Luka's arm around her shoulders, her arm across his back for stability.

"Take the day after he gets his wits about him but I want you back here at nine sharp. We have a lot to do before the weekend." He flashed a quick smile.

"Yes, sir." She whipped the door open, not bothering to close it behind them, making their way as quickly as possible to the elevator.

Chapter 33

Once he was up and walking, Luka came around quickly. In only a few minutes he was sitting in his chair rubbing his temples and looking pained.

"Could you reach in there and grab a bottle of water for me? Please?" He pointed to the long low cabinet that stretched from one wall to the other forming another work surface behind his desk.

Natalie opened the cabinet where he had pointed and found a case of bottled water. She took two, cracking one and handing it to him before opening hers. Natalie leaned against the edge of his desk, facing the chair next to his.

Her phone rang, its sudden vibration making her jump. Natalie looked at the display and groaned.

"Who is it?"

"My mother."

"You don't want to talk to her?"

She rolled her eyes. "I haven't talked to her since before your mother called me. I've been dodging messages since." When he looked like he wanted to chastise her, she quickly cut him off. "I wasn't in the most conversational mood."

That halted any further comments. Luka frowned and fiddled with a button on his shirt. Natalie felt bad for bringing it up again. She had thrown it in his face just as she had believed he'd thrown her secret in her face. Point taken. Natalie promised herself and Luka she would move on.

Natalie took a deep breath and pressed the button to take her mother's call. As she suspected, she was not happy.

Valerie Swenson was nearly explosive by the time her daughter answered. "Natalie Marie, where have you been? I've been trying to reach you for almost a month! I was getting ready to call the police." Her voice was shrill and worried.

"Sorry Mom. Summer courses are really short and I was always studying and then it was time for finals. I was going to call you, promise." She stopped herself making up any further stories. Luka was staring at her. "I was going to call you soon Mom." She left it simple and true.

204

Having made her point, Valerie began to calm down. She sighed and changed the subject. "Well, why don't you tell me what you've been doing the last few weeks when you weren't talking to your mother? Were your summer classes hard?"

She could tell her mother had forgotten the names of the classes but remembered that she had taken more than one. She had to give her mother credit. Valerie listened very well and always got the gist of things even if she didn't remember every specific detail.

Talking about school was good. It was uncomplicated and normal. Two things Natalie really wanted more of in her world but chances of that were looking less and less likely. "They weren't all that tough. I had a Philosophy class that was pretty cool and English Composition so there was a lot of writing."

"No wonder you were busy, they both sound like a lot of work. How is Avery? Still with that boy?"

Natalie smiled at Jason being called "that boy." "Yes, Mom. Avery is still with Jason. They're inseparable. It's hard to get her alone these days, but she's happy."

The heavy pause on the other end was one Natalie had fought hard for though now she found almost sad. Her mother had so many things she wanted to ask, all things Natalie used to hear in her head and had discouraged, often rudely, so many times Valerie no longer asked. Things like friends were only recently okay to discuss after Natalie offered up Avery for discussion. Avery had even spoken to Valerie a few times when she'd been around during calls.

"Why don't you tell her?" Luka regarded her, his expression serious. "I think it's safe, don't you?" He'd been able to hear the other side of the conversation. Natalie flicked her thumb to turn down the volume. Luka grinned.

Why not? She thought. It would be kind of fun to give her mother something to make her believe her daughter was becoming more normal. "Mom, um, I've met someone." She stumbled over the foreign words.

Valerie was silent for a long time.

"Are you okay Mom? Breathe." She kidded nervously.

"Uh, that's great honey." Valerie's response was slow and deliberate. She obviously felt it necessary to tiptoe around Natalie.

Putting a hand over the mouthpiece, Natalie told Luka. "I'm a menace. My own mother is afraid to talk to me."

He rested a hand comfortingly on her arm. "Then show her the new you."

Taking a deep breath again, Natalie rolled her shoulders back and tried to start undoing years of damage. She opened up. "His name's Luka and we started dating this spring." She left out that she had thought he was dead for most of that time. "You'd like him. He was one of my tutors since last fall. That's how we met." The words rolled off easily once she'd begun. Natalie hadn't realized how much she'd wanted to tell her mother about her life and now she had something she *could* tell her. It felt good.

"Is he nice to you? She asked cautiously. "Does he understand...?" She let her voice trail off.

Natalie tipped her head, thinking hard about that question. He had been nothing less than a gentleman to her, he had saved her life when she'd been hurt and alone and he had only caused her pain out of a misguided defensiveness.

"Yeah Mom. He's nice." Natalie felt her cheeks grow red. "And yes, he understands."

***

The next fifteen minutes, while Luka got his sea legs back, were spent on very new ground for mother and daughter. Valerie let Natalie steer most of the conversation and she in turn offered up some information on Luka that she didn't mind sharing with him sitting four feet away from her, able to hear every word. Natalie had only blushed when her mother asked if he was cute. Luka had sat back and smiled, shrugging an "of course." Cocky, but charmingly so.

Promising to call soon, Natalie slid the phone back into her front pocket. "That was kind of cool. I like talking to her so much more over the phone. It's less complicated."

He furrowed his brow thoughtfully at her. "You haven't been home since we've started working together have you?"

"You know I haven't. Tickets are expensive and I don't have a car. Besides, I really haven't wanted to go." She admitted somewhat shyly now on the heels of such a positive conversation with her mother. "Maybe I will soon." She could find the money if she needed to and now she was going to have a paying job. Though how she was going to explain that to her mother was beyond her. "Are you ready to go?" Temporarily closing the door on the subject.

"I think I can get out of here without drawing too much attention to myself." He pushed off the arms of the chair and stood, wavering only slightly.

They made it only as far as the elevator when Whiting's voice could be heard above the smooth mechanical gliding noise coming from inside the elevator shaft. It would be at their floor soon.

"Hey, nice job you two." He smiled proudly. Natalie wanted to slap him.

Luka turned to face him, expression fixed. "Thank you sir. We're heading out now. Is there anything you need before tomorrow?" Very politely, very definitely, Luka worked to establish a boundary with Whiting.

"I came up to check that you were coming back alright." He gave Luka an appraising once over. "And I wanted to make sure Natalie wasn't suffering any ill effects herself." He added cheerfully.

Natalie was confused. "How could that have hurt me?"

"Rebound of course." Whiting informed her without changing his mood. "Sometimes, when people are attacked, they hit back." He searched both their faces for evidence of damage.

Neither intended to give him anything.

"No, sir." Natalie made her voice as calm as she could manage.

He eyed her for a moment, not quite willing to believe her. "Okay." Whiting snapped back to Luka with a tight smile. "Bright and early tomorrow, you have work to get back to Luka. And Natalie, you begin your training."

In the car with Natalie at the wheel, they felt free to speak openly.

"Do you mean I could have been hurt too?" The thought had never crossed Natalie's mind.

He kept his focus on the passing landscape, she glanced over at him several times.

"Luka. Did you know that?"

"Yes."

"Then why did you insist I do it?"

"You had to. Whiting would have counted you a liability and gotten rid of you. It's happened before. Remember those rumors about him being popular with the young interns? They didn't leave because of failed romances. They were sent back to avoid suspicion and then all met with various 'accidents.'"

She felt her body go cold.

Luka read her silence correctly. "You're right to be worried. This is not a group to underestimate. That's why I wanted to keep you far away from them." He offered her a sincere look. "Now that you're here, I'm going to do everything I can to protect you."

"I don't need protecting Luka." Natalie bristled. "Is that why you wanted to be the one to take the hit? To protect me from some sort of blowback? What if I'd lost control? Would you let me give you brain damage?" The idea that he would sacrifice himself for her did not sit well. How could he be so careless with himself?

He turned to face her, a glance told her how unpopular that idea was. "You pack a hell of a wallop but I knew you wouldn't do that to me. You're not like that." He shifted to face forward again. "My guess is the more you work with it, the more powerful you'll get *and* the more control you'll have."

"You almost sound jealous." She baited him, watching him from the corner of her eye.

Luka tipped his head and nodded in agreement. "A little bit. It would be handy to be able to scramble someone's brain like that." His features went grim. "My bigger concern is the look on Whiting's face when he looks at you now. He's too eager for my taste. I don't like it."

Chapter 34

No one was home when they arrived at the Van Slyke home, which was good. Luka was still a little groggy.

"Are you hungry?" He headed straight for the kitchen.

"Um." She thought about it. It was about eleven o'clock. Not quite lunch yet her stomach growled at mention of food. "A little."

Luka opened the fridge and dug around emerging with the makings for cold meat sandwiches and an apple to share. He laid it all out on the long black granite countertop covering the elegant cherry cabinets. In keeping with the rest of the home's design, it was traditional design, new, and very nice.

"Do you know anyone who *isn't* rich?" Natalie asked, taking it all in and feeling incredibly inferior.

His hands stopped on the bread wrapper. "It isn't a crime to come from money. And yes, as a matter of fact, I do know people who aren't rich. It doesn't matter to me if you have money or not." Shrugging, he went to the sink to wash his hands. "What about you? Does it matter to you if people have money?"

She pulled up a black leather barstool and sat down to talk over the long, dark surface at him. "I think it's a lot easier to say you don't care about money when you have it."

Luka was drying his hands on a dishtowel and laid it down at her comment. "Natalie, do you think so little of me that you really believe that?"

"Well," she squirmed uncomfortably seeing the offense in her remark. "I do think it's easier when you have it." She put her head down and revealed some of her insecurities, borne of equal parts small town and blue collar parents. "When you come from this," she raised her hands to indicate the finely appointed house, "it's easy to be comfortable in 'nice' and benevolent in 'not so nice' knowing you're only visiting. When you come from the shallow end of the economic pool it can be hard to see people with all of this. Who needs so much? I have a hard time being here because it reminds me of what I come from." She shook her head, "And it isn't this."

"Is it bad to remember where you come from? Do you think just because you come from a certain place you have to go back there if you don't want to?"

Natalie shrugged.

Luka pushed, walking around the counter to stand next to her. "No really. What did you think was going to happen after college? Were you going to back home and work at the Dairy Queen for minimum wage?"

"Don't make fun." She defended some of the people she knew had gone from high school to do exactly that. "Not everyone can afford college. If it weren't for the scholarship I'm guessing came from Whiting, I'd be doing that very thing."

"I'm not making fun." He shook his head. "That might be a choice for some people but *you* chose to go to college. However the funding came through. That changes things. It changes you and what you know is out there. It changes how people see you and how you see yourself." Luka put a hand on her back, his palm circled, massaging over her hips. "Did you see yourself going back home after school? When you still had a choice that is?" His voice tightened in frustration.

She leaned back into his hand. The comfort of his touch softened the blow, knowing her future was set now. Oddly, danger aside, it was calming. "I honestly thought I was going to wash out after the first semester. Then I met Ivy and you and everything changed." Natalie peeked up into his warm gaze, liking what she saw there. "I haven't considered my future really, not since then."

"Why not?" His brows knitted together.

Natalie shifted. "I don't want to say."

Smelling he was onto something, Luka wrapped his arm around her back and pulled her up against his chest. "Tell me," he prompted, kissing the tip of her nose.

She turned to put her arms around his neck and pulled him in for a kiss.

Drawing his head up, Luka smiled knowingly at her. "Thought you could distract me did you? Well, I'm not that easy."

Natalie leaned in close, determined. Luka slid his hands down to hers, tightening his grip on them. Trapped, Natalie tried another tactic and draped her hands on both sides of his neck, one finger and thumb rubbed his earlobe gently. Experience had taught her that weakness.

"Nat, I'm serious. Why didn't you think about your future? Were you going to do something?" His face paled.

She watched him glance sideways at the forearm resting just under his nose. Of course he would think of that. If she had wanted to kill herself, she would have done it before the long car ride with her parents from Minnesota to California. The real reason was far more tame if not mortifying to expose.

"You can't laugh." She said severely, acknowledging defeat.

Luka held up a finger and crossed his heart.

"It was you. When I met you I might have developed a small crush. It got me through some difficult times in the beginning when I was trying to get my legs under me. Then, later," she refrained from telling him it was after she realized she loved him, "I wanted to be like you. I wanted to be as controlled as you were. You seemed to have it all figured out. I wanted that. I figured until I had that I couldn't really consider anything."

Again he kissed her nose, then her lips. "And now that you know me better do you still think I've got it sorted out?" He halfway teased. "Or have you seen me for the fraud I am?"

"I think you had it all figured out before you came here, but now that you're no longer in control your confidence is shaken. You and I have traded places because I do way better when someone takes my control from me. Now I can just put my head down and go. As long as I don't have a huge problem with the decisions, I find it kind of liberating." She wiggled her brows at him.

Luka stared at her in disbelief. "I don't think I've ever her myself summed up so neatly before. That was pretty impressive." Hands now forgotten slid from her hips to fall to her thighs.

"Sorry." She frowned, fearing she had overstepped. When had they gotten so serious?

He remembered himself and gave her arms a reassuring rub before going back to his sandwich preparation.

Natalie was standing next to her barstool, fidgeting with a napkin. She'd taken it from a ceramic chicken napkin holder. It was just the right amount of properly placed kitsch to give the model kitchen a "lived in" look.

Luka finally spoke up as he put the apple on a cutting board. "Here I thought lying was what I had to worry about. Turns out you use that as a cover. You're actually incredibly astute. Whiting had it right, you are quite a an asset." He saluted with the knife in his hand. A paring knife.

"I didn't mean to offend you. I'm sorry Luka." The knife's efficient slicing brought a picture to mind and she found it hard to concentrate. Their talk of control and the emotional drain of the day had her a little fatigued. Having had it recently been brought to the forefront of her mind, her memories went back to another time. Back when a knife much like that one, kept in her room to avoid detection, used to be her only tie to sanity. The sense of release she would get when it would lay open her skin, allowing the blood to run. The reassurance of knowing at least her body was the same as everyone else's. Same blood, same flesh. It was as controlling an addiction as an alcoholic's craving for a drink, never far from her conscious thoughts. As much as she knew it was wrong, she had been unable to stop herself when the blade had gone a little too deep...

"Stop!" Luka had put the knife down, his hands braced on either side of the white plastic board, the apple only partially sliced.

Natalie panicked. Entranced as she was by the knife's rhythmic motion she hadn't noticed its hypnotic effect on her. She hadn't felt her defenses coming down. His reaction meant Luka's had been down as well and he'd not only heard her ruminations, he had gotten a clear feel for what she'd felt. Knew how deeply her addiction had run. How close she had nearly come.

"Please." His voice was shaky. "Is that," he cleared his throat, trying to sound stronger than he felt. "Is that how it felt to do it? Is that why *you* did it?"

She knew he couldn't ask the bigger question in his mind. "I don't know if she did it for the same reasons as I did, but yes, it did make it seem bearable. Like if I did it I was real. It wasn't just a nightmare I kept reliving day after day."

He pushed himself away and staggered to the table, pulling out a leather side chair and collapsing upon it.

Without a word, Natalie finished preparing their lunch. Tentatively she tested if she could hear him, he was closed up again. She made sure to do the same, it was safest for now.

Carrying their plates to the table, she set his down in front of him and laid a hand on his shoulder. "I'm not thinking of doing it again. It was the knife. It just made me remember, that's all."

"I know it was only the memory. It was so strange to think not only was I feeling you but what it was like to be her too. I mean to be inside *those* thoughts. Andjela hadn't had them much after I hit puberty and started to hear things. She was leaving for college when I was just starting to figure things out, you know. It hit me when I was twelve, we had a year to talk about it, and then she went off to school. She shot herself two years later. She was better at helping me than she was at helping herself I guess. I was lucky, I never felt bad about what I had. She taught me it was okay."

"Wait, you never actually heard her thinking those kinds of thoughts before she left? You never heard them once?" Andjela had gotten beyond the confusion and self-hatred before she'd left and yet she'd killed herself two years later? That didn't sound right. After all, once Natalie had come to understand what she was hearing, it hadn't been too difficult to justify her separate realities into a cohesive one.

And there was one big discrepancy she hadn't considered before. Luka. He was an in house lie detector and Andjela had passed. Even if he'd been too young to understand what she was thinking or not caught on at the time, certainly he would have recognized those thoughts looking back now. Wouldn't he? And why would Andjela all of a sudden use a gun when she'd always been a cutter?

Luka was staring at her, the discrepancies not dawning on him. He was too emotionally involved and to reopen that wound was more than she was willing to ask based solely on a feeling. "I was fifteen when she died. I didn't really look into it myself. The school psychologist called, said she had killed herself and, with her history, no one questioned it. I don't think anyone could have handled going into some sort of long drawn out explanation of exactly what had brought her back to that place." His focus shifted inward. "We were all too busy blaming ourselves I guess."

Natalie had an idea except she was afraid to voice it. It wouldn't be fair to plant the seed in Luka's mind. She could see she was already losing him to the guilt again as it bubbled to the surface. *That* guilt ruled a large part of Luka's mind still.

Natalie made a secret promise to him that she would do her own investigating. She would see if she could find out what had happened five years ago to his sister, because she was not entirely certain it was suicide. Their family might be too troubled to look into it, but she wasn't. Luka had given her back her life. The least she could do was return the favor.

Chapter 35

The side door off the kitchen opened and in walked Bill Van Slyke. Tall and big shouldered, he could have been a linebacker if it weren't for the extra fifty pounds or so he carried around the middle marking him an armchair quarterback at best. His dark suit had to be tailored to fit shoulders that big and not hang anywhere else. His shirt collar had been pulled loose, his dark striped tie sat cocked at an angle, giving him a harried look.

"Hey Luk." He said it like the American version. Bill's voice was loud and boisterous, instead of being irritating, Natalie found herself smiling unconsciously at his exuberance. Bill ran a large hand, big enough to palm a basketball, over his chin then mussed his brown hair already graying at the temples. He took in the scene with large eyes an unusual shade, closer to amber than brown that danced mischievously hinting at a sharp mind and quick wit. Natalie liked him automatically.

Luka shrugged off his funk and pushed away his sandwich to turn and face the door. His face lifted into a near smile. "Hi Bill. How was Los Angeles?"

Bill shrugged, "Ah, typical. *He* wants to keep the business he's built with his own two hands and chose over his family, *she* wants him to sell it all and then some to pay her everything she's 'due,'" he used air quotes and rolled his eyes. "Of course they both say they have nothing but the kids' best interests at heart." He shook his head. "A few more years and I'm retiring early to learn carpentry. I'm going to build my own great big bookcase, put all of my case files on it and then set fire to it." He laughed at himself.

Grinning, Luka pointed out, "Natalie's dad works at a cabinet shop, maybe he could help."

Natalie felt her smile freeze in place at the sudden attention and mention of her family. She chuckled with them nervously.

Turning his eyes toward her, Bill raised his brows in interest. "Really? Do you think he could teach me to do something honest with these?" He held out his hands, bigger now that she was really looking at them.

The initial fear that the incredibly wealthy divorce attorney would find her hardworking and skilled father unworthy seemed silly now that she was here with him and sharing a laugh. Natalie felt herself thawing, warming even to the idea of the two meeting.

"Yes, sir, I think he could teach you a thing or two."

Bill waved a big hand, "Don't call me anything but Bill. Good to meet you by the way." He stuck the long fingered hand back at her and Natalie took it, watching it engulf her own. Bill was respectful of his power, though he was still firm. It was a handshake a man would say, "You could trust." "Are you going to be here for dinner? Elise called and said she was grabbing some fish for me to grill." He did his best to look exasperated, "I no sooner touch down and the woman's got me working. Never a moment's rest."

Natalie looked askance of Luka. This was his domain, his decision.

He could see she was comfortable here with Bill, and Elise had been more than kind this morning. "Sure Bill. I was thinking we should do some running around before that, when should we be back?"

"Six or so sounds about right." He ran his hand through his hair, leaving it tousled with a big chunk standing straight up in back. "You two have fun, I'm long overdue for some barefoot time and a cocktail."

Bill walked past them with a lofty step that belied his bulk, his garment bag rolling along behind him.

"What running around did you have in mind?" Natalie took advantage of the break Bill's entrance had provided and changed the subject.

He pointed at her dress, "I was thinking we should probably do something about your supplies. Maybe get some things to last you until we can get back to your dorm to get your stuff."

Natalie sat down. "I hadn't thought about that. I suppose I'm going to have to move. What about school?" She asked more of herself than Luka. "What am I going to tell my parents?"

"Exactly what I'm saying about this all getting so complicated. We have to make something up, something that can cover it all and not be so tricky we lose track of it." He ran a finger along the outside of his plate, wiping up a drip of mustard and sucking it off his finger. "The more general the better I'm thinking. I'm not sure Whiting's plans for Avery and Jason, they're probably on his radar already if they're at Prestige. Most people there are, I guess." He frowned. "It will depend, I suppose, on their next few years. Whiting was probably okay with me telling me what I did because they're going to find out soon enough. We might have even sped up their timeline."

Avery and Jason at Optimax? She hadn't considered it before and her mouth went dry at the prospect. Shrugging it off, she found the idea of either of the two with strong abilities ludicrous.

Luka's continued dogged denial that he had only ever lied to cover his telepathy made her roll her eyes, but this was admittedly her forte and even though she knew he wouldn't ask her, she knew *she* had to come up with the story.

"Let me think about it for a little while. I can probably come up with something easy to remember."

Luka's concerned expression told her he knew she meant him. Sadly, he believed for good reason she could carry it off.

Without commenting on how he was going against his own personal philosophy having to live a lie, Luka nodded at her statement of fact. "I leave it to you."

"Thanks." She smiled tightly.

Chapter 36

They ran to a local supercenter that sold food, clothing, toiletries, you name it. Natalie bit her lip when she rang up her purchases and put it on her credit card, knowing she had nearly maxed it out. Hopefully she would get paid before the bill came due. Her parents would not be happy to see her charging up the card for a non-emergency. Luka offered to kick in, saying it was his fault she was here but she declined. She had made the decision to come here and the repercussions were hers to deal with.

Dinner was served a little after seven with a cocktail hour beforehand. No one made any comments on the fact that Natalie was under the legal age. Luka was only barely legal and they knew she was younger than him.

Afterward when they were sitting around at the outdoor table, uncleared from dinner, Bill brought up an uncomfortable subject.

"So Natalie, if you are going to be staying on at Optimax, where will you be living?" He took a long pull of his scotch.

"Um," she was caught off guard. It was something she was wondering too, although until she discussed her financial compensation with Whiting, she had no idea what she could afford. Or if she would be living alone. She had toyed with the idea of talking to Luka about that in a few months, but it appeared Bill was going to help her out there in his own bold fashion. Testing, she lowered her guard to see if he might have something to say about it before Bill brought it out in front of everyone. She popped a cherry tomato in her mouth that had been sitting on the edge of her plate.

I've been meaning to ask you about this. It's kind of early but we would have eventually gotten to this point anyway. What do you think of getting a place together? We might as well give it a try, don't you think?

She could hear how anxious he was in his tone. Sneaking a peek under her lashes at him, she could see him twisting his napkin in his lap. *Are you sure? If you're nervous maybe we shouldn't do it yet.*

The napkin wringing stopped. *We know more about each other than most couples who've been together for years and before I left school we were just about living together anyway.*

Natalie was done chewing and gave her answer out loud for everyone. "Actually, Luka and I have been talking about that and we think it might work for us to get a place together." She let her eyes track back and forth between the two of them, searching for signs of disapproval.

Elise was rubbing at the sweat on her glass, sitting nestled in the napkin formed to it to catch any condensation before it might drip on her. "I think," she said slowly, staring at her glass, hazel eyes fixed. "It's a lot of change to take on all at once. Are you sure you're up to it?"

Natalie wished Elise hadn't seen them fighting their first night here. That probably didn't help. She held her chin up and defended her decision. "There's no way to know unless we try."

Elise broke her gaze from her glass and regarded her steadily.

Bill was slow in his own deliberations, staring across his cut crystal lowball at them both. Natalie was growing more uncomfortable under his scrutiny, shifting in her seat. She wasn't breathing at all when he finally spoke.

Nodding to himself, he said, "I think I have a good solution that can get you two a few months' trial period without a lease should things go poorly. Not that they would." He held out a reassuring hand. "My firm has an apartment between here and town we usually kept for a consultant. She's out on maternity leave and the apartment is empty. If you would be agreeable, I could get it for you until she comes back. Should be a few months at least. She's a consultant, like I said. She might not be back for a while." He pulled at his drink again, eyeing them over the rim.

"That's very kind of you Bill." Luka fidgeted with his napkin. "But as interns I don't know as that is in our budget. I'd imagine it's a pretty nice place."

"Bah, don't worry about it. Keep it clean and we'll count it even." Bill waved off Luka's concerns. "If you don't take it, I have to find someone else. We have a contract that clearly states the unit must be rented out eighty percent of the time to be a justified expense for tax purposes. You would be doing us a favor." He lobbied convincingly.

Natalie was fairly certain Bill was full of it. They weren't clients of the firm so it shouldn't matter whether they stayed there or not but he seemed determined and she had to admit that something non-binding and cheap fit their needs right now. Neither one of them had any idea what the future held for them so a lease could be a problem and, for Natalie at least, rent could be a big problem. There were so many unknowns.

Are you comfortable with this?

It's only temporary and we don't want to get into a lease we can't get out of if Whiting has relocation in mind.

Yes, that bothers me too. I guess we do this then.

If you don't want to do this then why did you ask?

I do want to do this. I just don't want to be in bed on a Saturday morning and have some out of town attorney come in to crash in the corporate apartment.

Oh, I never thought of that.

Luka rubbed the back of his neck. "Bill, that sounds like it's just what we need but we don't want to get in the way of someone else's plans. I mean, does anyone else have access to it for impromptu overnights and what not?"

"No, no. There are only two sets of keys and I have them both. Nobody's going to come barging in on you if that's what you're worried about." He grinned at them both. "You'll have privacy."

Natalie glanced over at Luka. *Can he hear us?*

No but he's been a divorce attorney for thirty years. He can read people better than me, I would bet. He gave a short laugh.

Bill continued to eye them, his glass hanging near his face partially obscured Natalie's view of his features. All she could see were his eyes, focused entirely too intently on her. "Are you two doing it?"

"Bill!" Elise's head whipped up from where she'd been watching her ice melt hypnotically.

Luka and Natalie stopped "talking" in shock, Luka replied before she could find her tongue. "That is an asinine question Bill."

Undaunted, Bill threw his head back and howled in laughter. "I wasn't asking about your sex life." He choked out, wiping at his eyes. "I was asking about your head thing." He pointed a finger back and forth between them.

"Oh." Luka swallowed his righteous indignation. "Um, yeah." It was surreal to have their ability brought up in casual conversation. Natalie found herself wishing Bill *had* been asking about their sex life. "Sorry." She cringed to think how they saw her. It seemed every time she turned around she was making a bad impression. Now she was rudely talking to Luka under their noses and they knew about it. She kept forgetting that.

Elise lay an icy hand, cold from holding her drink, over Natalie's sweating one and smiled warmly. "There's no need to apologize. Luka's told us about your special connection and in a way I envy it, though I don't know as I would trust *Bill* in *my* head." She twisted her lips wryly at his feigned offense then continued speaking genuinely to Natalie. "I hope you don't mind that we've spoken freely of you, but Luka is like a son to us and when we saw how upset he was, we had to do something. I asked and it all sort of spilled out. He didn't think he was giving away any secrets."

Natalie looked over at Luka who was squirming in his seat. She didn't want to think about the time Elise was referencing, though it did bring her some morbid pleasure that he had suffered through his fake death. She was sure it wasn't as much as she had.

Don't be so sure.

She startled, unable to keep her eyes from finding his. *I'm out of practice. I'd forgotten how intrusive you could be.* She glared jokingly.

Luka grinned at her, his hand moved to muss the hair that used to be so unruly. It was so short now it fell immediately back into place.

"Thank you Elise. I'm glad Luka has you and that you're right here when the rest of his family is so far away." She refrained from saying his "real mother" for fear of offending Elise and could tell by her expression the gesture was noticed and appreciated.

221

"I wanted to extend the same offer to you Natalie. I'm sure we're going to be seeing quite a bit of you from now on." Her gaze wandered over to Luka who smiled affirmatively. "It seems we know more about your 'gifts' than your own family and are maybe a bit more understanding of what life can be like for you. I would like to offer an ear to you should you need one, or a stand in for motherly advice while you're away from home." She gave her hand a little squeeze before returning it to her glass, leaving Natalie's feeling strangely lonely.

The simple gesture moved her and Natalie took a few moments to downplay its effect. "That is very kind of you both. I don't know what to say. You've been so welcoming, and understanding." She wished she could offer something in return but could think of nothing she could give them.

They don't want anything. They're just really nice people and they like to help.

"He's right. We don't expect you to do anything in return." Bill set down his glass.

"I thought they couldn't…" Natalie stuttered, trading glances with Luka.

"Don't worry, I can't hear anything you're saying but I don't have to. You've got a very expressive face Natalie. You should never play poker." Bill joked. "My wife is offering to help out of the kindness of her heart, nothing more. It would be an insult for you to try to offer something back." His hand rolled tenderly over Elise's shoulder. "We never had our own children so I think having Luk here has given us a taste of what we missed."

It was Elise's turn to squirm.

Bill slapped the arms of his chair and stood, pushing it back. "What do you say we go take a look at that apartment? If you two like it, you can stay there tonight. Maybe have some privacy from us old folks."

All were in agreement and after they finished their drinks they took two cars loaded up with Natalie's purchases as well as a bag for Luka. The apartment was not far away. It was less than twenty minutes and only a hop and a skip from work for them both.

"This is a perfect location." Natalie said, shutting her door and walking to the front of the car to wait for Bill and Elise still in their Mercedes convertible.

Unanswering, Luka swiveled his head to take in the buildings.

The apartment complex was in actuality closer to a small cluster of villas in the Spanish style positioned around a central courtyard complete with a fountain and tiled walks. Natalie loved it the second she laid eyes on it.

Bill and Elise walked up the path, joining them at the rod iron gates connecting the stucco walls surrounding the villas. Bill jiggled the keys dramatically before inserting them in the gate and swinging it open, motioning them through.

Their apartment was the second on the left out of a total of six, three on either side of the fountain. Bill led them through, Natalie held Luka's hand to let her eyes roam the picturesque little setting without having to navigate. The fountain was gurgling softly, the tiles swept free of leaf litter from the tall tropical plants hanging above and other exotic bushes that filled in the tan stucco canvas the walls provided.

Each unit's door was two steps up from the walk and its number marked by Spanish tiles. To the side of the blue front door marking their unit was a side window covered with a gauzy linen drapery. Bill opened the heavy wooden door and stepped aside allowing Luka and Natalie first entrance.

Natalie gasped upon entry, Luka squeezed her hand. The unit's golden hardwood floors were gleaming in the glow of the moon's first light. Luka flipped the switch and the room came to life.

The great room was large enough for the black wooden dining table and matched chairs without making it feel crowded. Over a half wall was a large kitchen outfitted with a mixture of black and stainless appliances. The countertops were a deep blue tile Natalie had come to appreciate as part of California heritage and matched the blue rugs and towels someone had used to soften the room.

Letting go of Luka, Natalie explored down the hall to her left and saw a reasonable bathroom with a tub and shower on her left and a small bedroom to her right. It was a little larger than Luka's back at the college and this queen size bed fit while still

223

allowing both sides to have mission style nightstands that matched the long, low dresser at the foot of the bed. A large picture window let in light from the side yard over the left side of the bed.

"What do you think?" Luka asked from the doorway. He was twisting and swiveling, assessing everything about the place.

"I like it." She toned down her reaction so as not to overwhelm him.

His head came around. "Me too." He smiled at her.

They went out to tell Bill they would take it and were rewarded with a back slap for Luka and arm squeeze for Natalie. Bill was far more comfortable with himself than her father. Natalie liked it. She felt bad for her dad that he wasn't able to express himself the way Bill did. Maybe some time with the big man would let some of that rub off on her dad. It could be arranged if Bill was serious about that hobby.

Keys in hand, Luka and Natalie bid good night to their benefactors promising to have them over for dinner the next week after they'd settled in. Their lodging was secure for the night and Luka and Natalie plopped down on the couch to watch tv intertwined, and promptly fell asleep, only to awaken and move to their bedroom for the duration.

Chapter 37

When they made their entrance to Optimax Friday morning, the lobby was less crowded than it had been the past two days. *A lot of people take Friday's off in the summer.* He answered her mental query. *Button it up.* He reminded her.

Natalie gave him a tight lipped nod in reply and did as she was told. She'd grown lax being with him so much. That would not do here.

Jonathan was on duty at the front desk and smiled in recognition at their approach. Luka veered left toward the elevators but he called out, "Ms. Swenson" and they both stopped. Jonathan was holding out an unmarked key card for her. Walking slowly back, Natalie took it from him.

"Thanks Jonathan."

"Welcome to Optimax" he gave her a toothy smile. The epitome of sunshine, Natalie couldn't help smiling back, even if he was a bit overzealous.

Together they made their way to Luka's office, Whiting called out as they walked past. "Do you have a minute?"

Exchanging a glance, Luka gave Natalie's arm a quick stroke with the back of his hand before moving away from her, creating a more professional distance. When they both stood in front of his large, dark wooden desk, Whiting spun his chair to face them, hands steepled with his thumbs resting on his chin.

They waited politely, allowing the senior man control of the room. After an eternity, Whiting lowered his hands to his lap and looked to Luka first.

"Luka, they're waiting for you in the lower rooms. After we're done here I'd like you to head down. Natalie, you'll be down there as well until your instructors say you're ready. Even then, we encourage all of our employees to make use of the facilities as often as they need to stay in tip top condition. I would assume Luka has filled you in on some of our little secrets?" He winked conspiratorially.

Whiting made her feel unclean. Hiding her distaste for him, she merely said, "Yes."

"Then you'll be pleased to know you will be starting out in the lower facilities as well. Getting your hands dirty from day one. Now put your things in your offices and Luka will show you around."

At Natalie's look of confusion, Whiting pointed out his door. "You're across the hall from Luka. I took the liberty of having some things sent up for you."

Returning his attention abruptly back to his computer, Whiting dismissed them in not so many words. Natalie crossed over to the aforementioned office and saw that indeed, where there had been nothing but an empty desk the night before, now sat a computer and pile of office supplies on top waiting to be organized however she saw fit.

Granted, Optimax was a cover for a secret agency that had been manipulating her life since junior high, but still, this was her first job and her first office and she felt a swelling of pride in her breast.

Luka came in behind her and slid an arm around her waist. "They move fast, don't they? Ready for your tour?"

Whiting hollered, "Luka."

He held up a finger that he would be a minute and backed out of the room. While he was gone, Natalie sat down in her chair and spun it in a quick 360. The cabinets behind her desk were expansive; she wondered what they were for. In the center was a wide section with bypass doors and on either end were large swing door cabinets. All three had locks on them, the center section's held a gleaming silver key.

Sliding off of her chair and onto her knees, Natalie was grateful for the choice of tan trousers and coral top today for ease of movement. She turned the key and slid the center section of cabinetry's bypass doors open on one side to reveal an empty pull out drawer. Doing the same on the other side, Natalie found one lone manila file folder without an external marker.

Pulling it out, she held it to her chest and sat back on the cream carpet. Natalie was staring in disbelief at the contents when Luka came back.

He cleared his throat to announce himself, she barely moved.

"Luka," she said in a hushed voice, "do you know what this is?" Not hearing an answer, she glanced up.

Luka was staring at her, lips tight. He nodded once, slowly.

"Is this what we're supposed to do? Is this the kind of stuff he's planning to send us out on?" She let the file rest on her crossed legs, closing it as if by doing so she could remove its contents from her mind.

He closed her door before crossing the room, lowering himself to sit beside her. "That is the kind of stuff he uses people like us for, yes." Pointing at the file, he continued. "Ours really is a rare ability. I was the only one that had come through Prestige with enough sanity left to be brought on here in a long time so he was pretty excited. Then, Ivy must have told him about *us* because he was asking a lot of questions from day one about you. Remember, I told you he was always asking personal questions?"

She nodded.

"Well, it was creepy really and then when I told him I was quitting, he told me all of it. He brought me down to the lower facilities where all the training goes on. Told me I could help save lives with my ability." Luka tapped a finger on the folder lying in her lap. "We went out on this the next day, an experienced agent and myself. This guy was rumored to be selling locations of American troops to al-Quaeda. I went in to meet with the guy and 'listen' and the other agent did the rest. The second I got back I called my mother and asked her to call you."

Natalie's dark eyes were huge. "Luka, this guy's dead. You got this guy killed." Her hand rested on the file. "He was an American. He had kids and a wife."

"He was getting his own people killed, Nat. What about *their* families? Which is the greater crime?"

She turned away from him, opening the file again to stare at the picture of the man Luka had helped to kill. He looked like any other suburban soccer dad. She traced his features with a finger, unable to stop the picture the words made in her mind of how he must have looked after it had happened. "Single shot to the back of the head," was written in the file.

"Did he know what was coming or did they sneak up on him?" She whispered. "Were you there when it happened?"

"Natalie don't." Luka's voice was rough.

Turning her head to look him in the eye, Natalie saw that his conscience was not entirely clear. His eyes were troubled over the life he had helped end. It eased her mind to know the gentle man she loved had not done his part easily.

"If I'm going to be doing the same thing, I need to know if you were there. If he begged you to let him go." The film in her head of his death had him begging for the sake of his children. She couldn't be a part of that.

Luka turned his head, "He knew." He left it at that, Natalie's stomach turned and she took a steadying breath.

Standing slowly and with considerable effort, Luka held out his hand. "Come on. Whiting wants you to see the facilities. He said you've got an appointment with the doctors for a physical. From there you meet with the personal trainers for a program setup." He held out a hand. "Come on, they're waiting."

Natalie took his hand, needing the help given the current wobble of her legs. She stumbled against him but quickly recovered herself, letting go to straighten her top. Luka watched her out of the corner of his eye. Neither one spoke.

They made their way to the elevators and Luka swiped his card alongside the number pad, pushing a red button marked "HELP." A voice crackled through the speaker.

"Yes?"

"Luka Bailey to training." He said it slowly and concisely. The elevator began to move and he spoke out of the side of his mouth. "Voice recognition. Say it the same way every time or they route you to the first floor."

Natalie didn't say anything. Now she knew the answer to her prior question if everyone there was in on the corporate secret, obviously not if they had a "secret knock."

The doors opened on very different surroundings than the rest of the building. The main parts of Optimax were white and sterile with each floor having its own serene color palette, each one generic in its own way.

This floor was dark. Concrete floors met concrete walls rising up to concrete ceilings. All of this was illuminated by lighting along the ceiling and some uplighting every ten feet or so along the floor. It felt like a bunker, very military.

"They made this in the fifties during the Red Scare. Optimax built on top of it, only they weren't Optimax at the time. I forget all the names they've had, but this has always been below it even when they've knocked down the upper building like they did about fifteen years ago and put this one up."

"It's cold." Natalie rubbed her arms.

"Yeah, I don't imagine they do much to heat the place. It's so far underground it stays the same temperature year round." He led her down the long, bleak corridor that came to a "T." They took first a left then a right before coming to another door. This one was similar to an old metal bank vault, except the keypad to its right was too advanced for any bank she'd belonged to.

Luka placed his thumb on a square and typed in a code. The seal releasing made an audible sighing sound and Luka stepped aside to let the door open itself. Natalie followed him in and scooted forward the last few feet when she realized the door was closing itself behind her. The security measures were straight out of a movie. A movie where the good guys could be just as bad as the bad guys. Natalie pictured the photographed man face down in a pool of blood, Luka standing next to him. She shuddered.

Chapter 38

The cavernous room that opened up in front of them was domed, shaped like an egg. They stood in the narrow end. Along the right wall lay a bank of monitors, several people stood in front of them dressed just like normal office people in trousers, shirts and ties.

To the left was a cubicle fully encased by glass with a large black metal desk set in the middle. A tall woman sat behind it, head bent studiously over a file, red hair slicked back into a neat bun. As Natalie stared in at her, the woman looked up and blinked. Her blue eyes were piercing. Then, glancing at Luka standing with her, the woman rose and walked out, coming straight for them.

Natalie wanted to hide behind Luka, to break the woman's intent stare but she stubbornly stood her ground, determined to appear strong even when she didn't feel it.

"Hello Bailey, Mr. Whiting called to say you were bringing down a new recruit." She extended her hand. "Ms. Swenson I presume?"

Reaching out, Natalie had nearly made contact when Luka's hand flashed out to knock hers away. Furious and equally embarrassed, Natalie glared at him. "What the…"

Pointing, Luka's finger directed her eyes back to the woman's palm. A blue arc ran the length of her palm. Natalie's eyes bulged and she looked up, bewildered, at the redhead.

Smiling modestly, she held the hand up and Natalie watched the arc sink back into the woman's pale flesh. Wiggling her fingers for Natalie to see, she flashed her teeth. "Monica Devries." Her hand returned to her side and she spun on her heel, efficiently striding off and called over her shoulder. "Keep up."

Natalie shot a quick confused glimpse over to Luka whose face was tight. He was radiating his displeasure at Monica. The fear that he could not protect her here or in the field was of great concern to him and it was beginning to sink in. Not for the first time, Natalie wondered what she had done coming here.

They caught up with Monica, now standing in the larger dome part of the egg shaped room. Against the far back wall was a gigantic screen with a map of the globe in a grid. Opposite the wall, back about twenty yards lay a bank of computers with two men spinning in chairs to access all of them. As they typed, the grid zeroed in on an area then came out to focus on another area. Meanwhile, a white haired man in a dark suit stood with his hands in his pockets, rocking on his heels and calling orders to the men behind him on the computers. Each time his mouth moved, the grid changed.

Their party stopped at the edge of the computers. Monica stepped forward and spoke quietly in the suited man's ear. His eyebrows rose as he turned his head. His visual appraisal of Natalie was so thorough she had a passing thought that he might be able to see through clothes.

His assessment complete, he returned to his task of calling out regions for the computer operators. The grid went back to its malleable state. Monica returned to them, her lips upturned in the corners.

"The general likes you." She walked past and Natalie and Luka had no choice but to fall in behind her.

Natalie jogged to catch up while Luka's long legs brought him abreast of their guide in a few strides. "Who's the general?" Natalie asked.

Monica didn't slow nor did she turn her head. "The general is the ultimate authority as far as you're concerned. What he says, you do. No questions. Isn't that right Bailey?" She taunted him over something Natalie couldn't read.

Luka's teeth ground audibly together. Natalie reached out and touched his arm, asking with her eyes. He shook his head. Monica's laughter up ahead drew Natalie's attention back to her although not before she saw Luka's eyes narrow in hatred.

"Come on Bailey. You have to admit it's ironic." She twisted to see him and shrugged. "Fine, I'll tell her. When Mr. Bailey here tried to leave us, the general had a 'talk' with him and showed him the error of his ways." She smiled, intentionally oblivious to his glare.

"What does she mean?" Natalie whispered when Monica turned her back and led on down the hall.

He sighed, giving in to the fear he heard in her voice. "The general can send a shockwave, like your blast only ten times stronger. It scrambles your brain but while he's in there, he picks through and finds what he needs." Nodding at her look of dismay, Luka continued. "He found exactly what he needed to blackmail me into working for him. I told him I'd be cooperative if he would leave you alone. He said he'd think about it, he could sense how strong you were but he also saw your scars and worried you wouldn't be stable. I capitalized on that and had him convinced to let you go and he could keep me."

Natalie finished for him. "And then I came here and gave them a show. No wonder Whiting was so excited."

"Yep. They'd resolved themselves to just having me until you came here and showed them just what you could do. They couldn't pass that up even if you *were* unbalanced."

"Sorry." She started to see what Luka had been willing to sacrifice for her. Guilt lay heavy in her heart at her doubts about him and his suffering while here. She reached out and touched his hand.

He tightened his lips in a forced smile before turning his attention back to Monica who had turned down another hall. Natalie was surprised. She hadn't seen it from the back of the "egg."

"It's a huge complex."

"I guess."

They passed through the long corridor with large windows down both sides opening into sunken rooms, each filled with people doing all sorts of things that agents might need to know in the field. A large room to their right outfitted with black mats had people fighting each other hand to hand, several rings were going at once with bodies being thrown down and popping back up to try again. On the other side, through a long narrow window Natalie could see paper targets in human shapes and the backs of agents as they held handguns and long guns, firing randomly. Reaching the end of the hall, Monica stopped abruptly and pointed to the door straight ahead. There was no window.

"I think they're waiting for you Swenson." She dropped the formality of the "Ms." "Bailey, I think you could do with some more firearms training."

"Thank you Monica." He ground out tightly. Giving Natalie a last unreadable look, he turned and stalked away, disappearing into the firing range doors. The loud popping of gunfire filling the corridor before the door cut off the sound once again, leaving Monica and Natalie enduring an awkward silence Monica brought to a quick end.

"They're waiting in there." She repeated, less patient. "Go on. Come back to my office when you're finished." She shooed her through the doors.

Three hours later, after Natalie had been poked, prodded and run through every testing device and procedure she thought she could endure, she finally emerged ready to be done with this place.

Monica didn't bother to come out of her terrarium, merely waving her through to the elevator pointing at her card and giving a thumbs up that it would get her back. Figuring the rest out on her own, Natalie got herself back to her office and had just sagged down into her chair when Luka's head popped in.

"How did it go?" His expression was difficult for her to read.

She'd grown too accustomed to hearing him in her head, and quite honestly, right then, she didn't have the energy to read him like a normal person. Shrugging her shoulders, she met his hooded eyes with her tired ones.

"I feel like I've been beaten to death, resurrected and then beaten down again."

"Yeah, I remember." He empathized. He knocked his knuckles once on her doorframe, pushing off. "I'm just wrapping up a report and then I was thinking we could go to lunch. Are you hungry?"

Whether she could eat or not, Natalie wanted to spend some time outside in the sunshine with him. Being in here and in the "lower facilities" as they called them had her feeling like she was in a whole other world.

"Sure, I'll just be putting this stuff away." She pointed to the small mound of supplies on her desk. "Hey Luka," she called out softly to his back. He spun around. "Did you put that file in my drawer or did Whiting?"

"I did." He answered the next question before she asked. "I needed you to know before anyone else said anything." Though guarded, she could see the pain it caused him to have admitted his part to her.

"I'm glad you told me first."

He gave her a quick nod and retreated to his office. Natalie had another ten minutes of peace without any intrusions from Whiting before Luka returned.

"Ready?"

"Yes, I am."

Chapter 39

The warmth of the sun on her upturned face help to push the last of the chill from Natalie's body that hadn't been entirely due to the air conditioning inside the monolithic structure. Absentmindedly watching the ducks marching across the lawn toward a small pond beside the building, Natalie rubbed her arms.

Luka's arm slid around her, helping to rub warmth into her skin from where he sat beside her at one of their many picnic tables. Due to their late lunch hour and the Friday factor, they were the only people out on the lawn. They spoke quietly but freely.

"Is this real?"

"Seems like a weird spy movie or comic book doesn't it?" His low voice rumbled against her comfortingly.

"Yeah, I can't believe all of this is happening. A secret agency and this whole hidden facility right here under our feet and nobody knows it's here." She shook her head in disbelief. "It's hard to wrap my head around it."

Leaning in, Luka kissed her head. Natalie lay against him, reveling in his warmth. They stared at the pond, enjoying the calm and peace they brought each other. A passing airplane's engines surged in the distance.

"I suppose the afternoon is going to be some sort of obstacle course and firing range thing?" Natalie rolled her eyes, letting Luka pulled her to her feet.

"Close," he said entirely serious. "Whiting has you working with the personal trainers this afternoon. They'll have your test results by now and they'll design a fitness routine for you."

Natalie ran an inquisitive eye over Luka's body. Never a slouch, he had definitely put on some more mass and streamlined his muscle tone until he was even more enjoyable to look at.

"Can they make me as hot as you?" She tried jokingly to detract from the real trepidation she felt.

His hand still held hers. Rubbing the back of it with his thumb, he winked at her. "You'll put me to shame."

He was right. Whiting barely let them stop in their offices. Luka had wanted to check his email, apparently he was waiting on something for a report he was working on. Natalie was honestly putting off asking him about it, worried it was another job he would have to go on that would make someone else turn up dead.

"Luka, take care of that report. I need it by end of day. You can go down tomorrow. Natalie, go find Monica and let her know you have an appointment for your fitness program." He barked from his office without bothering to call them in or get up.

"Yes, sir." They both yelled back.

Natalie gave his arm a quick touch, he smiled reassuringly and she headed back down, adjusting on the fly to this new alternate reality she found herself in.

Monica was waiting. She led Natalie to the corridor off the right side of the egg. It was a mirror image of the left side. The windows on one side looked out onto an enormous gym filled with the gleaming metal of exercise equipment, much of which was currently in use.

At Natalie's curious gaze, she inclined her head and looked glib. "Go on. Unless you want me to push you." She raised an eyebrow holding up her palm, a thin blue line glowed as it rose in a low arc.

"I'm fine." Natalie scooted around her to let herself in. Monica's mocking laughter was cut short by the door closing behind her.

If Natalie thought she'd been in shape before, the fitness program designed and then conducted by her new personal tormenter, Dan, proved her wrong. Not only did he run her through almost an hour of cardio work, he also had her lift an inordinate amount of weight over and again with every part of her body. It was more than she'd ever done on her own.

"Do I really need to be able to bench a hundred pounds?" Natalie puffed, weight bar resting on the metal holders above her. Her arms dangled like dead things down from her fatigued shoulders. If someone had a gun to her head, she couldn't have moved.

Dan snorted. His shorter stature brought him eye level with Natalie, though his shoulders were twice as wide. She'd seen action stars with bodies like his before but never a real person. Even with Luka's new body he had nothing on this guy. His wire rimmed glasses were the only thing breakable about him. The light brown eyes that blinked at her from behind them held a tiny hint of amusement she hadn't thought him capable of after the past hour of agony.

"No guns here. You'll do that Monday." He held out a hand for her to take and pulled her up.

Jellylike, she let him pull her up while she stared perplexed at him.

"What? It's not like you're the only one around here who has any sort of psychic ability."

"Well, yeah, but I heard no one here was a telepath." She didn't say any more, not sure who knew what or should know about the specifics about her or Luka's talents.

He studied her strangely, her near slip making him curious. "You heard right. No one here is a telepath. I can only see pictures of what you're thinking." He shrugged. "Sounds cooler than it is. I see a picture but I have no context. For all I know, you want to shoot *me*." He winked and flashed a charming smile.

Natalie smiled back weakly. "I was thinking I couldn't lift another weight if there was a gun to my head." Being tired definitely made her more susceptible to others' talents. Natalie would have to be more diligent and start working with Luka again. She hadn't practiced any of that since he'd gone away. Obviously she needed some more practice, especially since breaks were going to be hard to come by here. She had to build up her endurance, so to speak.

Dan tipped his head thoughtfully. "You're lucky. We're done for today. You have the weekend to heal. I'd recommend some steady doses of potassium and ibuprofen for those muscles. We start back up on Monday and we'll meet three times a week."

He went to work putting away her weights. Natalie straightened her rumpled tee shirt. It was wet in places she didn't know she could sweat. The locker room had cabinets full of shirts and shorts to borrow but she would have to remember to pack some that fit better and didn't bunch when wet because if today was an indicator, she was definitely going to get sweaty.

"So, what are you doing this weekend?" Dan asked, his back to her.

"I don't know. I think I'm going back to campus to get some of my stuff since it looks like I'll be here for a while."

"Oh, well, if you wanted somebody to hang out with or you need help getting settled in you could call me."

Natalie looked down and saw that Dan was adjusting weights in the racking, staring up at her expectantly. He tried to sound casual even though his focus was anything but. She couldn't imagine she had impressed him with either her performance or with her at present stunning appearance. But had he just asked her out? He had to be at least five years older than her.

"That's really kind of you Dan, thanks. But Luka's going to be helping me get situated." She refrained from saying he was her boyfriend. It was presumptuous of her to assume he meant it in a romantic way. He probably was just trying to be nice to her since she was new here.

Dan's eyebrows knitted together. "Luka? The new guy?"

"You know him?"

"Yeah, he's not one of mine but I've seen him here. Kind of quiet."

Natalie had to think back to when she had first met him and he had been so cold. It made sense Dan would think he was quiet.

"Just at first. He's a great guy once you get to know him." Hearing herself she thought she sounded like she was making excuses for him. She tried to recover awkwardly. "He was my tutor at Prestige so we got to know each other pretty well."

"Huh." Dan gave her his back while he went back to cleaning up.

Feeling like she had just complicated a situation that might result in far more physical pain on Monday than she had been previously scheduled for, Natalie said her awkward goodbye and went to the locker room to change.

The plain, red faced girl who looked back at Natalie in the locker room mirror looked like she'd run a marathon. After dressing, she tried to smooth out her hair pulled into a sloppy ponytail and went upstairs via the stairwell to avoid as many people as possible.

When she got to their floor, she stuck her head in Luka's office. He was staring at his monitor, lips pursed in concentration. Natalie rested her head against the wooden doorframe and watched him, feeling peace return to her heart and mind.

Sensing he was being watched, Luka glanced up. His feelings for her were evident in the way his expression eased when he saw her.

"Hey, how was it?" His fingers finished keying his sentence and he leaned back.

Natalie walked in and stood behind one of his guest chairs. "That man has no mercy." She joked. "I think if he has his way I'll be able to dead lift a horse by the time he's done with me."

Luka's eyes clouded for a moment. "Close. It's important to be able to drag your partner out should the need arise or have the stamina to fight for prolonged periods."

"This is real, huh?"

"Yes, it is."

Natalie sat down, laying her hands on his desk. Luka forced a half smile and reached to take her hands, giving them a squeeze. He glanced up at the clock.

"I'll be done with this in a few minutes and we can go. Are you going to wait in here or your office?"

There was nothing for her to do in hers. "I'll wait here if you don't mind my staring."

"I don't mind at all."

Ten minutes later, Luka switched off his computer, slid it into the cabinet against the back wall and locked it.

"Are we supposed to lock up our computers?" Natalie asked.

He nodded. "Yours doesn't have much on it yet, but it's a good habit to get into. We have to leave nothing on our desks and the cabinets must always be locked."

Natalie hurried into her office to conduct her lockup properly. "Okay." She came out and had her hand on her door handle, glancing up at him questioningly.

"You can leave it open. The cleaning crew is background checked so they're clear to come in. Whiting doesn't want us leaving anything out is all. Just in case."

Just in case of what, she didn't ask. It was hard to conceive that her first job was one that would require her to drag a body and hide all of her things lest they fall into the wrong hands. And that was the office portion. The field was going to be a lot hairier.

Chapter 40

They went straight back to their new apartment where Natalie made a beeline to the shower. Just as she was rinsing her hair, she heard the door slide open and shut. Hands slid around her waist. Natalie had to keep rinsing to open her eyes but his hands continued to make it hard to concentrate. When he started "helping" her with the soap, she gave up completely and let him help to his heart's content.

Once they had both gotten dressed they made dinner and spent the evening in, intending to get up early and do their run to Prestige and back on Saturday. Natalie called Avery to let her know her plans. Luka called his mother to give her an update on what had happened.

It must be something to be able to confide in someone not involved, she thought.

Not really. It means Whiting is more than willing to use her as leverage. Especially now that he's lost you.

He hasn't lost me. He's got me. She pointed out.

Do you think he'd give you up to keep me? He'd get rid of me before he'd lose you.

Natalie mused silently over that one.

"Natalie, did you hear me?" Avery hollered shrilly, Natalie pictured the stomping foot in her mind's eye.

"I'm sorry." She flushed at being caught not paying attention. "Luka just said something. I'm back."

Avery sighed exasperated. "What I *said* was Jason is with the guys this weekend so I'm single. What do I need to do to persuade you to stay the night?" Sensing Natalie's pending refusal, she pleaded. "Come on, he's getting you the rest of your whole life. Give me another night. He won't mind."

Natalie flicked her eyes over to where Luka was sitting, speaking to his mother. She said nothing of Avery's "whole life" comment, instead mouthing, "Do you care if we stay over?" He gave her a thumbs up.

"Sure."

Avery squealed and Natalie pulled the phone away from her ear, glimpsing over at Luka to see if he caught any of that. He was frowning at his phone, mumbling quietly into the mouthpiece. Natalie got off the phone and waited for Luka to hang up.

"What's wrong? Is your mom okay?" Her first thought was of Whiting. She said a silent prayer. Not a believer necessarily, she figured it couldn't hurt to think good thoughts.

"Yes, she's fine." His voice was tight with anger. "She wants me to check in with Ericka."

Natalie's heart threatened to implode. "Ericka? Why?"

Luka struggled to keep himself calm. "I told you, her parents are friends with mine. I guess she's been complaining that she's all alone now that I'm gone. Her parents are worried about her."

She bit her tongue at her initial response. Trying to be a good person, thinking of how she would feel if her only friend left, Natalie tried to be gracious. "Then you should."

He didn't hide his shock at her support. "Really?"

Shrugging, she told him truthfully, "You *are* all she has. It's not like you're going to feed into her delusion that you're a couple. Maybe this time apart has helped. She probably just misses having someone to talk to." Natalie knew that feeling all too well. That had been her life before Prestige.

Luka's expression turned thoughtful. "You're probably right. I'll have her over for dinner and then, while you're with Avery, I'll grab some of my stuff I've been meaning to pick up so I can put the rest of it in storage."

"You mean now that you're back from the dead?" she teased.

Guilty, he nodded. "Yeah, I couldn't come back and risk you or your friends seeing me."

"Wait a minute." Something clicked in her mind. "Didn't your mother tell Ericka about the accident? Didn't you think I'd find out?"

He looked down his nose at her. "I wasn't worried you and Ericka were going to compare notes and we couldn't risk Ericka spreading it amongst my parents' friends. She would, you wouldn't." He snorted. "It's really easy to disappear at college. No one knows anyone and people come and go all the time."

Grudgingly Natalie acknowledged his point wondering if there was ever a time in her life when she could have disappeared and had anyone notice.

Luka set down his phone and patted the cushion beside him.
Natalie folded one leg underneath the other as she lowered
herself to the soft, dark leather.

"Our have to's are done. What's next?" He wrapped an arm
around her shoulders bringing her into his side where she fit
perfectly.

"I think a night of this would be fine with me."

***

The next day's car ride got them to Prestige just before lunch.
When they were close, Natalie called Avery and Luka called
Ericka. Both girls were giddy except for very different reasons,
Natalie was guessing. She told herself not to be catty. It was *her*
Luka had chosen and she trusted him knowing how he felt about
them both. He disliked Ericka nearly as much as she did only
he'd been saddled with her care for most of his adult life and was
easily guilted into doing it again.

Luka dropped her off at her old dorm promising to call later.
He was coming back after breakfast to pick up her things and
they could be back home before dinner.

Natalie leaned over and kissed him before hopping out of the
car and waving goodbye. Luka gave her a wink and held up a
hand in return. Her insides were squishy just thinking about
him.

I love you. She said to herself, forgetting he could hear.

Me too.

Natalie waited for Luka to drive out of sight before she cut
back across the road making a beeline for the tutoring center. It
was Saturday but Ivy was usually there until the early afternoon.
Natalie broke into a jog. She wouldn't have much time before
Luka got to his place with Ericka and she didn't want to have to
make up a lie should Luka see her. He would question why she
would want to see Ivy and she didn't tell him what she was up to.

Ivy was in, glancing up and removing her glasses upon
Natalie's entrance. Today's color was purple, matching her
purple dress partially obscured by a cream cardigan. She dressed
the part of a mom. Again Natalie wondered if she had kids.

"Natalie, what a pleasant surprise." Her tone was, however, not as enthusiastic. Why was Ivy upset with her, she wondered?

"I didn't know if you'd heard, I'm going to be working at Optimax. I'm leaving school." She watched Ivy's face for a reaction. Given what Whiting had said about the conspiracy to manage kids like her, she assumed Ivy knew everything.

"So I'd heard." She didn't disappoint. "What brings you back for a visit?" She was stiffly polite.

Natalie took a deep breath, exhaling slowly to calm herself. "Ivy, did you know Luka's sister?" She watched Ivy's face closely.

Her features froze, eyes hardening. "Why would you ask me that?"

"Because I know why she was sent here. The same reason Luka was sent here and I was sent here. Because I know how much they wanted a talent like ours." Natalie appealed to Ivy's affections for Luka. "And I want to know what happened to her that made her kill herself."

Ivy's expression softened only mildly, her hands lay flat on her desk, pointer finger twitching. "Andjela was a deeply troubled girl. She'd been close to her breaking point for years and being away from home pushed her over the edge. There was nothing anyone could have done for her. I've told Luka all of this before, why don't you ask him?"

"He's told me all of that. But I think it's strange she killed herself after she'd come to terms enough with who she was that she was coaching Luka. She hadn't hurt herself in a while." Natalie shrugged, thinking aloud. "It doesn't seem right that she would all of a sudden do that out of the blue, and *then* to use a gun when her preferred tool had been a blade." Natalie knew firsthand, once a cutter, always a cutter. If she were to go back to that dark place in her mind again, she would never think to use a gun. It would be a knife. She knew Andjela would have been the same.

Ivy stood, hands stiffly at her sides. Natalie noticed Ivy intentionally eased her shoulders away from her neck, forcing herself to appear relaxed. "I'm sure you ask out of concern for Luka but you shouldn't stir up old ghosts. Andjela didn't handle her time here away from her family well. End of story. As to why she chose to use a gun and how she got it, I guess we'll never know."

Natalie pushed back. "Had she gone to The Company yet?"

Staring at Natalie, Ivy's dark eyes flashed something too quickly for Natalie to comprehend, and she knew she was on the right track. Ivy knew something about Andjela she wasn't sharing. Was Ivy protecting Andjela, Luka, or The Company?

"I don't know what you mean."

"Optimax. Had she gone for her internship yet?"

"Why would you assume she would have interned there as well?" Ivy played dumb.

Natalie gave her a look that told her she knew better. Ivy gave her a wry smile.

"You are an asset Natalie. But even assets can become liabilities. Leave this alone." Ivy warned her. She gave Natalie a gentler smile, the kind that had so endeared her at their first meeting. "Please."

Natalie studied Ivy, considering her possible motives. She'd been the one who'd helped her get her life back on track. She'd given her Luka. Ivy's secrets might truly be meant to protect Luka and his family. Didn't Natalie have her own secrets? It didn't necessarily mean Ivy was doing wrong, she had to remind herself.

"I just hoped now that we all know about," she hesitated, "everything, maybe there was something else you could tell me that would help Luka rest easier about it."

Ivy put a comforting hand on Natalie's shoulder. "It's natural to want to ease the minds of your loved ones, but you have to know there's nothing more to tell."

Nodding, Natalie rested her hand on top of Ivy's and returned her smile. "I'm going to miss you Ivy."

"As will I, Natalie." She said softly. "Goodbye dear." Ivy drew Natalie in for an embrace, a hint of a sniff in her ear, before shooing her out.

Natalie left, her suspicions intact regarding Ivy's involvement, although she couldn't think of what she could be hiding. The tickling warning climbing up her shoulders, warning her there was more even to the monster that was Whiting's deceit, refused to leave her. Picking at it in her mind, she busied herself the whole way back to Avery's.

Breaking into a jog the second she cleared the center's doors, Natalie made it back to her dorm out of breath and had to give herself a minute to recover before making her way upstairs. She was going to have to get some more ibuprofen from Avery. Her muscles were screaming at her, making her silently curse Dan, her new nemesis. He was lucky she hadn't taken him up on his offer to hang out. If he had been within reach, she'd have decked him.

Chapter 41

"Come on in woman!" Avery answered at the first knock. By her outfit, Natalie could see they were going out. Avery had already put on her favorite jeans with just the right balance of "fade and rip" and she'd topped them with her Heaven tee shirt. Avery said it was a techno club in Charring Cross she'd gone to once on winter break in England. They'd talked about going there someday on a girls' weekend.

Natalie stepped eagerly into Avery's wide arms, closing her mind down for damage control. If Avery was angry for her going away, she didn't want to know unless she physically said so. She didn't.

They talked girl talk and Avery confessed she was head over heels for Jason and they had plans to move in together after the summer.

"I thought you would like living alone. Remember how mad you were when you found out you had a roommate?" Natalie teased her.

Avery colored and laughed. "Well, you've changed my mind about rooming with someone."

"I guess that goes for both of us." She grinned, excited to share. "We've got a place too."

"Oh. my. Gawd, listen to us we're so domestic." She giggled, taking a poke at her New York friends. Then, in a rapid change, Avery stuck out her lip in a mock pout. "We're going to have to try extra hard to keep in touch now that you're going to be so far away."

Natalie agreed, waiting a few seconds and glancing around to make her question less suspicious. "Hey Avery, I'm just curious. Did you apply to school here or did they recruit you?"

Avery furrowed her brow. "They contacted me. Weird huh? They actually wanted me to come here even though I had the worst grades and no sports affiliations whatsoever." She rolled a shoulder upward. "I figured Dad's checkbook had something to do with it." Her eyes narrowed at the mention of her father.

Natalie searched her own memory for any mention, outward or inward, Avery might have made of medications or ailments. There was only one. "Do you still get those headaches?"

"You know, I don't. Ever since Ivy taught me how to do that meditating thing, I haven't had any problems. Thank you by the way for introducing me. Ivy's better than just a tutor, she's like a sensei." Avery leaned in, conspiratorial. "She's been trying to get me off my meds for a while now. I'm afraid of the headaches, I don't want them to come back. She got me convinced finally, just this week I cut my doses down to half so we'll see what happens." She confessed nervously.

Ivy had taught Avery the same control techniques as her. She'd assumed Ivy's interest in her friend had been due solely to her accompanying Natalie to the center. It had never occurred to her that Avery might have her own working relationship with Ivy. She certainly spent enough time there even after Natalie and Luka had relocated the majority of their sessions.

"Have you ever tried to figure out what causes your headaches?"

"Ah, *yeah*." Avery rolled her eyes. "I've been to every doctor known to man. The only thing they were able to figure was that it was hormones since they started when I got my first period. It was kind of good though." She lowered her eyes wickedly. "They put me on birth control by fourteen and dot, dot, dot." She winked.

Natalie made herself laugh at Avery's joke, yet she couldn't help feeling sad for her too. She'd lashed out at herself and her father by being promiscuous, whereas Natalie had turned her rage inward. Both of them had been dealing with the fallout of their talents with no guidance and both were damaged because of it. Part of her hoped Avery would come to Optimax but, she realized with a stab of guilt, part of her wanted to keep her safe from the risks just like Luka had tried to do for her.

She couldn't think of any way to ask Avery about her talent without sounding like a kook so she left it for the time being. "What do you want to do tonight? Your pick." She offered cheerily.

"It's Saturday night and we're two super hot chicks, so what's better than going out and making men who can never have us drool?"

Natalie laughed hard. She was going to miss Avery. "Anywhere in particular you have in mind?"

"Well, I heard about a party that's supposed to be stellar."

Natalie hadn't been too excited by parties in the past but gave in for this last hoorah. It even struck her as a fun idea. "All right. But am I dressed right for it?" She looked down at her jeans and long sleeved lavender tee. It had a ghosted image of the Eiffel Tower up one side. Both were buys from her recent shopping spree.

"You look awesome." Avery waved a dismissive hand at her concern. "We have a few hours. Have you had lunch yet?"

She shook her head.

"Could I buy you lunch at Mel's?" It was a hole in the wall greasy spoon not far from campus at the edge of town and one of their favorite haunts. Mel's prided themselves on having been in business and not remodeled since the forties. They had actually waited so long, they were now cool retro instead of old and outdated.

"Sure, I'm buying this time." Avery had picked up on the state of Natalie's finances and had always found different ways to get the check. Now that Natalie had prospects, she wanted to make up for it.

"Oh, now that you've got a big fancy job I suppose you've got a big fancy paycheck too." Avery studied her, concern creeping into her features. "How's that going anyway? Life at the mystery company?"

"It's fine. There's a lot to learn." She stayed vague.

"Is it really that bad or was Luka messing around?" Avery stayed serious. "I'll give him the whole 'I'm dead to protect you' thing. It's not what I would have done, a little dramatic even for me, but was it necessary? I mean what can they be doing, selling secrets to the Russians or something?"

For some inexplicable reason, she found herself *wanting* to tell Avery about Whiting and the training and the underground facilities they'd been right on top of and totally unaware. Sitting here in their old room, her new life seemed like a dream and the threat to Avery a faint nagging whisper in a far away corner of her mind. She leaned in and stared into Avery's blue eyes.

"We actually get to stop people from selling secrets but I don't think it's so much the Russians anymore." Natalie confessed.

Avery blinked and gasped.

Once the words were out, Natalie felt a familiar old feeling gathering in her stomach, dread. She shook her head, clearing it. What had she just done? Why would she tell Avery the truth? There was no excuse for that. She couldn't understand what could have come over her. Forcing a short laugh she winked. "Gotcha."

Avery was staring at her, mouth agape. She snapped it shut again. "You know, you two are both a couple of asses. You deserve each other as far as I'm concerned."

Before Natalie could respond, Avery stormed out, leaving Natalie sitting on her bed, stunned. "How am I going to fix this?" She mumbled to herself. Believing Avery would return once she'd cooled down, Natalie stayed put. She lay down on her old bed and stared up at the plywood bottom of Avery's upper bunk, pushing on it with her feet for old time sake.

It was faster than she thought. Avery was back in less than twenty minutes. "Hey." She called out from the doorway.

"Hey." Natalie sat up. "I'm sorry. I shouldn't have teased you like that." Her apology was sincere.

Coming to sit beside her, Avery sank down on the bed. "I think I've been pretty cool about this whole thing. Your dead boyfriend turns out to be alive and you go to work with him at a place he says is so scary he would rather break your heart than have you come looking for him." Whether she was trying to make her blue eyes gigantic or it was an effect enhanced by Natalie's guilt she couldn't be certain. It worked.

"Oh Avery, I know it sounds awful and I wish I could tell you everything but I can't just yet. I need you to believe me." Natalie meant it with all her heart.

Big blue eyes stared into her nearly black ones, searching. Finally, Avery smiled tentatively. "I trust you Nat." She took hold of Natalie's hands and demanded, excitedly back to her old self. "If you promise to tell me as soon as you can."

"I promise."

Shaking herself out of the serious moment, Avery perked up. "So, about that lunch you owe me."

"Sure, I'm starving."

They went out for a late lunch, conversation easy and light. Avery let Natalie buy and Natalie was feeling quite pleased with herself by the time they were going out to their party. That too was surprisingly enjoyable, mostly because Avery was in rare form, dancing and singing on the bar in the basement at one point and starting an impromptu sing along when "I Got Friends in Low Places" came on. Natalie's face and sides hurt from laughing so hard by the time they stumbled out. She could feel her defenses shorting out with the effects of the two beers she allowed herself but was riding high on the euphoria of the evening, too much so to notice when she started to hear Avery in little bursts.

She started talking just to drown out the sounds in her head. "So do you call Jason to check in at all when he's gone?" Natalie directed Avery's mind down a safe path.

"Yep. I wanted to call him pretty quick here if you don't mind. What's Luka up to this fine evening with his woman out gallivanting with her best friend in the whole wide world?"

"He's out with Ericka." She laughed.

Avery stopped, sobering up fast. "Ericka the psycho? Are you kidding me?"

Natalie shook her head. "It's fine. His mom said she's been lonely with him gone so she asked him to look in on her. I bet having him gone so long has given her some perspective." She repeated the same sentiment she'd shared with Luka.

Grabbing Natalie by the arm to pull her in close, Avery's eyes had lost all remnants of humor. It wasn't often Natalie saw Avery's dark side, she saw it then. "That girl almost killed you because she *thought* you had taken her guy. Now she *knows* you've taken him away from her and you've sent him to her on a platter? Are you an idiot?" Her grip was painfully tight.

Her panic was contagious. Natalie felt herself growing more frantic by the second. Glancing around them she got her bearings. They were roughly twenty minutes if they really hoofed it back to his place. One look was all it took to confirm her friend was on board.

"Let's go." Avery nodded in agreement to the question that didn't need asked.

They moved fast, several times breaking into a flat out run. Those didn't last long, Avery didn't have the footwear and Natalie's abused muscles didn't have the stamina. After what seemed an eternity, they walked up Luka's front step. Natalie led the way up the stairs, dropping what remained of her cheesecloth of a defensive shield in her mind and called for him.

Natalie? Stay out!

She heard the alarm in his voice and needed nothing more to tell her Avery's instincts had been right. A constant jumble of rage and sadness had the tenor of Ericka's voice but was otherwise unrecognizable. If any of her previous reading on the subject could be trusted, Natalie would say Ericka was having a psychotic break.

They reached the top of the stairs and ran down the hallway to stop at Luka's door. Natalie had to jump twice with her hand over her head to hit the key hidden up there and knock it down. She and Avery heard it clatter on the ground, losing it on the mixed hue tan and brown carpet.

Avery cursed and Natalie held up a finger over her lips. "Sorry." She whispered contritely.

"Aha!" Natalie exclaimed despite herself, instantly clapping a hand over her own mouth. Listening in on what was happening inside, she heard no breaks in Ericka's "disjointed rambling."

With all the stealth her shaking limbs could manage, Natalie slid the key into the lock.

Nat, please, no! Call the police and wait outside! He pleaded desperately.

His pleas were meant to warn. They served only to cement Natalie's intentions. Fear gripped her as she turned the key and opened the door.

I'm coming in. Tell me what I need to know.

He felt her resolve and told her what she needed. *We're in the bedroom.*

Chapter 42

Natalie's breath caught in her chest and got stuck, crushing her with its weight. He was saying something else but she couldn't hear it over the aftershock of that last announcement. *We're in the bedroom.*

She held out a hand to stop Avery from rushing in beside her. "Avery, go call the police. I've got this."

"I can't leave you up here with that nutcase," Avery fired back in a heated whisper.

Torn between keeping Avery safe and maintaining her secrecy, Natalie stared frozen at her friend's frightened eyes.

"I'll be fine. Trust me. I know what I'm doing." Natalie rested a reassuring hand on Avery's arm.

Avery wanted them to go in the hall together to call the police. She didn't have any interest in running into the eerily quiet apartment. Natalie heard her panic rising. She fought hard against the urge to go with Avery and let qualified professionals go in. Avery nearly had her convinced when she "felt" Luka again and broke away.

Seeing her friend's mind was unchangeable, Avery nodded once, tight lipped. She was already reaching into her purse for her phone as she strode back out into the hall.

Natalie, free of distractions, spun back to the apartment. Focused and running with her senses wide open, Natalie had to filter out the neighbors' noisy thoughts and concentrate solely on Luka and Ericka.

The lights were all on in the unit, the scent of garlic hung in the air. A glance over her shoulder filled in a few more blanks. Two plates sat on the counter, wine glasses empty, the bottle beside them half full said they'd been eating and hadn't gotten much past dinner before things broke down.

Fortunately given their limited consumption, she hadn't had much to drink so that might not be a huge factor in the way things were going to unfold here tonight.

Luka's voice was quiet. She reached for him but got nothing. Irritated, she spoke to him even though he was blocking her.

I'm here. If you leave me blind you can't complain if I get hurt. It would serve you right, she thought, her fear making her testy.

Luka sent out a sketchy *get out* and shut down again. Natalie was getting ready to charge in, the justifiably pissed off girlfriend when she felt terror creeping into her mind, affecting her senses though she didn't know why she should be so frightened. Ericka had beaten her up before but that was when she'd gotten the drop on her and she'd been armed. This time, Natalie had the advantage.

She let herself be filled with righteous indignation, taking a deep breath and stepped around the corner into the bedroom doorway. "What the hell?" She had meant to finish with "are you doing here" except those words died on her lips as she made sense of the scene playing out before her.

Luka lay, fully clothed on top of his bed. Ericka straddled , hovering over him, also clothed. Her weight was supported on one arm and her knees. What she had in her other hand, resting against his chin was what had stopped Natalie mid sentence. Former raven haired beauty Ericka, looking pale and drawn, sickly even, had a gun braced in both hands, too close to miss. The mechanical beast in her hands might have been small by gun standards, but to her it looked like the biggest, blackest cannon she'd ever seen.

At Natalie's intrusion, Ericka turned her head to face the threat. Her wild eyes narrowed but she stayed where she was.

"Get out," she hissed.

Natalie held out her hands to show she wasn't a threat. "Ericka, listen. It doesn't have to be like this. Let's talk this out."

Ericka's voice rose, quaking in her wrath. "We don't want to talk. Luka and I want to be alone. You don't belong here."

Risking a step, Natalie advanced slowly. "Look Ericka, I don't want to get in the way of your and Luka's happiness, I see that now. I just came by to get something." She played to her delusion. The lack of coherent thoughts in the woman's head gave Natalie nothing to go on. She was fighting blind and Luka's life hung in the balance. She had to swallow to keep her voice even. "I'm leaving but I can't leave you like this. Not if I think someone's going to get hurt." She felt her eyes riveted to

254

the gun, pressing firmly enough against Luka's flesh to make an indent around it's tip. Her lungs stopped working and she didn't notice.

Following the direction of Natalie's stricken stare, Ericka glanced back over her shoulder to the gun and, smiling a little off kilter, swung it around bringing it to bear directly on Natalie. "The only way someone is going to get hurt is if you don't leave right now."

Though it should have been the opposite, Natalie found the ability to breath again staring at the red mark the gun left on his skin.

"Ericka." Luka rushed, now as fearful as Natalie had been seconds ago. "Ericka, look at me."

She was not going to be distracted from her new target.

"Ericka do you remember what you asked me before Natalie got here?" He fought to regain her attention. "Do you remember what you wanted from me? I'll do it. Okay? We'll go away together."

Natalie listened, fascinated to see Ericka's deranged expression turn instantly to one of joy as Luka's words registered in her scattered mind. "Really?" The arm with the gun, now forgotten began to lower itself.

"Yes," Luka went on, gaining momentum. "Sure. We can go anywhere you want. Anywhere in the world."

Ericka's head started to turn back to Natalie and Luka rushed to keep her focus.

"No one else will get in the way. It'll just be me and you."

She smiled at him, lowering her face to his and Natalie felt the hair on the back of her neck rise. Luka kissing that siren's lips made her throat clench and Natalie took a few steps toward them, thinking she might be able to get the gun now that she was distracted.

By some cruel stroke, Ericka felt Natalie advancing and whipped the gun back up. Natalie had no doubt Ericka was going to pull the trigger and felt a cold sensation sweep through her as though she had fallen through the ice, plunging her into a frozen lake. She'd done it once, going in up to her waist before her father caught her. No one was going to catch her this time. Her teeth began to chatter.

No! Luka roared, he was back in her head again. *She's tied to me, it's something like a talent. She's been latched on, in my head for years. While I was gone she went off, she can't be reasoned with. Nat, you have to get out! She's going to kill you!*

But she couldn't run. The shock of knowing she was going to die was too great. She could only stand and close her eyes, waiting for Ericka to pull the trigger.

When the gun's report echoed through the room with a deafening roar, Natalie waited for the pain from where the bullet tore through her. It didn't come. It dawned on her that she had miraculously been spared, that Ericka had missed with her one bullet. Hoping to see Ericka standing with an empty gun, she opened her eyes.

The reason for her being spared had nothing to do with bad aim or lack of ammunition. He was currently wrestling the gun from Ericka's death grip, waving their four interlocked hands around and shaking the bed violently in the process. He had flipped her over and was trying to pin her arms, her legs were flailing, trying to come up and knock him off of her.

Natalie shook herself out of her trance and dropped to her hands and knees to crawl out of the line of fire. She had gone around the foot of the bed and was coming up the far side, intent upon taking Ericka by surprise and hopefully capturing the weapon, when the gun went off again, and the bed stopped moving.

Natalie had no need to look to know who'd been hit. She felt the shock as strongly as if the bullet had pierced her flesh. Jumping to her feet, Natalie stood and challenged Ericka, gun or no gun.

The blood spreading across Luka's bedding could have been water for all the color it added. There was no dramatic gushing of red blood, only a darkening of sheets. That was probably good. Natalie couldn't have handled the reality of all the blood. As it was she stared at his face, ashen with pain and the rapid loss of blood from the wounded side he now held with both hands.

Rage, fury, hatred, none of those words could adequately describe the surge of emotion that flowed through Natalie at the sight of her lover now bleeding to death right in front of her. It was her fault he was hurt again.

"Luka!" She screamed it inside and outside of her head.

His eyes were closed but she could tell he was still breathing and his face was contorted in agony. She could hear him struggling to breathe through teeth clenched against the pain. *God damn it, get out! She's going to kill us both you fool.*

Natalie felt it when his defenses crumbled, leaving his mind completely open to her. She felt the searing pain and the growing numbness of his body with each terrible drawing of breath. She felt his grim satisfaction at having created a distraction to let her sneak away, and his frustration with her for not making use of it.

His eyes opened when he heard her call his name. He glared at her, angry for her for not doing as she was told, worried she was next.

Natalie felt her anger gathering; the coming storm. She laughed, nearing hysteria.

Ericka began to swing the gun back to Natalie, hate in her eyes and accusations on her twisted lips. She would blame Natalie for this even though it had been her finger that had pulled the trigger.

The building energy in Natalie's mind looked for somewhere to go. Her tenuous hold on her own sanity told her where to send it and Natalie felt her own lips curving in a predatory smile, the cat who had the mouse cornered. She gave a little chuckle as she turned the full force of her attack on Ericka and released it.

Inside Natalie's head was a cacophony of sound, between the pounding waves of energy in her ears, Ericka's inner screams that never reached her lips and Luka's roar of fear as he felt Natalie blast Ericka with everything she had.

The only sounds Avery heard from the hallway after the gunshot were Natalie yelling, a loud crack and then dead silence.

Chapter 43

Sirens piercing the stillness of the apartment, too late to be of any use but cleanup, shook Natalie from her daze. She ran on shaky legs, collapsing on the bed beside her fallen love. Taking the blanket hanging over the edge and wadding it up, Natalie pressed it against his side to help staunch the flow now soaking an impossibly huge area around him. Too spent to cry she sat staring at him, thinking he was far too pale.

A tiny voice in her head told her to look over the edge of the bed where she'd seen Ericka fall after slamming into the wall so hard she'd made a hole in the sheetrock. Natalie refused to listen. Whatever was down there, she didn't want to have the image burned into her mind's eye. Ericka was not a threat right now and that was all that mattered.

Male voices registered on the periphery of her senses but Natalie couldn't tear her eyes from Luka's face. She barely saw his pulse in his throat nor did she see his chest moving.

"I told you not to die again," she whispered hoarsely.

He said nothing.

Natalie felt hands on her shoulders. They were gentle.

"Nat, it's okay. The paramedics are on their way up." Avery was beside her.

"There's too much blood," she heard herself say in a monotone.

"I know honey." She rubbed Natalie's back with a few short strokes before asking, puzzled, "Where's Ericka?"

Natalie didn't answer right away. Avery didn't have to ask again. The police spilled into the room, a male voice called out "over here" and another one muttered "sweet Jesus." The first male voice spoke into a radio, "we're going to need a bag up here." Natalie didn't understand why they would need bags. What they needed was bandages. Something to stop Luka's blood. It was hard to imagine there was anything left inside him, it was everywhere.

Finally something metallic was rattling behind her and stronger hands roughly pulled her off the bed, shoving her aside. She watched, numb, as the two paramedics worked frantically on

Luka. His eyes hadn't opened and then she couldn't see his face past the backs of the working medics. Instead, she watched his hand. She barely blinked. Staring at the fingers, believing that if she saw one twitch or move it meant he was going to be okay. They pulled him from the bed, laying him on the stretcher. One pulled the stretcher, along with one of the officers helping to guide it. The second medic sat astride Luka performing chest compressions the other twisted backward to squeeze a blue bag strapped to the bloodless face breathing for him.

Avery wrapped an arm around Natalie's shoulder and tried to pull her in for comfort. Silently refusing, Natalie stood wooden, staring at what had to be all of Luka's blood now staining the bed they'd once shared.

"He's going to be okay. He's in good hands now Nat." Avery was no more convinced of the truthfulness of that statement than Natalie.

Don't know what the hell happened here. That girl's not strong enough to have thrown her that hard and he was already bleeding by the looks of things. What the hell?

"Miss?" The authoritative male voice was soothing. "Miss? I'm Officer Murdock, I'd like to ask you a few questions." He moved into her sight line and Natalie blinked.

"Let's get her to the hospital. She's not answering any questions right now, Roberts."

"Let me go with her, please." Avery was pleading with the officer.

"Sure. Let's get her to the car. You can ride in back with her."

The ride was a blur. Natalie didn't hear much of what anyone said, nor did any of it stick. Avery was answering all the questions, including giving the doctors her parents' number.

Natalie heard her croaking voice tell them not to call her parents. She hoped they would listen. She was over eighteen. Bob and Valerie fretting around the hospital was not going to help things at all. The only person she wanted to see was Luka. They put her in a bed talking about needing rest. Her teeth still chattered and she was having trouble controlling her breathing but that didn't matter. She wasn't hurt. Luka was and she wanted to see him. A nurse came and there was a pinch in her arm.

"Where's Luka?" she croaked again.

The white coat with a clipboard, Doctor something or another, answered her with the generic doctor speak. "He's in surgery. Are you family?"

She shook her head. Sad. Everything they were to each other, none of it mattered to a doctor when there was no blood or legal document binding them.

Avery jumped in again. "She's his girlfriend. You should tell her as soon as you know anything."

"We can do that," the doctor agreed easily.

Natalie marveled at how simple it was for Avery to get what she wanted. It was almost like no one could disagree with her. It had always been a little bit that way but now, this visit, even Natalie couldn't say no.

Her numbed mind wrapped itself around the evidence, happy to have something non Luka related to dwell on. Avery had been working with Ivy and she'd recently cut her medicines in half. Now she had gone from being able to get her way *most* of the time to having everyone wrapped around her little finger.

"Avery?" Natalie asked hoarsely when the doctor had left and they were alone.

Avery sat down on the edge of Natalie's bed, careful to avoid sitting on the wires of the monitor hooked up to Natalie's finger. "What do you need Nat?"

Natalie focused on Avery's big blue eyes. They were ringed with pink, bloodshot from crying and her strawberry blond hair was thrown every which way in a disheveled mess of waves. "Have you always gotten your way?"

Snorting, Avery smiled weakly. She looked tired. "Everyone here wants to help. They're all really nice. You'll see."

She remained unaware of her talent. Natalie kept her mouth shut, feeling her heart sink still lower. Whiting would love Avery. It was a matter of time before she was with them as well. At least if she had a few years head start, Natalie could hope to protect Avery when she joined her under Whiting's watchful eye. Maybe she could even swing it to be her partner. She'd heard they liked to pair a junior partner with a more experienced agent, and by then she would be one.

Taking her friend's lack of a response for exhaustion, Avery patted her arm. "Get some sleep Nat. There's nothing more to do for now. I'll wake you if we hear anything on Luka."

Not having the energy to argue, Natalie felt the past few hours settle around her neck, a yoke pulling her down into the dreamless sleep only true fatigue can render.

What seemed only minutes later, Natalie was awakened by the sound of angry male voices. She blinked in the bright light of the morning sun streaming in between the slats of the white industrial blinds. Blinking, she turned toward the speakers.

One was the doctor she vaguely recognized from last night. The other was a uniformed officer who might have been at Luka's apartment. Or not, she hadn't really given a lot of to his face, what with having just killed a woman at the time.

She was sure of that. Her loss of control had not just stunned Ericka, it had caused her death. Natalie felt her stomach heave and was thankful it was empty. Her retching drew the doctor's notice.

He was at her side calling for a nurse in seconds. "Take it easy Miss Swenson." He kept his hands to himself, speaking in a calming tone of voice. "That's a side effect of the sedative we've given you. It can make some people feel nauseous."

That explained why she was having trouble focusing. The thoughts hopping around in her head were all jumbled and hard to understand clearly. It was like she was in a crowded stadium trying to hear someone two seats away. Not trusting her voice, Natalie nodded at him. It hadn't been like this for nearly a year, the defenseless state reminded her how far she'd come.

Dr. Jansen, a short bearded fellow who looked more college professor than doctor proceeded to examine her. She followed his finger, looked into the penlight and answered questions about who she was and what day it was.

The police officer was less concerned with her well being and stood at the foot of her bed, staring at her with his best cop face on. Natalie felt her stomach getting ready to go again.

"Ms. Swenson." His tone was no more friendly than his expression. "I don't know if you remember, but my name is Officer Murdock. I'm the investigating officer on this case. Now that you're able, I would like to ask you some questions about what happened last night. Is that all right?"

She got the distinct impression it was a rhetorical question. "Um, yes sir." Her tongue felt thick, her mind continued to short out. Snippets of a hundred conversations and thoughts assaulted her, she blinked and winced.

The nurse came in with a cup of ice chips. "Are the lights bothering you dear?"

Natalie accepted them with a weak smile and shook her head. The nurse and doctor conferred a stone's throw away, their faces cloudy. Officer Murdock had successfully made them enemies in less than five minutes. She didn't hold out much hope she would be on friendly terms with him when this was done either.

Officer Murdock opened a black notebook he'd retrieved from his blue, city issue trousers. He clicked his pen and began his questions. Gray eyes focused intently on her to detect any falsities she might try to run past him.

"Ms. Swenson, what is your relationship to Mr. Bailey?" He watched her eyes and she thought maybe her chest. Was he listening to her racing heart?

Keeping her arms rolled to minimize the exposure of her scarred skin in the short sleeved gown, Natalie slipped her heart monitor off of her finger. It had an alarm on it that brought an unexpected smile from the officer.

"You'll have to keep that on Miss, doctor's orders." He pointed at the poker faced doctor maintaining a professional distance while still making it abundantly clear Officer Murdock was intruding upon his territory.

She slid it back on and forced herself to remember Ivy's first lessons. Her heart began to cooperate and slow itself. "I'm sorry. I'm just really scared about Luka." That was true enough. Just saying his name made her throat close up. She shook an ice cube onto her parched tongue.

Pointing with his pen at her arms, he raised an eyebrow. "What happened?"

The truth wasn't an option, not unless she wanted them to see her as unbalanced. She dragged up a made up accident she'd given her gym teacher once when she'd seen them in volleyball. It had worked because there were no new purple ones at the time. "I fell through a window a few years ago."

Officer Murdock nodded and did give her a more genuine smile after that. "Your concern for your friend is understandable but let's try to get through these questions. Okay?"

She nodded, watching him just as closely.

"So am I to understand that you and Mr. Bailey are friends?"

"We're dating." It sounded so minor when she put it that way. "We've just moved in together and had come back here for some of our things."

"And he was alone with another woman in his apartment when you found him?"

His diving in aggressively took Natalie by surprise, leaving her stunned and sputtering. "No. No, I was spending the night with my old roommate and he was going to have dinner with Ericka." Her name brought a taste of bile with it. Natalie took another chip of ice. "Ericka has a history of being, um, unpredictable, and we thought we'd come check on Luka."

"Has she ever shown an inclination toward violence before?"

Natalie gave him a careful nod, sucking on her ice. It was the only thing providing any moisture in her mouth.

"Why was Mr. Bailey, Luka, seeing this woman if she's been violent on previous occasions?"

"She's not violent with him, she's violent with me."

He tipped his head, knitting his brows. "She's violent with *you* so *you* intruded on their evening?"

He was making it sound so backward. There was no way to explain it all to him without giving him too much. Natalie had been a great liar for the better part of ten years. It didn't take much to tell partial truths. But he was getting her flustered. She again reverted to Ivy's teachings to calm herself down.

"Luka had asked me to check in with him later, to touch base. That's all I was doing. I had no idea she had a gun until we got there, and then she flipped out. I didn't know she would shoot him." Natalie felt the warm tears instantly running down her cheeks in hot streams.

Her oversimplification and sincere emotion seemed to strike a chord with the jaded officer. He gave her a moment to compose herself before continuing.

"What happened in the apartment last night Ms. Swenson? In your own words could you please help me to put this thing to rest?" He stood with his pen poised, not knowing she could never answer that question to his satisfaction.

She shook her head. "I don't know. She had the gun and was sitting on the bed with Luka when I came in. All of a sudden I heard the shot, and then I heard another bang and when I looked, she was gone." She shrugged in feigned bewilderment. "Maybe Luka kicked her off when she shot him. You know, like a muscle spasm."

Officer Murdock lowered his pad and pen, clicking the pen to retract it back into its plastic sheath. "A muscle spasm? That woman was thrown into the wall hard enough to break her neck and crack her skull. She was dead instantly." A vein throbbed in his high forehead below the close cropped dark hair.

He was still glowering at her, Natalie holding her ground silently when Avery came in. She surveyed the situation and came to her friend's aid.

"What's going on here? Are you interrogating her after what she's been through? Officer Murdock," she leaned in to emphasize the fact that she was reading his nametag. "Should you really be here right now? I'm sure you have other things to do than bother Natalie." She tore into him. "Why don't you find out how a nutcase like Ericka was able to get her hands on a gun in the first place? That might be time better spent." She waved a hand at Natalie's slumped form. "Surely you don't see her as a threat." Her confidence borne of years of affluence and entitlement with few limitations was awe inspiring when seen in action.

Natalie watched in pure amazement as the veteran officer slid his pen in his shirt pocket, returned his notepad to his trousers and nodded to them both. He mumbled his apologies, recognizing his intrusiveness, and exited the room.

Natalie stared open mouthed at Avery. Had she really never noticed this before?

"Wow, what a jerk!" She had her hands on her hips and one foot in front of the other, possibly poised for a dramatic stomp should the officer have required it. "Are you okay?"

All she could do was nod her head. "Anything on Luka yet?" she asked hopefully.

But Avery, unlike the officer, was not to be distracted. "Natalie?" She leveled a steady gaze down her nose at her friend, watching her, equally uneasy. "What happened?" Weight shifted from foot to foot. "What happened in there? With Ericka?"

Shrugging, Natalie attempted to recall what all Avery might have seen. Had the police arrived before Avery had come back? She couldn't remember. "I, um, I don't know. When I got there Ericka was holding the gun on him and then she got mad when I came in. I tried to talk to her, I really did. Then she kind of lost it and Luka tried to take the gun from her. They were struggling and the gun went off." It was unnecessary to convolute that part. Grimacing, Natalie turned her eyes to a nubby pull in the cornflower blue bedspread covering her legs. "I heard a big bang and then, then I went to Luka and there was so much blood. I really don't know what happened after that." She finally dared meet her friend's eyes. "I really don't."

Natalie could hear her heartbeat in her ears, in stereo with that rotten monitor giving away her nerves.

For several long moments Avery watched Natalie. What she was thinking was impossible to know, her features were uncharacteristically benign. "Is this something to do with what you two do now?" She raised her brows. "What Luka was trying to protect you from?"

The monitor surged and Avery's lips pulled tight to her teeth. "Are you dangerous now? Or was this because of her?"

Open mouthed, Natalie made a tiny squeak. Her friend's intuition had nearly guessed it exactly. Still she didn't dare tell her any more than Luka had risked. Not before Bradley decided it was time.

A quick nod and wave of her hand and Avery lifted her chin. "I don't want to know any more than that." Taking control of the conversation and diverting it from that volatile place, she let her shoulders sag and she took a step toward the bed. "We haven't

heard anything from the doctors yet. Luka's still in surgery."
She sat down on the edge of Natalie's bed and took one of her
hands in her own.

Natalie twisted her arm to keep it protected. There were still
those secrets. Things she couldn't bear to share, especially now
that her character had suffered such a blow in her friend's eyes.

"He's lost a lot of blood Nat. The doctor who saw him go into
surgery said the bullet went in at an angle. It hit his liver and
punctured a lung."

The heart monitor told everyone in the room and hallway how
terrified Natalie was for Luka. The doctor stepped into their
private moment. "Miss, why don't you let Ms. Swenson rest?"

Natalie looked down at the heart monitor on her finger and her
legs elevated so comfortably as she lay useless and unharmed.
They were treating her for simple shock, pampering her in this
bed while Luka fought for his life, alone, somewhere in this
hospital.

How could she be laying here indulging in her self-serving pity
party? Luka and his mother were the victims here. His dead
sister too. His father was gone and now both children were
going to be lost because of some sort of something going on
between the school and Whiting's Company. It's injustice grated
on her and she made a fist, punching the bed in a blow that
missed its mark by miles.

She had made a promise to him that she would find out what
happened to his sister and she hadn't done it. Natalie was going
to find an answer she could give his mother. It might give her
some peace in the face of the guilt she was sure to feel once she
heard the girl she'd asked Luka to "look in on" had tried to kill
him. She wondered if his mother or Ericka's parents had known
how her psychic talent had tied her to him. Had that been what
had made her so unbalanced without him? What was that even
called, psychic vampirism? Or just plain codependent to the nth
degree?

Natalie slid her feet over the side of the bed and eased her
weight onto them. Avery watched her, eyes wide going straight
to the doctor who was beginning to object. Avery got to first.

"Nat, what are you doing? You should stay here."

Furious with herself and the spinning room, Natalie wobbled, enjoying in the feeling of the blood returning to her limbs. "There's nothing wrong with me. I'm fine and I'm leaving."

She made a line for the faux wood cabinet on the wall at the foot of her bed. A quick inspection revealed only a plastic bag with the name of the hospital on it. Incensed, Natalie clenched her fists and ground her teeth together. This wasn't happening, she fumed to herself.

"Nat, hey, calm down."

She felt her heart follow Avery's direction. Awed, she fought to keep her head of steam.

"Check the bag. It's from the gift shop downstairs. Your stuff was pretty messed up. They threw it away when you got here so I got you some shorts and a sweatshirt."

Natalie glanced up at that. It was summer in California, no one else would buy a sweatshirt but her.

Avery gave her a small grin. "I know you're always cold so I figured that's what you'd want."

If she weren't so pissed, Natalie would have hugged Avery right there. Instead she only tightened her lips for the ghost of a smile.

A quick visit to the bathroom and some finger combing and Natalie was ready to check out. She gave herself a moment to put her mind back together as well, overhearing everyone else's fears wasn't going to help her to focus on what she needed to do. Returning to her room, Natalie heard nothing. Her shoes lay in the bottom of the cabinet. Several large spots darkened the brown leather. Natalie touched one with her finger expecting it to come up wet and red, but it was already dried.

"So where are we going?" Avery laid a hand on her shoulder.

"I have to do something. Sorry Avery, but I need to do it alone."

Avery patted her pocket and Natalie heard the jingle of keys. "If you want to go somewhere, you're going to need some wheels."

Natalie made a snap decision she was sure she was going to regret but she was tired of hemming and hawing around. "Avery, I need to go see Ivy."

Avery kept her mouth shut but Natalie saw her eyes were troubled. When her concentration slipped, Natalie had a quick flash of intuition. Was it possible Avery knew something?

Chapter 44

A quick stop at the nurse's station where Avery asked someone to call the minute Luka was out of surgery, and they were off to Prestige. On the way, Natalie explained to Avery about Luka's sister having killed herself while here at school five years ago.

"That's sad Nat, but why do you think there's something weird about it?" She stared out at the scenery whipping past. "This is a totally different thing that happened to Luka."

Natalie didn't think they had to worry about a ticket. As a matter of fact, Avery could probably get a police escort if she asked. Her meds were working their way out of her system quickly. She was going to be unstoppable when she cut out the rest. Nothing would please Avery more, she mused.

Sighing, she filtered what she was going to say. Judging by the strength and value of Avery's ability, she was going to be joining Natalie soon enough at The Company, still, Natalie didn't want to be the one who had to tell her. Not yet. Let her have her fun at school planning her future before it was taken over. That wouldn't end well for whoever tangled with Avery.

"Because I think she was murdered for something she found out." It almost sounded too conspiracy theory here in this car during the bright light of daytime.

Avery was darting suspicious glances at her intermittently.

"I'm not crazy. Look, I know it sounds weird but there's something there. Something that doesn't make sense." She explained to Avery about her suspicions about Andjela's death, leaving out any talk of The Company and abilities. She was rewarded with a thoughtful silence.

After a few miles, Avery's shrill voice penetrated the stillness of the vehicle.

"Do you think Ivy's in on it?"

Natalie shook her head before she considered Avery might not be able to see. "I don't know if she's in on it, but she knows something. I'd like to get a look at her files. Remember she's in contact with the school psychologist, I'm guessing she's got some record."

"Then that's where we start." She dipped her head once decidedly.

They arrived at the school by ten, not considering the fact that it was Sunday morning. The center was locked but Natalie had an idea for that. She glanced around and saw the call box for security on its bright red post. They had been positioned around the campus for safety and guards were always on duty, ready to be dispatched on a moment's notice.

Walking up, she pressed the button and waited. In seconds static buzzed forth surrounding one word, "What?"

She leaned down to put her mouth near enough to be clear. "I'm at the Tutor Center on the edge of campus and I need someone to help me. I've fallen and I think I twisted my ankle."

"Would you like medical assistance?" He was probably excited to pass this to 911 if he was like most of the security guards she'd seen.

"No, just a little help getting back to my room." Natalie made herself pant, elevating her voice in false pain.

Pause. "I'll be right there."

"What do you suppose that's supposed to accomplish?" Avery whispered putting her back to the speaker.

Natalie just shrugged. Let Avery wonder. She'd find out soon it was her Natalie was banking on.

Sure enough, the guard was a few years older than them but already soft in the middle with the exaggerated attention to protocol reserved for those who want desperately to be taken seriously.

"Avery, could you ask him if he could let us in?" Natalie dropped the ruse at once.

"What?" Both Avery and the guard whose shiny nametag said Paul, were taken aback.

Natalie pointed to Paul. Avery rolled her eyes and humored her crazy friend.

"Paul, could you let us into the Tutoring Center please? My delusional friend here thinks that you should."

Paul studied her, serene expression on his face and agreed easily.

While he let them in and stood outside the doors, Natalie avoided eye contact with Avery. She had already begun opening

270

or trying to open drawers on Ivy's desk, searching for what she wasn't sure.

She found nothing in her desk and moved on to the locked file cabinet behind it. Locks were a good indicator she was on the right path for what she wanted to find.

"Ah, hello?"

Natalie glanced over her shoulder to see Avery, hands on her hips, foot forward. "What? I knew you could talk him into it."

Her reply took her by surprise. Not what she said, but how she said it. It was curiosity brought on by years of confusion. It was all too familiar. "How'd you know?"

Sighing, Natalie turned and rested her back against the cabinet feeling much older than her nineteen years. "You have a gift Avery. Have you noticed, when you aren't medicated out of your mind, how you can get whatever you want from people? It started around puberty with the headaches?"

Avery didn't respond, her focus was inward, looking back over years of hollow victories. No one had ever given her the "no" she'd needed as a teen for guidance.

"My dad, he used to say I should be a politician or a salesman." Her frizzy curls bounced with the shake of her head, eyes downcast in hiding. "Because he said no one could lie to me or say no." When she looked up, Natalie winced at the raw emotion in her blue eyes, dark with pain. "That was why he sent me away. When his company was hiding what they were doing. When he knew what they'd done. He couldn't help telling me. All I had to do was ask. It scared him. He sent me to school in Connecticut first and I got kicked out. After the second school booted me, they said I had antisocial behavior and sent me to the doctor who sent me to a specialist. He loaded me down with drugs and it got better. It never went away though. Not completely. I always pushed, waiting for someone to say no. They never did, it was like they couldn't."

All Natalie could think to do was offer a brighter future. For now. "You can use that gift now to help. We can figure this out between the two of us."

Avery bobbed her head distractedly and Natalie went back to her search.

Of course there were no keys to be found. She dug around in a nearby closet for spare supplies and hidden amongst the paper towels and boxes of pens was a flat head screwdriver. In minutes the lock was destroyed and the drawer slid open.

Inside were tens of files, some of which belonged to people she knew. She grabbed hers first, flipping through it. They must have made a copy for Whiting. Gasping at the contents, Natalie saw the additions Ivy had made to it since her arrival at Prestige.

Strong telepathic ability… shows promise… good control unless stressed… paired with older student with similar ability… Questionable stability. Recommend further analysis to determine suitability.

Natalie set her file on the top of the cabinet and searched the B section. She saw Luka's file as well but left it closed, reading it felt like spying. Grabbing it, she laid it on top of hers. She would give it either to him or his mother, it wasn't right for it to stay here.

"Avery, you have a file. Want to see it?" She held it out behind her and felt Avery take it from her.

Andjela's file was not in there. Not surprising considering these were current students and she was not.

The next drawer down contained only a few names.

"Bingo," Natalie muttered victoriously. In a section separated by a metal divider from the rest of the files marked "Parachute," Natalie found what she was looking for. There were a handful of files, the third one from the front marked Bailey, Andjela. She hadn't seen it written before and hadn't recognized it was traditional Serbian spelling like Luka. Thought of his family losing both children brought a sniffle and she blinked back her tears. She tried not to let herself think about him struggling for life. If he died, part of her would too.

Not usually a positive person, Natalie made herself picture Luka awake and smiling that wide grin, hand ruffling his hair. The things that made him *him*. A tiny flicker of hope caught fire within her breast and she clung to it desperately.

Just as the drawer was sliding shut, Natalie saw a name that made her grab it and pull it back open. *Christiana Santiago*. On a whim, she pulled the file and stacked it beneath Andjela's.

"Oh my God. These are my school records, discipline records, doctor's notes; they know everything. Why would a college *tutor* have this? What does this mean?" Avery's disturbed voice behind her made her jump.

Natalie pressed her hand to her chest, quieting herself. "It means they've been trying to teach you how to control your talent." She didn't turn around, finding it easier to have this conversation without seeing the devastation it might bring.

"Do you have one too? A talent or whatever you call it?" she asked in a small voice.

"Yes."

"Luka too?"

"Yes."

"Does it have anything to do with your work?"

"Yes."

Avery fell silent again. Natalie gave her privacy, keeping herself closed off. This couldn't be easy to process. It was still fresh in Natalie's mind.

She flipped open the file. Inside the front cover was a picture of Andjela. It was the same image she'd seen in Luka's scattered memories after she'd jumbled his mind the last time. She looked at Andjela's black hair and green eyes. They had the same sparkle. That was strange. She was happy in that picture. Natalie checked the date. It would have been her freshman year. It was probably her school photo they took at orientation for student id cards.

Déjà vu. Andjela's file read exactly like Natalie's. They could have lived the same life. Both were great students until the seventh grade then it was in and out of the doctor's office with constantly changing medications and doses. The cutting started later, when she was fourteen, and stopped when Luka said it did. Her grades came up the last year of high school as well and the meds stayed the same.

That meant she was handling her problems much better. When she came to Prestige she began to work with Ivy, she was paired with another student, and from there she flourished. Grades, ability, she even became active in school politics.

Natalie snorted thinking how maddening that would be to be telepathic in politics. Sharing what you knew could prove entertaining for the masses however. She still thought law was the way to go with this ability, if one got to choose.

Reading on, Natalie saw a change in the tone at the start of her second year. She'd been referred to the Parachute Project. Ivy oversaw it with Bradley Whiting. He was the liaison for Optimax's intern project it said.

A man's voice hummed on the periphery of her hearing and seconds later, the lights flicked on.

"What are you doing in here?" Ivy's voice was icy. "Put those files down right this instant."

Chapter 45

Natalie shot a quick glance at Avery who was blinking in confusion at Ivy. "Ivy, what is all of this?" Her entire posture was one of injury. "I trusted you. I told you things and you put them in *here*?" She laid her palm on the sheets in front of her.

Ivy's lips slowly came down to cover her bared teeth. Natalie watched the change as Avery used her gift on Ivy. Ivy's ability to block her telepathy apparently didn't work against Avery.

"It's my job to track your progress Avery," Ivy replied coolly. Avery could get her to answer, not like it.

"For what? Who wants to know?"

"The Company."

"But what is The Company?"

"An agency of the government. They're technically under the CIA's banner. They've been working to utilize the special abilities of paranormals like us since the Second World War. You're flagged as possibles when your behavior meets certain criteria and then you're tracked until you can be sent here for training. If your ability is strong enough, you go on to intern at Optimax where you're trained to use it and tested further for suitability. Both of you will be welcomed at the Company based upon your strengths."

"What about Jason?"

Ivy shook her head back and forth one time. "His is too weak. At best his charisma will make him friends and bring him success but he will never be an agent."

"Ask her about the Parachute Project." Natalie kept her eyes glued to Ivy's face, catching the slight narrowing of the eyes and pinching of the nose before she smoothed out her features.

Avery asked and Ivy couldn't refuse.

"Parachute was an experimental project using students that had been trained and sent into the field without going through the additional training through the internship program. They were trained here on campus quickly and ineffectively. They weren't prepared for field work." Her chin quivered for only a second before she wiped her expression.

Natalie caught it and instinctively lowered her blocks enough to send out "feelers" and try to hear Ivy.

Immediately Ivy snapped her head around and glared at Natalie. "I've told you never to do that."

"Why not?"

"Because my thoughts are my own. You people can't leave well enough alone sometimes." Her voice broke.

The wheels in Natalie's mind were working, trying to tie together information and assumptions. "What did Andjela get when she read your thoughts?" She asked softly.

Ivy tightened her lips intending to keep mum. Natalie sighed in exasperation. "Really Ivy. Either you can answer my question or Avery can ask and you can answer it, but that just seems really lame."

A sideways glance at Avery showed her to be spellbound by all of this. She remained frozen, perched on a table facing a chair, feet on the seat and elbows on her knees.

Seeing she was defeated, Ivy's shoulders slumped and she leaned back against the wall. All of a sudden she looked twenty years older and exhausted from the strain of keeping her secrets locked away and her guard up for so long.

She let it come down with a long, drawn out sigh and Natalie heard it all. For Avery's benefit, she repeated what she was hearing like she was reading aloud. Ivy drooped against the wall, no fight left.

My Christiana was one of the first. She was a year ahead of Andjela and they knew each other, though not well. Tina, that's what I called her, she was a blocker like me but she could project it. She could put armor around someone else to protect them or a bubble to keep someone's powers contained. She was very valuable. Ivy's tone surged with pride, her eyes lit from within before being quickly extinguished again.

They sent Tina and Andj to training here on campus. It was only a few weeks. Some basic hand to hand, minor weapons handling and they were off on their first mission. Two green agents sent in on what was supposed to be a relatively simple task.

The NSA had picked up chatter about a computer programmer who'd designed a guidance system so basic yet effective it could be run on a laptop. Back then, that was an accomplishment. No one knew what he looked like but there was going to be a deal with the North Koreans. They picked up where and when and sent the girls. It was in a public place and the programmer was just a guy, no weapons, no bodyguards, nothing. No danger and a great test run for them both. That's what Whiting told me. Andj was supposed to read his mind, find out who was their guy and Tina was going to project Andj's demands directly into his head. No one would even know what they were talking about. It was a revolutionary way of doing things with no intrusion on civilian life whatsoever. No one would even know it was happening.

Her eyes dimmed with the memory. *You can guess it didn't go as planned. The North Koreans didn't trust the guy and didn't want to pay him. They went in early and saw our girls talking to him. We caught most of it on the recording of their communication devices so we know what happened.*

Andj couldn't "hear" the North Koreans because their thoughts aren't in English. She didn't learn the language because she wasn't supposed to be there when they showed up. She was in the process of taking the disk with the system from the programmer and Tina was focusing on them when one of the Koreans took a few shots.

Tears ran down Ivy's face yet her expression remained slack and gray. She could have passed as a corpse at that moment. Natalie's voice broke as she spoke Ivy's thoughts for Avery. Even Avery sniffled, picturing the scene and hearing the pain in the mother's memory. She'd heard her daughter die and been helpless to stop it. Worse still, she'd sent her in herself.

The press played it off as a mugging with some bystanders as collateral damage. Obviously we had to protect the identities of the girls and fake names were given to the papers. I was Tina's only living parent so they gave her to me to be buried. Andj's family had to be lied to. No one had known of her double life. We capitalized on her history and pretended it was suicide. I called her parents myself and attended the funeral. It was awful.

All three stood, faces wet and hearts heavy with unwanted knowledge.

"Is that what you wanted Natalie? Is that why you came here?" Ivy asked her, no malice behind the words. It was an honest request.

"The family has been consumed by guilt for years believing they failed her. Luka," her voice cracked, "Luka has never forgiven himself for not 'hearing' her." She thought bitterly that every time she spoke to Marta Bailey, it was about death. Again she forced her mind to wrap itself around a picture of Luka awake and smiling at her. "It's time to give them peace."

Reanimating, Ivy pushed herself off of the wall and agreed. "I suppose you're right. There have been too many secrets."

"What happened to this Parachute Project?" Avery wanted to know.

"It was couched after that. Agents need more time to mature. More training and now we only pair junior agents with more seasoned agents. We haven't had a tragedy like that one since."

With Ivy's burden lifted, she dropped her animosity toward them. "How is Luka?" She asked, lowering herself into the chair behind her desk. Natalie didn't ask how she knew already. Most likely it had something to do with Whiting and his information sources.

Mutely, Natalie shook her head. "Still in surgery. Speaking of which, I'd like to go back to wait for the doctor. If you don't mind." She looked askance of Avery.

Avery was already gathering up her file, handing it back to Ivy. "Yep."

Ivy appeared surprised at Avery's return of the personal information.

She just shrugged and in typical Avery fashion responded flippantly. "Why don't you keep this until I ask for it back."

Ivy's smile was tolerant. That was the best she gave. A new respect was there between them.

Natalie frowned down at the stack she held. It was all so personal she didn't want anyone reading it or knowing those things about her. Yet, at the same time, the purpose of the file was to give information and someday there might be a situation that would require someone to access that information. It might even help her or save Luka's life. For that reason alone she didn't keep it to burn. Reluctantly, she handed her file back as well.

Raising her brow, Ivy waited for her explanation. Natalie didn't give one. Instead she gave a small wave with a "subdued thank you," turned on her heel and walked out. Avery was right behind her.

Chapter 46

When they arrived at the hospital Avery took ownership of her ability, using it to its capacity. They waited in the doctor's lounge with coffee, not from the machine but from the barista downstairs, staring at a show about nothing on a tv bigger than anything Natalie had at home.

"I could get used to this." Avery reveled in her coup. "It sure beats the waiting room."

"Yeah." Though comfortable, Natalie could not find pleasure in the situation.

"The nurse said she's going to find out how it's going and she'll come fill us in." Avery reached out and touched her hand. "It shouldn't be too much longer."

It wasn't, although in place of the nurse, the surgeon entered. The front of his green scrubs were damp with sweat, he plucked the cap they all wore as a sort of medical hair net off of his black hair streaked with silver. Natalie was struck by how sure of himself the surgeon was as he crossed the floor in a few long strides, unexpected given his shorter stature. He had to be not much more than Natalie's height, shorter than average for a man.

When he got close he came to a stop, offering his hand to first Avery then Natalie. She tried to read his mind but was amazed to find that she couldn't. A flash of a smile and she knew he was one of them.

"You know I'm only supposed to speak to immediate family." He gave them a stern frown making his blue eyes cloud over ominously. One hand pinched his chin, the other crossed his stomach, supporting the elbow for a proper "Father Knows Best" pose.

Natalie gave Avery a slight nudge with her elbow but the doctor gave a cough and pointed, finger bouncing between them. "That won't work on me so don't try it."

"Why not?" Avery was too surprised to be polite.

His stormy eyes bored into hers. "Because you, young lady, are not the only one who can do things like that."

"But Ivy…" Avery began.

"Is she still teaching young minds how to control others?" His demeanor shifted to a more pleasant one. "She was my teacher long ago. She was pretty mad when I told her I was going to be a doctor." Shaking his head in disbelief at the memory, he chuckled. "You should have seen her face when I told her I wasn't going down the path they'd chosen for me."

"You were able to choose?" Natalie felt herself gaping in shock.

His eyes twinkled mischievously. "Back then Ivy was younger and easier to get around." A shadow fell again over his merry expression. "Not anymore from what I hear."

Shrugging off what she considered superfluous conversation, Natalie pressed him for details. "Is Luka out of surgery Doctor?"

Appraising the girls, clearly breaking all the rules, he stuck out a hand. "Doctor MacCutchan. The one that got away."

Natalie smiled shakily, taking his hand and giving her name at her turn. "Doctor, please."

Doctor McCutchan's playful grin disappeared. "Natalie," he paused to be sure he got the name right. At her nod, he continued. "Luka's injuries were severe. He's lost a lot of blood. We were able to repair the damage to the lung, he lost a portion of his liver but he still has over seventy percent. Plenty to live a normal healthy life." He gave her a meaningful look. "Even the one *he* has in front of him."

It all sounded good but Natalie had known enough doctors to recognize his tone. There was a "but" coming.

"We lost him twice on the table," he kept talking over Natalie's gasp. Avery touched her shoulder. "And with being down as long as he was, there is a certain risk of brain damage. We can't be certain until he wakes up how extensive it might be."

Everything around her fell away. Natalie stood, staring at the doctor with tunnel vision. The roar of blood in her ears drowned out the actors' meaningless drivel and canned laughter coming from the giant tv. All she could see was the doctor's face, studying it for any signs or hints of hope or maybe some hidden meaning he wasn't sharing. He was stone faced. Then his lips moved again and Natalie willed her pulse to quiet itself so she could hear.

"They're moving him to a private room now. If you would like to wait with him you can. The anesthesia will be wearing off soon and then it's a waiting game." Completely somber and straight faced, Doctor MacCutchan had played this game before. He knew how to keep his cards hidden.

"Private room? In this place? Wow, luka must have more money than he let on." Avery sounded off, trying to lighten the mood.

The doctor corrected her. "Actually, I heard it was someone named Whiting, not Bailey who arranged it. Said he was his boss. Is that who's running things now?"

Natalie didn't know exactly what he meant by "running things" nor did she care. All she wanted now was to see Luka's face, to hold his hand and tell him she was there for him. "What room?"

"Top floor, room six fifteen. It has a nice view of the trees."

Doctor MacCutchan himself led them to the room. They arrived just as Luka's gurney was disappearing into the doorway. Natalie's feet froze.

"It's okay Nat. Go on in," Avery urged.

Natalie looked from the doctor to her friend and gave them a brave smile. "I'd like to be alone with him. I'm sorry Avery. I don't mean to be rude." She rambled, trying to make them understand what she wasn't sure she did herself.

Avery wrapped her arms around her and kissed her cheek. "I have some things I need to do. Call my cell when he wakes up. Okay?" She pulled away and Natalie saw that her eyes were wet.

"Thanks Avery." She pulled away, fingers tingling with the need to feel him.

As any good friend can and will, Avery read Natalie's mind. She patted her arm and left. "I'll call his mom." Natalie only wondered for a moment how she would get that number, then realized she could get anything she wanted from the nurses.

The doctor gave her a grim smile and assured her he would check back in a few hours, he was due in surgery right then. "A gallbladder waits for no man."

Chapter 47

The lights were dim. The nurse working to adjust his monitors and settle him into his room informed Natalie it was more gentle on his eyes should he wake up. Natalie approached him, studying the changes in his face.

His fight for life had taken a toll already. Luka's normally olive skin was ashen, his closed eyes were sunken and had shadows beneath them, the weight he had lost during their separation left his skin pulled unnaturally thin and tight, exposing his cheekbones more than was normal. Even his shiny black hair looked dull and lifeless.

Real life sick and dying was never as glamorous as it was in film. He didn't look relaxed, his features were pinched in pain even in unconsciousness. Here there was no one to do his makeup or shift his gown back onto his shoulder where it had been pulled forward to be tied while he was lying in a drugged induced slumber.

Luka had the look of someone who has haphazardly dressed before passing back out in his bed. And still he was beautiful in Natalie's eyes and her heart was pained at the mere sight of his sunken shell, lying helpless and smaller against the crisp white sheets.

"You can sit honey. I'll be out of here in a minute." The nurse told her over her shoulder, adjusting the dials on the standing monitor beside the bed. "You can pull that chair over and sit with him. They like it when you talk to them." She advised. A strong dark hand smoothed her coarse bangs against her high forehead.

Glad to have a task, simple thought it was, Natalie hooked her hand under the seat of the heavier looking side chair and dragged it to the bedside with a loud scraping noise announcing her progress at every inch. Settled, she tentatively reached out to touch Luka's hand.

"Press the call button if you need anything honey. If he wakes up in the night don't hesitate. Call us right away. Okay?" The nurse gave her tired shoulder a squeeze and Natalie smiled faintly back without taking her eyes from Luka's face.

They were alone. Natalie had his cool hand held in hers, stroking the back of his hand with her thumb like he did with her when she needed reassurance. His hair had been plastered down from a hairnet or something during surgery she was guessing. Natalie all too willingly ran her hands through it to sweep it off where it pressed the edges of his face and ears.

Busying her hands with the physical gave her something to think about other than whether he was going to wake up at all, or wake up as the same Luka she loved. She went on to straighten his gown and bedding the best she was able.

That done, she sat down again to wait. Her hand wrapped around his and she tried to talk to him inside his head but the anesthetic made a barrier to his thoughts she couldn't cross. She'd heard people in comas could hear what was happening around them and sometimes woke up when they heard the voices of those they loved. Although it was too soon to tell if Luka would be in a coma, Natalie clung to the hope that he would wake up and laugh with her again. His hands would touch her; his arms would hold her close. Now that she had him back, Natalie felt the threat of his loss all too well.

Natalie talked to Luka about what he'd missed when he had been gone. She told him how it had been when she had thought he was gone from her for good and how she didn't want to be away from him like that again. She went on to tell him about her day, what she had learned. She talked until she was hoarse and her voice was raspy with use.

The nurse came back with a pitcher and plastic cup. Thanking her profusely, Natalie poured herself a glass and went back to her one sided conversation about anything and everything.

Natalie tried to hear him again when she guessed the anesthetic had faded, but it was hard to make sense of anything. It was all jumbled, mixed up. She was reminded of his mind after she had blasted him except it was far worse. There was nothing stable to cling to and she had no idea if Luka, her Luka, was in there or not.

"Please come back to me Luka." She whispered hoarsely, swiping harshly at the flood coursing down her cheeks. "I've never asked you for anything." She laughed bitterly. "I've never asked anyone for anything. My whole life I've been by myself

and I kind of thought that was how it was going to be for me."
Her thumb stroked his hand. "But now you've come and ruined
all of that. When you kissed me for the first time I told myself
you'd given me back my life. Saved me from being lonely
forever or doing something to end all of that." She thought
about her scars and how it had been a daily struggle not to add to
the collection. "But I was wrong. You didn't give me my life,
you took it. It's yours and I didn't realize that until I thought you
were dead. You took it with you. Now, here we are. I just got it
back and you're trying to take it away from me again. You can't.
I won't let you. I'm asking you to stay here with me."

Natalie stood, strained voice cracking and giving out. Her free
hand stroked his hair, sweeping it back again and traced the
outline of his face. Eyes so full he was blurry right in front of
her, she leaned forward and kissed his head then nose then lips.
Finally whispering, "I love you Luka." She kissed him again
and let herself fall back in her chair, discouraged by his lack of
response.

Natalie hadn't known it until then but she had expected him to
wake up or stir or show some sort of sign of life at her emotional
outpouring. She had told him things she didn't dare let him hear
in or out of her head. She had told him her most private
thoughts. Not getting anything, even an eye twitch, Natalie felt
defeated.

Her shoulders drooped and she leaned forward to lay her head
on the bed beside him, one hand still on his. The mental drain
soon caught up with her and Natalie felt herself slipping into an
exhausted sleep.

She dreamed of Andjela's mission gone bad, Ivy living with
lies and trying to make things right by training students more
thoroughly and bridging them slowly to the agent life. She
dreamt of her life without Luka and could picture nothing but
sadness.

Don't be sad.

How can I not be? There's so much loss.

I'm *here with you.*

"Excuse me Miss." A firm hand was shaking her shoulder
gently. "Miss we need to examine him."

Natalie blinked back to the hospital room, looking over at Luka, still unmoving and felt her ember of hope fading. It had been a dream. She had heard his voice in her dream.

The nurse removed his hand from hers, taking his pulse at his wrist. Movement at the doorway caught her eye. Turning, Natalie saw Doctor MacCutchan walk in.

"Hi Natalie, just thought I'd stop in before I head out." He approached, joining the nurse in her exam. "Let me see that." He removed her stethoscope from around her neck and smoothly interposed himself between her and Luka, effectively taking over the exam. The nurse put up her hands and took a step back.

"By all means Doctor. I got other patients. This one's all yours." She had a ghost of a smile on her lips as she left. He had not irritated her, she had been pleased to have handed off one responsibility. She had others.

"Has there been any change?" The doctor asked her, eyes and hands still moving over Luka's body. "Have you been talking to him? He can hear that, you know."

Snorting, Natalie gave a half laugh. "Yeah, I've been talking."

The doctor gave her a strange look. "Good." Belatedly adding redundantly, "It helps."

Natalie stared at the good looking doctor trying to gauge his age. "You can't be much younger than Ivy, Doctor. How did you know she was at the school still? She had to be a student, for all you knew she could have left by now."

His head turned toward her, eyes clouding over. "She was my mentor. We were students at the same time but I got out. The head of the Center then wasn't like Ivy. He was hard, he broke more students than he helped. Ivy wanted to change that. I knew she'd stay." The corner of his mouth ticked up in a wistful smile. "Ivy wanted to change the world. That was what was so great about her."

Her desire to ask more questions was forgotten when she heard him.

Nat.

Eyes snapped to his face, searching for an outward sign that he was waking.

"Did you see something?" Doctor MacCutchan studied the monitor as well as Luka's face for an indication of what Natalie had seen.

"No," she said quietly without taking her eyes from Luka's unchanged expression. Was she imagining that he was a tiny bit less gray?

To try to tie him to his body and bring him back, she spoke aloud. "Luka, I'm here." She clasped his hand tight in both of hers.

Natalie you sound so far away. His voice was pained.

"I'm here in your room with you. Can you feel my hand?" She tightened then loosened her grip.

Sort of. He was hesitant.

"Luka you need to wake up now. Concentrate on where I'm touching you. Tell me if you feel it." One hand kept constant contact. The other hand ran up and down his arm, fingers curving to give her nails purchase. She knew that he liked that from times spent curled around each other, touching just for the sake of feeling each other. "Do you feel that?"

Um, yeah. He was more certain.

Doctor MacCutchan watched silently, not interrupting. Natalie saw him out of her peripheral vision but he was not her focus. Only Luka. To the doctor's credit, he could tell something was going on and his knowledge of the presence of Natalie's talent gave him respect for the unknown. He trusted that she was talking to him. In running with her senses wide open, Natalie picked that up as well as some scattered thoughts about his college life and some private moments with Ivy. She brushed that aside as unimportant.

Natalie leaned over and kissed Luka's cheek, following it with her hand. She slid the backs of her fingers lightly across his skin. He was a tactile person, always touching and very much enjoyed being touched in return. Natalie had found that after years of not having anyone touch her, she more than just enjoyed his touch, she basked in it. It had awakened parts of her soul she'd long forgotten. She did that now for him, reviving his body and uniting it with his mind.

As Natalie's hand stroked his shoulder, she saw his eye twitch then his mouth.

"That's it Luka. Wake up. Talk to me."

I am.

"Not like that. I mean speak to me with your voice. I want to hear your voice." She flicked a nervous glance up at the doctor at his surprised intake of breath. He hadn't realized the extent to which they were communicating.

Luka's long dark lashes fluttered against his cheeks before his eyes opened, blinking in confusion at the dim, white room. "Nat? Where are we?"

Smiling through tears, Natalie nodded at him. Words failed her.

Doctor MacCutchan was in his element. He buzzed the doctor on duty and began explaining to Luka that he was in the hospital but would be fine. The floor doctor on duty entered, repeating MacCutchan's examination and using his penlight and finger to check for obvious brain damage. Finding none and ascertaining that Luka knew who he was, he left amidst promises of a return for further testing soon. But first he would have a nurse bring up a tray of food.

When they'd gone and left Natalie and Luka alone, he squeezed her hand. She'd kept her hold on it the entire time.

Luka's eyes were losing their bright expression, his lids threatened to close.

"You look tired, you should rest," she suggested, adding teasingly, "As long as you promise to wake up." The doctors had both assured them that was no longer a concern at this point. The fear of coma was behind them.

Slowly he shook his head. "I want to know what happened, after Ericka shot me."

Natalie's joy faded thinking about the life she'd taken. She had let those thoughts remain untended in the shadow of Luka's life threatening injuries. Now they came rushing back, taking the wind from her chest. She brought her defenses up, protecting herself from the disgust she was sure Luka would feel for her. Ericka was sick yes, but she had killed her.

Natalie was a murderer. "I hit her." She whispered it, unable to look him in the eye instead studying the dark hairs on his forearm. "I hit her and she flew back into the wall. She broke her neck, cracked her skull. She died instantly. I'm sorry."

Luka said nothing. Natalie imagined his condemnation through his silence. She started to pull her hand away from his, knowing he would not want to be with her right now. Maybe in time he would forgive.

"What are you doing?"

She risked a glance at his face and saw his brows knitted, confusion in his eyes. "I killed her Luka." She kept her voice low. "I killed her because I was angry."

His grip was amazingly strong for someone who had just been at death's door. He wouldn't let her go. "You saved me Natalie."

She stopped trying to pull away.

"You did what you had to do to save my life. I can't fault you for that."

She searched his face but saw no misgivings. Relief flooded through her and she leaned in to kiss him again, feeling it was not enough, wishing she could lay with him. Her body ached to be against his.

We need to work on those defenses. When you get emotional, you have a terrible time keeping them up. He teased. *Come up here.* He patted the bed beside him.

There was not much room and she couldn't ask him to scoot over, but her need to touch him was irresistible. Natalie sat on the edge and leaned against the raised head so she was essentially sitting next to him, curved against his side. He slid his arm around her, holding her as close as they dared. When his heart monitor sped up briefly she grinned. He chuckled.

"Natalie?" He asked in the dim quiet. "When I was under, I heard some things."

She knew right away what he was referring to, what he'd heard while she lay with him. "Your sister didn't kill herself." She confirmed it for him.

The breath whooshed out of him as if he'd been kicked. Natalie waited for him to regain his breath before going on to explain. "You knew she was like us, but she was already an agent. Did you know that?" She didn't wait for an answer. "Ivy and Whiting had this project, they'd take people like us, good ones, and train them at the school. They didn't go through Optimax's internship for more training. They sent out Andjela

289

with Ivy's daughter when they weren't ready. They both died. They told you she'd shot herself to explain the wound." Natalie stroked his chest. "She didn't kill herself." She repeated.

A choking sound in his chest and Natalie felt his hand come up to cover his face. His guilt poured out of him, she could see his face was wet under his hand. She pulled it away and kissed his cheek. Luka turned toward her and pressed his face into the side of her neck and hair.

"Thank you." His voice was rough with emotion.

Natalie kept her face to his head. *You didn't fail her.*

A soft knock at the door startled them. Natalie barely kept herself from jerking and possibly hurting Luka's damaged body.

She felt Luka's love for the tall woman in the dooway and would have known who it was even if she hadn't had black wavy hair and a long lean body she'd passed on to both of her children.

"Luka." Warmth was clear in her voice now as she said his name. The cold words she had spoken to Natalie had been feigned. Marta loved her son.

"Hi Mom." He raised his hand in salute.

Natalie started to rise, Luka's hand around her shoulder tightened. "Mom, this is Natalie."

Smiling easily, Marta advanced and held out a hand. "I'm pleased to meet the girl who has stolen my son's heart. Finally." She added with a feigned serious look at her son.

She took the proffered hand and shook it, noticing Marta had given the children many visible traits but one. Her eyes were warm and brown, the color of milk chocolate. Natalie would never meet the one who had given them their stunning green.

An older woman wearing a bright pink shirt marked, "Volunteer" walked in, a flower basket held in front of her face.

Marta took it with a "thanks" and placed it on the windowsill.

"Did you send those?" Luka asked Natalie.

"No."

"Mom?"

"No. I called the Van Slykes when I landed but that was less than an hour ago." She slid the card out of its holder and opened the small envelope.

"Who else knew I was in here?"

Marta's smile grew stiff. "It's from Bradley Whiting." She cleared her throat and read.

Just then, Natalie's phone rang.

"Hello?"

"Natalie, its Mr. Whiting calling. Did you get my flowers?" As always he sounded amused.

"Yes, thank you." *It's Whiting.*

Luka's mouth tightened.

"I heard what you did. Incredible. I want you back here on the double. Luka can take a week, we'll expect him back for desk duty by next Monday though."

Natalie bridled at his orders. "Sir, I will be more than happy to bring Luka back a *week* from next Monday but I'm staying here in the meantime. Surely you know about the investigation into the incident." She flicked her eyes up at Marta and saw her eyes were tight but not angry. "It would not look good if I were to leave and we don't want them following me, checking into things there. I think it's best to handle things here and come home when I bring Luka back. It won't raise any suspicion then."

Whiting mulled that over for a tense minute. Luka looked worried. Finally Whiting laughed. "You have a bright future Natalie Swenson. I'll give you your time, but not a minute longer."

"Thank you, sir." Natalie flipped her phone closed with a sigh. Her head fell back against Luka's shoulder and he turned to kiss her head.

Marta was watching them tenderly. "Natalie I'm glad you found him. I feel better knowing you two will be watching out for each other."

"Thank you Mrs. Bailey." Natalie smiled at her.

"Please, it's Marta."

"Mom, have a seat. I have food coming and I'm going to want to pawn off everything but my jello."

Marta sat on the chair Natalie had vacated and pulled out her phone. "I'm hungry too. Let's see if we can't find something better." She gave Natalie a wink and, although the color was wrong, the playful twinkle was all too familiar.

End

Keep a close eye, Luka is healing and Natalie and Avery will be working hard for their first mission. Be there when they take their first steps as agents.

Acknowledgements

It's been a long journey for this book and for its author. A good friend convinced me to enter this work into the 2012 ABNA contest put on by Amazon and Penguin Publishing for breakthrough novelists and out of five thousand entries I made it down to the last two hundred fifty. In addition, I was given two reviews by professionals at Publishers Weekly and both were flattering as well as humbling. There are some things to work on but also to be proud of. When is this not the case in this life, right?

Immediately I was excited to share this story with readers but then life intervened. After a deeply emotional loss and complete life renovation I'm back and so is Whispers. Without the help and support of my editor, Karen Reckard and most amazing personal assistant, Jaime Radyalac I wouldn't have been able to keep moving my writing forward. But when I didn't have the time or energy they both were there to go over and above what needed done. For that I will be ever grateful and thank you is just woefully inadequate but that is what I have. So thank you. Also my mom and daughter have been there with hugs and love when I questioned my choices and my ability to do this on my own. Again, thank you but that doesn't begin to cover it.

And to the wonderful readers who reached out to share their thoughts. You have no idea what those kind words can mean to a writer who sends their heart out into the world in the form of characters and a story born of the writer's imagination. If they are received and loved only a fraction of how much they are by the author then that is more rewarding than any paycheck.

Despite the heavy subject matter some of the characters are dealing with I hope they brought a few smiles too. Avery and Jason never cease to make me laugh and Natalie's strength in her struggle gives me hope that she will just keep getting stronger.

This book started as a standalone but by the end, as usual, the story took over and now I see some seriously cool possibilities. So stay tuned...

www.ingramcontent.com/pod-product-compliance
Lightning Source LLC
Chambersburg PA
CBHW030957260626
47169CB00002B/586